Blood Kin

BLOOD

KIN

HENRY CHAPPELL

Texas Tech University Press

This book is typeset in Minion (text) and Walbaum (display). The paper used in this book meets the minimum requirements of ANSI/NISO Z39.48-1992 (R1997). ∞

Designed by David Timmons

Printed in the United States of America

Library of Congress Cataloging-in-Publication Data

Blood kin / Henry Chappell.
    p.   cm.
ISBN 0896725308 (cloth : alk. paper)
1. Texas Rangers—Fiction. 2. Young men—Fiction. 3. Texas—History—Revolution, 1835–1836—Fiction. 4. Texas—History—Republic, 1836-1846—Fiction. I. Chappell, J. Henry.
PS3603.H376 B56 2004
813'.622

2003023040

04 05 06 07 08 09 10 11 12 / 9 8 7 6 5 4 3

Texas Tech University Press
Box 41037
Lubbock, Texas 79409-1037 USA
1.800.832.4042
ttup@ttu.edu
www.ttup.ttu.edu

For Jane, who believed

Author's Note

BLOOD KIN could not have been completed without the help and support of family, friends, and colleagues. I am eternally grateful.

Judith Keeling believed in this project from the beginning and never let me take the easy way out. Her sure editorial hand and uncanny feel for my characters greatly improved the novel. Dr. Jim Brink and Johnny Boggs carefully read the manuscript and steered me away from numerous blunders. Alan Huffines, George Nelson, and Stephen Hardin gave me more insight into 1840s San Antonio than I could have gleaned from weeks of research and reading. Juan Cordova and my daughter Jamie Chappell Ambrose helped with the Spanish dialogue. Steven Jent directed me to folk music popular during the Republic years. During the tentative early stages of the project, my friends in the DFW Writers Workshop provided invaluable critique and encouragement.

As always, my wife, Jane, tirelessly supported the project, proofreading the early drafts and encouraging me through the rough spots. Just as reliably, my daughter Sarah endured her distracted father with patience and humor.

Several books were essential in helping me establish the novel's historical and cultural background: Bill Groneman, *Battlefields of Texas* (1998); Ernest Wallace and E. Adamson Hoebel, *The Comanches: Lords of the South Plains* (1986); W. W. Newcomb Jr., *The Indians of Texas* (1995); T. R. Fehrenbach, *Lone Star: A History of Texas and the Texans* (1983); Rupert N. Richardson, Ernest Wallace, and Adrian Anderson, *Texas: The Lone Star State* (1981); Charles M. Robinson III, *The Men Who Wear the Star* (2000); Walter Prescott Webb, *The Texas Rangers: A Century of Frontier Defense* (1977); and Noah Smithwick, *The Evolution of a State, or, Recollections of Old Texas Days* (1983).

The settlement of Bastrop probably was named by Stephen F. Austin in honor of his friend Baron de Bastrop, who selected the site in 1823. In 1834, the Texas and Coahuila legislature changed the name to Mina in honor of Mexican martyr and hero Francisco Xavier Mina. Maps from the Revolution and early Republic period reflect the name change. The name reverted to Bastrop in 1837 when the town was incorporated under Texas law. To avoid confusion, and because Noah Smithwick wrote in his memoir that he could not remember the town ever being called Mina, I stayed with the name Bastrop throughout the novel.

Although the major battles and events in this work closely follow accepted history, the exchange of gunfire between Texian rebels and Mexican soldiers at Bastrop, Noah Smithwick's ambush of the Mexican patrol on Camino Real, and most of the skirmishes between rangers and Comanches are fictional. Other than Noah Smithwick, John Moore, Major Williamson, Mathew Caldwell, Jack Hays, Antonio Peréz, Juan Castro, and a few minor figures mentioned in Smithwick's *Evolution of a State,* the members of the ranging companies are products of my imagination.

For these and other liberties, I ask for the reader's indulgence.

History is brutal; only future peril lies in omitting or obscuring man's continuing brutalities.

T. R. Fehrenbach, *Comanches: The Destruction of a People*

Whoso sheddeth man's blood, by man shall his blood be shed: for in the image of God made he man.

Genesis 9:6

BLOOD KIN

The Raid

Chihuahua, Mexico
September 1828

FROM HIS GOAT PEN, Miguel Oropeza watched the dark band of mountains north of the Rio Bravo del Norte. A nearly full moon sat a hand's width above the eastern cordillera. He pulled his serape under his chin and enjoyed its warmth. The goats milling around his legs provided warmth, too, and a measure of comfort.

He welcomed any comfort now, for it was time for the coming of the savages. For the past twenty-eight years, the hordes had passed unseen by this community of goat herders, either by choice or by chance. And each of those twenty-eight autumns, Miguel and his kin supposed that after years of brutalizing northern Mexico the Comanches had at last tired of raiding or had been wiped out by some plague, but nearly always the reports came from the south: haciendas and villages burned; hundreds of horses and mules stolen; men scalped; women and children carried away.

Most years he walked along the raiders' highway—a wide horsemen's path coming out of the mountains north of the del Norte—to help families of neighboring villages load the discarded bodies of their loved ones into carts to be carried home for burial.

The raiders had not always passed him by. On an autumn afternoon in his eighth year, they rode in from the north and spoke calmly in poor Spanish of their intentions. He witnessed his father's pathetic begging and his mother's shrieking appeals to the Saints and the savages. He saw his sister's look of disbelief as they bound her and jerked her by the hair onto a warrior's horse.

His neighbors cowered out of sight, weeping and praying while the young savages coursed and lanced a half-dozen bleating goats and heaved them into the well. He stood with loose bowels and listened to his sister's fading pleas.

Since then he had hated his father and himself, the Spanish authorities, and then the so-called Mexican government so preoccupied with putting down revolts and maintaining the huge estates to the south that it did nothing to protect its northern citizens from butchery.

And now the butchers were returning. He felt their approach. The six-year drought had broken. The water holes and tinajas were full. The night smelled of curing desert shortgrass. Lately his wife, Ilena, had prayed that their communal stock farm would be passed by again. Miguel considered the absurdity of praying to be passed by so that someone else could be slaughtered. He, on the other hand, prayed that the northern barbarians would all die horribly of smallpox or cholera. He had once prayed for a Comanche syphilis epidemic, but retracted the request when he realized that they would bring the scourge to Mexico.

He owned a musket that he had never fired, and his neighbor Benito kept a matchlock blunderbuss beneath his bed. But they had no powder, ball, or flint. Just as well since he had only a vague idea of how to charge a gun.

Captain Guzman's dusty lancers rode through two years prior, in midsummer when no Comanches would be about. The young officer told Miguel that he and his men had ridden from Monclova to hunt down and destroy Comanches and that soon the citizens of northern Mexico could rest easy.

Miguel studied the lethal-looking weaponry as he nodded politely and ignored the captain's boasts while the women scurried about preparing nine goats they could ill afford to offer. The lancers left, heading east, after two days of ogling, eating, and shitting too close to people's homes. Miguel had heard nothing of them since. He assumed they had been called away to put down some forlorn revolt.

But he remembered the lances. He and Benito cut stalks of lechuguilla and sotol and tipped them with honed sections of barrel hoop.

Now he had something to fight with. No more pathetic appeals for mercy. No more offering of gifts. He would hide his family if he could. Failing that, he would fight. Dying horribly would surely be better than living with the memory of his daughters, young women now, being dragged away by smirking warriors.

Still, he recalled his paralysis at the sight of the mounted wild men, braids hanging to their waists, devilish figures painted on horsehide shields adorned with dangling scalps. And their sniggering and contempt at his father's begging, the heat in their eyes as they leered at his comely sister.

Miguel sat in the dust and leaned back against the water trough. He penned his goats at night to discourage coyotes and wolves, although lobos sometimes slipped in downwind of the dogs and jumped over or gnawed through the fence to go on a killing spree.

A few nights before, he woke to goats' bleating and the sound of quick movement on sand. He found himself facing two wolves and a pen full of dead and dying goats. The wolves stood watching him impassively. He thrust his sotol lance and yelled "Ha!" They stiffened but did not retreat. Then, as if by some mutual signal, they turned and bounded over the fence and into the darkness.

Now as he sat looking between its spiny members toward the del Norte, the fence seemed to afford no protection at all. The wolves were coming, and a fence would stop them no more than would a single man thrusting a crude lance.

A dog barked. He looked back at the darkened jacales. Were his neighbors all asleep, or did they feel it too? Everyone in the northern provinces knew the meaning of a wet summer and a September moon, but few mentioned it. There were only the knowing glances and the women's silent, feverish work, their eyes forever seeking their children.

Miguel checked the moon's position. Three hands now. In its light he could discern individual goats. The sweet coffee-colored nanny he would never slaughter; the yellow horned brute he could not turn his back on and would eat next; the raffish tan billy. He could see two scrawny chickens roosting in a mesquite, trace the lines in his hands, pick out dead grasshoppers impaled on the spines of his fence by butcher birds. He much preferred dark nights and a brilliant firmament.

His favorite nanny gently butted his shoulder and nuzzled his cheek. He stroked her ears. Gentle stock always calmed him. Maybe the devils would not come this year after all, or would pass by this wretched collection of huts and goats in favor of the horse-rich ranches to the south.

He stood, yawned and stretched. Perhaps he should just go on to bed. He rubbed his eyes and started to turn toward the gate, but a pinpoint of light just below the northern horizon stopped him. He stared until the dry wind forced him to blink. Still there. Now another. Two more. His pulse beat in his ears. Only four fires. Vaqueros, perhaps. But no. The points of light spread until the mountain resembled a dark vessel riddled with pinholes and lit within.

He ran through the gate, breaking the leather keep, then frantically retied it. He slipped into his jacal and knelt next to his wife's bed and cupped his hands around her ear. "They're here," he whispered. He nudged her and repeated himself. She opened her eyes, propped herself on an elbow and looked at him, calmly, as if she had been expecting him. Moonlight poured into the room. He nodded.

"Where?"

"North. Their fires nearly cover a mountain."

"Tell everyone. I'll gather what we need. Don't wake the children yet."

Ilena sat up and began working up her coarse black hair into a knot. Miguel lit a candle with an ember and set it on the table. His oldest daughter, Reyna, raised her head. "What is it?"

Ilena went to her, knelt, and put her hands on the girl's shoulders. "We have to go."

"The savages?"

"They're still a half day's ride away," Miguel said. "We'll hide in the mountains. I know a place."

Ilena waved him away. "Go."

He ran door to door beating and yelling that the Comanches were upon them. Villagers burst from their homes. Women clutched their solemn, confused children.

Miguel found Benito next to the blacksmith's shed and grabbed his arms. "Gather your things."

"They'll run us down. Do you think they can't follow the tracks of an entire village?" Benito's eyes bulged. His sweaty hair was plastered to one side of his head.

Miguel shook his friend. "We can't stay here. They'll be upon us before sundown tomorrow."

"How do you know they won't pass us by again?"

"Benito, we discussed this! Gather Marcella and the children!"

"We can offer them goats and burros. If we run or fight they'll kill us all."

"We'll fight."

"We'll die. Come to your senses, friend. This is our only hope."

"Will you offer them Marcella?"

Benito's lip curled. "Go to hell!" He covered his face with his hands, ran them through his hair, then turned and ran toward his jacal.

Now old Oscar Reynoso yelled, "Gather your flocks! We'll give them everything! We mustn't provoke them!"

"The church!" a woman yelled. "We can barricade ourselves in the church."

Miguel raised his hands. "Friends! We can hide! They won't trouble themselves for a few goats and burros!"

But his neighbors were already breaking up fencing and sheds for breastworks.

He shook his fists. "Fools! Cowards!" Dogs barked. Skinny Nestos Rocha began hacking a stable post with an ax.

Miguel ran home. Reyna and his younger daughter, Cecilia, were bundling bedding, corn, lard, and utensils. Ilena took a crucifix from above the hearth. Eight-year-old Agustin sat on the edge of his bed, chewing a cold tortilla.

They said nothing. Miguel carried the bundle to the stalls and secured it on his old burro's back. Across the back of his younger burro, he hung two full water jars. He took the pack basket from Ilena and worked his arms into the straps, grabbed his sotol lance from the top of the stalls, then opened the goat pen. Using the butt of his lance as a staff, he started the eleven goats westward. Without looking back, the Oropeza family followed their flock into moonlit desert toward the black, looming mountains.

• • •

Looking eastward from near the head of the canyon, Miguel saw late in the afternoon of the second day of their exodus black smoke billowing ten miles distant. He walked up a faint game trail and found his family sitting on blankets in a clearing among gnarled juniper and ocotillo. Behind them, a mountain crag rose three hundred feet into the failing light.

Agustin's mouth and fingers dripped purple from the ripe prickly pear he'd eaten. He smiled, showing purple teeth. Ilena, just beginning to grow stout in her thirties, sat grinding corn with her pestle. Reyna and Cecilia busied themselves weaving a thatch arbor. The Oropeza goats browsed about nearby. Miguel stopped at the edge of the clearing and admired his family. "This is a good place. We'll be safe here."

Ilena looked at him, then turned her eyes back to her work.

He knew she had started to speak. "What is it?"

She shook her head. The girls kept their eyes on their work. "When will we go home, Papa?" Agustin asked.

"I think we'll enjoy this place until winter comes. There's a good spring nearby. And it's very pleasant, don't you think?"

The boy nodded solemnly. "When will we see Ignacio?"

Ilena stopped her pestle. Miguel swallowed and fought images of Agustin's young friend bleeding in the dust.

"Silly Agustin," Ilena said, "you look like a peccary who has been eating cactus all day. Your head is purple." The boy showed his teeth again. Ilena smiled sadly at Miguel, then went back to her grinding.

That night the family lay side by side beneath their blankets, and the goats crowded around them. Miguel and Ilena clasped hands across their children's thin bodies. The wind moaned in the canyons. The burros sniffed and snorted and stamped their hooves on the rocks.

Now Miguel thought this the evilest place he had ever known. He slept fitfully, sweating but cold, and Ilena squeezed his hand and stroked his thumb with hers. The children lay deathly still save for the gentle, steady rising and falling of their backs and bellies.

He woke to a canyon and desert floor still in shadow. Behind him the gray mountain crag rose into the canted morning light. Ilena knelt, breaking twigs for a small fire. She coughed, and her breath showed in the cool air. "Is it safe to build a little fire?"

"Surely. We can't make it through autumn without building a fire."

Ilena shaved off thin slivers of dried juniper, then arranged the kindling on it. She fired a knot of dead grass with her flint and steel, then eased it into the tinder and blew the nascent flame to life. Miguel watched, transfixed. The night's evil seemed to dissipate with the meager smoke.

"What is it about a fire, Ilena?"

She smiled and shrugged.

"Or maybe it's you building the fire."

She laughed. "I know you. It won't work."

"We have time if nothing else."

She shook her head in mock exasperation. Agustin awoke and rubbed his eyes. He crawled over Cecilia, who slapped at him and covered her head with her blanket.

Ilena handed Agustin another cold tortilla and some jerked meat. "Good morning, little peccary. You're still purple."

Agustin smiled shyly and stuffed half the tortilla in his mouth. Reyna sat up, stretched, and prodded her sister. Miguel knelt and held his hands over the fire. The girls, still frowsy and glum, joined him.

Reyna cleared her throat. "What will we do today?"

"You're hoarse," Ilena said.

"It hurts to talk."

"I'll heat some water. We have a little coffee. We can finish our arbor this morning. It's miserable with no shade at midday." The girls nodded.

Miguel stood. "I'll refill the water jars." He started toward the nearly empty vessels. The burros pricked their ears and snorted. Goats bleated. Miguel looked down the canyon toward the desert floor.

Ilena rubbed her thighs. "What is it?"

"Hide," he whispered.

"Where?"

"Anywhere. Go!"

The girls grabbed Agustin. Four riders came out of a dry wash sixty yards away. "It's too late," Miguel said. "Just keep quiet." The calmness in his voice surprised him. He walked numbly across the clearing to retrieve his lance. He remembered this feeling in his legs and bowels. His family stood wide eyed, but silent. Miguel admired them for an instant. How handsome, stoic. When had Reyna grown taller than her mother?

It was all quite simple now. No more decisions. No bargaining. No attempt at appeasement. He would simply react as the situation required. No member of his family would be taken alive. Ilena had agreed.

The riders came on. They rode Spanish mustangs and wore only breech-clouts, leggings, and moccasins. Oily braids dangled against their thighs. The lead rider carried a lance. The others carried short bows. Miguel guessed none was over twenty years old.

He held the lance at port arms and stepped in front of his huddled family. He heard their uneven breathing; felt his wife trembling against his back. The leader smiled, turned, and spoke to his companions. The second rider nocked an arrow.

The Comanches pulled up five feet away. The lancer looked amused as he took in the goats and two burros. He spoke to his companions in a sonorous, buzzing tongue. They all laughed. He regarded Miguel, then the women. "We are hungry," he said in Spanish.

Miguel swallowed. "We have nothing to offer."

The young warrior snickered. He looked at the girls. "You have many good things."

"We want no trouble. Let us be please."

"Then what is your need for the lance?"

"Hunting."

The Comanche turned again and spoke to the other warriors. They laughed. "Hunting goats, pig?"

Miguel felt Ilena stiffen. "There is no need to be rude."

"No. No need. We will help you with your hunting." He spoke again in Comanche. The other warriors nocked and shot arrows from horseback. The women shrieked, Miguel cursed, and the entire herd lay struggling, smearing their blood on the dry juniper needles and prickly pear. Their dying bleats echoed down the canyon. The leader spoke again, and arrows dropped the braying burros. No sound came from Agustin's gaping mouth. The girls turned away and covered their eyes.

Miguel gripped his lance and measured the distance to the lead Comanche. The warrior's eyes narrowed; he lowered his lance tip at Miguel's chest. Fresh scalps dangled from the butt.

Miguel spat. "Butcher."

The young Comanche smiled coldly. He nodded to one of the others, who dismounted and strode toward the girls. Miguel stepped out to meet him, lance ready. The young man stopped, obviously surprised.

Miguel caught his scent. Sweat, wood smoke, and tobacco. Arrogant bastard. Blood under his fingernails. Torso greased. He'd run this strutting cock clean through before he'd give up his girls. The warrior gathered his wits and laughed.

He heard in this boy's laugh two hundred years of Mestizo humiliation. He stepped and thrust. The Comanche moved easily out of the way. Another warrior raised a bow, and Miguel felt a blow like a mule's kick to his breastbone. Yet he kept his feet and looked in surprise at his chest and a ragged, finger-sized hole in his shirt. His breath left him.

Ilena and the girls screamed. Miguel turned and saw the arrow stuck in the ground ten feet behind him and then the growing blotch of pink froth soaking his shirt. The desert and canyon walls, the mountain and sky swirled. Then the ground rushed at him.

He opened his eyes. What was all this commotion? Footfalls and shrieks. Or bleats. His lance! He needed his lance! But it was so dark. He groped and tried to draw his knees beneath him. "Ilena, the wolves are at the goats again! Reyna! Cecilia! Agustin! Where's Mother?" He could not hear his own voice. "The wolves have returned! Where is my lance?" He rolled onto his back. The wolves were all around now, killing the goats, and he had misplaced his lance. "Where are you, Ilena?" he said.

I
REVOLUTION

One

Mexican province of Coahuila and Texas
March 9, 1836

ISAAC WEBB SAT HIS HORSE and listened.
The mist-darkened woods crowded the narrow road. He shivered.

A courier named Stanton wiped the drizzle from his face and continued.
"Not a one left alive. Bastards stormed the walls before dawn three days ago.
Had the bodies piled up and on fire before noon." He handed a slip of paper
to Noah Smithwick. "Orders from Major Williamson."

The angular, dark-bearded Smithwick glanced at the note. "That's the
Major's hand. Were you in Béxar?"

"Hell no. We heard it from a Tejano named Lopez. He has family there."

Isaac licked his lips with a dry tongue. A few hours ago he and his father
were on their way to Bastrop with a wagonload of hides and honey to trade for
coffee and cornmeal. Now this.

"What about the officers?" Smithwick asked.

"All dead. Bowie, Travis, Crockett." He shook his head. "Shit. Bowie dead.
I never thought that sumbitch could be killed."

Felix Gross tugged his beard. "What now, Smithwick? This ain't just talk.
We can't fight four thousand Mexicans. And where in hell is Houston?"

"Word is, he's headed for Gonzales," Stanton said. "He'll try to marshal an
army there. There's a chance he ain't heard about what happened at the
Alamo."

Smithwick turned in his saddle to face Gross. "What would you have him
do, Felix? Retake Béxar by himself? We never thought Santa Anna would show
up this soon—and sure as hell not with four thousand men. It takes time to
raise the militia."

Isaac looked westward along Camino Real, the muddy, rutted so-called
road that connected Saltillo, the capital five hundred miles to the south, and
Nacogdoches in the pinelands to the northeast. He listened to the arguing.
These men had seemed like giants. Smithwick, Gross, Choctaw Tom Crosby.
Now in drenched buckskin, rainwater dripping from their beards and rifle
barrels, he saw them as Santa Anna might see them: a gaggle of pale, undisci-
plined rebels who'd stepped in over their heads.

Smithwick slipped Williamson's orders into a coat pocket. "And we let Cós
surrender and leave with his army."

Gross said, "I knowed we should've shot that skunk."

Choctaw Tom Crosby had been following the conversation with his eyes. He scratched his ear. "Wouldn't have done a drop of good, Felix. Anyway, I can't see standing a soldier up and shootin' him just because he ain't on my side."

Gross shifted his chew to the other cheek. "Hell, what's Santa Anna gonna do about it? Show up with four thousand men and kill us all?"

"Gets worse," Stanton said. "Lopez said Gaona's on his way to Bastrop with seven hundred men—cavalry and dragoons, I expect. And Sesma is headed for Gonzales with another twelve hundred. Aims to burn the settlements and run Houston down before he can raise an army."

Smithwick looked down the road toward Béxar. "Gaona's coming right at us." He turned back to his men. "The Major wants all but two of us to ride back to Bastrop to cover the withdrawal of the citizenry."

"I ain't stayin' here to be run through by no Mexican lance," Gross said.

"I don't blame you, Felix," Smithwick said. "Tom? What about you? We have good horses and no family to worry about. We'll watch the road at Plum Creek for two days. If the Mexicans don't show, we'll ride back to Bastrop."

Crosby shrugged.

Isaac considered riding back to Bastrop with Felix Gross. There were nineteen volunteers there now. But Smithwick's demeanor calmed him. And two men could stay out of the way of an army advancing along the road. "I'll go with you, Captain."

Smithwick looked surprised. "What about your family?"

"They'd be gone by the time I could get back. I couldn't do 'em no good even if I could find 'em."

Smithwick studied him, eyes mirthful. "Brave Horatius."

"Who?" Isaac wondered if Captain Smithwick had forgotten his name.

"Never mind. How about it, Tom? Suppose I take Isaac, and you and Felix ride back to town."

"You're the captain," Crosby said.

Gross turned his horse toward Bastrop. "*Captain.* Everybody's a goddamn captain."

"Your turn tomorrow, Felix," Smithwick said. He nodded to Crosby. "Good luck to you, Tom."

Crosby returned the nod. He, Stanton, and Gross rode eastward at a trot.

Smithwick watched them disappear around a bend in the road. "We'll go on to Plum Creek and reconnoiter from there. We ought to make it before dark."

"What'll we do when the Mexicans show up?"

"Slip away and ride for Bastrop. They'll never know we're about." He drew his rifle from its scabbard and laid it across his pommel. "Of course the Comanches are another matter."

Two

ISAAC SAT with his back against a live oak and wondered what a Mexican soldier might look like. Below him, Camino Real crossed clear-running Plum Creek. He could see two small bass holding in an eddy.

The air had warmed little in the two days since a norther left skim ice around the edges of the slow pools. The steady drizzle had long since soaked his buckskin pants and homespun shirt. A sodden wool blanket draped around his shoulders provided scant warmth. The woods along the creek smelled of earthen decay, and the sprawling, Spanish moss–laden live oaks in the hills above him dripped so that he saw rather than heard Noah Smithwick stepping out of the woods on the far side of the road.

"All clear, Captain?"

"All clear save for three red hogs and a gaunt wolf bitch." Smithwick crossed the road in two strides and bounded up the steep bank. "You're lookin' peaked, Isaac. Get up and stomp around a bit."

"I swear, I'm about to freeze to death." He pulled himself to his feet using his rifle for support. "By god, a fire would go good about now."

"I hate to see a man treat his weapon that way, Isaac. That maple stock wasn't made to be used as a staff. I'd have thought a good Arkansas boy would know better."

"Well, he would. Sorry, Captain. My nerves and this weather have about wrung all the sense out of me." The reproach stung. Noah Smithwick was a veteran of the battle of Concepción and widely regarded as one of the ablest men in the Texas colonies.

Smithwick pulled the plug from a dried Spanish gourd and took a drink of water. "I'm about wrung out myself. Did you seal your pan and frizzen like I showed you?"

"Yes sir. Here's your beeswax." He handed Smithwick a small horn container.

"Good man. Not many know that little trick. It'll gain you favor in weather like this. Would you care for a bite of cornbread?"

"Believe I would."

"Watch the road." Smithwick walked back through the trees toward the draw where they'd picketed their saddled horses. His waterlogged pants now hung half a foot too long, and Isaac could hear his feet squishing in his moccasins.

He returned shortly with a parfleche bag full of cornbread and jerked venison. Isaac's mouth watered. He hadn't realized how hungry he was. His ranging company had left Bastrop before he could gather provisions.

They ate sitting cross-legged, facing the road, with their rifles across their laps. The drizzle had stopped and the sky began to clear. The late afternoon sun shone through the thinning clouds, turning the western horizon to copper.

"About to clear up and get cold sure enough," Smithwick said.

Isaac nodded. "We'll be froze by mornin'."

"Better froze than quivering on the end of a Mexican lance. Hell, or a Comanche lance."

"I've never laid eyes on a Comanche. I thought they stayed west of here."

"Usually do. They've been raiding further east of late. They're keeping Gonzales up in arms. They make me pine for the Karankawas."

"I never seen a Kronk neither."

"Bucks six feet tall. And besmeared with alligator grease. Handsomest race of people you ever saw. And fighters. Haven't seen one in years."

"What went with 'em?"

"Never were many of them. I think we've killed them out. Colonel Tumlinson smote an entire camp three years ago and that seemed to be the end of them. In '23, when I came to Texas, you couldn't turn your back on a horse or woman without a Kronk relieving you of one or both."

"I hear they ate their enemies."

Smithwick laughed. "With much zeal."

"Lord." Isaac had never heard of zeal. He wondered if it went well with all meat, or if the Karankawas reserved it for their more gruesome meals.

"It's just their way."

"Tonkawas eat people too, don't they?"

"For ceremony. Otherwise they're a friendly, helpful people. Not nearly as clannish as the Kronks."

"We've got three that come around all the time bringin' pecans and squirrels," Isaac said. "They speak a little English and Mexican. Everybody says they're bad about stealing, but they ain't took nothin' from us."

Smithwick nodded. "The Tonkawas make superb scouts. But I'm afraid they're going the way of the Kronks. They lack the Comanches' insolence."

"Insolence?"

"Stubbornness. Pride. You think the Mexicans are merciless? They'll run you through with a bayonet and be done with you. The Comanches will stake you out and kill you a little at a time for a week. They'll revive you just to keep killing you."

"I wish they'd get killed out like the Kronks."

"It'll be a job. The Mexicans have tried without success for two centuries to subdue them. That's why we're here."

Isaac shook his head. "I ain't following you."

"The Mexican government wanted a line of Anglo settlements between itself and the Comanches. Now we're a threat to Santa Anna's domination and he wants us out of Texas."

They sat in silence. Isaac chewed his jerky. "Ever run across a Comanche?"

Smithwick rubbed his beard. "I have. After I buried a tot. The child's mother had managed to get away from the devils and stumbled into our camp on Brushy Creek. I won't say what they'd done to the poor woman. We caught the heathens asleep out in the open and still managed to kill only one." He shook his head. "They just disappeared before we could reload. You never saw anyone mount and ride like they did." He ran his index finger along the outside of his rifle's trigger guard. "We'll be dealing with the Comanches soon enough. We might remember Santa Anna fondly before we're through."

"I hope we live to," Isaac said.

Smithwick laughed and pulled his pistol from his belt and laid it in his lap. "Damn thing was chewing into my belly."

Isaac studied the weapon. "I wish I had a pistol."

"I'd just as well give this one to you for all the good it does me."

"Don't it shoot true?"

"I might be able to kill a horse with it if I shoved it in its mouth first." He hefted the pistol. "They call it a Pennsylvania model. I traded my big Kentucky for it thinking it would be lighter and handier. I'd trade it back in a heartbeat."

Isaac studied Smithwick's rifle in the failing light. "I've never seen a rifle like that. Where's the pan?"

"There is no pan. It's a swivel-bore percussion gun." He pointed to two small caps beneath twin hammers. "These take the place of the flint and pan. They ignite the charge when the hammer comes down. After the first shot, I can twist this second barrel into place. I can get off two shots in about as many heartbeats."

"Be damn. Where'd you get it?"

"Picked up the barrels and action in New Orleans. I put the oak stock around it—she's a little on the heavy side."

Isaac found Smithwick's refinement settling. The man rarely swore, and Isaac suspected he spoke something like proper English. "Captain, would you tell me the truth about something?"

"Certainly."

"We got so much as a prayer?"

"Just a prayer. This is a different army than we faced last year. But they're a long way from home. The longer we can hold out, the better our prospects. I doubt they can live off the land. But when they've backed us all the way to the Sabine, we'll either fight or give up Texas." He paused. "Your folks should make it across fine."

"I reckon I should've gone back."

"No, you were right. You'd never find them. They're long gone by now."

Isaac hoped they were long gone. He suspected that Smithwick usually got his way without resorting to intimidation. "It's got dark on us."

Smithwick stood and stamped his feet. "Go pile up out of the wind. I'll post first watch."

Isaac felt his way through the oaks to the draw where the horses were picketed. They nickered at his approach. The sky was clear now; a gibbous moon had risen in the east. He rubbed the horses' flanks and stroked their muzzles, and they seemed glad for his company. He was glad for theirs. He scraped away the forest duff to get to dry ground, then sat with his back against the bank and wrapped himself in his blanket. It would be a long night. He thought wistfully of his feather tick at home and wondered where his family was and about his mother's reaction when his father returned from Bastrop alone. He found the North Star and then followed the handle to the dipper. A horse swished its tail.

Then someone shook him. "Time to get up, Isaac," Smithwick said. "It's almost dawn."

Three

ISAAC COULD FIND NO PLACE that provided shelter from the wind and a good view of the road. He finally sat where he'd posted watch the previous afternoon. Within minutes his teeth were chattering. His buckskins had dried little overnight, and the wind cut at his face and hands.

He could just see the road and the dark line of trees and brush on the far side. He pictured Smithwick curled in his blankets out of the wind. He doubted he could cock his rifle; he could barely feel the trigger.

Night before last Isaac had gone to bed with his belly full of ham, beans, biscuits, and coffee. The siege at Béxar might as well have been in some distant country. His father, Cyrus Webb, considered all the talk of revolution the banter of filibusters. Let those in the prosperous bottomland settlements talk of occupying Mexican armies, he'd said. Why would the Mexicans care about his stump-riddled hill farm?

Isaac and his father, his mother, Ruth, and sister, Esther, arrived in DeWitt's Colony eight years ago. While they unloaded their wagon on a bench above the Lavaca River and Cyrus cursed the mosquitoes, an alligator slipped out of the shallows and took one of their four hounds, a rib-sprung bitch named Hortense. She yelped twice, then disappeared beneath the tannin water.

They called in the other three hounds, reloaded the wagon, and struck out for the hills north of Bastrop where his mountaineer father could farm the thin soil with no worry of alligators and little aggravation from mosquitoes. Let the river bottom plantations prosper. Let the settlement roosters strut and crow for authority. The Webbs worked their place, raised their beans, corn, and tobacco, waged war against wolves, coyotes, and bobcats, and rode into Bastrop to trade for staples. After years among the Choctaw, they found the local Tonkawas' company preferable to that of their hard-shell neighbors. The Webbs had come from the Ouachita Mountains of Arkansas to be good Anglo citizens of Mexico.

But they knew no Mexicans. Isaac thought he'd seen a Tejano at Gonzales but couldn't be sure. Other than a few Lipans and the Tonkawas, black slaves and freedmen, he knew only Anglos. In Bastrop, he'd heard much talk of Comanches. The Anglos blamed all horse thievery on them, while the resident

Tonkawas and Lipans accused each other. Yet except for Noah Smithwick and a friendly Tonkawa called King Sol, he'd met no one who had actually seen a Comanche.

Isaac snugged the damp blanket around his neck. A faint glow had formed along the tops of the eastern hills. He mused on how quickly life could turn. The morning before, he and his father arrived to find Bastrop in an uproar. Doors and windows flung open, families loading wagons, dogs howling. They stopped the mules in front of McAllister's Mercantile and got out of the wagon. A big sandy-bearded man rode up. "What's in the wagon, farmer?" he asked. His hands were huge, his broad face wind burned.

Cyrus Webb spat, looked at the man. "I don't know ye."

"I'm Captain Samuels."

Cyrus studied Samuels's civilian clothing. "Says who?"

"Major Robert Williamson and the Provisional Government of Texas."

"That don't mean nothin' to me."

"I'll ask again. What's in the wagon?"

"You aim to buy what's in it?"

"I might need to requisition it. Pull those hides back and let's have a look."

Cyrus turned to walk into the mercantile. Samuels rode around the wagon to block the door. "Mister, I asked you what the hell is in that wagon."

"None of your business."

"I don't appreciate your demeanor."

"Go to hell then."

Isaac watched his brown, rawboned father cradle his rifle. Others had gathered to watch. Cyrus seemed calm.

"I'll see for myself," Samuels said. He started to dismount. With one hand, Cyrus pointed his rifle at Samuels's chest. "You'd best keep your big ass on that horse."

"I'll have you arrested."

"Have at it."

A tall young man with a dark beard and unkempt shoulder-length hair stepped out of the mercantile and nodded cordially to Samuels. "Captain," he said. Samuels nodded officiously. The young man thrust his hand at Cyrus Webb. "Smithwick's the name. You'll be?"

Cyrus kept his rifle on Samuels. He seemed to study Smithwick's hand. After a moment he took it. "Cyrus Webb," he said. "I've heard of you." He glanced from Smithwick to Samuels.

"Pleasure, Mr. Webb. Do I hear some eastern Tennessee in your words?"

"You do."

"North Carolina here."

"Well. A man can't help where he's born at."

Smithwick laughed. Some in the gathering nervously followed his lead. Samuels remained stern. "Noah, this man refuses to cooperate. I suspect he's a Mexican sympathizer."

Cyrus regarded Samuels coolly. "I might sympathize with a Mexican if I was to ever see one. Can't say for sure."

Smithwick smiled and cleared his throat. "Mr. Webb, we're about to see Mexicans in force. Our spies tell us General Urrea is on his way from Refugio with a thousand men."

"General who?"

"General José Urrea."

"Never heard of him."

Samuels shook his head in exasperation. "Beloved Texas is being colonized by half-witted hill men. Moses Austin is rolling in his grave."

"Urrea's cavalry overran San Patricio less than two weeks ago," Smithwick said. "He's marching toward Gonzales now. He'll surely make his way here."

Cyrus nodded. "All because a band of fools overran Béxar last December."

Angry mutterings moved through the gathering.

"My god, man, where's your sense of honor?" Samuels said. "A good number of those *fools* you speak of are under siege at this moment."

Isaac was uncertain as to the location of Béxar and as to what constituted a siege. He visualized angry hordes of uniformed soldiers storming a stockade.

Cyrus laughed coldly. "Mister, I was killin' Creeks while you was still hangin' on the tit."

Samuels's nostrils flared. "That's it. Boys, arrest the traitor."

No one moved.

Samuels spat. "Goddamnit!"

"We'll have to fight or run, Mr. Webb," Smithwick said. "Santa Anna won't rest until he's whipped or we're all dead or driven across the Sabine."

Samuels looked upward as if contemplating the clouds, then sighed and shook his head. "For god's sake, Noah, deal with this imbecile, if you will."

"Certainly, Captain. I'll be along shortly."

Petulantly, Samuels turned his horse and rode toward the east end of the settlement. Cyrus lowered his rifle. "Arm was gettin' weary. I can't help you, Smithwick. I've got to get back to my women."

"Fight or run, Mr. Webb."

"I've done my fightin'. You pups will have to do it this time."

"What'll you do?"

"Get my women across the Sabine and wait for this mess to clear up."

"What about the boy? I'd guess he's nudging six feet."

"I can't do without that boy."

"We're raising a company to see to the safety of the women and children and to watch for the Mexican advance. We're shorthanded."

"He ain't but fifteen."

"Sixteen, Pap."

"Just turned," Cyrus said.

"How old were you when you shot at your first Creek?" Smithwick asked.

"Goddamnit now." Cyrus's eyes showed mild panic.

Isaac had never considered the question. He attempted the arithmetic.

"We'll provide Isaac with a horse."

"Just *requisition* one, I reckon," Cyrus said.

"There's a war on, Mr. Webb."

Isaac arrived at a range of ages between thirteen and seventeen. "I never thought about it before."

Cyrus and Smithwick looked at him. "Thought about what?" they said in unison.

"I'm as old as you were."

"Shut up!"

"What's your name, son?"

"Don't you open your mouth!"

"Isaac."

"Well hell. I told you to keep quiet. I ought to whop you one."

"That might be a job," Smithwick said.

"It ain't our fight, Smithwick."

"Santa Anna won't see it that way."

"He ain't took Béxar yet."

"He will. I've seen the fortress." He shook his head. "Why would any man follow an Alabama lawyer?"

Isaac met his father's gaze. He could see the old man thinking.

"I just need men to see the woman and children and old folks eastward," Smithwick said. "And watch the road. I'm not talking about throwing your boy at the Mexican army."

Isaac cleared his throat. "That don't sound too . . ."

"Hush! Where's all the men at?" Cyrus said.

"Some at Béxar. Some in my company. Most went to Gonzales to wait on Houston."

Cyrus snorted. "Ran off and left their women and younguns."

"No. And you know it."

Cyrus studied Smithwick. "Well." He looked Isaac up and down. "Anything happens to this boy, your hide'll hang on my smokehouse wall."

Smithwick nodded.

"Right alongside mine," Cyrus said under his breath. He handed Isaac the rifle.

• • •

Isaac shivered. Birds chittered in the trees. He watched the frosted road, and noted ice in the ruts. He stood and tried to stomp but couldn't feel his feet. He shuffled about until feeling began to return, but his toes remained numb. He thought of his father's stories of frozen digits turning black and falling off.

The morning sky was virtually cloudless, and the sun rising above the oaken hills provided no warmth. Twice he mistook the sound of foraging squirrels for Smithwick coming to join him. The wind had nearly laid, but the air felt colder than ever. Mexican soldiers now seemed a remote threat. Surviving the cold had become everything. Pacing made him feel better. He'd keep moving. Mexicans be damned. Surely he'd hear them coming down the road in time to hide.

Two does appeared along the far side of the road. Isaac never tired of watching deer. He stood motionless. They made their way to the creek and drank, raising their heads now and again to listen and test the air currents. Their delicate hooves made no sound on the frozen mud.

One doe jerked her head up and looked toward the woods opposite Isaac. Then the other one did the same. Another deer coming. A buck maybe. Then again it seemed unlikely in late winter. The rut had long since ended. He'd recently seen shed antlers. He waited. The larger doe stamped. Isaac backed into a tree and eased to the ground. White tails went up, then down. Isaac began to suspect wolves. Then both deer snorted and bounded up the bank right at him. He raised a hand, and the deer leapt sideways and spun, kicking up duff, then jumped the creek and disappeared in the brush. The sound of their headlong flight faded in an instant. He scanned the far side of the road. He never missed a chance to watch unsuspecting wild things, and he had the wind in his favor.

A soft thud came from the trees. He stiffened, then recognized the sound of horses' hooves moving through the oaks. The head and chest of a Spanish mustang appeared from the shadow, then the rider, a man wrapped in a buffalo robe. Three more riders followed.

Long braids, shields, and bows. Isaac shivered and tried to silence his breathing. One man wore a white coat with red epaulets. Another wore a dark shako topped with a red plume. All carried short bows slung across their backs and quivers full of arrows. Two appeared to be boys; the other two middle aged. The older men held muskets across their saddles. They watered their horses at the creek.

One of the elders stood in his stirrups, drew a leg up, and placed a knee on the horse's back. Pulling aside his breechclout, he pissed in the road without dismounting. A boy said something and they all laughed. Several times one or more glanced in Isaac's direction, but they remained at ease.

Each took something from a hide bag, and they sat their horses, chewing and talking. None seemed bothered by the cold. Isaac concentrated to control his shivering. He wanted to close his eyes and think of an oak fire and coals six inches deep, but he dared not look away from the Indians. He could hear his own breathing.

He prayed that the horses would not smell the mustangs and nicker. What if Captain Smithwick awoke and walked unaware into the midst of these wild men?

The Indians laughed again and one sang a snippet of song. Isaac considered picking a target. Shivering though he was, he wouldn't miss at this distance. Would they bolt or melt into the trees and hunt him down? The shot would warn the Captain but would also give them away.

He shivered so that his bones ached. Surely they would hear his breathing or look up and see his white face. Though he knew the difficulty in spying any motionless creature, he wanted to cover his face with his blanket.

The cold seemed unbearable. His thoughts strayed to yesterday's scene in Bastrop, then to the Comanche's buffalo robe, which seemed to transform into a mule's luxuriant winter coat that he now felt wrapped around him. No, not a mule's coat. One of his mother's quilts. Heavy and warm. The aching in his bones had subsided. He heard horses on the road but could not find the riders. Then silence. How long had he been here? Someone was coming through the woods. Just squirrels, maybe. Or the Mexicans. He had to stay awake and watch for Mexican soldiers. Or was it Comanches he'd been worried about? Yes, someone was coming. He tried to roll away, but he was too sleepy, unable to lift his exhausted arms.

He felt a blow against his jaw. They had him. Why couldn't he move? "Isaac," a man said. "Isaac! Wake up, son. You've damn near froze to death!"

Four

"THOSE HEATHENS were wearing parts of Mexican uniforms," Noah Smithwick said. "They love anything showy." He laid a wrist-sized piece of oak into the fire. "Caught one of Gaona's patrols along the road, I imagine."

Smithwick had pulled off Isaac's wet clothes and wrapped him in four blankets. His shivering had abated so that he could speak. He felt the cold air on his face. The barebacked horses grazed the meager grass in the sunlit clearing. "Awfullest lookin' men I ever saw," he said.

Smithwick laughed. "I imagine so. You barely lived to tell me about it."

Isaac clasped his hands between his thighs. The sudden warmth pained his fingers. This time yesterday he'd been on his way to Bastrop. Now he'd nearly frozen to death within earshot of four Comanche raiders fresh from their massacre of a Mexican cavalry patrol hunting for Texians like himself. "I was restin' easy when you showed up," he said, and laughed softly.

"About gone is what you were. I didn't know if you'd make it or not. Winter before last a boy turned his dugout over in the middle of the river. Swam back to the bank but crumpled over before he made it down to the ferry. Still breathin' when we found him. We hauled him up to old man Roberts's place, built up a big fire, stripped him, and rolled him into every quilt we could find. We even got Otis Crocker to strip and crawl in with him to warm him up." Still hunkering, Smithwick moved to one side to avoid the smoke. He shook his head. "He slipped away in spite of it all."

Isaac wormed deeper into the rough blankets. "You ain't worried about somebody smellin' our smoke?"

"I am. But I worry more about your daddy nailing my hide to his smoke-house."

That afternoon, they found Bastrop deserted save for nineteen rangers, several dozen dogs, untold numbers of cats and chickens, a few milk cows, and an abundance of half-wild swine. Choctaw Tom Crosby met them as they rode in. "We're supposed to get across the river, break up the ferry, and sink every boat," Crosby said. "We'll see if Gaona's boys can swim."

"Where's Major Williamson?" Smithwick asked.

"On to Gonzales, where we'll be headin' soon as we can sink these boats. This boy cause you any trouble?"

"He's a hand. Says he got a little cold watchin' Comanches."

"Comanches. Lord."

"Seems they got to one of Gaona's patrols before it got to us. The bucks were wearin' Mexican army garb."

Crosby took a drink from a jug. "Sooner we get east of the Brazos, the better."

"I'm guessin' that ain't water," Smithwick said.

"Best water I've had. Try a swig."

Smithwick took a pull and nodded his approval. Isaac expected him to offer the jug. He didn't.

"By god, this is a forlorn sight," Smithwick said, looking around. "All these years of work."

Isaac listened to the howling dogs and tried to imagine his family fleeing eastward: his father on horseback, cussing the mules and the dogs; his mother driving the team, Esther in the seat next to her; the three hounds snuffling in the woods on either side of the road. He swallowed and looked into the hills to the north.

With axes, they chopped holes in the bottoms of dozens of dugouts and canoes, pushed them into the current, and watched them sink. The Colorado ran fast and green, and the steep banks, covered with oak, elm, and sycamore, rose on either side.

Isaac, Smithwick, and Crosby led their horses onto the ferry. Felix Gross worked the rope. Isaac stroked his horse's neck.

"Felix, I see you've found a more agreeable line of work," Smithwick said.

Gross pulled the rope hand over hand. "Where in hell is that son of a bitch Williamson? Off to Gonzales, that's where. And we're left to face Gaona's cavalry. I'd like to know who picked out our officers. Nobody asked me about it."

"Your optimism is infectious," Smithwick said. He winked at Isaac. "Don't worry about old Felix. He'll stick when the time comes."

Felix spat an amber stream into the river. "Fixin' to get every one of us shot, lanced, or bayoneted." He looked at Isaac. "Now we're gatherin' up boys."

Isaac's ears went hot.

"Why Felix, Noah tells me the boy's right steady," Tom Crosby said. "Sat dead still while a gaggle of Comanches watered their horses at the creek."

Isaac looked back at Bastrop. They were nearly across the river now. He'd sat dead still all right.

The ferry bumped the east bank, and they led their nervous horses onto the gravel. Felix grabbed Isaac's arm as he stepped from the ferry. "How many was there?"

"Four. Captain Smithwick is lettin' on bigger than it was. I was too scared to move. About fouled my britches."

Gross smiled more with his eyes than his mouth. He squeezed Isaac's arm. "Damn right," he said.

• • •

They camped just above the east bank. From one of the deserted cabins, Isaac had gathered two threadbare quilts to add to his bedroll. The ranging company was spread amid huge oaks in a grassy flat against hills rising to pine forest. A waxing moon, nearly full, sat just above the eastern horizon. Noah Smithwick raised a Dutch oven lid to check a ragged chunk of pork loin. Tom Crosby sipped milk from a gourd ladle. "Easy livin' on the fruits of other men's labors," he said.

Isaac folded one of the quilts in half and laid it as close to the three-foot fire ring as he dared. He lay down and propped his head in his hand, stared into the fire, and basked in the heat of the oak coals. "Somebody might be livin' on the fruits of your labors, Tom. Nobody's watchin' your place."

Crosby wiped off his milk mustache with the back of his hand. "They'd find the livin' right sparse."

"I don't feel right helpin' myself to these people's quilts," Isaac said. "They'll need their stuff when they get back." Now fire blind, he looked at Noah Smithwick but couldn't make out his features.

Crosby took another sip of milk. "We need their things right now. You freezin' to death or me starvin' won't help nobody. And them comin' back to their farms is too far down the road for me to see."

"I find myself in the uncomfortable position of agreement with Tom Crosby," Smithwick said. "What we know this night is that seven hundred Mexican soldiers are headed this way on the San Antonio Road."

"Still don't feel Christian," Isaac said. He wondered what his family had left behind.

Smithwick stared beyond the flames. "The Almighty may well take the matter up with us shortly."

Crosby rubbed his thinly bearded chin. "I wonder if it makes any difference if you die fightin' Catholics instead of heathens."

Felix Gross walked into the circle of firelight. He held two jugs. "A bit of fortification, boys?"

Smithwick laughed. "I'd much prefer fornication, Felix, but lacking that, I suppose fortification will do."

Crosby spat into the coals. "Speakin' of heathens."

Gross arched his brows. "Heathen? Why I've been a good Catholic ever since I crossed the Sabine. I'm a man of my word." He hoisted a jug. "See there? I say we pass these around and all behave like the proper Catholics we said we'd be."

Isaac didn't know what he was, but he doubted he was Catholic. "I don't recall sayin' that."

"I reckon DeWitt failed to read that part of the agreement to your daddy," Gross said.

Isaac moved closer to the fire. "As I recall, we rode down from Arkansas and lit where it suited us."

Gross took another swallow. "Goddamn hill men. We'll soon be overrun by 'em." He winked at Isaac. "The sooner the better, I say."

Smithwick accepted one of the jugs. "We all can't be men of education and refinement like you, Felix." He took a long pull.

"Refinement? I expect we'll be dead or squattin' in Louisiana before long," Gross said.

Smithwick belched. "A man of vision and hope."

Gross handed the second jug to Crosby and drew a cheroot from a coat pocket. He shoved a finger-sized stick halfway into the coals. "A man of practicality," he said with the unlit cheroot between his teeth. He withdrew the stick and lit his smoke.

"Why not just light out for the Sabine?" Isaac asked. He found it a compelling question, one he'd taken to asking himself a dozen times every waking hour.

Gross studied the glowing tip of his cheroot. "Well, I can't say I ain't thought about it, and I don't believe there's a man in the company that ain't thought about it. But I put down roots here in '30, and I can't abide nobody marchin' in here from five hundred miles away runnin' me off my place." He shook his head and tossed the cheroot into the fire. "Of course, now, we wouldn't be worryin' about any of this if we didn't have a bunch of rich planters at Washington and San Felipe raisin' hell just because Santa Anna says they can't bring in any more niggers to pick their cotton."

Smithwick slapped his thighs. "It goes deeper than that, Felix, and you know it. And why resent a man because of his means?"

"They showed up with their damn slaves and stock and took up all the best bottomland and commenced gettin' richer while the rest of us is up in the hills killin' our mules jerkin' stumps out of our cornfields."

"A true democrat," Smithwick said.

Isaac had no idea what a democrat might be, and he had no intention of asking in front of Gross. "Land seems like the one thing we got plenty of. Besides, we couldn't abide the gators eatin' our dogs down in the bottoms."

Gross shook his head in exasperation. "I reckon a man would have to know better to care."

"We're doin' good," Isaac said. "Our place ought to last us another five years yet. It's downright level next to our last place."

"Goddamn," Felix said.

Smithwick leaned toward Gross. The fire lit his sharp features. "Felix. We're under the rule of a dictator. Our government—if you can call it that—funds no schools and offers no protection, yet it taxes the life out of us and shoves the Catholic religion down our throats."

"I don't pay no taxes," Gross said. "I swap for what I need. Anyway, we knew all this when we came."

Smithwick rolled his eyes. "We thought we had a constitution. But Santa Anna does whatever he pleases. He kept Austin locked up for more than a year, and now here he comes with an army to run us off our farms. Has he done one thing to help us with the Comanches? Hell no. Lets us make the province fit for men, and how does he repay us?"

Gross picked his front teeth with his thumbnail. "We ran Cós out of Béxar."

"Cós chose to occupy Béxar. He got just what he deserved."

"The Mexicans think Béxar's theirs. And we can't forget our mighty invasion of Matamoras."

Smithwick studied his hands. "Absolute lunacy there. I'll be the first to admit it."

Gross nodded emphatically. "We've shit in our own spring, and now we're fixin' to drink."

Isaac had not known the arrangement was so complicated. After wearing out farms in Tennessee and Arkansas, Cyrus Webb found a patch of unoccupied land in Texas and unloaded his wagon. And no one in Arkansas had ever seemed ready to take up arms over the absence of schools.

The Captain crossed his arms on his chest. "We've whipped the Kronks and Tonkawas and established profitable agriculture. Why shouldn't we be in charge of our destiny?"

Having thrown away his cheroot, Gross now stuffed his pipe. "It ain't what we said we was goin' to do."

"All agreements were voided when Santa Anna abolished the constitution," Smithwick said.

Isaac remained confused on the issue of the constitution. Numerous things were said to have upset his father's constitution. None, as far as he knew, had ever abolished it.

Gross lit his pipe. "Neither here nor there. My wife and boys have piled everything we own into two wagons and are runnin' for the Sabine. I aim to cover 'em."

In the moonlight, Isaac saw the horses grazing on the hillside and the forms of men huddled around a dozen fires. Across the river, the deserted log buildings and homes stood dark like burned-out hulks. The barking of the settlement dogs and the lowing of abandoned cattle mingled with the howling of wolves in the hills. Somewhere along that road, he thought, seven hundred Mexican soldiers were huddled around their own fires.

Five

NEXT MORNING Isaac woke to find camp occupied by eleven wet dogs.

"Wretched curs swam the river last night," Felix said. He pointed to a bushy gray and black brindled mongrel. "Woke up this mornin' and that sumbitch was layin' across my legs. Had to lay there a spell after I shoved him off before the feeling came back to my feet."

Tom Crosby squatted by the fire. "I don't know why we couldn't have somethin' good to eat swim across the river and walk into camp. Why didn't we shoot some of them hogs and haul 'em across before we sunk the ferry?"

Smithwick banged the coffeepot on a rock to settle the grounds. "Nothin' to keep you from eatin' dog, Tom." He glanced at Isaac, then back at Crosby. "I hear young dog ain't too bad."

"Who said?"

"Oh, that big old Lipan chief. What's his name?"

"Castro? Hell. No tellin' what that murderin' heathen eats."

Felix poured himself a cup of coffee. "You surprise me, Tom, you bein' a Choctaw." He blew on his coffee. "Of course, now, y'all got whipped right off. The Lipans ain't been properly whipped and civilized yet."

Crosby stared sullenly into the fire. "I don't reckon we ever ate dog."

"I knew some Choctaws that ate two mules one winter in Arkansas," Isaac said.

Smithwick shook his head. "That's different. Me and John Webber ate a mule one time when we were running tobacco down in Coahuila. As I recall, it ate just fine."

"I never tasted mule either," Crosby said. "And I don't aim to." The brindled dog snuffled up and nuzzled his elbow. Felix looked mirthfully at Isaac. Crosby cracked a smile and scratched the mongrel's ears.

The other dogs sniffed about the cook fires. Isaac spotted a lanky black and tan hound swaggering about carrying a hog's foot. "What're we gonna do with all of 'em, Captain?"

Smithwick dipped a piece of cold cornbread in his coffee. "Looks like our ranks are swelling."

By midmorning, Isaac had coaxed the big hound to within arm's length with a scrap of cornbread raked through the previous night's pork drippings.

She circled warily, wagging her tail, but kept just beyond Isaac's reach, unwilling to drop her pig's foot.

The other dogs erupted when a man rode in from the south. Isaac looked up, and the hound dropped the pig's foot and snatched the greasy cornbread from his fingers before he could lay hands on her. She dashed away twenty yards and stood with her ears pricked, licking her lips. As soon as Isaac walked away toward the rider, she dashed back and snatched her pig's foot.

"Be feedin' that bitch all the way to the Sabine," Felix said.

"I aim to feed her all the way home."

"Now ain't that gonna be a sight. Folks runnin' for their lives in front of the Mexican army and here we come draggin' along a pack of mongrel dogs."

"She looks like she might be blooded."

"A blooded hound in Texas. That'd make her better born than any of us."

They walked to the gathering that had formed around the new arrival. The short, stocky, red-bearded man dismounted and stepped from behind his horse.

Isaac stopped. "Lord have mercy."

"That's Major Williamson," Felix said. "Three-legged Willy."

A wooden peg extended from Williamson's right knee to the ground. His withered calf, ankle, and moccasined foot were drawn back at a right angle as if he were about to hop on the other foot. He wore buckskin breeches and a black woolen coat.

The deformity and short stature didn't seem to diminish the Major's sense of authority. He handed his rein to Tom Crosby. "Boys, General Houston is marshaling an army of volunteers at Gonzales. Our orders are to remain here until further notice or the arrival of Gaona's cavalry."

"Wait here to be lanced," Felix said under his breath.

Williamson's eyes sought the source of the comment. "What was that, Felix?"

"I said this is our best chance." Laughter rippled through the group.

"How could I ever doubt you, Felix?" he said. "Noah, keep two guards posted along the river. The Mexicans will have hell crossing, and that should give us all the time we need to carry the news to the General and any citizens who might be straggling."

"Where's Samuels?" Crosby said.

Williamson nodded. "I'm afraid the good captain has taken his leave to see his family across the Sabine."

Smithwick spat. "Why sure."

Nicholas Wren ran from the trees at the base of the hill. He burst into the gathering. "Captain. Major." He bent and rested his hands on his knees.

"Catch your breath, Nick," Williamson said.

Wren coughed and spat. "We missed some company last night. Must've hurt their feelings 'cause they took three of our horses when they left."

• • •

Isaac slept little the next week. Although the men blamed the thievery on Comanches, Smithwick admitted that the horses could just as well have been stolen by Lipans, Tonkawas, or even Caddos. At times, Isaac stood watch along the river and in the hills above the horse pasture. The older men seemed to trust him and he began to move easily among them, although he wondered if they knew the same terror he felt alone at night with his back against a tree and wind whispering in the pines and the purling river or the horses' restless movements below.

Days went by pleasant or cold and wet. After a particularly hard rain, the rangers gave up all pretension of stewardship and simply occupied the most comfortable dwellings on the east side of the river. No one seemed inclined to forage given the abundance of hogs, chickens, eggs, and milk cows.

The dogs lived well. The big hound had taken to following Isaac and sat with him on watch if she wasn't running game in the hills. Isaac and Tom Crosby talked of hunting with her, but remembrance of the horse thievery kept them near the settlement. Sometimes the hound's deep baying continued through the night or faded into the distance, but she never missed her morning handout.

Nearly all of the men had family fleeing eastward. Isaac took solace in this and fantasized of a triumphant reunion with his parents and sister. If they made decent time, it seemed unlikely the Mexicans could catch them. They could go back to Arkansas, or given his father's wanderlust, to Missouri.

Texas had been fine, but in the last two years he had felt a sharp yearning for and curiosity about young women. He'd seen a few around Gonzales and San Felipe, daughters of prosperous citizens who felt little regard for mountain families scratching a living from the thin soil of the oak and cedar uplands.

Six

UNCLE JIMMY CURTIS was drunk. Isaac knew it the instant he heard the old man staggering down the bank to post sunrise watch. The waxing moon sat atop the western hills, but the day's first tentative twitterings had already replaced the furtive rustling of night things. Below him, the yet rising Colorado gurgled and whispered.

"Good morning, Uncle Jimmy. Are you up to this?" Isaac had no idea whose uncle the old man was, but everyone, including Captain Smithwick, addressed him as such and treated him with deference.

"Who's down there?"

"It's me. Isaac."

"Young Isaac Webb!" Uncle Jimmy stopped. Isaac still couldn't see him but suspected the old man had paused to pull on his jug. The spastic rustling continued to baritone accompaniment:

Run your sow with a ten-foot pole,
Twist that groundhog out his hole,
Ground-haawwwg!

"I'm comin', boy." He staggered into the clearing. "There you are. The Mexicans would sure as hell never find you. All clear you say?"

"I ain't seen a thing. Where's your rifle?"

Uncle Jimmy looked at his jug, then at his gnarled, empty hand. His buckskins swallowed him, and the moon turned his sunken, bewhiskered jaws cotton white. "Well I'll be goddamn."

Isaac sighed. "Where'd you leave it?"

"You're a good boy, Isaac. A fine boy. I'm just an old man. Can't do nothin' right."

"Now that ain't so. I'll get your rifle and you can sit right here and watch the river." Isaac wanted to get away before Uncle Jimmy turned weepy as he'd been wont ever since word came that his son-in-law Wash Cottle died at the Alamo.

"Wash was good boy too—you know it?"

Isaac cringed. "I know he was and I know you miss him." He had never met the man.

Uncle Jimmy sobbed and wiped his eyes with his sleeve. With his finger still in the jug handle, he put both hands on Isaac's shoulders. "I want you to promise old Uncle Jimmy something, Isaac."

"Anything you want." He'd promise to give away his firstborn if it would get him away from Jimmy's breath.

"There's fixin' to be some dyin'. Promise me you won't get yourself in some place you can't get out of. Promise me that, will you?"

"I promise I'll be careful."

"These fools don't care nothin' about you. Sam Houston don't know you any better than Travis knowed Wash Cottle. Don't go gettin' hemmed in for some dandy wantin' to hold on to his niggers and make hisself a name. Promise me that, son." His eyes were unfocused but ardent. His head wobbled. He shook Isaac's shoulders.

Isaac nodded. The ache in his throat surprised him. "I promise. You just sit right here on this stump, and I'll fetch your rifle."

Uncle Jimmy embraced him and patted his back with the jug. "You're a good one all right, Isaac. I knowed it as soon as I laid eyes on you."

Isaac led him to the stump. The old man crumpled and sat with his head hanging between his knees. Isaac turned away and wiped his eyes, much to his vexation. "I'll be right back."

He strode up the path toward the ranger encampment. He hoped old Jimmy had left his rifle with his bedroll. He shook his head. Some company this was. What kind of officer would send an old drunk to guard the river against seven hundred advancing Mexicans? They had gotten damned careless. Sleeping past daybreak. Eating other people's hogs and chickens. And here he was blubbering like a woman at a tent revival. Some of the men now doubted that the Mexicans were coming. Santa Anna had made his point, they said, and had turned back toward Mexico. Isaac had to admit that the theory seemed plausible. Gaona should have arrived days ago.

Sis jogged down the hill to meet him. She'd bayed in the hills all night. He palmed her soft muzzle. "Left me on the river by myself, and now you expect me to feed you." She sniffed and licked his palm and whipped her tail.

Lately he'd felt guilty about befriending the big hound. Now she'd follow him east causing who knows what kind of problems. And her owner might return to find her gone. Then again, a real houndsman wouldn't have abandoned her in the first place. He smiled. What would his father think of him bringing home a handsome black and tan hound from a deadly fracas with the Mexicans?

He followed the path to three large cabins set against the wooded hills. There had been a fourth until Otis Crocker and Tom Crosby piled too much wood into the fireplace one cold night and nearly burned themselves up along with the cabin. Now a blackened stone foundation and chimney stood off to his right.

A rooster crowed, and several dogs barked at his approach. The moon had dipped below the horizon. Dew-wet grass had soaked his breeches from toe to thigh. Smoke from the chimneys rose straight up. Clear day ahead.

He took the leftmost footpath to the low log house where Uncle Jimmy had been sleeping. He heard men snoring well before he reached the stoop. Sis curled up in the dirt, and he eased the door open. The leather hinges made no sound. His eyes had adjusted to the dark woods, so the coals in the fireplace made the single room seem well lit. A half-dozen men lay on the floor. Two others lay in beds. He longed for his own bedroll, but he'd settle for a nap after breakfast. He found Jimmy's rifle propped in a corner along with his bedroll and stood for a moment to let the coals warm his wet shins.

Another cock crowed. The men continued their snoring. Isaac padded back across the room, stepping over sleeping rangers. Tom Crosby suddenly sat up. "By god, it ought to, for what it cost," he said. He lay back down and rolled over. Isaac suppressed a laugh and stepped back into the cold dawn. Sis looked at him expectantly.

They walked down the path, Isaac carrying a rifle in each hand. In the growing light he could see that Uncle Jimmy's weapon, plain as it was, with no engraving or checkering, had been lovingly cared for. He noted the perfectly knapped flint. Maybe he didn't really know the old man.

They came to the riverbank, and Sis raised her nose to the breeze and moved haltingly.

Isaac nudged her ribs with his foot. "What you smell, gal? Uncle Jimmy ain't *that* ripe, is he?" She wagged her tail but kept her nose pointed eastward across the river, ears pricked, brow furrowed.

The settlement looked deserted. He heard nothing but the river, the stiff westerly wind, and the whipping grass and brush. They stood watching the road. The sun edged above the eastern hills and lit Camino Real so that he could see the ruts two hundred yards away. Sis growled.

A distant glint caught his eye. It danced and elongated and moved toward him along the road. Sis let go a short bark. Her erect hackles formed a dark ridge along her spine to the tip of her tail. The sound of his own ragged breathing startled him. At a bend, beyond the last log building, sunlight struck the bit, cheek, and chest of a big palomino, then polished black boots, white breeches, and red plume, and now Isaac resolved the scene before him. A column of gleaming lance heads ran from the far edge of Bastrop, around the bend, and into the low hills to the west.

Seven

NOAH SMITHWICK STOOD on the doorstep holding a coffeepot when Isaac ran into the bare yard. "Wha—? Ain't that Uncle Jimmy's gun?"

Isaac had forgotten about the second rifle. "They're here, Captain. And Uncle Jimmy's passed out drunk on the riverbank." He leaned on the two guns to catch his breath.

Smithwick wiped his eyes with the back of his free hand and nodded gravely as if the Mexicans' arrival had been inevitable and he'd foreseen it months ago. "How many?"

"Hundreds of 'em. Hell, thousands, I don't know. Comin' through Bastrop carryin' lances. You've never seen nothin' like it." A good spit seemed in order, but his tongue was dry as parchment.

Smithwick glanced at his coffeepot, then looked about as if trying to decide where to put it. He tossed it toward the fire ring. Sis loped over to investigate. "Go get Uncle Jimmy. I'll be there soon as I can roust the boys."

Isaac ran back down the hill. Behind him Smithwick bellowed, "No, god-damn it, I ain't joshing you! Get the hell up!"

The trail bent to the right. Sis, having given up on the coffeepot, nearly knocked Isaac down as she passed him. He broke out of the trees and found a sea of white fatigues, shakos, lances, and horses on the far side of the river. A man wearing a blue jacket and red sash strode along the bank, looking up at Isaac, pointing and shouting in Spanish. Seventy yards below, Uncle Jimmy lay on his face in the little clearing. A few yards beyond, the bank dropped away twenty feet to the river. Sis threw her head back and bawled as if she'd treed a panther.

As Isaac started down the steep trail, a half-dozen soldiers formed up at water's edge. He ran, leaping deadfalls and brush. The clearing and the river rushed at him. The riflemen each dropped to a knee and aimed. Thirty feet from the clearing, he turned sideways in the trail, and, holding the rifles out for balance, dug at the ground with the balls of his feet. He leapt over Jimmy, then realized, with grim fascination, that he couldn't stop. At the far side of the clearing, at the edge of the drop-off, he hooked the trunk of a young sycamore with his left arm, and his feet flew from beneath him.

He hit the ground on his side, and the impact drove the air from his lungs.

Pain shot up his rib cage. His left arm felt as if it had been ripped from its socket.

No shots. He'd probably fallen from the Mexican's view. And he still held both rifles. His breath returned; he gasped. "Shit! Oh lord." He smelled the damp earth. The thought of raising his head above the brush made his skin crawl.

He lay resting, praying. Sis nuzzled his face. He heard the voices of the Mexicans and the snorts and whinnies of their horses. Still, no shots came. Surely, they couldn't get across the river. Surely they wouldn't risk the deep, fast water for one man. He thought of Smithwick and the others saddling horses and striking eastward in a panic. And here he was with God only knows what broken. All to save a man too drunk to know he was about to die; too drunk to know that he, Isaac Webb, had just damn near killed himself.

With his good arm, he dug the butt of his rifle into the mud, drew his knees beneath him, and tried to pull himself up the bank. The pain in his ribs nauseated him. Tears dripped into his open mouth. "Damn it; goddamnit!"

He churned the bank with his knees and clawed the ground with the rifle butt. The bastards had deserted him. Smithwick sent him down here. Damn right, he'd go rouse the others.

Shots came from across the river, and the balls struck the bank well above him. He could hear the Mexican officer bellowing at the riflemen. So this was it. They'd just spray the bank with lead until they struck flesh. He hoped they hit him in the head right off, if they hit him at all. Far better than being slowly shot to pieces. Or lying there for days with a hole in him. If they hit him, he'd just start screaming and they could hone in on the sound and finish him off.

A shot rang out above him. One of the Mexicans screamed and Isaac heard shouts and thrashing in the shallows. Encouraged, he dug with his knees and the rifle butt and pulled himself screaming and cursing into the clearing and crawled face-to-face with Noah Smithwick.

"By god, Isaac, I thought sure they'd killed you."

"Damn near did," he said, nearly weeping with relief. Another Mexican volley cut the sumac above his head and reminded him that two could die as easily as one.

Smithwick crawled to Uncle Jimmy and shook him. "Wake up, Uncle Jimmy, you drunken old shit."

Jimmy rolled onto his side and propped himself on his elbow. "What in hell, Cap'm? Is it my watch?"

"For god's sake, Uncle Jimmy, we're under fire. Keep your fool head down. Isaac, can you run?"

Isaac nodded and rubbed his bad arm. "I'll run, but he'll have to carry his own damn gun."

"Why that's my rifle you've got there," Uncle Jimmy said. "You've got mud all over it."

Isaac shoved the rifle at the old man. The pain in his arm made him dizzy. "Goddamn you."

Uncle Jimmy's eyes settled on his jug. "How about a drink, Cap'm?"

Smithwick ignored him. He looked at Isaac. "After their next volley, I'll scatter 'em with a shot. Keep low and head up the bank. Don't stop until you get in the woods. The Major and the boys have already lit out." He lay the butt of his rifle downhill, poured a palmful of powder from his horn, and dumped it down the barrel.

"Here, just shoot mine; it's loaded," Isaac said.

Smithwick shook his head. "You might need it." He pulled a loading block from his possibles bag, positioned a patch and ball at the muzzle, and ramrodded them down the barrel. He pinched on a cap and looked at Isaac. "When you get to the horses, wait for us. I'll drag Uncle Jimmy up the hill."

"Cap'm, I can't leave you two here. I'll help you."

Smithwick shook his head in exasperation. "We don't even know if you can get yourself up that hill."

"I believe I've broke some ribs."

The Captain gripped his rifle. "You gotta go."

"Let that pup go and we'll have us a little snort, Cap'm," Uncle Jimmy said. He drank from his jug.

More gunfire came from below. Balls hit the bank ten feet below them. Sis calmly scratched behind her ear.

"They're feeling their way to us," Smithwick said. "Get ready." He got to one knee, aimed and fired toward the Mexican riflemen.

Isaac heard more shouting below as he pushed himself to his feet using his rifle as an alpenstock. He started up the hill, but jagged pain sent him to his hands and knees. He crawled through the brush, keeping his nose almost to the ground. Below him, Uncle Jimmy said, "The hell, they are. We'll leave after we've had us a drink."

The Mexicans fired again, and Smithwick cursed. Isaac crawled faster. Were he on his feet he'd be safely up the bank and into the trees by now, he thought. He worried that Smithwick was hit, but he heard his rifle again, followed by another shot. "Aggravatin' bastards!" Uncle Jimmy yelled.

Smithwick laughed triumphantly. "By god, Uncle Jimmy, you've shot one of their horses!" Isaac heard the two men thrashing through the brush behind him. The Mexicans' shots fell short again, then another volley cut branches from the trees over his head. Muskets, he thought. If they were shooting long rifles, he wouldn't be crawling up this hill. He threw up a prayer of thanks.

He scrambled up the bank and onto the forested bench, out of range of the Mexican guns. Sis, who'd dutifully followed him up the bank, sniffed his sweaty hair. He rolled onto his good side and looked back. The shooters were standing with their officer, watching Smithwick dragging Jimmy up the bank by his collar. Hundreds of soldiers were erecting tents, gathering firewood, and seeing to their horses.

Isaac's breathing had slowed, but he felt as if he had a thick blade between his ribs. He studied the Mexicans. These were professional soldiers. Small men, mostly. Some looked to be a full head shorter than he and the Captain. But they watched with the casual interest of seasoned fighters. Yes, the Texians were escaping, but there would be another fight another day. Smithwick's marksmanship had disrupted their shooting, but, after each of his shots, they had re-formed to take careful aim.

His head was clear now. And he knew this: even terrified he could fight. He hadn't fired a shot, but he could have. He'd be afraid the next time too, but he'd fight. And Captain Smithwick would stick.

He watched the soldiers. Their uniforms and weaponry looked out of place against the forested riverbanks. These men were invaders. They had nothing invested here and had come only under orders. Certainly the whites and Tejanos were invaders, too, in the eyes of the Lipans, Tonkawas, and Comanches. But his people had come to stay and make a life here. This was his home as much as any place had ever been home. He'd met his enemy.

He thought of Smithwick's assessment that the longer Texians could hold out, the better their prospects. They'd wear down Gaona and his men; harry them and disappear into the hills. These were soldiers of open battlefields and roads. They fought with cannon, musket, and bayonet, but this was country suited for the long rifle, the bow and arrow, and the quick skirmish. He remembered the Comanche boys wearing the ridiculous shakos and fatigues. Four raiders had wiped out a Mexican patrol. The hapless soldiers probably never saw their killers.

Smithwick heaved Uncle Jimmy over the top of the bank. The old man fell on his face, then turned to study Isaac. He looked sober now. "Lord, Cap'm, this boy ain't gonna be good for much."

Eight

ISAAC DECIDED that the riverbank skirmish may have killed him after all. After fetching the horses, Smithwick and Uncle Jimmy helped him onto a laconic sorrel mare named Fanny. He nearly passed out in the saddle.

Uncle Jimmy stood ready to catch him. "By god, Cap'm, he's pasty. Maybe we ought to fix him a travois."

Smithwick tightened his cinch. "A travois. And drag him over this road? Might as well leave him for Gaona."

Isaac saw no humor in the remark. If Uncle Jimmy's sudden sobriety was any indication, their situation was grim indeed. "I'm ready, Captain. I'll feel better after we put a little distance between us and those damn lancers." He was nearly dying where he sat. Why not go ahead and move?

Smithwick scratched his head beneath his formless gray hat. "Maybe I ought to tie you on your horse."

Isaac took a deep breath and fought his nausea. "Hellfire; let's ride."

Smithwick smiled. "Let's be off, Uncle Jimmy, before I have to shoot the boy for insubordination."

The old man kept his eyes on Isaac. "I reckon I can take it if he can." He slid his rifle into his scabbard and climbed into the saddle. "Left my damn jug on the river."

Smithwick stepped into a stirrup and grabbed the saddle horn. "Fetch it if you've a mind to." He started eastward on Camino Real. "We'll just have to take her slow. Two of the boys are afoot. We'll catch them soon enough."

Sis howled from the riverbank. "Givin' 'em hell, ain't she," Jimmy said.

Isaac's throat ached. No sense trying to call a worked-up hound. "Leavin' my dog." His two companions gave no reply.

The morning was cool and clear. The horses stumbled and lurched through ruts brimming with water. They rode for three miles, then took the southeastward fork toward Cole's Settlement. Late morning, they stopped and Smithwick wrapped Isaac's ribs with strips of blanket. "Hang on," he said. He snugged the last strip. Isaac heard Uncle Jimmy say, "Catch 'im," and the muddy road spun and rushed at him.

He woke after dark to suffocating pain. He could draw only shallow, cutting breaths. Smithwick and Jimmy sat by a small fire, watching him. The pines swayed overhead, but the air near the ground was still. The smoke leaned eastward and hung only a few feet above the ground.

Smithwick got up and came to Isaac's side. "You're busted up, but you'll make it. I never heard of a man dying of broken ribs."

His words were a comfort. Pain was best not borne alone. Isaac tried to relax and breathe. "I ain't never hurt like this. I don't know how I'm gonna make it." The few words left him breathless.

"Yeah, but I heard of a fellar dyin' when one of his broke ribs tore a hole in somethin' or other," Jimmy said.

Smithwick shook his head and sighed. "Lord, Uncle Jimmy." He pulled back the blanket. They had wrapped the strips over Isaac's filthy homespun shirt. Smithwick checked the snugness with his finger. "I need to tighten these, Isaac. You ready?"

Isaac nodded and looked at the tops of the pines.

Smithwick untucked the first strip, then tightened it.

Isaac saw a flash of white light. "Oh lord." The treetops spun.

"Now then." Smithwick tucked the wrapping under to hold it in place. He snugged the other two strips as Isaac fought for consciousness. He stood and looked at his work. "That ought to help."

It did. Although his lungs felt even more constricted, Isaac found the stabbing pain much less intense. "Thank you, Captain."

Smithwick smiled and nodded. "We'll catch up to the boys tomorrow. I expect Gaona is still building rafts and looking for river fords. I do worry about a patrol swimming across and overtaking us."

Uncle Jimmy spat into the fire. "Left my damn jug on the river."

• • •

They rode east at sunup. Isaac had slept surprisingly well, but he nearly passed out again when his companions helped him into the saddle.

Shortleaf and loblolly pine rose a hundred feet on either side of the road. Their huge overstory shaded out underbrush so that the forest floor was a nearly open carpet of pine needles.

Several times, they left the miserable ruts, but found the spongy forest even worse and returned to the road. Clouds had gathered again to the west, and the air had grown much cooler. Isaac began to see his breath. Wild things busied themselves in preparation for the coming weather. Squirrels crisscrossed the road; nuthatches ran up and down the massive, scaly trunks. Several times, the riders rounded a bend and sent deer bounding into the pines.

Isaac found that if he rode perfectly erect, he could breathe and endure the pain in his ribs. Whenever he sagged, the cutting pain returned.

His mood darkened along with the sky. More cold rain meant misery and even worse traveling. Already the horses were mired clear to their hocks. He dreaded wet buckskins and sodden blankets.

They rounded a bend to find Sis standing in the road whipping her tail as if she'd been waiting for them all morning.

"Well now," Isaac said. His mood brightened.

"Isaac, I might have to buy that hound," Uncle Jimmy said.

"I don't imagine you can afford her. If Pap ever lays eyes on her, she'll never be for sale."

"Your daddy a dog man, is he?"

"Me and him both."

Uncle Jimmy spat. "I had a good brace of hounds when I first come to Texas, but I swear, I believe them damn Lipans got 'em. They just up and disappeared one night."

"Maybe a panther got 'em. Or a bear," Smithwick said.

"Hell, these dogs treed panthers and bears. Them Lipans got 'em for sure. Goddamn heathens." Jimmy dug in his nose and studied Isaac. "I believe you're doin' a little better."

"The Captain has got me bound up so tight these broke ribs can't move." He wanted to get down and give Sis's ears a good scratching. If he were alone, he'd sweet-talk her a little.

Smithwick smiled at Isaac's remark. "I can't forget your daddy's promise. He'd be damned displeased if he saw you now."

Isaac touched his sore ribs. "I done it to myself. Any fool ought to be able to run down a riverbank."

Uncle Jimmy stared at the road. "I won't forget what you done for me, son."

Isaac face flushed. "Followin' orders."

"Nobody would fault you for leavin' my drunken hide on that river."

"I wouldn't leave you nowhere, Uncle Jimmy. Anyway, you had some grievin' to do."

The old man tugged his beard. "Well, I've done it. If you have to haul me off another riverbank, it won't be because I'm drunk."

Smithwick doffed and reseated his hat. "Boys, I'm touched."

"A man can't say a word in this comp'ny without somebody makin' sport of him," Jimmy said.

Isaac's resentment evaporated. He could never stay angry after an apology and often as not managed to feel guilty for having been mad in the first place. How could you stay upset at a surly old man who had humbled himself enough to express remorse and gratitude?

They rode on. Isaac tired and slumped in his saddle. The wind picked up; cold drizzle stung his face. As they approached a bend, Smithwick's piebald mare nickered and tried to turn around in the road. Smithwick allowed her to face the wind. She snorted and pricked her ears. He patted her neck. "We'd best get off this road for a spell."

They rode into the pines south of the road. Isaac clenched his jaws as Fanny struggled on the boggy ground. A hundred yards into the woods, Smithwick stopped and dismounted. Sis milled around the horses' hooves and raised her nose westward and sniffed.

Uncle Jimmy slid out of the saddle and tied his reins to an oak sapling. He looked at his rifle. "Goddamn this rain," he whispered. "Be a wonder sure enough if this sumbitch shoots."

Isaac dismounted with difficulty. His rifle was still muddy from his fall on the riverbank. With his thumb, he wiped the mud from the flint. "Who do you think it is, Captain?"

"Be damned if I know. But if it's Gaona's cavalry, we'd best stay out of the way. If it's just a patrol . . . well, hell. We'll have to see."

"What about Comanches?" Isaac asked.

Smithwick looked toward the road. "We don't need any trouble with them. Just stay put. I'll ease back a ways and see what we've got."

Uncle Jimmy laid his rifle into the crook of his arm. He shook his head and pinched the loose skin below his chin. "I don't know, Cap'm."

Smithwick waved off the old man's concern. "I can stay clear of anybody on the road. Just stay put and keep these horses quiet." He pulled his hat down and started through the woods parallel to the road. He made no sound on the wet duff and quickly disappeared into the gloom. "Goddamn, this don't feel good," Uncle Jimmy said.

Isaac had no idea whether or not he could fire his rifle. He mounted it, pointing toward the road.

Uncle Jimmy's eyes widened. "What?" he whispered too loudly.

"Seein' if I can shoot." Mounting the gun had pulled at his ribs, but he could shoot. Working the ramrod might be something else altogether. He handed Jimmy the rifle. "Can you hold her for a spell?"

"Now where do you think you're goin'?"

Isaac turned his back to the old man. "I can't shoot good when I've got to piss."

Uncle Jimmy took the rifle. "Lord. Get busy and be done with it."

Isaac finished and took back his rifle. They waited. Drizzle fell through the pines and steam rose from the horses' backs and nostrils. Isaac shifted his weight from one foot to the next to relieve the pain in his side. Uncle Jimmy chewed furiously.

Sis and the horses pricked their ears. Isaac glimpsed movement seventy yards to the west—sudden darkness between two young pines—then Smithwick ran low and silent out of the mist, his wet hat brim sagging over his eyes. His rapid breath hung about his head, and he motioned for the two to come near. He hunkered and they bent to listen. "Three coming," he whispered. "Slow and easy. Talking things over. One of Gaona's patrols, I imagine. Carrying lances and muskets."

"Shit," Uncle Jimmy said.

Isaac heard his pulse. "What now?"

Smithwick searched their faces. "We can stay out of their way, or we can see that they don't make it back. Our shots might draw attention, but I expect the dragoons and most of the cavalry are still trying to cross the river. It's a long way from Bastrop to the nearest ford this time of year."

Uncle Jimmy stopped chewing. "We can't run forever."

Isaac shivered. "Tell me what to do."

"We'll have to light out, after the shootin'," Smithwick said. "You up to it?"

Isaac could not imagine riding at a gallop. Yet the prospect seemed distant in light of the coming violence. "I don't see no choice. I'll ride. I don't aim to get you two killed." The words tumbled out. Suddenly he could recall no compelling justification for this war. He wanted only to get through the fight, then flee.

Smithwick stood and patted Isaac's shoulder. "Well then." He looked at Jimmy. "Take the horses over this little rise and tie them in a draw where they can't smell the Mexicans' horses again." He nodded toward Sis. "I don't know what to tell you about your dog. Keep her quiet or we'll have to uh . . ." He shook his head. "I'm sorry. I don't know what else to do. Move along, Uncle Jimmy. They'll be right in front of us by the time you get back."

The old man gathered the reins and strode away through the woods.

"Lay down where you can see the road and fix you a rest," Smithwick whispered.

Isaac lay down forty yards from the road. Sis wagged her tail and licked his face. Stumps, vines, and low brush blocked his view. He pushed himself up, expecting the Mexicans to appear at any instant. He found another spot and lay down with identical results. After two more tries, he lay prone behind a small log and fashioned a rifle rest with his coat and hat. Now he'd have an open shot.

Thirty yards to his left and slightly back, Smithwick lay seemingly calm, watching the road. Could just as well be deer hunting, Isaac thought. He needed to make water again, but dared not get up. Sis snuffled about behind him. He hissed and she came to him and sniffed his ear. He put his left arm about her shoulders and, with his right, swept her feet from beneath her. She lay sullen with her tail tucked between her legs. He sighted down his rifle barrel. Sis started to get up and he cuffed her on the back of her neck. "Sit still, goddamn you," he whispered. Smithwick scowled and held a finger to his nose.

Sis laid her ears back and curled up with her back tight against his side. Her warmth comforted him.

He watched the road and considered the span of Smithwick's scouting foray. Surely the Mexicans were nearly upon them. Where in hell was Uncle Jimmy? The old man would get him killed yet.

The drizzle continued. He was shivering again. He felt exposed without his hat. Rainwater ran down his forehead and into his eyes and dripped off his chin. He licked it off his upper lip but it did little for his thirst.

Sis raised her head and growled. Isaac nudged her with his hip. He kept his eyes on the road but pictured her long ears pricked, brow furrowed, and sad eyes bright and alert.

The chink of a bit came from somewhere on the road to his left, still out of sight. His heart thumped against the wet, needle-covered ground. A horse snorted. Three riders came into view, moving haltingly. In the gray afternoon light, they appeared as shadows, depthless and colorless.

The wind moved the tops of the pines, and water dripped from the needles. He watched the riders but heard nothing of their movements. Nor did he hear Captain Smithwick, but he felt him, felt his tension as surely as if he were only inches away.

The riders halted and looked about, obviously conferring, although Isaac could not hear their voices. They sat their horses, lances pointed skyward, one man in front and two on either side and slightly back.

Isaac aimed at the lead rider. He eased the serpentine back and felt the trigger in his finger joint. He drew a breath. The front sight steadied. Why didn't the Captain shoot? Hell, they hadn't discussed what they'd do when the time came. And Uncle Jimmy? He exhaled. The riders moved slowly ahead. Perhaps Captain Smithwick lacked a clear shot. Why hadn't they talked about this? He swallowed and drew another breath. He put the bead just ahead of the leader's chest, tracked the slow progress, took in his trigger slack, and exhaled. Please, God, let the powder be dry. Let her fire. He wouldn't miss. Shaking or not. He squeezed. Squeezed. It was always this way; anticipating, cringing. Don't flinch. Squeeze. Came the click of the flint, the hiss, the boom, and searing, white smoke, and Sis sprang to her feet, ears back, tail up, looking for something to tear to pieces.

Isaac recovered from the recoil to see the lead horse bolt without its rider. To his right, Uncle Jimmy was kneeling, clawing at his powder horn and cussing the rain at the top of his lungs. The old man had crept unheard into position.

The two remaining Mexicans spurred their horses. Smithwick fired and a second rider fell. The third horse bucked and reared, and its rider fought to stay in the saddle.

Smithwick got to one knee, swiveled his second barrel into position, cocked and fired at the bobbing lancer. "Shit! Missed!" He drew his pistol and ran toward the road.

Isaac had started to reload, but upon Smithwick's charge, he threw aside a palmful of powder and followed his captain.

Smithwick broke out of the woods, and the soldier, who now had control of his horse, turned, lowered his lance, and charged. Isaac could see the thin mustache, sparse chin whiskers, and the resolve and desperation. Smithwick fired and blood and bits of the lancer's coat and collarbone flew into the air behind him, but he held the rein, gripped the lance with his good arm, and kept coming.

Smithwick leapt toward the woods, but in a heartbeat the Mexican expertly closed on him. As he turned to parry the blade, Isaac burst out of the woods, screaming, and swung his rifle like a club and caught the soldier flush on the side of the head.

The Mexican fell from his saddle onto his back. Isaac, unaware of his ribs now, straddled him and came down with the butt of his rifle. He looked into already unknowing eyes as he thrust and felt he could ram the stock through granite and that nothing would do short of destroying this man who had nearly killed the Captain. He raised the gun again.

Someone grabbed him from behind and lifted him off the ground so that his blow fell short. He clawed at the powerful brown hands clasped about his belly and the bony arms strong as ironwood. He recognized Uncle Jimmy's voice. "Isaac! Goddamn, boy, he's finished! Let him be! You'll bust your rifle."

Isaac relaxed. "I'm done, damn it!" With his feet off the ground, he towered over Jimmy Curtis and could feel the old man's chin in his back.

Uncle Jimmy eased him to the ground. The pain in his rib cage returned. He braced himself with his rifle and dropped to his knees. Sweat dripped from his chin and tears streamed down his cheeks. "He didn't cut you, did he, Captain?" He spat blood. He'd nearly bitten off the tip of his tongue.

Smithwick sat in pine needles along the edge of the woods. He looked at Isaac.

"You ain't cut, are you, Captain?" Isaac repeated.

Smithwick blinked.

Uncle Jimmy cleared his throat.

Isaac started to stand. "Captain?"

Smithwick wiped his mouth with his sleeve. He laughed softly. "Hell no, son, I'm not cut."

Uncle Jimmy bent and rested his hands on his knees to catch his breath. "He was dead before he hit the ground. I heard his skull split from way over there."

"I'm obliged, Isaac," Smithwick said. "He had me for sure."

Uncle Jimmy worked his finger around the inside of his cheeks to dig out the dab of chew he hadn't swallowed during the fight. He glanced at the two other bodies lying in the mud. "Well, they ain't causing no trouble." He picked flecks of tobacco from his tongue. "Cap'm," he said between spits. "This boy's hell when his blood's up."

Nine

ISAAC KNELT IN THE MUD. He doubted he could stand without crying out.

"Why this one ain't but a boy," Uncle Jimmy said, bending over the bludgeoned soldier. "No older than Isaac if he's that old."

Isaac had no intention of looking at the faces of the dead. Keeping his back straight and rib cage still, he slowly stood. "Good lord." He caught his breath. "Let me help you, Uncle Jimmy."

The old man shooed him. "Hell no, son, you're half killed yourself."

"I won't argue with you. We aim to bury 'em?"

Smithwick strode up carrying a musket in one hand and his own rifle in the other. "There ain't time. It pains me, but we'll have to just drag them off the road." He looked disgustedly at the musket, then pitched it into the woods. "I'd say his lance was the better tool."

"What about that one Isaac shot?" Uncle Jimmy said.

"He got hung up in the stirrup somehow," Smithwick said. "Horse dragged him a ways, then tromped all over him before she shook him loose. I left him in the woods. That dragging didn't do his looks much good."

"Hellfire," Uncle Jimmy said.

Smithwick glanced at the young Mexican. "Their damn horses took off. We could use a couple, but we don't have time to catch them. We'd best tidy up and get moving. Isaac, stay put. You've had a right busy morning."

"I thank you, Captain." He watched his companions drag the muddy corpses off the road. Their voices sounded unnaturally loud in the dripping woods. In a few seconds he had stopped the voices of two men forever. Before the Mexicans rode around that bend, their breath had shown in the cool air, and they had smelled the dank woods and heard the creak of their saddles and the chink of bridles. He, Isaac Webb, had killed two men, one at close range with his rifle stock. He'd felt the man's—or the boy's—skull buckle. He should feel something beyond the cutting pain in his side and the bracing cool air in his throat and the drizzle on his face. Had he been a second later swinging his rifle, the Captain would have been run through. A barred owl issued its mad, quavering call. Had these Mexican soldiers prayed for their own safety? Had they survived the siege at Béxar, and issued thanks as he just had?

Sis nuzzled his hand and pricked her ears toward Uncle Jimmy and

Smithwick as they stepped out of the woods. He stroked her soft muzzle. "I didn't shoot nothin' for you gal."

They rode on. By nightfall, the drizzle had turned to rain, and the horses sank to their hocks in the deeper ruts. The trees rose black and foreboding on both sides of the road. They talked little. The air grew colder; Isaac's fingers and toes were numb.

Around midnight, the horses shied from a deep mud hole, and Smithwick turned to the right and rode into the woods. He looked over his shoulder. "Hell with it. We're stopping for the night."

They rode a half mile into the woods, unsaddled and tethered the horses, wrapped themselves in blankets, then lay down in the rain. Isaac fell asleep at once.

He awoke well after daybreak, shivering and hungry. During the night, they had ridden out of pine forest, and he looked about surprised to see post oak– and live oak–covered hills, and grassy savannahs. The rain had stopped, and the sky had cleared, leaving the morning bitter cold.

Uncle Jimmy sat with a blanket about his shoulders. He regarded Isaac with mirth. "Well Cap'm, looks like we ain't gonna get the boy's food after all. I expect he'll be wantin' his share now that he ain't died."

Smithwick had just fired a handful of dry tinder with his flint and steel. "A smart man always keeps a little tinder in his saddlebag."

Isaac watched the little flame consuming the pine whittlings. He felt better already. He cleared his throat and tried to speak. Nothing came out. He swallowed and tried again. "How'd you keep it dry, Cap'm?"

Uncle Jimmy said, "Goddamn boy. You sound like a bull frog."

"Rolled the shavings up in a ball and coated it with tallow. Just break her open and she'll light every time."

"Be damn," Isaac croaked. His mother could spare a little tallow. He'd make some fire starter when he got back home. He smiled. His father would scoff at the idea, then use it and let on like he'd thought of it.

Smithwick added a few twigs he'd gathered from standing deadwood. The little fire smoked, but as the wood dried the flames grew. "I worry about this smoke, but not enough to freeze to death."

They moved closer and sat eating wet cornbread and jerked venison dipped in honey. Sis watched with interest. Isaac threw her a few pieces of jerky. Uncle Jimmy shook his head in disgust. "Well, hell then. Here girl." He pitched her a piece of dried meat. She caught it and gulped it down, wagged her tail, and watched Uncle Jimmy expectantly. "Go see the Captain," he said. She did, and he obliged.

They rode for Cole's Settlement. Isaac's ribs felt much improved, and the three rangers made good time riding single file along the edge of the woods to avoid the quagmire of the road. "A man would drown in some of them ruts," Uncle Jimmy said. The sun warmed their backs and the open country improved Isaac's spirits.

Midmorning they came to a cabin on a low hill to their left. From the road, they could see the open door and windows and chickens scratching in the yard. Somewhere in the woods behind the house a cow bawled piteously. They rode up the footpath. Two gray cats padded out to greet them, mewing. Sis bounded up to meet them, and they arched their backs and hissed. She laid her ears back and trotted back to Isaac. Smithwick helloed the house. No answer. "Left in a damn big hurry, I'd say."

The cow continued her bawling. "Needin' milkin' bad, I expect," Uncle Jimmy said.

They dismounted and stepped inside. "Good puncheon floor," Smithwick said. "I expected dirt all the way out here."

Isaac had never seen such fine furnishings. Maple bed and feather tick against one wall; oaken table and cane-bottom chairs near the middle of the room; empty Dutch oven just inside the cold fireplace. Sis set about sniffing every item in the cabin.

"These folks were doin' just fine," Smithwick said, looking around. "Their furniture was brought in. What's that stink?"

Uncle Jimmy sniffed a large pail sitting on the table. "Damn. Whole pail of sour milk. I reckon them cats drank their fill before it went bad."

"And no tellin' what else," Isaac said. He pointed to dried, milky raccoon tracks on the table.

Smithwick sat on the edge of the bed. "Headin' east with little more than the clothes on their backs. Looks to me like they just ran out the door." He nodded toward an open trunk at the foot of the bed. "Took only what they had to have, if they took that much."

Uncle Jimmy picked up the pail of sour milk and stepped outside. Seconds later the milk splashed in the woods.

Smithwick looked around the room. Sunlight streamed through the two propped-open windows. Rain had blown in and wetted a small dresser. "We ought to get moving, but the place holds me. Somebody set store by this little farm."

Uncle Jimmy stuck his head in the door. "Cap'm, I'll run back here and see about this cow. You'd take a drink of milk, wouldn't you?"

Smithwick nodded. "Best hurry." Jimmy could be heard striding into the woods. Isaac felt the feather mattress, touched the smooth maple headboard. He hoped his family had loaded a few pieces of furniture in the wagons. They owned nothing as nice as this, but their cabin was bigger and just as comfortable. He'd helped his father lay in the floor. His mother vowed she would never live on dirt. He felt the Captain's reluctance to leave. They could have a fire going by the time Jimmy returned. He'd noticed a smokehouse out back. There probably were a few hams still hanging there. The old man could have the bed, and he and Smithwick could throw their bedrolls out in front of the fire. He tried to remember how his own bed felt. Or how it felt to be unafraid. Just rise in the morning. Eat until he was full. Do whatever needed doing. Split wood. Hunt for venison. Crack pecans. Plant in the spring. In a matter of hours, running and fighting had become his life.

Uncle Jimmy stepped inside with a pail full of fresh milk in one hand, and in the other a large, cured ham. "Drink hearty," he said. He held the ham up by a rawhide thong. "We'll feast tonight."

"Just don't seem right," Isaac said.

Smithwick took a ladle from above the hearth. "I'll eat your part then. A guilty conscience is hard to abide."

Uncle Jimmy licked his lips as Smithwick dipped a ladleful of milk. "That old cow thinks I done her a favor. Drink up, Cap'm."

They drank their fill, then poured bowls for Sis and the cats. The sun lighted the woods and the horses' flanks, and Isaac could imagine no threat coming east along the road. The previous day's skirmish seemed like some fantasy conjured while sitting next to his father in the wagon seat. He touched his tender ribs. They must have been badly bruised, not broken. He wanted nothing so much as to wrap up in dry blankets and sleep, dry and without pain.

Uncle Jimmy shoved the ham into his saddlebag. After considerable work at positioning, he gave up closing the bag and allowed the shank to protrude.

They closed the windows and door, gathered ears from the corncrib and scattered feed for the chickens, took a last look, then mounted and rode down the path and into the quagmire.

Ten

NEXT DAY they rounded a bend and saw two men afoot, walking east, an eighth of a mile ahead. Smithwick and Uncle Jimmy sat their horses and squinted. Dawn had broken muggy but clear, and gnats swarmed around their heads. The old man thumbed his nose. "What you think, Cap'm?"

The two men seemed unaware of the rangers' presence. "They don't look Mexican," Smithwick said.

Isaac casually spat. "Tom Crosby ain't Mexican."

The two older men looked at him. He nodded eastward. "That's Choctaw Tom. And I believe the other is old Felix." It felt odd knowing he had better eyes than his experienced companions. "I'm sure of it." There could be no mistaking Felix's bouncing gait.

Smithwick helloed them and they broke for cover.

"Now hell," Uncle Jimmy said. They rode ahead to the spot where Crosby and Felix left the road.

"Come on out, boys," Smithwick yelled.

Felix's hat appeared above the knee-high grass seventy yards off the road. He stood up and dusted himself. "Well, I want you to look, Tom. I reckon we're all saved for sure."

Crosby crawled out of a young, dense oak motte. "By god, we thought sure the Mexicans had you. Where in hell have you three been?"

"Now listen to that," Uncle Jimmy said. "I believe they've been worried about us."

Smithwick said, "Tom, it's gettin' right warm. You're liable to find something you don't want in that thicket."

Crosby slapped his neck. "Goddamn skeeters. What in hell do you expect, ridin' up behind us like that?"

"Where's everybody else?" Isaac asked.

"They're just up ahead," Felix said disgustedly. "You'll recall that some manner of heathen left us short two horses, and of course we can't leave old Jim Leach and Andy Dunn afoot. Some of us been taking turns walkin'." Andy Dunn and Jim Leach were the two oldest rangers, a fact that Uncle Jimmy Curtis liked to point out.

Smithwick loaned his horse to Felix. Tom Crosby swung into the saddle behind Uncle Jimmy. They caught up with the rest of the company two miles further on. "By god, Noah, you're a sight for sore eyes," Williamson said. Isaac thought the Major looked sallow and haggard.

Smithwick set the butt of his rifle on his foot. "They're comin', Major. We caught a patrol on the road about thirty miles back. I imagine Gaona's wondering where they are."

The men gathered around.

"How many was there on the river?" Otis Crocker asked. "We lit out without lookin'."

Smithwick looked at Isaac. "What would you say? Five hundred?"

Before Isaac could respond, Uncle Jimmy said, "Seb'm hundred if there was a one. Thousand wonders we got off that riverbank." He shifted his chew and looked down the road toward Bastrop, nodding gravely as if pondering some subtle tactical matter.

"Ambushed 'em, did you?" Nicholas Wren asked.

"We laid for them," Smithwick said. "Isaac here got two of the three. If he hadn't gotten the second one, I'd have been run through for sure."

The men all looked at Isaac. "For a fact," Uncle Jimmy said.

Williamson nodded impatiently. "All well and good. But now Gaona knows we're about. General Houston needs to be alerted; our current pace won't do."

"Major, we don't even know where Houston is," Felix said.

"*You* don't know, Felix," Williamson answered, wagging his head. "*I* know he's drilling the militia at San Felipe. This company could use some discipline."

Felix spat and stared past Williamson.

The Major continued, "Noah, you and Crosby come with me. We'll ride for San Felipe. The others will just have to catch up. As it is, we're shirking duty."

Felix shook his head slowly. The rest of the men stared at Williamson. Smithwick smiled, nodded. "Major, with your permission, I'll stay with these boys."

"Permission denied. The fight lies ahead."

"For god's sake, Will, these are our neighbors. We don't even have enough horses to go around."

"They're grown men; they'll have to fend for themselves. And you'll address me as Major."

Smithwick sighed and stared at the ground to gather himself. "My apologies—Major."

"Go ahead, Captain; we'll make out," Felix said.

Isaac took off his hat and ran his fingers through his sweaty hair. He'd been better off before they caught up with Williamson. Without Smithwick the company would go to hell in an hour.

"Lieutenant Petty will command the stragglers," Williamson said.

Felix looked in disbelief at the Major. "George?"

"No, Lieutenant Petty."

"The man has no experience," Smithwick said. He grinned sheepishly at Petty. "This ain't personal, George."

Petty, tall, broad, and florid, said, "Why I was at Concepción and Béxar."

"Hell, you never shot a ball," Otis Crocker said. "Laid up in the back of the gunnery wagon every time I seen you. I don't know what you'd have done if we hadn't dumped the cannon."

"I was under the weather," Petty said, now even more flushed.

Crocker rolled his eyes. "Bent over with the clap is what you was." The entire company, except Petty and Williamson, laughed.

"You'd hold a case of the clap against a man?"

Crocker shook his head. "I'd be the last to hold it against a man. I've had the ailment more than I ain't. But I never shirked a day of work on account of it." Even Williamson laughed.

Isaac remained uncertain as to the nature of the disease, although he gathered that you contracted it through relations with sorry women. He wondered how sorry they had to be and if you could tell by looking. If you could, then Petty and Crocker deserved whatever misery they suffered.

"Major, please," Smithwick said. All laughter dissolved.

Williamson's eyes narrowed. "You ain't shirking a fight are you, Noah?"

Smithwick's jaws tightened for an instant. "You know better than that. I'll ask you the same question."

Williamson said, "I'll let that comment go only because you're the one that made it, my friend. Hang back if it suits you."

"Thank you, Major. You oughtn't ride alone."

"Anybody's free to come so long as he's mounted."

Smithwick said, "Uncle Jimmy, you and Tom accompany the Major. Give our regards to the General if you find him."

Williamson rode away. Crosby and Uncle Jimmy followed. The remaining rangers watched without comment. After the three had ridden out of sight, Smithwick said, "Who wants to walk for a while? I'm gettin' a little footsore."

"Hold on now," George Petty said. "I'm the only commissioned officer. I'm in charge here. The Major said so."

"Goddamn," Felix said.

Otis Crocker spat. "Commissioned by who?"

Petty drew a slip of paper from a breast pocket, unfolded it. "Why it says right here. It's signed by . . . well, hell, I can't tell who it's signed by. Probably Henry Smith."

Felix bit off a chew of tobacco, nodded thoughtfully. "Henry Smith signed your commission, did he?"

"I expect so." Petty looked accusingly at Smithwick. "He ain't really a captain. Everybody just calls him that because the Major lets him boss us around."

Isaac looked at his fellow rangers and thought of the columns of disciplined soldiers he'd seen on the banks of the Colorado.

Felix said, "Where to, Captain?"

"Damn it, now!" Petty looked at the impassive faces around him.

"Hush, George," Otis Crocker said. "I can't hear the Captain for your big mouth."

Petty sat his horse and glared at Crocker.

Isaac dismounted. "I'll walk a spell. It might do my ribs some good. Fanny's about to jar my teeth loose."

"Good of you, Isaac," Smithwick said. He nodded to Petty. "That all right with you, Lieutenant?"

Eleven

WALKING PROVED more miserable than riding. Isaac carried his rifle in one hand, then the other. The weight pulled on his sore ribs regardless of which arm bore it. His walking companion, nineteen-year-old Ezra Higginbotham, a massive, towering Mississippian, was about to win their argument.

"Now hell, Isaac, let me carry that rifle; I can see it's about to kill you." Ezra had a reputation for being as kind as he was huge, although in a recent altercation at Refugio, he'd broken the wrist of a boatman named Broussard. According to Felix, Broussard drew a knife, then refused to drop it when Ezra grabbed his wrist. The big man clamped with one hand and twisted with the other. Broussard let go of the knife.

"I guess I'd better give it up before you take hold of me."

Ezra rolled his dark eyes. A light southern breeze blew his black beard, making his face look lopsided. "I never aimed to break old Broussard's wrist." He spat. "Should've broke his neck. He had no cause to mistreat that nigger just for upendin' a pirogue."

"Felix said the boy dumped the alcalde in the river."

"Don't matter. Why, I never stepped in a pirogue I didn't turn over."

"I don't imagine you ever stepped on a riverboat you didn't turn over."

Ezra smiled. "I aim to try one of these days." He reached for Isaac's rifle. "Give it here."

Isaac let him take it. "Good of you, Ezra. I thank you." He rubbed his sore ribs. "Just don't lean over the gunnel." They laughed.

The mounted rangers had gradually pulled ahead and disappeared around a bend in the road. The late afternoon sun shone through holes in the darkening clouds building to the west. Free of his weapon, Isaac quickened his pace. With a rifle on each shoulder, Ezra strode easily through the muck. Both men were wet to their knees, and their weapons, buckskins, and faces were spattered with mud.

"I never killed nobody though," Ezra said after a while. Sweat rolled down his forehead and dripped from his beard.

"Well." Isaac was breathing hard trying to match Ezra's strides.

"Two of 'em, huh?"

Isaac nodded. "I don't feel any different. It's like it never happened. It seems like somethin' I thought up or dreamt. I don't even remember bein' scared, but I know I was. I don't reckon I thought. I just done, and this time I done the right thing."

They walked on. Ezra seemed to be considering Isaac's explanation. "I just hope I don't come undone," he said after a few minutes. "Goin' along talking about it with somebody, it always seems like I'd do good in a fight." He paused. "But when I'm by myself, 'specially at night, I get to worryin' that I'll shit in my britches or start blubberin' or shoot one of our boys in the back of the head."

"I don't know what to tell you," Isaac said. His father had told him there was no predicting how a man would perform under fire. He might fall apart next time somebody shot at him. "Uncle Jimmy told me about two boys at Concepción rammed eight or nine balls down their barrels. Thought they was shooting, but all they was doing was rammin' powder and balls."

"Hell," Ezra said.

They walked in silence. After a while, Isaac said, "What did you think when that boatman came after you with his blade?"

"I don't recall thinkin' a thing. I just caught his arm."

"That's what I figured."

Ezra nodded as he walked. "I never thought about it like that."

They began to encounter chattel strewn along the road. Pails, cane-bottom chairs, small trunks, a feather mattress, pitchers, a vanity, two dressers, a stool.

"Somebody's lightenin' their load," Ezra said. He stopped to examine an overturned trunk.

Isaac stood in the road and looked at the scattered wares. "Looks to me like somebody got scared and took off. Look there; they left a handcart." He hoped the rest of the company hadn't pulled too far ahead. The sun sat atop the western hills. A few minutes before, the road had seemed hot and still, the air oppressive, the woods and prairie dead. Now in the slanted light, the hills and draws and mottes looked sharply formed. Birdsong had been replaced by rustling in roadside brush. The best time of day. But the scattered wares seemed foreboding.

Ezra righted the trunk and unbuckled the leather latch. "Woman's stuff." He looked through linens and cotton dresses, carefully laid them back and gently patted the top of the pile before closing and securing the trunk. "I wish I had some way to pack that feather tick."

Isaac shook his head. "This takin' other people's stuff . . . I just can't get used to the idea. I keep thinkin' they might come back for it."

"I suppose they could, but it don't seem likely. I hate to see somethin' go to waste."

There was a rustle in the grass, then footfalls. Sis jogged into the road, tongue lolling.

"Now I want you to look," Isaac said. "Where in the hell have you been?" She'd disappeared shortly after their stop at the abandoned cabin.

Ezra patted his thigh and Sis bounded to him, turned broadside, and demurely pressed her ribs against his shins and wagged her tail. "Found a farm and lay around for a few days eatin' some poor soul's chickens is where she's been," he said. "Probably been eatin' better than we have."

"I expect so. Uncle Jimmy took the rest of that ham with him." His mouth watered at the thought. They'd get by on game and mush until they could find another deserted smokehouse. He knelt and scratched the dog's ears. "She don't look a bit poor, does she?" Sis licked his palm. "I'll carry my gun a while." He didn't plan on walking into the ranger encampment with Ezra carrying his rifle.

Ezra smiled and handed Isaac the weapon. Sis jogged ahead and disappeared around the bend for a moment, then ran back excitedly as if she wanted to report her findings.

They rounded the bend. A dozen campfires burned just ahead. A woman's moan stopped them. "Goddamn, did you hear that?" Isaac said.

"Somebody's sick or shot." Darkness hid Ezra's face. He looked like a huge oak broken off just below the first limb.

Sixty yards from the nearest fire, Isaac yelled, "Comin' in, boys. Don't shoot."

Felix answered, "I never aimed to shoot 'til I heard who's comin'."

Someone stepped into the road just ahead. "By god, Isaac, you've fell in with a bear."

"Otis, I've never seen a bear half as big as Ezra Higginbotham," Isaac said.

"I swear," Ezra said under his breath.

Another moan off to the right. Then an older woman's crooning voice, and Isaac made out a wagon and team of oxen and figures standing about a fire. "What in the world?"

Felix walked out of the firelight into the road. "Some poor girl is tryin' to push a baby on out, but it's wantin' to come ass first. She's havin' a time of it."

"Lord." Isaac had never heard of a woman surviving such a birthing.

"It don't look good," Otis Crocker said.

Felix spat. "How in the hell would you know, Otis? You wouldn't go over there and pay your respects to the family."

"The Captain told me. Anyway, I wasn't the only one wouldn't go. It ain't easy listenin' to a girl whimperin' like that."

The other rangers stood about the fires, talking softly and looking absently at their feet or the night sky, and glancing in the direction of the girl and her family. Sis's silhouette appeared and disappeared against the fires. "Where's the Captain at?" Isaac asked.

"Over there talkin' to the girl's grandpap," Felix said. "I don't know what he's tryin to do."

Isaac took off his hat and started toward the wagon. He heard Smithwick say, "We won't do it. I can't abide it."

Ezra looked in that direction, then turned back toward the rangers' fires.

"I'm fixin' to eat somethin'," he said. "I won't have no idea what to say to them folks."

"I don't blame you," Crocker said.

Isaac stepped into the circle of firelight. The Captain stood next to a stooped, elderly man wearing wool and homespun. "We don't want your help or your company," the man said. "If not for your kind we'd be home right now where Catherine would at least know a measure of comfort. And Franklin would be there."

Both men looked at Isaac. To his right, a middle-aged woman bent working over someone wrapped in blankets. He cleared his throat. "Captain, I wondered if there was somethin' I could do."

"I don't know what it would be, Isaac, but I thank you." Smithwick said. "You'd best have a bite of supper."

"You can help me move this child," the woman said. "I've got to get a clean blanket under her."

Isaac started for the girl. The old man stepped into his path. "Hell no! Don't you touch her! We don't need no help from you!"

Isaac stopped. The woman stood to face the man. "I won't have it, Daddy!" she said. Her eyes were wild and rimmed with tears. "Where were you when Mother and Saree lay in their deathbeds?"

The man stopped and wagged a finger at the woman. "Don't you talk to me that way. I never put up with it when you was a girl and I won't have it now."

"You just hate in these men what you hate in yourself."

He waved her off with both hands. "Goddamn all of you."

Isaac saw the girl, Catherine. Young, no older than he. Dark hair about her shoulders, ashen, sweat beaded on her upper lip. Her eyes fluttered. She licked her pallid lips.

The woman knelt by her feet. "Help me, boy."

He propped his rifle against the wagon and went to Catherine's side.

"I'll get her legs and you get her shoulders," the woman said.

He slid his hands beneath her shoulders and started to lift. He smelled her hair and sweat and something else he vaguely recognized. She tensed, then cried out. Tears streamed down her cheeks.

"Wait a spell," the woman said. "It'll pass."

The girl whimpered and furrowed her brow.

"This one's about done, sugar," the woman said, stroking Catherine's cheek.

Isaac stood. "Reckon we ought to be movin' her?"

With her fingers, the woman wiped the tears and sweat from the girl's face. "I don't have no idea what we ought to be doin'. All I know is this blanket is soaked." She studied Isaac. "Don't you get peaked on me now. I wish you men were half as good at takin' care of trouble as you are at startin' it."

The girl relaxed. Sweat soaked the blanket on her chest. "Now then," the woman said. "You about ready?"

Isaac nodded and took Catherine's shoulders again. They were harder and denser than he had expected. The woman clasped the girl's legs behind her knees and said, "Lift."

He raised Catherine's arms and shoulders as the woman stood and pulled her legs, but her bottom and swollen belly didn't budge. Smithwick and the old man stood watching as if transfixed, then the woman said, "Damn it," and they rushed to help. The four eased the girl a yard to one side and onto a clean blanket.

The woman wept. "Why the little thing made no sound; that wasn't nothin' to what she's had to bear." She turned away, fists clenched. "Lord, I don't know. I might've just killed her. I don't know what to do."

Isaac's throat ached. He wanted this girl to know that he tried to help her. It mattered even if she died that night. She needed to know that twenty men running from an army found her plight reason enough to stop, that her life mattered to a stranger. "Where's her man?" he croaked.

The woman wiped her eyes. Her hair was steel gray, the color the girl's dark hair would be if she were to live to middle age. Isaac saw Catherine's slight overbite and dark eyes in her mother. She set her jaw. "Ran off with that James Bowie. Look where it got him."

"Every bit of it foolishness," the old man said. "You men have brought this down on us."

"Why if you was one year younger, you'd be right with 'em," she said.

"You ought to have told that man of yours what you're tellin' me."

"There's no tellin' him anything." She looked at Smithwick. "My husband is off somewhere east of here doin' somethin' for Houston." She smiled sadly. "Captain Adair, he calls himself."

"A man of the Republic," Smithwick said. "These times call for terrible sacrifice, Mrs. Adair. He surely didn't anticipate your troubles."

Catherine cried. "It's comin' again," Mrs. Adair said. She knelt by the girl. The old man put his hand over his eyes. Smithwick lightly touched his back. "We won't leave," he said. "We'll see this through with you."

"Miz Adair," Felix Gross said from the darkness near the wagon, "I ought to be seein' to your oxen."

Twelve

CATHERINE CRIED OUT through the night while Isaac dozed fitfully in his blankets. By dawn her cries had ceased, and the men sat sleepily around their fires.

Smithwick walked out of the woods where the horses were hobbled and started across the road. Isaac rose and followed him. Mrs. Adair and the old man sat wrapped in their blankets by the weakly glowing coals. The girl lay perfectly still and ashen where Isaac had left her the night before. Her eyes were closed, her countenance peaceful. Five feet to her right, on a horse blanket, lay a small, linen-wrapped bundle.

Smithwick took off his hat. "My condolences. The young lady? Is she, uh . . ."

"Still with us," Mrs. Adair said, expressionless. "I don't see how; I never heard of a woman livin' through a birth like that." She glanced toward the girl. "She's bad off."

The old man said, "We ought to pick up and move on, but I swear I ain't got it in me. I don't believe I can get up from here."

Catherine lay so still Isaac wondered if she'd died since her family last checked on her. His head hurt from lack of sleep and coffee. He wanted to offer condolences, but every phrase that came to him seemed weak.

Felix walked into the camp, took in the scene, doffed his hat. They stood in silence. After a few minutes, Smithwick said, "Would you like us to prepare a grave, Mrs. Adair?"

She nodded, then lay down on the damp oak leaves and closed her eyes.

• • •

Isaac and Felix walked behind Mrs. Adair's wagon. The clumsy oxen, driven by the old man, Winfred Porter, moved so slowly over the muddy road that Isaac felt he might tumble over his own feet. The ranging company was strung along the road for a quarter mile. There was little talk.

Isaac found his eyes drawn to Catherine Druin's pale forehead just visible above the tailgate of the wagon. She had not spoken or responded. Her lips moved as the wagon jounced along the road.

"Nothin' more worrisome than a sick girl," Felix said. "Wonder why that is?"

"Maybe because we're used to women takin' care of us when we're busted up. We're always dyin' or gettin' ourselves killed, so we don't pay any attention to it. But a sick girl is a sad sight sure enough."

Felix scratched his head under his hat and moved his rifle from the crook of his arm to his shoulder. "Right comely, ain't she?"

"Right pitiful. And her man killed at Béxar. I don't believe she'll make it. Do you?"

"I say she will," Felix said. "It's been my experience that a woman is harder to kill than a man." He pulled a plug of tobacco from his pouch and bit off a chew. "A man will live through a war, fightin' damn near every day, live through gettin' shot and snakebit," he said, chewing thoughtfully, "and then take a cold and just up and die. A woman, now, might be born peaked and be sick with one ailment or another every day of her life, but she'll still whelp you a dozen younguns and live 'til she's ninety." He nodded toward the wagon. "I don't expect this one's done yet."

Isaac found Felix's prognosis heartening. "How old would you say she is?"

"Hard to say with a young woman. Sixteen. Seb'mteen." He looked at Isaac. "Now hell."

"Now hell nothin'. I just wonder how old she is."

"When she comes to, you can just hop up there and ask her. Of course her daddy might have somethin' to say about it."

"You know him?"

"Know of him. Hard-shell Baptist from Georgia. They say he was hell on the Kronks when he first moved to Texas. I imagine that's why he's a captain and me and you are afoot. I hear he lives way upriver of Bastrop. Not another farm within a dozen miles. He's full of grit; I'll give him that. The girl had been livin' in Gonzales with her husband."

"What in hell are they doin' all the way up here?"

"Her grandpap told me that he and Mrs. Adair were down at Gonzales seeing to the girl after the boy took off to Béxar. They followed Houston out of town, crossed at Burnham's, then headed north when they got word that Sesma was on their tail. Just lost and runnin' scared when we found 'em."

"Good words Captain Smithwick said over that baby's grave this mornin'," Isaac said. "I never knew he was so handy with Scripture."

Felix laughed. "Yes sir; good words sure enough. I don't know if they was Scripture or not. I imagine he made it all up. We didn't have a Bible, and he's right quick on his feet."

"Sounded like Scripture." Isaac dismissed Felix's conjecture. Nobody lower than the Almighty could compose words like, "My harp is also turned to mourning, and my organ into the voice of them that weep."

Chattel littered the roads. On both sides, cabin doors and windows hung open. Starving dogs howled and ran from their yards and warily followed the rangers. Cattle lowed and hogs grunted and wallowed in the puddles and deep ruts.

"I expect we'll eat better for a few days," Felix said. "Cole's can't be too far."

That night they camped in an open stand of blackjack oaks. The girl lay still as death, and her mother and grandfather went wordlessly about their camp chores while the rangers watched awkwardly from a distance.

Isaac built a fire and laid out his bedroll so that he could see Catherine sixty feet away in the back of the wagon. The rangers butchered two hogs. He ate distractedly. Just before dark he was sitting on his bedroll arguing with Felix and Ezra about the best way to skin a squirrel and whether red squirrels were easier to kill than cat squirrels, all the while glancing at the girl. He looked up and Mrs. Adair had caught his eye as she leaned over the side of the wagon to stroke her daughter's hair. He looked away for a second, then raised his eyes again to see her still watching him. After a few seconds she turned back to her daughter.

He slept poorly, fretting over Captain Smithwick's assertion that the girl would have to take water shortly or die. The Mexican problem now seemed distant, yet he thought often of how expertly the lancer turned on Captain Smithwick.

As he tossed in his blankets, he realized that he hadn't thought of his family in days. This was his life. Mud and gnats, lice, fleas, and scummy water, numbing fatigue and morning headaches from marching into the rising sun.

Next morning they pushed on. Isaac rode while Ezra and Tom Crocker walked behind the wagon. He agreed to the arrangement before he realized that he wouldn't be able to keep an eye on Catherine. He rode to the front of the column alongside Smithwick and Felix. Midday, they came to Cole's Settlement. A dozen or so low log buildings stood abandoned on either side of the road. Scrawny, half-wild chickens, skittish as quail, scratched about, and spoke-ribbed dogs greeted the company with hysteria.

Smithwick halted the column. "Let's see if we can find this girl a bed."

"I say we push on," George Petty said. "Gaona could be right on top of us and we wouldn't know it."

Otis Crocker dismounted and looked about. "George, help me catch a few of these chickens."

A shot rang out at the rear of the column. Fanny lurched and Isaac fought her to a standstill while other horses bucked and curses flew and rangers dismounted wild eyed, looking for cover. Smithwick sat his horse, calmly patting her neck, looking at the dying chicken flopping in the middle of the road. Simon Hicks, bug eyed and skinny as a heron, sauntered over to pick up his kill. He held it up and nodded sheepishly.

"For god's sake, Simon!" Petty shouted. Laughter rippled through the column.

Felix said, "Simon, if you're gonna use up ball and powder, why not shoot a hog or beeve?"

Smithwick dismounted. "Some men have a taste for chicken, Felix. I say we settle in for the day and eat our fill."

Coons and cats had taken over most of the buildings. Tables, chairs, and beds were covered with chicken shit. "I can't see these people just runnin' off without their things and not even closing their doors," Smithwick said. "Surely they knew it's a good three-week march from Béxar to here."

After searching several cabins, they found one that had been secured before the owners fled.

Much to Isaac's disappointment, Smithwick sent Ezra to fetch the girl. Moments later, the big man stepped back inside and laid Catherine on the bed as if she were the most fragile thing in the world. Her eyes were shut. She made no sound.

Mrs. Adair covered her daughter, then looked sternly at the men, who realized suddenly that they were staring.

Isaac stepped into the afternoon sun, shaking his head at the realization that he was smitten by a teenage widow who'd been near death and unaware of him from the moment he'd laid eyes on her.

He looked up to see a swath of cloth or paper tacked to a tree and fluttering in the wind toward the middle of the settlement. "Look there, Captain."

Next to a blacksmith's shed, they found a half page of the *Washington Democrat* spiked to a huge, gnarled live oak. Smithwick pulled it from the trunk. In the bottom margin someone had written a note in booming cursive. "The Major's hand," Smithwick said. He read it and swallowed. The color left his face.

"What does it say, Captain?" Isaac could read print, but cursive vexed him. "Fannin surrendered."

"Well, hell," Felix said. "I reckon he's got more sense than Travis had."

"What'll happen to 'em?" Ezra asked.

Smithwick licked his lips and swallowed. "It's already happened. Says here Urrea lined them up and shot them all."

Thirteen

FROM A RESPECTFUL distance, Isaac watched Catherine sipping broth from a tin cup. She seemed to be gaining strength by the hour. A day out of Cole's Settlement she'd taken a few sips of water. Next morning she took a little broth and appeared to whisper to her mother. By the time they made their present camp in the Brazos River bottom a few miles north of Washington, she could sit up for a few minutes at a time. Her face still held no color, but she seemed able to take in her surroundings and occasionally touched her face and hair and spoke to her mother.

Smithwick had chosen to pass through Washington, certain Gaona would raze the settlement within a few days. Yet things could have been far worse. Isaac's ribs barely hurt. And the company had plenty of food. The smokehouses in and around Cole's had been full of hams and bacon, and, using cornmeal for bait, the rangers caught a couple dozen chickens before fleeing northward. Bagged or lashed together, the outraged birds had squawked and flapped throughout the three-day ride from Cole's to Washington.

"She just needed to lay still and heal up," Felix said. "There'll be some other healin' to do too, I expect."

Isaac couldn't think of Catherine as a widow; she seemed just a girl about his age. But she'd already lost a child. He couldn't forget that. And did she grieve for her dead husband who'd surely been a grown man? What use would a widow have for a sixteen-year-old boy? Ridiculous thinking. Every man in the company probably was in love with her by now.

"You ain't hearin' me, are you?" Felix said.

"Huh? Yeah, I heard you."

"What'd I say?"

"You said she needed to heal up."

"Then what'd I say?"

"Probably somethin' that didn't make a drop of sense."

"That's what I thought. You never heard a word."

"Gentlemen, I do appreciate your concern, but could you give us a bit of privacy? I need to tend to my daughter." Mrs. Adair stood beside the wagon, hands on her hips.

Isaac's ears went hot. "Oh . . . yes ma'am. I was just tryin' to make sure everything is all right."

Felix was laughing. "Just tryin' to be helpful. Isaac here is the helpfullest boy that ever was."

Mrs. Adair spread another blanket over Catherine, then peered beneath it.

Isaac and Felix walked through camp. The morning was already hot and muggy, and gnats bedeviled them. "Spring is upon us," Felix said. Given a choice, Isaac would take cold and damp over hot and buggy any day. Felix found the preference odd. But then he seemed oblivious to swarming insects.

Most of the chickens had been freed to scratch about, but their capture and travels had left them disheveled and wilder than ever. Huge oaks shaded camp, but added to the feeling of dankness in the bottom.

They nodded in greeting to George Petty, who sat sullenly against an oak. He ignored them. After news of the murder at Goliad, Petty, in a fit of terror, tore up his commission so that he could not be identified as a Texian rebel should he fall into Mexican hands. Most of the men considered his actions a display of abject cowardice, although Felix pointed out that no one else in the company had a commission and therefore couldn't be tested. Smithwick allowed that they'd be hard pressed to convince Gaona that a group of twenty heavily armed Anglos were actually good Mexican citizens and patriots.

"Poor old George," Felix said as soon as they were out of earshot.

The Brazos boomed wide and muddy just below camp. Every man in the company longed to put the river between himself and the advancing Mexicans, but fleeing settlers had sunk the Washington ferry. There had been much discussion of raft building, but the swirling currents and floating trees dampened enthusiasm for the project.

They found Ezra laying a slice of ham into a skillet. Sis sat five feet away, watching with interest.

Ezra nodded at the big hound. "I made the mistake of throwin' her a scrap of fat. Now she's settled in for breakfast."

"It takes a cruel man to eat in front of a hungry dog," Isaac said. Perhaps small talk would take his mind off Catherine.

Ezra watched the melting fat spreading over the bottom of the skillet. "Every man has his shortcomings. Even me."

"Eatin' like a bird ain't one of 'em," Felix said. He sniffed the frying meat. "I hope Gaona's boys are goin' hungry. Seven hundred men could go through a lot of pig and chicken and we sure as hell didn't leave much in our wake."

Smithwick strode up looking more haggard than usual. "We ought to ride down the road tonight and see who might be following us."

Ezra turned the slice of ham with his patch knife. "Who ought to?"

"Present company."

"When would we ride?" Isaac asked. It had become clear that avoiding Mexican cavalry took priority over reinforcing Houston.

"Dusk. We might be out a day or two."

Felix lit his pipe. "Well, Isaac, you'd best get back over there and watch that girl for a while."

Washington smelled of mud and hogs and cold ashes. The moon lighted their faces as they rode through the settlement. The log buildings, the dogtrot cabins, and the frame mercantile stood black and silent. There was no breeze. Hogs grunted and popped their teeth from the shadows. Dogs bristled and howled. Isaac imagined Sis tied to a tree back in camp, bawling at the top of her lungs and chewing on the rawhide tether.

They rode southwest, struck high ground, and stopped to looked over the dark river bottom; no sign of campfires except those in the ranger camp to the east. The Brazos ran silver in the moonlight.

Four miles south of Washington, they sat their horses atop a grassy ridge. The moon hung high and full, and Isaac guessed the time to be near midnight. A few hundred yards out, a wolf howled, then another joined it. Their voices peaked and quavered, ebbed and peaked again before ceasing. Then, much closer, came the answer. The hair on Isaac's arms stiffened. He shivered. Fanny pricked her ears, snorted and stamped. He stroked and patted her neck.

"Hell," Ezra said, exhaling. "I never have got used to that."

"Wolves rarely howl this time of year," Smithwick said. "I suppose they're complaining about us."

"Nope. Look there. Along the road." Felix's normally low, gravelly voice sounded unnaturally high and thin.

Just like in Bastrop, Isaac thought. Odd how light plays off of polished metal two miles away. Suddenly he felt very exposed on this open ridge beneath a full moon. He fought the urge to dig his heels into Fanny's sides.

Smithwick sat his horse, apparently calm. "Cavalry. Heading for Washington."

"What in hell are they doin' marching this time of night?" Ezra whispered.

The captain laughed softly, his face in shadow beneath his hat brim. "Why Ezra, they're hunting *us*."

Fourteen

JUST SOUTH of Tinoxtitlan, someone challenged them from the rank brush along the river. "Just hold her right there, boys, and state your business. We're all over you."

Isaac had been dozing on his feet, trudging along a muddy riverbank trail. The voice roused him, and his aching legs and hips reminded him where he was. Gnats and mosquitoes had deviled him for forty miles; he no longer bothered to scratch the welts on his face and the backs of his hands.

"Texians out of Bastrop," Smithwick answered from the front of the column. It was nearly sundown, and the canopy of newly leaved oaks and sycamores along the Brazos blocked the dying sunlight. Isaac could not see Catherine or the wagon though he knew it was only fifty feet ahead. The exhausted rangers left the rifles at rest across their pommels.

"We're in bad shape," Smithwick continued. "Gaona's cavalry picked up our trail at Washington. We ain't stopped since midnight before last."

"And just who would you be?"

"Noah Smithwick. For god's sake, man! Do we sound Mexican?"

The picket laughed. "Why hell, we're all good Meskin citizens, ain't we? Welcome to Tinoxtitlan, Captain. Foller me."

Isaac heard laughter ahead, then Smithwick saying, "Oh you had us covered, did you?"

"A little fellar like me learns to bluff," came the tenor reply. The column began to move. The Adair wagon's axle squealed; for the first time in over a day, laughter and low talk rippled through the company.

A half mile further on, the dense woods opened, and Isaac made out low log buildings and dogtrot cabins on either side of the trail. Near the center of the settlement a head-high campfire threw pale light on gnarled boles and waxy leaves. He heard fiddle music and singing:

Oh Rose, Rose, coal black Rose;
I ain't never seen a girl I love like Rose.

Uproarious laughter, then sudden silence. "What in the world, Clarence?" The voice from near the fire was convivial, deep, projected authority.

"Brung you some reinforcements, Colonel."

"Well, hell, I was hoping you'd captured the Mexican army. Who do we have here?"

"We're a ranging company out of Bastrop. I'm Smithwick."

"Boys, get down and take a rest. I'm Colonel Bain; this here is Captain Bob Childress."

The rangers dismounted. Several of Bain's men took the reins and led the horses into the dark woods. Isaac walked past Catherine's wagon. She was sitting up, propped against a meal sack. Her eyes glistened. Did she return his gaze? And why would she?

He stepped into the firelight. Tinoxtitlan smelled of decaying logs and mold and swine. Bats fluttered and dipped above the flames. Two dozen or so men stood about the fire, silently regarding the newcomers. A black man hoed coals out of the fire and into an adjacent cook pit.

Smithwick extended his hand to a lanky, rawboned, middle-aged man sitting on an overturned milk pail. "Colonel, Gaona's force chased us out of Bastrop; he picked up our trail just south of Washington. Five hundred men if there's a one. Cavalry and dragoons. They may still be on our tails."

Bain stood, shook the Captain's hand. "You're aware of Fannin's fate?"

"Major Williamson left word in Washington."

"Where is the old judge?"

"He and a few of the boys went ahead to reinforce General Houston." He glanced back at his rangers. "We've been slowed by a lack of horses. And we've picked up two women and a older gentleman along the way."

Bain looked at another, larger, gray-bearded man sitting on a block of oak. "Hmmm . . . Well. Bob, what do you think?"

Bob Childress shook a jug to ascertain the level of its contents. "I'd say Gaona's got bigger cats to skin than us. He ain't about to march up here from Washington. I say he's huntin' for Houston."

Smithwick nodded politely. "Well, me and two of the boys waylaid one of his patrols halfway between Bastrop and Cole's. I'm afraid he's lookin' for us."

Bain studied Smithwick. "That's more than we've done."

Childress pulled on the jug, wiped his mouth with the back of his hand. "But he don't know who laid his boys out. He didn't see you do it, did he?"

Smithwick shook his head.

"So far as he knows, Comanches done it," Childress said.

"We didn't scalp or mutilate the bodies. Just laid 'em off in the woods."

Childress spat; pointed the mouth of his jug at Smithwick. "There's your mistake."

"We've already evacuated the women and younguns," Bain said. "Saw the last few on their way east this morning. Now we're tryin' to figure out what the hell to do. We've got scouts out lookin' for Houston; they should've been back by now."

Felix Gross cleared his throat. "Uh, Captain; we ought to find this girl a clean bed."

"Of course," Smithwick said. "Colonel, we've got a sick woman under our protection. She lost her husband at Béxar and her baby during birth. She nearly went with it."

Bain nodded. "She can have my quarters. Who's looking after her?"

"Her mama and grandpap are with her."

Isaac's face burned. He should've spoken up before Felix.

The black man who had been tending the coals stood up. "Colonel, water's boilin'; I'll have pone comin' out directly. These gentlemen are hungry, I imagine."

Bain said, "Excellent, Luther. A little pone will take the edge off their appetites. Tactical matters should never be discussed on an empty stomach. Boys, we've got more pork than we know what to do with."

Two hours later, Isaac drained his coffee cup, spat out the dregs, poured another cup. He, Ezra, and Felix sat on their bedrolls about a small fire and listened to the two fiddles and bawdy refrains of Bain's men. The moon sat overhead and the buzzing of tree frogs seemed to fade in and out with the rise and fall of the music.

The scalding coffee comforted Isaac. He sipped and dozed, luxuriating in his exhaustion. Some of the company had joined in the bonfire revelry. Isaac enjoyed a dance tune, but tonight, coffee and blanket seemed more inviting.

"I want you to listen to that nigger stroke that hoe," Ezra said. "Listen. Just scraping with a case knife. Right in time with the fiddle."

Isaac sipped dreamily. The music and song warmed his insides as much as the coffee.

O get up gals in de mawnin'
O get up gals in de mawnin'
O get up gals in de mawnin'
Jus' at de break of day.

Surely Gaona wouldn't follow them here. Colonel Bain said as much. A light breeze blew in from the river. Get up gals in de mawnin'; get up gals in de mawnin' . . .

"Isaac, you ain't checked on young Miz Druin yet tonight," Felix said. "You can't doze off yet."

"Felix, hell." He pictured Catherine resting on Bain's feather tick. The image only made him sleepier. If Catherine was well, then he was well. He'd have time for worry after a good night's sleep. Surely the Captain was discussing their next course of action with Bain and Childress. He'd be ready tomorrow. He needed sleep, could drift off anytime, but the mild night and his friends and his full belly, the coffee and the breeze that kept the mosquitoes away, all these needed savoring. Ezra stirred the coals and Isaac felt the heat on his face. Sis laid her head in his lap. He stroked her ears.

"Somebody comin'," Felix said.

Sis growled. Ezra said, "Surely it ain't the Mexicans."

Felix stood and looked down the dark river trail. "Why no, they surely wouldn't come in here and upset such a contented bunch of men as these."

Several horses nickered from the rope corral back in the woods. Two riders appeared along the trail, coming from Washington. They rode by the three rangers and into the clearing. The music stopped.

Isaac downed the rest of his coffee. "I swear." They got up and walked toward the others. The two men had dismounted, a tall, powerful-looking, middle-aged man in black woolen pants and buckskin shirt and a small black man who looked to be less than twenty years old.

Everyone stood. Smithwick, Bain, and Childress walked out to meet them.

Bain extended his hand to the older man. "By god, Thomas, I thought sure we'd lost you." He nodded toward the young black man who stood with his hat in his hands. "Bobby. Good to see you again."

The boy nodded. "Yes sir, Colonel. Good to see you too."

Thomas gave his reins to one of Bain's men. "Could a fellow wet his whistle around here? I have news, but I'll not give it with a dry tongue."

Childress raised the jug. "I'd offer you a sip of tongue oil, but I've learned better."

Thomas took a gourd dipper full of water from Luther and gulped it down. "You're a quick study, sir." He gave the gourd back to Luther. "Gentlemen, Houston and our militia have crossed the Brazos below Washington by steamboat and are marching toward Harrisburg. He hasn't announced his intentions, but he looks to be in full retreat."

"I don't believe it," Bain said.

"You would if you saw Santa Anna's army. I saw it on the west bank at San Felipe. A thousand men easy. Thank God, Baker sank the ferry."

"Good man, Mosley Baker," Childress said.

Thomas nodded. "Burnt the whole settlement so as not to leave a thing for the Mexicans. But Santa Anna turned south, probably heading for the ferry at Fort Bend. I expect he's across the river by now."

The men listened in silence, their features pale and unmoving in the firelight. Bain took the jug from Childress. "Love of God." He took a drink.

"I ain't through yet," Thomas said. "Filisola and Urrea are on their way to Fort Bend with a thousand men apiece. Probably about there by now."

"What kind of force has Houston raised?" Bain asked.

"Not quite a thousand, last I heard."

"And Gaona," Smithwick said. "If he's turned southeast, that'll put four thousand Mexicans at Fort Bend. I'd retreat too."

Thomas looked at Smithwick, obviously noticing him for the first time. "I don't believe I've had the pleasure, sir."

Smithwick extended his hand. "Noah Smithwick."

"Well sir, your reputation precedes you. It's a pleasure. I'm Thomas Adair."

Smithwick shook his hand, then stopped suddenly. "Adair? Captain Adair?"

Fifteen

ISAAC WATCHED old Andy Dunn lashing a sack of supplies onto a rude twelve-foot-square raft made of oak, sycamore, and sweet gum logs of wildly varying diameters. He and Jim Leach, the two oldest men in the company, had spent the previous three days lashing the logs together with the help of two of Bain's men, a Georgian named Spencer and a Tejano named Sanchez. Word was, the men planned to raft back down the Brazos to San Felipe, which the Mexicans would have already passed. Where they'd go from there was the subject of much speculation.

"They'll drown before they get around the first bend," Felix said. He stood leaning on his rifle and stroking his beard as he watched the men's final preparations. "Crazy bastards. Old and senile."

Isaac swallowed a mouthful of biscuit. "I expect the old boys are tired of travelin'. I hear Spencer and Sanchez have been afoot for awhile. There's never enough horses."

"I'd rather be afoot than driftin' along the bottom of this river. I expect it's right cold down there."

"They might make it."

"Hell."

The young black man, Bobby Durham, picked up one corner of the raft. Three other of Bain's men did the same. They waded knee deep into the river and eased the lashed logs into the water. The deceptively fast current snatched the raft from the hands of two men upstream. Bobby moved to block it, slipped and fell backward, and disappeared beneath it.

"Look at that!" Felix said. He laid down his rifle and ran along the bank. Other rangers did the same, some splashing into the river. Three men dove onto the raft as if pinning a calf. The raft spun in the current as it drifted downstream. Bobby popped up wide eyed and coughing. He looked about, then pounced on something. "Got it! My damn hat!" He held it up like a boy showing off his first squirrel.

Ezra and Isaac got to the young man at the same time. The current nearly took Isaac's feet from beneath him.

Bobby smiled and put on his hat. Water gushed from the brim. "Obliged. I made out fine."

"By god, this water will shrivel a man's ballocks," Ezra said.

Bobby started toward the bank. Isaac and Ezra each grabbed one of his arms to steady him. His head came to Isaac's chin.

A dozen rangers had subdued the runaway raft and were dragging it onto the gravel. Some laughed. Others cursed. Felix said, "Gonna ride this brush pile clear down to San Felipe, huh? Where are our two admirals now?"

Old Andy Dunn leaned high and dry on a twelve-foot ash pole. "Anybody ain't got better sense than to set an empty raft in the middle of the river ought to get wet."

Smithwick came walking down the trail from the makeshift officers' quarters. "What's all this commotion?"

Felix dropped his corner of the raft. "We just dunked the whole company tryin' to keep this raft from gettin' away so Jim and Andy can drown in the river."

"A gallant army," Smithwick said.

Felix picked up his rifle. "Got mud all over it. I want you to look. Captain, can't you order these two coots to stay?"

"They're determined to go. Besides, they're both seventy if they're a day and we're short two horses."

Felix spat. "They're gonna drown, Noah. That river is colder and faster than it looks."

"This is a volunteer company, Felix," Smithwick said gently. "I've talked to them and they've made up their minds. There's always a chance."

Both ranging companies had gathered on the riverbank. The morning sun had cleared the trees on the far bank; Isaac appreciated the warmth on his wet thighs. Bain and Childress strode up and looked over the scene.

Childress grinned. "I see the Texian navy has yet to set sail." He nodded toward the beached raft. "A little light of cannon if you ask me."

Even Andy Dunn laughed. He still leaned on his pole. Jim Leach poked the grub sack with an arthritic finger. "Still dry as a bone, Captain. She floats plenty high."

"Damn," Smithwick said. "I was hopin' we'd delay the launch a few weeks on account of wet grub. A man just can't abide soggy cornbread."

Bain held up his hand. "Gentlemen, enough of this. You men launch if you're launching. Else prepare to march."

Smithwick nodded solemnly. "That's right, boys; the fate of the Republic is in sway."

Bain turned to Andy. "About ready?"

The old man raised his pole and jabbed it into the sand. "I'm waitin' on these boys to put her in the river."

"I've been ready since sunup," Jim Leach said. As far as anyone in the company knew, Old Jim hadn't slept since they got word of the Goliad massacre.

Three rangers eased the raft into the river until it just floated. The four men boarded. Andy and Sanchez stood fore and aft, poles ready. Spencer and Leach sat Indian style in the middle.

"Keep her topside up," Smithwick said. Several of the men wished them luck. Isaac thought of the earlier debacle. On the other hand, the river had been in view for most of the forty miles between Tinoxtitlan and Washington and he didn't remember any rapids. Maybe they'd make it. They could reprovision in what was left of Washington. They could always shoot a few hogs.

Andy and Sanchez strained to pole away from the bank, but their collective weight had them sitting on the bottom. Isaac and Ezra waded knee deep and dragged the raft into the current.

The officers waved farewell. No one spoke except Sanchez and Andy, whose voices could just be heard above the hiss and gurgle of the dark green river and morning birdsong. The smooth surface of the water reflected the riverside sycamores and willows.

They poled into the main current. "Look at 'em go now," Thomas Adair said. "They'd better not nod off or they'll wake up at Velasco."

Isaac had never heard of Velasco, but assumed it must lie far downriver. He wondered if any of the men on the raft were having second thoughts. If they were on the Colorado, he'd want to ride downriver with them. He'd grown used to the dry, open, oak-sprinkled uplands around Bastrop. The lower Brazos country seemed close, oppressive, and foreboding. Verdancy and decay filled his nostrils. Yet the past three days in Tinoxtitlan had been comfortable, with plenty of good food and merriment. The two ranging companies and their officers got on well, and friendships had formed the first night.

He watched the tiny, fragile raft now swept two hundred yards away on the booming Brazos. For the first time that morning he thought of home and family.

No one spoke. The raft disappeared around the bend.

"Well, that's pretty well that," Smithwick said. "We'd best get moving before I take up residence. I've grown right fond of this humble settlement."

An hour later, the last few men ferried across the river. Thomas Adair cut the cable with several ax blows, and Bobby Durham and two black men, Saul and Homer, laid siege to the ferry with picks, axes, and pry bars, knocking and ripping loose boards and timbers and tossing them into the current.

The Texians sat their horses and looked down at the destruction. "It'll take Gaona's boys awhile to gather up the makings of *that* ferry," Smithwick said.

Isaac watched the drifting lumber. "Maybe they'll build rafts."

Smithwick chuckled. "I hope so."

The midmorning heat and humidity made Isaac drowsy. Somewhere ahead, in the shadows beneath the leafy canopy, Colonel Bain yelled, "Let's go find the General." They rode southward along the river toward San Felipe.

Sixteen

TWO DAYS LATER, just north of the Rio Navasota confluence, the road turned back toward the river. They had kept cold camps, and had arisen to a breakfast of hardtack and water. Now the midmorning sun rose above the trees, and sweat stung Isaac's eyes.

The two companies descended a steep, rutted hill, Isaac and Ezra in the rear, officers at the head, and the Adair wagon near the middle of the procession. Catherine sat awake and alert now, and spoke often with her mother, though Isaac could never hear her words. Captain Adair usually rode with the other officers but occasionally fell back to check on his wife and daughter.

The forest closed in on them along with a dank, sweet smell that Isaac took first for the ripe smell of wet forest. The tender leaves stirred. He gagged.

"Lord," Ezra said. "Somethin's deader than hell."

Felix spat. "Not somethin'. Somebody."

Isaac drew his shirt up over his nose. "How can you tell?"

"I can tell."

The other rangers gasped and cursed. Bain ordered a halt. "Let's go see what we've got," Felix said.

Isaac glanced at Catherine. She held her nose while her mother tried to comfort her. George Petty glared as they rode by. "Who told them three to break rank?" he said.

Felix glanced over his shoulder. "Poor old George. Bless his heart."

Two hundred yards further on, they found Smithwick and Bain, green faced, sitting nervous horses while a swirling column of vultures rose three hundred feet above the river. Scores of others hopped from rock to rock in the shallows and flapped and croaked in the trees like a swarm of giant, roosting grackles.

Smithwick shook his head. "Raft must've caught on something, and the current pulled it under. I don't see any sign of it, but there lays what's left of old Andy." He pointed toward a bloated, pecked corpse bobbing in an eddy. "Hell, not one of 'em could swim. I imagine the buzzards will show us the rest."

Isaac recognized Andy's brogans but nothing else. "We aim to bury 'em?" He hoped not.

"He'll fall apart," Bain said. "I'd let the buzzards clean him up."

"We ought to gather him up some way," Felix said. "Old Andy fed me for a week when I first came to DeWitt's. I'll do it myself if I have to."

The Brazos ran clear and shallow below them. The morning sun filtered through the treetops and lit the sandy riverbed. Just downstream of Andy Dunn's corpse, a gentle riffle hissed and gurgled.

"Damn fool thing for them boys to do," Felix said. "I knowed right off."

The sycamore overhead seemed alive with the flapping vultures. "Filthy, devilish birds," Bain said.

Isaac fought his rising bile. He stared at the pale boles across the river, and wondered if Smithwick and Bain planned to pitch camp at this very spot. The two men glanced alternately at the corpse, the birds, and some spot on the far bank. Other rangers began to arrive and gag and cuss.

"Well," Smithwick said.

Bain spat. "First man we've lost. It don't bode well, Captain."

Isaac vomited from horseback. The two older men glanced at him, then paid him no further attention.

Smithwick said, "Isaac, best ride back and ask Miz Adair if she can spare a quilt. I don't know what we'll do if we run across the other three."

• • •

Midmorning two days later, they looked across the Brazos at the blackened remains of San Felipe, and Isaac remembered that they were at war. A steady rain formed black puddles in the charred remains of the cabins and frame buildings. Ashes clung to the wet moss in the trees and swirled in eddies. Despite the still, sodden air, Isaac caught an unmistakable whiff of burnt flesh. There was no sign of the ferry.

"Mosley Baker is a thorough man," Felix said. He and Isaac rode near the end of the column. Ahead, Captain Adair rode alongside the wagon that carried his wife, daughter, and father-in-law.

The swollen Brazos, muddy and wrinkled with swirls and eddies and pocked by rain, carried limbs and planks and kegs. Otis Crocker licked his lips. "I'd hate to think of one of them kegs bein' full of whisky."

"I'm glad we're on the east side of the river," Isaac said.

Felix watched a one-wheeled wagon tumble by in the current. "You wouldn't get me on no raft. This river was a lot tamer when it drowned Jimmy and Andy and them. I expect Santa Anna has already crossed at Fort Bend."

Isaac looked eastward along the road, then back toward the San Felipe ruins. A few days ago Santa Anna stood on the far riverbank glowering at a few defiant Texians. What lay to the east? He drank from his gourd, but his mouth remained dry.

They rode east. The horses slipped in the ruts and hock-deep holes. At times, the canopy closed and the day felt old until they emerged from the shadow of the dripping, moss-laden oaks. The rain slowed to an intermittent sprinkle; the air stilled and the rangers cursed the mosquitoes. Despite the heat, Isaac put on his coat and gloves, pulled his collar up and his hat down. Sweating was preferable to the itching and maddening whine. Felix lit his pipe and rode on.

An hour down the road, they came to a fork. One prong ran northeast toward Louisiana, the other southeast toward Galveston Bay. Bain ordered a halt.

"What the hell now?" Felix said. "I never came all this way to run to Louisiana. I don't see what there is to talk about."

Smithwick rode to the rear. "Captain Adair will be taking his family to Louisiana. I expect our army and the enemy lie just ahead." He looked at Isaac. "Expecting some weather, are you?"

Isaac unbuttoned his coat and fanned his face with his hat. "Damn skeeters."

"You're red as a plum," Smithwick said.

"Skeeters like me." He stared into his hat. What difference did it make if the girl left? She didn't know him from a hole in the ground. He put on his hat and looked at the wagon. Catherine was sitting up, facing the rear with her back against her hope chest. Her wet hair was pulled back in a tight bun. "Well."

"Be safer for her that way," Felix said gently. "Nothin' but trouble to the southeast."

Isaac nodded. Why should he care? They were in a war, after all. He might die tomorrow.

Captain Adair rode back to meet them. He looked at Isaac, then briefly at Ezra, Felix, and Smithwick, then back at Isaac. "Mrs. Adair tells me you men have been a help and comfort. We thank you." He looked down the road toward Harrisburg. "I have to see my family to safety. I've left them long enough."

Felix took his pipe from between his teeth. "God bless you, Captain. You've pulled your weight and half of everybody else's."

Smithwick extended his hand. "Good luck to you and your family, Thomas. Texas will be a free republic when we meet again."

Adair shook their hands, then rode to the front, speaking to his men, who waved and offered their good-byes. He rode back and nodded to his father-in-law, who flipped the reins and started the oxen along the northeasterly fork.

"Be damn," Isaac said. His arms and eyelids felt impossibly heavy.

Ezra stroked his beard. Colonel Bain turned his horse toward Harrisburg. The others followed. Smithwick said, "I believe I'll ride with you boys for a spell."

Isaac appreciated the Captain's gesture; he suddenly felt alone. He looked at his haggard company. Forty-one men slouched on gaunt horses and mules. *Texas will be a free republic when we meet again.*

"No wagon to slow us down now," Smithwick said. "Be in Harrisburg by dark."

The rain had ceased. The sun burned through the clouds, lighting the dark green oak leaves and the coffee brown rainwater in the ruts. Isaac rode past the fork and watched Catherine disappear beyond a slight rise.

Seventeen

AROUND MIDNIGHT, Bain ordered a halt and sent Bobby Durham ahead to reconnoiter. "Can't see the skulkin' little bastard after dark," the Colonel said. The young ranger returned an hour later and reported wounded Texians camped near the burned-out ruins of Harrisburg.

They pushed on. Isaac smelled the charred settlement before he saw the rebel campfires. A few dozen Texians suffering from fever, snakebite, broken bones, and various wounds lay on pallets beneath lean-tos in woods along the river. A bearish, bearded man named Cheatam was making rounds, changing bandages and offering food and water. His eyes glistened in the firelight.

"You look a little feverish yourself," Smithwick said, after the rangers had picketed their horses.

Cheatam nodded. "A physician has his duties. How's your outfit holding up?"

"Very well, save for a bit of extra flatulence in old Felix Gross."

The doctor wiped his brow with his sleeve. "Just wait. This country is rife with fever. I pray I'll be returning to drier climes."

"I have every confidence," Smithwick said.

Cheatam shook his head. "I wish I shared it. Santa Anna has Houston and maybe a thousand Texians cornered fifteen miles east along this fetid bayou. Word is, Cós is on his way with another four hundred men."

"Nonsense," Bain said. "Cós pledged never to lead troops in Texas."

The doctor smiled. "I'm afraid El Presidente absolved the good general of his promise. Deaf Smith caught a courier carrying orders." He shrugged. "That's what I'm hearin' anyway."

Isaac looked at the pallid faces of the wounded. Santa Anna, the butcher, a half day's ride to the east. Someone moaned out in the moist darkness.

Smithwick drank from his gourd, then nodded thoughtfully. "You think Houston will engage?"

The exhausted doctor laughed. His eyes held no humor. "He'll either fight or retreat into the bayou. He sure as hell can't surrender."

The officers rubbed their beards. Smithwick cleared his throat. "I say we go to our army."

Childress nodded.

Bain slapped his thigh. "We'll leave at first light."

Dr. Cheatam said, "Rest and eat, gentlemen. I'm afraid you'll have to forage for meat; it's scattered about the settlement. Santa Anna was thoughtful enough to cook it for us. Only wish he'd thought to draw and bleed it first."

. . .

Sleep eluded Isaac. He doubted anything ever dried in this moldering country. He lay shivering in the forest duff, his coat over his head against the swarming mosquitoes. Ezra and Felix snored on either side. He'd never been both cold and beset by mosquitoes.

He sat up and looked around. No sign of Sis. She was probably off rolling on a dead horse. She'd show up for breakfast. The communal fire still flickered just off the road. He got up quietly, threw his blankets about his shoulders, and walked toward the flames. Moving felt good. The fire cast a pale glow into the moldy tree trunks and the hanging blue green moss. A gaunt, red-bearded man sat shivering on the far side of the fire. Isaac nodded. "Mornin'."

"Mornin' to you," he answered in a tenor voice. "Shakes run me off my pallet. What brings such a strappin' boy out of his blankets in the wee hours?"

"Damn skeeters. And I'm soppin' wet."

"Skeeters botherin' you, huh?" He studied Isaac. "Mountain boy, ain't ye?"

Isaac nodded. "Ouachitas. Skeeters ain't botherin' you?"

The man began stuffing his pipe. His hands shook so that he dumped more tobacco in his lap than in the bowl. Isaac started to help, but the man held up a hand. "I've got her." He drew a burning stick from the fire and lit his pipe. "Skeeters bother me? Hell no. Growed up in South Georgia. But that don't keep me from gettin' the fever from time to time. Have all my life."

Isaac sat cross-legged as close to the fire as he dared. "I'm Isaac Webb."

"Pleased. I'm Stokes."

"Good to meet you, Mr. Stokes."

"Just Stokes." His drooping hat brim hid his expression. He drew on his pipe with sunken cheeks.

Isaac considered the red hair and beard and pictured pale blue eyes glistening with fever. "Cup of coffee would go good about now."

"It would sure enough."

Isaac started to get up. "I'll fetch the makin's."

"This bayou be blood red tomorrow," Stokes said.

Isaac sat back down, drew a labored breath. "What am I s'posed to say to that?"

Stokes stared into the blackness. "I'm tellin' ye; there's never been such a murderous horde of men. Nor a more ruthless flock of officers." He puffed on his pipe.

Isaac pictured the burning corpses at Béxar and the prairie littered with the bodies of Fannin's men. He'd been perfectly content contemplating coffee.

Why would Stokes tell a man who was about to ride into battle that he was doomed? Maybe the feverish old swamp rat was delirious. Yet he doubted it.

"They'll kill every man," Stokes said. "I seen it in their faces. Devils, I tell ye. Away from home, vengeful, murderous. I hate to miss it."

"Why in hell would you hate to miss gettin' killed?"

"What?"

"You've been sayin' how murderous the Mexicans are."

"Murderous Mexicans? Son, they kill only because they're ordered to kill."

"What're you sayin' then?"

Someone yelled from the woods, "Love of God. Pipe down!"

Isaac repeated the question in a loud whisper.

Stokes pointed his pipe stem at Isaac. "You've got me wrong, son. Santa Anna don't know it, but he made Houston's army. I seen it wrought. Béxar; then Goliad; women and younguns with red eye and fever, piled up waitin' to get on a ferry. A month ago, these Texians didn't amount to spit. And they won't amount to nothin' a month from now. But this day, they're the terriblest men that ever lived."

• • •

Bain halted the rangers six miles east of Harrisburg. The sun had nearly burned away the morning fog. Much to Isaac's relief, the light breeze and brisk pace had kept the mosquitoes away. He and Felix sat their horses near the rear of the column.

Felix shook his head. "What the hell now?"

Isaac stood in his stirrups, trying see over the heads of his companions. "I smell a creek."

Shouted curses rang out in front. Smithwick rode to the rear. "Somebody tore out the damn bridge."

"Goddamn Meskins," Ezra said.

Smithwick smiled. "As likely Texian as Mexican, I'd say. Creek's up but sluggish." He looked at Sis who lay panting in a mud puddle. "Can she swim?"

"She got across the Brazos some way," Isaac said. "Showed up two days after we busted the ferry up."

Smithwick looked at Ezra. "What about you boys?"

"Hellfire," Felix said. "Let's get movin'."

Isaac, too, felt the urge to go. To meet his enemy. To finally end the gnawing fear and tedium.

"Well then," Smithwick said. He turned his horse and rode for the creek. The line moved forward and soon Isaac heard splashing and shouting, then black water came into view. The creek was forty yards across and smooth, but Isaac sensed power in the dark current. Already, riders were emerging thirty yards downstream from their entry point and quirting their horses up the steep, muddy bank.

On the far side, Bobby Durham yelled something and pointed upstream, but Isaac couldn't make out his words over the splashing and shouting. Ezra turned. "He's sayin' gators, Isaac. Best put Sis across your saddle."

"Lord, I never thought of that. He saw a gator?"

"He's pointin' at something." Ezra followed Felix into the creek. Isaac whistled and patted his leg. Sis shook off the muddy water and reared up on the saddle fender. He grabbed her scruff and pulled her up and across the pommel. The mud-encrusted hound beat her tail against his hip and licked his chin. He laid his rifle across Sis's back and rode into the water.

"Lot of time and trouble for a dog," George Petty said from behind.

Fanny proved a good swimmer. Half a minute later she struggled up the bank and onto the muddy road. Isaac had just let Sis down when George Petty screamed, "Get away, goddamn you!" He was midstream, flailing at the water with his rifle butt. "I'll kill you, you devil!" Isaac glimpsed a thick, armored tail and gentle swirl. Petty rode out of the creek, a plume of slobber on his beard. "I never come all this way to get eat by a damn gator." He quirted his horse up the bank.

By early afternoon, they'd slowed to a walk. The few wispy clouds provided no relief from the sun. Sweat dripped from Isaac's chin. Sis kept disappearing into the brush and waist-high grass only to return a few minutes later soaking wet.

"Gators gonna eat you yet," Isaac told her.

Ezra pointed to a set of six-inch-deep tracks. "Look at them ruts. Something heavy in that wagon."

Felix laughed. "Shit. Cannon, I expect."

"Hellfire," Ezra said.

Broken tumbrels, Mexican sandals, empty jugs, laudanum bottles, and fly-blown mules littered the road. Vultures flapped away at the rangers' approach. On either side, dense oak mottes punctuated gently rolling savannah colored red and yellow by wildflowers. The air smelled of brackish water.

A low, distant boom sounded in the east. Colonel Bain raised his hand. They stopped, sat their horses, and listened. There was only the sound of birdsong, swishing horse tails, and ragged breathing. Then came a thump and shock wave billowing toward them like thunder. A flock of cormorants flushed from the edge of the bayou. Smithwick turned and looked back at his men. "That'd be cannon, boys."

Isaac's stomach fluttered. He looked about, but Sis was nowhere in sight. The sharp clap of a rifle volley rose over the fading cannon roar. Smithwick turned to Bain. "Colonel?"

Bain shouted, "Ride!"

Isaac set Fanny at trot. He guessed the rifle fire to be less than three miles distant. He managed only shallow breaths, and his bladder suddenly felt ready to burst, yet he wanted nothing so much as to see this thing played out. He thought of Stokes's words. Blather of a fevered old man?

The column bunched into a shifting phalanx, horses kicking mud, spattered riders maneuvering for purchase on the road and in the grass. Isaac sensed they were again drawing near the bayou. The horizon rolled away, and gulls swarmed overhead. He heard no further cannonade. The rifle fire slowed and spread.

Three Mexican soldiers broke out of the brush on Isaac's left. He reined Fanny and mounted his rifle. Someone shouted as he laid the front sight on the nearest soldier's chest. Felix jerked his barrel down. "They're unarmed, son!"

The bare-headed soldiers raised their hands. "*¡Nos damos por vencer! ¡No tiren por favor! ¡No tiren!*"

Smithwick shouted, "Hold your fire." The soldiers dropped to their knees.

A volley cut all three down. Four rebels ran out of the brush screaming and bashed the dying men's skulls with rifle butts. Isaac sat transfixed. Smithwick and Bain shouted that the men were unarmed and had surrendered.

The oblivious attackers bludgeoned on. Gunfire continued to the east, just out of sight beyond a strip of oaks. Smithwick and Bain fell silent.

The largest attacker came down a final time with his rifle butt, then met the officers' stares with wild blue eyes. Splotches of blood covered his face and blond beard. He laid his gory rifle into the crook of his arm and said slowly, calmly, "Remember Goliad?" He held Smithwick's gaze, then looked defiantly at the rest of the company. The other three rebels had stopped their mutilation and now stood, chests heaving, facing the rangers. "I do," he said. "I goddamn remember." He turned and walked back through the oaks toward the battlefield. The other three followed.

"Lord have mercy," Felix said.

Isaac looked at the smashed bodies and thought of Stokes's prophecy. *Terriblest men that ever lived.*

The rifle fire was sparse and sporadic now. They rode through the trees, crested a low hill, and looked over the battlefield.

Dead soldiers, horses, muskets, leather helmets, and broken rifle stocks littered the prairie and the marsh bordering a narrow lake. At first Isaac tried to ride around the dead, but soon gave up and allowed a nervous Fanny to step over the staring faces and dismembered bodies.

Buckskin- and homespun-clad Texians were whooping and searching the corpses. Several hundred rebels seemed to be gathering beneath a stand of live oak near the lake. The rangers rode speechless. A rude breastworks lay in shambles, obviously blown apart by a cannon positioned near the top of a knoll. Scores of tents still billowed beyond the destroyed fortifications. A few dozen Mexican soldiers knelt, facedown, at gunpoint. Clouds of white smoke hung thick over the plain. Isaac drew his neckerchief over his nose.

A lank, clean-shaven officer rode out from the oak grove to meet them. "You boys just getting here?"

Bain nodded dully. "We're a ranging company out of Tinoxtitlan. I'm Colonel Bain."

"Pleased, Colonel." He held out his hand. "Sidney Sherman. Béxar and Goliad have been avenged. Caught 'em at siesta."

"Captain!" A small, frail figure ran toward them from the rebel cannon. "Captain!" Uncle Jimmy Curtis staggered and fell to his knees at Smithwick's stirrup. Tears streamed down his bloody, bewhiskered jaws and dripped from the end of his nose. He held a rifle broken off at the wrist. "Captain! Praise the Almighty; you made it."

"Good lord," Sherman said. He turned to Bain. "Once their blood was up, there was no holding them back. You might call it mutiny under different circumstances." Intermittent shots rang out along the lakeshore.

Uncle Jimmy looked up at Smithwick. "I done it, Captain." He sobbed. "I done it for Wash. Them bastards! I had to!"

"I know you did, Uncle Jimmy," Smithwick said. "God bless your heart."

Jimmy turned to Isaac. "Isaac, son, you made it too. You remember what you promised old Uncle Jimmy? I might've been drunk when you promised it, but I remember."

"I . . ." Isaac's voice caught. "I remember." He took a deep breath.

"You damn sure did," Jimmy said. "You're a good one all right."

Felix said, "Isaac, here comes that hound of yours."

Isaac looked over the lake. Hundreds of blue-jacketed bodies and shakos bobbed in the shallows. Sis nosed along the bank, skittering at the screams of the dying. The incoming breeze had pushed the smoke over the oak savannah west of the battleground. Rebels were searching the Mexican tents and collecting piles of muskets. Vultures gathered overhead.

II
COLEMAN'S FORT

Eighteen

Colorado River, north of Bastrop, August 1836

ISAAC STRODE AROUND to the front of the cabin carrying a sack of potatoes. He found his father and the Tonkawa King Sol squatting at the far edge of the bare yard dressing squirrels. The three hounds, Stout, Andy, and Sis, watched intently. King cut an incision near the base of a squirrel's tail, grabbed its hind legs with his knife hand, and peeled off most of the hide with the other. When the squirrel looked like it had a shirt pulled over its head, the Tonkawa excised hide, head, and all and tossed it into the woods. The three hounds bolted; Sis got to the morsel first.

Cyrus Webb looked up from his work. "Well, you throwed the head away."

The old Tonk picked up another squirrel from a pile of a dozen or so. "I don't like my meat lookin' back at me."

Cyrus gritted his teeth and strained to get the hide off an old boar. "Damn old red thing. He'll have to cook for a week." He stopped to rest. "I like the head meat on a squirrel and you know it." He pitched the heart and liver to Andy. Neither organ touched the ground.

Esther's slender bottom appeared at the cabin door as she dragged out a big cast-iron kettle. She stopped to wipe her brow. "Lord, I'm burnin' up in there; we'll cook and eat outside tonight."

Isaac held up the sack of potatoes he'd just dug. "Swap?"

"What a good brother." She took the sack. Isaac carried the kettle to the fire pit in the center of the yard.

Ruth Webb bustled out the door carrying a spadeful of coals from the fireplace. "Watch out; stay back." She dumped the coals into the shallow pit. "You men had better finish those squirrels." She hurried back inside with the spade.

Isaac drew his skinning knife and examined the rodent pile. There wouldn't be many brains in this kettle of burgoo no matter who did the cleaning. King had head-shot nearly every squirrel with his broken-stocked, sightless, smoothbore musket. Isaac doubted that he himself could do nearly as well with his long rifle, and he'd never been accused of being a poor shot.

Isaac, Esther, and King were standing over the kettle cutting up the squirrels and potatoes when the three hounds pricked their ears and growled. Isaac looked down the trail toward the river and saw a lone rider on a big bay. "Somebody's comin'."

King looked up for a second, then went back to his cutting. "Noah."

Esther said, "I hope he stays for supper."

Cyrus poked in the kettle with a long wooden spoon. "What do you suppose young mister Jonas McElroy would have to say about that?"

Esther looked imperiously at her father. "Who's tellin'? Anyways, I just said I hope he stays for supper."

"Why Esther, the Captain's a grown man." Isaac had given up trying to understand his big sister. What would a nineteen-year-old girl want with a man nearly thirty years old?

"I've noticed," Esther said.

Cyrus laughed, looked down the road. "Boy, your sister's about growed up enough for somebody besides me to keep a roof over her head."

"I might just end up a spinster," she said. "That way I can help Mama wipe your chin."

Cyrus tugged at a shock of hair that had fallen onto her forehead. "Not with them yeller locks you won't."

They dumped the last of the meat and potatoes into the kettle just as Smithwick rode into the yard. He nodded cordially. "Evening."

Isaac rushed forward, hand extended. "Captain. Awful good to see you. You'll be takin' supper with us, won't you?"

"Why sure he is," Esther said. She smiled and stirred the burgoo.

Smithwick returned the smile. "Miss Esther."

Cyrus said, "Evenin', Smithwick. Are the Mexicans upon us again, or are you just lookin' for a meal?"

Noah looked beyond the cabin. "I swear, Cyrus, I believe the corn is about to take over your stump field."

Isaac laughed. Cyrus nodded gravely. "The irksome weed takes hold, and a man can't get shed of it to save his life."

Ruth Webb stepped outside, her auburn hair dusted with cornmeal, sweat running down her cheeks. "If the young man would mind me and marry the Widow Duty, he wouldn't have to go around beggin' his meals. Good to see you, Noah."

"Always a pleasure, Mrs. Webb."

Esther stirred the burgoo with such vigor that Isaac thought she'd slop half of it out of the kettle.

Cyrus said, "Be eatin' in the saddle?"

Smithwick dismounted and handed the rein to Isaac. "Kind of you, Cyrus. Of course I've come to expect nothing less. King, good to see you."

The Tonkawa studied the bay. "That's a good horse."

Smithwick stroked his horse's neck. "Kind of you to notice."

King took a pipe from his parfleche pouch. "I had a horse like that once."

Smithwick laughed. "Whose was he before he was yours?"

"Some Wichita's. I never woke him up to ask him his name."

At dusk, with bull bats hunting overhead, they sat about the porch and yard, eating the burgoo. Smithwick finished his portion and patted his leg. Sis came over for an ear scratching.

Isaac wiped his bowl dry with a piece of cornbread. Seeing the Captain and Sis together again jolted him. "Heard from Felix or Ezree?"

"Lately, I've seen both the rascals about every day."

"I thought they were off catching mustangs."

"That enterprise lasted less than a month," Smithwick said.

Isaac noticed his father watching him. Ruth seemed to be staring into her bowl. Esther watched Noah, and King sat on a stump, scratching his full belly.

Cyrus cleared his throat. "Smithwick, you know you're welcome here anytime, but you didn't come all the way out here just to visit and sit for a meal."

"No sir. I've been workin' up to it." He rubbed his beard. Glanced at the women.

Cyrus said. "Son, they'll sit where they are. Say what's on your mind."

"Yes sir. You've heard about the Comanche raid on Parker's Fort?"

"Sure I have."

"They stole three women, a boy and a little—"

Cyrus raised his hand. "We know the particulars."

"Of course. My apologies." He nodded to Ruth. "The raiding continues. Secretary Sawyer has ordered Captain Coleman to raise three ranging companies to defend the settlements and punish Comanche raiders. Naturally he's seeking proven fighters."

Ruth looked at him in disbelief. "Proven fighters! Why Isaac ain't even seventeen."

"Yes ma'am, but he's a veteran."

Isaac mouthed the word, *veteran.* The fact had never occurred to him. Smithwick and Felix were veterans. He was a boy.

Ruth stood. "He survived a wretched war only by the grace of God. Bastrop is full of grown men to fight savages. He went with you only because his father had no better sense than to let him go. Had I been there, he'd have gone with us to Louisiana."

Cyrus studied his palms in silence. Esther chewed her cornbread and frowned at Ruth.

Smithwick adjusted his hat. "With all respect, Mrs. Webb, I know of two Mexican soldiers who would disagree with you if they could."

King grunted his approval.

Ruth waved off the comment and glared at her son. "Isaac, this is no business of yours."

Cyrus said. "Mother, were the Creek Wars no business of mine?"

"You were a grown man."

"Not when you run off with me."

Esther smiled. Ruth rubbed her temples. Cyrus spat, grinned. "I swear, Smithwick."

King Sol ladled out another bowl of burgoo and squatted next to Cyrus. He looked from Ruth to Smithwick to Isaac.

Smithwick said, "One-year term of enlistment. Every man will be awarded 1280 acres and twenty-five dollars a month."

"This is not about land or pay," Ruth said.

Isaac had not considered that he might be paid.

Cyrus said, "Why would I care about 1280 acres? When I wear this place out, I'll just move up the creek a piece. If the boy wants a piece of land, he can strike out and build wherever he lights."

"Cyrus, things won't work that way much longer. Folks are pouring across the Sabine by the thousands. And don't tell me you can't use twenty-five dollars a month."

Isaac said, "Seems like . . ."

Cyrus snorted. "I swap for what I need. Them bills ain't good for nothin' no way."

Smithwick said, "You never asked Isaac what he wants to do."

Isaac cleared his throat. "I could . . ."

"Noah, you've got no right," Ruth said.

Smithwick stood and doffed his hat. "Mrs. Webb, Miss Esther, a delicious meal. I thank you. I believe I've caused enough discord for one night. My apologies."

Cyrus said, "Damn it, Ruth."

Isaac set his bowl on the ground. "Mama, what if they come here?" They all looked at him.

"It's only a matter of time," Smithwick said. "Think of Esther."

"Hell, think of yourself," Isaac said.

"Watch your mouth, Isaac Webb. Cyrus, you go with him then."

Smithwick shook his head. "And leave you and Esther?"

"We'll move to Bastrop."

"Mother, our place would be pilfered and burned to the ground in a week."

"Mama, I made out fine fightin' Mexicans. I'll make out this time too. Better this way than to meet the heathens out here some night when they've got us outnumbered."

"I won't hear of it."

Isaac wondered when a boy got to make his own decisions. He sensed his time hadn't yet arrived.

King Sol swallowed a mouthful of burgoo. "I'll look after Isaac." He took another bite.

Ruth said, "Why King . . ."

Cyrus slapped his thigh. "There you go. Old King is the awfullest, meanest red nigger that ever lived. He won't let nothin' happen to the boy."

Smithwick said, "King, we've already employed Lipan scouts."

"They better not bother me," the Tonkawa said.

Smithwick put his hat back on and sat down. "Lord."

"When would I need to leave?" Isaac asked.

"First light tomorrow too early? Felix, Ezra, and Uncle Jimmy and a dozen or so of our old company are already on Walnut Creek building the stockade."

King got up and started for his horse. "I need my bow and blanket."

"I reckon not," Isaac said. Things happened fast whenever Noah Smithwick showed up.

Ruth started gathering the bowls. King rode into the darkness.

Isaac said, "Mama, I know you want me to be a gentler man than Pap, but this country won't abide it."

She nodded. "You could do worse than to be like your Pap."

"Well, I feel a damn sight better," Cyrus said.

"Captain, you'll be staying with us tonight?" Ruth wasn't smiling.

"It's awfully late. I appreciate your hospitality. I'll fetch my bedroll."

"No. You'll sleep in Isaac's bed." Ruth carried the stack of bowls to the dishpan at the end of the porch. The hounds gathered around Esther as she began scraping out the kettle.

"Yes ma'am."

"Just as well, Captain," Isaac said. "I won't sleep a wink."

Smithwick laughed. "By the way, I bumped into young Widow Druin at the dry goods store in Gonzales. She sends her regards."

Nineteen

SMITHWICK LOOKED over his shoulder and shouted above the rain, "There's a farm three hills north and up the creek. They've put me up a time or two. I expect they'll take pity on us tonight." He rode along a faint game trail up a grassy, oak-studded hill.

Rain poured off Isaac's hat brim. The Captain looked like a formless, gray specter only ten yards ahead. It would be dark in an hour or so. Ezra coughed a few yards behind him. Little comfort awaited at Coleman's Fort, which, at their current rate of travel, they wouldn't reach until around midnight. Here it was November and they still didn't have the bunkhouse built, and it had rained nearly every day for the past month. The ranging company had been sleeping in the open or crowding under lean-tos. His blankets hadn't been dry in weeks. A tight roof and hearth would suit him just fine.

That morning at sunup, he, Smithwick, and Ezra had ridden southeast from the fort on Walnut Creek, looking for Comanche sign. Several farmers around Webber's Prairie had reported missing stock. Captain Coleman refused to send more than three men, given the work that remained at the fort. Smithwick had jumped at the chance to escape another day of ax work.

The day had dawned clear; the rain started around noon and hadn't slackened. Smithwick seemed in fine sprits, perhaps relieved that they'd found no Comanche sign, which wasn't surprising. They'd seen not one moccasin print since the company formed in August.

They topped the hill and started down the other side. Isaac's piebald gelding, Squab, had proven himself more surefooted than old Fanny, who had pulled up hopelessly lame shortly after Saint Hyacinth. The little mustang trotted up steep, narrow trails with aplomb and seemed to enjoy rough terrain. Isaac considered him homely and too short, but he was nimble and sweet natured, one of the few good horses left in the company remuda when Isaac joined. The other men had passed him over because of his unusually bulbous eyes, which had earned him his name. Isaac had ridden one of the family mules from home and planned to return it as soon as they finished work on the fort. He wondered how many tons of stone and timber the beast had dragged over the past three months.

They topped two more hills, then descended into a broad, grassy bottom. The largest log house Isaac had ever seen sat on the far side. A pole barn sat off to the right and next to it a much smaller cabin and three other outbuildings he supposed were smokehouse, corncrib, and henhouse. Firelight shone through the cabin's two gun ports.

They rode into the yard. A gray and white feist bustled out of the barn, hackles up, barking furiously. A tall, lean black man ran from the smaller cabin. "Gyp! Hush!" The little dog growled and huffed about.

"Hello, Cedrick," Smithwick shouted.

"Why Captain, what the devil are you gentlemen doin' out in this weather? Bring these horses in the barn." Cedrick dragged open the pole door. Inside, the dirt floor was raked and dry.

"I'll see to these animals, Captain. Madam will be tickled to death to see you again."

They ran through the rain toward the cabin door. "I never thought about seeing a slave way out here," Ezra said.

Smithwick skipped and clapped his hands. "Move along boys!" He bounded up to the door and shook like a dog, grinned and rubbed his hands together.

"What in hell has gotten into him?" Isaac said. "By god, you're glad to be here, ain't you?"

Catherine Druin opened the door just as Smithwick turned to knock. "Why hello, Captain. We saw you coming. Get in here this instant."

Isaac's breath left him. Catherine stood backlit in the doorway. He realized those were the first words he'd heard her speak.

Smithwick said, "Pleasure's all ours, Mrs. Druin. You'll remember Mr. Webb and Mr. Higginbotham."

She smiled at Isaac. "I surely would. Good to see you again, gentlemen. Welcome."

Ezra said, "I swear."

Smithwick stepped inside and motioned for Isaac and Ezra to follow. "I apologize for these boys, but as you can see this weather has made them a little peaked."

She backed into the room to let them in. "Why sure. Who wouldn't be a little peaked after a day in this mess? Come in you two, before you take sick sure enough."

Isaac remembered to breathe. "Yes ma'am," he said. Damn Ezra Higginbotham had gotten in the first word. He looked at the puddle of water at his feet. His wet buckskin britches dragged the floor.

He shut his eyes against the sudden heat and light from the fireplace; opened them as Mrs. Adair stepped in from a door to the left. He'd never seen a home with more than two doors—one at each end of the dog run—let alone multiple rooms. "Welcome boys," she said. Isaac thought she looked much plumper and a little grayer than she had the past spring.

Catherine knelt at the fireplace and lifted the Dutch oven lid. "Just about done," she said. "Where in the world is Daddy?"

She wore her light brown hair in a bun and seemed much taller than he'd remembered; then he realized he'd never before seen her on her feet. She'd nearly outgrown her gray, woolen work dress. For the past six months he'd dreamed of a frail girl. Before him stood a healthy woman.

Mrs. Adair said, "Warm yourselves a little before the fire while we get the food on the table."

Isaac stood while Smithwick and Ezra moved toward the warmth. With a poker, Catherine knocked most of the coals from the oven lid. Her face and hands were brown from working outside. She glanced at him. "Mr. Webb, you're freezing to death. Get over here and get warm." He obeyed as he always obeyed women.

Isaac heard footfalls outside. Thomas Adair entered with the same flourish he'd shown that night in Tinoxtitlan. "My lord," he said, shedding his woolen coat, "look what my taste for venison has cost me. I'll have to restock the larder after tonight. Welcome boys." He shook hands all around.

Catherine picked up the Dutch oven by the bail and started for the table. "Well?"

"Well what?" Thomas said.

"Don't give me that."

"I don't have no idea what you mean."

"You don't have to say another word. I know the answer."

Isaac enjoyed the exchange. A close father and daughter playing a familiar game.

"Oh that," Adair said. "Why didn't you just come out and ask? It's hangin' in the barn. Fat as an October hog."

Catherine shook her head. "Well, the wonder of it all."

"I wish we had as much luck," Smithwick said.

Adair hung his dripping coat and hat on the door peg. "I doubt you boys were huntin' four-legged game. I've generally found the two-legged sort the more taxing."

"Thomas, you're about to flood us out," his wife said. "Come here and let me daub you off."

Isaac noticed the aroma for the first time. Ham and biscuits and beans. He'd forgotten it was hog-killing time. His mouth watered. Then he remembered he'd soon be eating in front of Catherine.

"You've made some progress here since my last visit," Smithwick said.

Adair pointed to the wall beyond the table. "Not near enough. Ran out of time and had to put up that wall there to keep from freezing. I'll knock her down or cut a door this spring and we'll finish the other half of the place.

Isaac guessed the cabin was already twice the size of his family's home. Board floor and colorful throw rugs. Oak table and chairs. A good place for a dance if the Adairs weren't Baptists. Probably even nicer in the adjoining rooms. He supposed Catherine sat at a dresser and primped before a mirror every morning.

They ate at the table, Catherine between her parents on one side and the rangers on the other. Isaac found himself seated on one end, facing Mrs. Adair. He thought it no coincidence that Ezra had situated himself directly across from Catherine. Adair asked for the blessing of the food, prayed for the Republic, the subjugation and conversion of the native savages, and the rangers' safe return to the fort. Then Isaac heard himself swallowing. The more carefully he tried to down his ham or biscuit, the louder his gulping. By the end of the meal, his throat had seized up so that hot coffee pooled just beyond the back of his tongue.

No one seemed to pay him any mind. Smithwick entertained his hosts with Felix Gross and Uncle Jimmy Curtis stories. Catherine sat with her hands in her lap, laughing, obviously charmed. Isaac wished the dandy would let a fart slip or gag on that last bite of biscuit.

About halfway through their third cup of coffee, Adair said, "I want to hear about you boys jumping that Mexican cavalry patrol."

Mrs. Adair folded her arms and looked at the ceiling. Catherine stared at her plate. Smithwick laid both hands on the table as if studying them. "I'm not sure that story is mine to tell. Isaac ought to recount it."

Isaac felt blood rushing to his face. "Oh . . . I . . . we were ridin' along and the Captain's horse smelled these Mexicans a ways behind us." Catherine was watching him. Adair and Smithwick nodded their approval. "We hid in the woods—no, first the Captain ran back down the road; I mean he stayed in the woods when he done it." They smiled. He wiped his forehead.

"Go ahead, son," Adair said.

"He came back, the Captain did, and when they came around the bend we waylaid 'em."

"I hear there's a little more to it than that, Isaac," Adair said.

Smithwick sipped his coffee. "He's a fighter, Thomas. Gentle as a baby 'til he's riled."

"He is that," Mrs. Adair said. "Gentle, I mean." Now Catherine blushed.

"Snores and talks in his sleep, though," Ezra said. "And you ought to see his bug-eyed horse." He looked at Isaac. "What else? Oh, and he won't let me within a mile of that blond-haired sister of his."

Smithwick leaned back in his chair. "Why Ezra, I took supper with Miss Webb this past August and Isaac sat right there and watched me."

"Watched you close," Isaac said.

Catherine threw her head back and laughed, much to Isaac's satisfaction. Adair said, "Mother, I believe this is the liveliest company we've had."

Mrs. Adair pushed back from the table. "Nothin' like a houseful of young men."

Adair raised his hands. "I take back every word of it."

Mrs. Adair said, "Captain, we'll be pleased to have you sleep in our guest bed. Cedrick will fix pallets in the barn for the boys."

Two hours later, the rain pattering on the barn roof hadn't lulled Isaac to sleep. "I believe she's sweet on the Captain."

Ezra pulled his blanket under his chin. "So is that sister of yours."

"She's sweet on Jonas McElroy too, but if she could snare the Captain she'd drop poor old Jonas tomorrow."

"They're both out of luck. He's after Widow Duty and I hear she's agreeable to bein' caught."

"I'm told she's somethin' to see," Isaac said. He rolled onto his side, facing Ezra. "Catherine's a grown woman; I mean just look at her."

"I did."

"And damn you for it. I need to just get over her. She's a widow, for god's sake. And I just turned seventeen. She don't want to be courted by a boy."

"Felix said her husband wasn't but twenty."

"Hell. A grown man." But, then, Catherine might still be in her teens. Girls often married at seventeen or eighteen. "I like to have died when she opened the door."

Ezra snored softly.

Cedrick woke them well before dawn and invited them into his cabin. The barn was pitch dark and bitter cold. The rain had stopped. Outside, the naked, wet tree limbs reflected moonlight. He and Ezra hurried to the tiny cabin. The Adair house was still dark. They squatted next to the fireplace and sipped Cedrick's coffee while he slipped into his master's cabin to build up the fire.

An hour later, Smithwick called them from the porch. Isaac managed to enjoy his bacon, biscuits, and coffee, even though Catherine sat across the table from him. "I apologize for the late breakfast, gentlemen," Mrs. Adair said. "Thomas sold our kitchen girl to pay for another span of mules. We're a little shorthanded right now."

"We miss Lucy. Cedrick was taken with her, but I needed the mules," Adair said.

Isaac peered out a shooting port. Nearly sunup. His time with Catherine was slipping away. He tried to think of small talk, but decided he'd never done or seen anything of the slightest interest to anyone.

He was cinching his saddle when Smithwick walked up behind him and said, "I brought you all the way out here; now you say something to that girl."

"Say what? You should've told me she was here so I'd have had time to think of somethin' to say."

"You'd have forgotten it on the ride out here. Tell her thank you for the hospitality."

"Her daddy won't ever get away from her long enough for me to say somethin'."

"I sure hope you like being a bachelor."

"You said you seen her in Gonzales."

"I did. In June. She told me she'd be living up here with her folks by fall. I'd say she's a woman of her word."

"You just wanted to see me fall over from shock."

"A man takes his pleasure when and where he can. You gonna talk to that gal or not? If you don't, I ain't bringin' you back."

"I don't need no help findin' my way back," he lied. He smiled in spite of himself. "Anyway, who says I'm sweet on Catherine?"

"Every man in the company. And especially Felix Gross."

"I should've known."

"And Louise Adair."

Isaac nearly shoved his rifle through the end of its scabbard. "Lord."

"She saw it right off."

"What does she say about it?"

"Nothin' yet. But she's watching. The old man has no idea."

"What about Catherine?"

Smithwick grinned, shrugged. "Couldn't say."

"Or won't."

They walked across the muddy yard. Catherine stood with her parents, shivering under a woolen shawl. Isaac and Ezra doffed their hats and nodded while Smithwick expressed thanks. Ezra and Smithwick started toward the horses; Louise and Thomas stepped inside. Isaac found himself standing alone, holding his hat and facing Catherine, Gyp sniffing his leg.

"Mrs. Druin."

She arched her brows in question.

"I'm pleased that you're well now. We was all worried."

"That's kind of you, Isaac. You'll visit again?"

He nodded. "First chance I get—we get, I mean." He swallowed. "If that'd be fine with you."

"I wouldn't have asked if it wasn't fine."

"Well. I'd best be off." He stood, rooted in the mud.

"Why sure." She waited. "Good day to you." She raised her brows again.

"Huh? Oh . . . I thank you." He turned and walked toward his horse, trying to remember what he'd just said, terrified by what he might have said. The door closed behind him. Smithwick and Ezra were mounted, stifling grins. He stepped into a stirrup. "Not one word, goddamn it."

They rode up the hill through the wet grass. At the top, King Sol sat his horse, waiting.

Twenty

"HERE IT IS spring, and you ain't been back to see that girl," Felix said. He hoisted his jug.

Isaac jabbed at the fire pit coals. They'd finished the stockade before Christmas, but he still hadn't grown accustomed to the nighttime feeling of confinement. The movement and murmur of twenty men obscured the night sounds, but Noah Smithwick's fiddle playing, rough though it was, seemed natural as chirping crickets.

"We ain't been back down that way, Felix. Anyway, I hired on to hunt Comanches." He hoped Catherine didn't think he'd snubbed her invitation.

Felix laughed. "Captain, let's hear 'Cricket on the Hearth.'"

Smithwick slid his fiddle under his chin. "At your pleasure, Felix." He positioned his feet as if preparing to dance to his music. The tune started rough but smoothed as he found the feel and rhythm.

Ezra said, "We been huntin' all right. If that's all we're supposed to do, we're earnin' our pay."

Isaac hated the tedium of their daily patrolling more than the thought of a Comanche attack. Stock was still disappearing from farms around Bastrop, but no one had seen a Comanche or even located workable sign. King Sol saw no mystery in the rangers' lack of success. They were camped too far northwest of their settlements. By the time the fleeing raiders made Walnut Creek, they'd split up so as to be impossible to track. The rangers, he said, should go home and stay ready to fight and pursue. Why should fighting men move far from home where they're of no use to their women and children?

Isaac lay back on his blanket. "What I need is some nasty weather. Then I'll ride over to the Adair place by myself and they'll take pity on me and let me sleep in the house. I'll lay there and listen to Catherine sigh."

Ezra said, "I'd have to go along with you. I can't abide a good friend ridin' by hisself in dangerous country."

Smithwick pirouetted, played on.

"Ain't that pretty?" Felix said.

King Sol sat on his blanket, dozing. The night was mild, and the breeze smelled of river and new growth. The two Lipan scouts, Castro and his son Flacco, had ridden home two weeks before to oversee their band's spring hunting. Isaac suspected their departure was more a matter of boredom than the need to rebuild their larder. Since August, the two had completely ignored King, though they were friendly toward the other rangers.

Several campfires burned within the stockade. Small groups sat about gambling and storytelling. Captain Andrews had replaced Coleman as fort commander after one of Coleman's lieutenants, a short weasel named Robels, whom Isaac despised, tied Billy Bales to a post for drunkenness. Bales passed out during the night, slid down the pole, and hung himself. Robels disappeared and Coleman stepped down under threat of mutiny. Thus far, Andrews had proven a popular, easygoing leader.

Yet Isaac and most of the Bastrop rangers considered Smithwick their captain. As best Isaac could tell, once you commanded a few men, as Smithwick had done that day on the road to Plum Creek, you were a captain from then on, at least informally. Smithwick had reminded him several times that he was just another ranger now, but he still answered when addressed as captain.

From the parapet, Jo Weeks said, "Captain, you'd best get up here and look at this."

Smithwick stopped playing in midstroke. "Interrupted in the throes of creative passion."

"Is that what that was?" Felix said.

Smithwick laid his fiddle and bow on his blanket and climbed the six-foot ladder to the parapet. "Be damn," he said at once.

Several of the rangers picked up their rifles. Isaac said, "What is it?"

"Somebody has built a fire on the bluff above the river," Smithwick said.

Felix scratched his head beneath his hat. "Who in hell would do that right here in the middle of Comanche country?"

Isaac climbed the ladder and looked over the stockade wall. The dark woods rolled away to the river. With his head above the wall, he could hear the tree frogs and the hiss and gurgle of the river. The dark bank on the far side rose to a three-hundred-foot bluff. A large fire flickered at the top.

Smithwick said, "I'll tell you who would build a fire right in the middle of Comanche country."

Isaac rested his arms on the ends of the stockade logs. "Lord."

Smithwick chuckled. "Damn right. I'd say the heathens are on their way back from a raid on the settlements. Be headin' out on the plains at first light."

"How far away do you think they are?"

"A mile as the crow flies, maybe. I reckon they can't see our fires for these walls."

Other rangers gathered along the parapet. "We ain't going after 'em tonight, are we?" Simon Hicks asked. Simon was terrified of the dark and often irritated the men by pissing too close to the fire.

Smithwick said, "Go on to bed, Simon. Why, we wouldn't be able to see where to put a foot down."

"Thank the Lord!" Hicks said. He backed down the ladder.

Smithwick kept his eyes on the distant fire. "Ezra, go wake Captain Andrews."

A few minutes later, Andrews rubbed his eyes with his knuckles, then looked across the river bottom. "We'll ride up there at first light," he said, after staring for a moment.

"We'll either ride tonight or they'll be safe on the plains by the time we make the top of the bluff," Smithwick said.

"Well, I hate to ask the boys to ride out after dark," Andrews said.

Smithwick seemed to be studying the river and bluff. "I'll save you the trouble of issuing an unpopular order."

Andrews sighed. "How do you aim to do that?"

"We'll ask for volunteers."

"Who do you think will go after Comanches in the dark?"

"You underestimate your men," Smithwick said. He started down the ladder. "Gather round, boys; gather round." He stood waiting at the cook fire. The men crowded around him. Isaac hadn't seen Smithwick enjoying himself this much since the trip to the Adair farm.

"Boys, Captain Andrews is asking for volunteers to ride with me, Lieutenant Wren, Isaac, Ezra, and Felix. You all know why. You've seen the fire up there."

Simon looked to be on the verge of palsy. "I thought you said we wouldn't be able to see to walk out there."

"We won't. But our horses will make out fine."

Simon's eyes darted to the faces of the other rangers. Isaac tried to recall being asked to volunteer. He caught Felix's sidelong glance.

"Speak up, gentlemen, this is what we've waited for," Smithwick said. "Volunteers only. I'm not a man given to coercion."

King Sol belched.

"Excellent, King. Who else?"

An hour later, the entire company started down the trail toward the river. Isaac fell in behind Felix. A newly waning moon lighted the river and the bluff ahead. They turned southeast along the faint river trail, crossed at a shallow ford, and rode into the cedar hills.

Isaac thought a buffalo herd could have moved as quietly. The dense cedars blocked the moonlight, and the horses stumbled often, sending rocks tumbling down the slope. Smithwick and King Sol led the company northwest. Isaac's rifle, carried across his pommel, kept catching in the brush; he gave up and carried it at his side with one hand.

Three or four deer flushed to their right; some of the horses shied and men cursed, but Squab pricked his ears and held his course. "Good old Squab," Isaac whispered. He wished for a pistol.

The trail grew steeper, more open. Isaac felt exposed. Some of the rangers' gray homespun shirts seemed to glow in the moonlight; Isaac was grateful for his greasy buckskins and Squab's mottled coat. He kept track of the moon and Little Dipper as best he could. He estimated an hour before sunrise when Andrews, no doubt acting on Smithwick's polite recommendation, ordered a halt. Word came back through Felix that Smithwick, King, Nicholas Wren, and Jo Weeks had ridden ahead. Although he did not relish the thought of scouting for Comanches in a pitch-dark cedar brake, he felt chagrined; he had grown accustomed to being one of the Captain's chosen. But Weeks, Wren, and King were all experienced fighters. Then again, so was he. But those weren't Mexican soldiers up there. He looked at the top of the bluff. Best to concentrate on the job.

They waited. Isaac wanted to talk with Felix, but no one spoke. He could not imagine slipping up on a Comanche camp. He'd seen a wildness that day on the road that he'd not seen in the Tonks or Wichitas or the friendly Choctaws in Arkansas. And men who pissed from horseback would not allow themselves to be knocked out of the saddle and bludgeoned with a rifle butt.

The air smelled of cedar; he shivered in the morning coolness. A fine time to be hunting with Sis. Two mules brayed somewhere above. The moon sat just above the hills to the east. If they started now, it would be sunup by the time they made it up the slope.

A few minutes later, Smithwick, King, Wren, and Weeks rode out of the brush. The rangers gathered around them.

"About a dozen asleep under a big oak," Smithwick whispered. "We walked right into the middle of their damn *caballado;* the mules set up to braying, and I thought sure the heathens would wake up. They must be worn out; they're running four dozen horses and mules if they've got a one."

Isaac drank from his gourd and wondered if two of the mules belonged to his father. Most of the stolen stock probably came from around Bastrop. "Any white women or younguns, Captain?"

"Can't say for sure. All I saw was some folks sleeping. You've never heard such snoring."

Isaac thought of Comanche pickets hidden in the brush, watching them. Maybe the loud snoring was a ruse.

Smithwick looked up the bluff. "Captain, I recommend we split into two groups. Half can go with me; half with Lieutenant Wren. My boys will go right at them; Nick's boys will flank them from the north."

Andrews rubbed his beard as if carefully considering the plan. "You've seen where they are. I'm in no position to argue with you."

Smithwick said, "Isaac, you and Felix and Ezra go with me and King." He then drew an imaginary line down the middle of the group. "You boys with me; the rest with Nick. Let's get movin'. We're about out of time."

King, Smithwick, and Andrews started up the hill directly toward the Comanche camp. Isaac, Felix, Ezra, and seven other rangers followed. The other group followed Wren up a draw to the right. A mockingbird warbled somewhere up the hill.

Smithwick stopped on a half-acre bench. "Picket your horses," he whispered. "We'll go on foot from here."

Isaac tethered Squab to a sapling, then checked the edge of his flint. A light breeze blew down the hill; otherwise the Comanche horses would have smelled them by now.

Smithwick pointed up the slope to the right. "Their remuda is just up there on another little flat. Follow me and stay clear of it. We're damn near on top of these heathens. Don't fire until I . . . Captain Andrews . . . gives the signal."

They clambered up the hill. Their moccasins made little sound on the grass and cedar duff. Isaac looked back to the east. Pale copper along the hilltops.

They cleared the edge of the bluff and crept across midgrass prairie toward a giant, solitary live oak a couple hundred yards out. The sun edged above the hills behind them. Isaac saw dark lumps on the ground beneath the tree. King dropped to his belly. The others followed his lead. Sweat dripped from the end of Isaac's nose. Even crawling in the knee-high grass, he felt exposed.

The mules brayed again. The rangers froze. The beasts had probably winded or heard Wren and the boys moving into position. The grass blocked Isaac's view of the Comanche camp. He kept his eyes on Felix's moccasins.

He checked his flint again. It would be a miracle if the rifle fired after being dragged for two hundred yards. The wind rustled the grass and crows cawed in the distance. He heard his own shallow, ragged breathing. Felix snaked ahead. Isaac let him gain a few yards, then followed. Felix lay alongside King and Smithwick. The grass thinned and gave way to ragged clumps of shin oak. The snoring Comanches lay forty yards ahead. The new sun shone on dusty buffalo robes. Lances and shields leaned against the trunk and bushes. The coals from the fire barely glowed; Isaac smelled the smoke. One of the Comanches rolled onto his side, and Isaac saw the placid face of a man he might kill.

He heard rustling in the brush beyond the tree. Wren had overshot the camp. Isaac waited for the Captain's signal. Surely now was the time. More rustling. Birds twittered. Isaac eased the serpentine back, laid the bead between the sleeping man's eyes. He hoped everyone wouldn't shoot at the same man.

One of the other Comanches sat up and rubbed his eyes. Isaac's heart banged against the dead oak leaves. The Comanche sang, "Ha-ah-ha!"

Someone in Wren's group fell or kicked dry brush. The Indian turned toward the sound. A rifle fired to Isaac's left. The Indian screamed and fell back kicking. The other Comanches rolled out of their robes. Isaac fired too late, and duff flew up where the man's head had been. More shots. Rangers were screaming curses, running at the camp. Isaac gained his feet and charged, Smithwick and Felix on his left wielding pistols. Something hissed by his face. He realized he was attacking with an unloaded weapon. But he'd make an easy target if he stopped to reload. Comanches were running bandy-legged through the grass, disappearing into a brushy draw fifty yards distant. A twang and hiss and Philip Martin gagged and fell clutching his face. Pistol fire and cursing. Isaac ran over a buffalo robe. The shot Comanche lay on his face, unmoving.

A young warrior sprang up in the grass, arrow nocked, five strides away. No time to reload. Isaac charged with his rifle butt raised. The boy drew his bow, but Isaac was upon him. He swung the buttstock, but the Comanche lunged; his forehead smashed into Isaac's chin. The boy dropped his bow and wrapped his arms around Isaac's waist. Isaac smelled hair and ash and sweat. The Comanche lifted him off his feet. Isaac came down with both elbows on the boy's collarbones, then dropped his rifle, grabbed the Comanche's ears and twisted. The boy screamed, let go his bear hug, and leapt away. Isaac landed on his feet and drew his knife, expecting the Indian to slash with his own blade. "Goddamn you, I'll kill you!" No fear now. He'd draw and skin this boy. Another volley near the head of the draw. The young warrior broke for cover. Isaac started to chase him, but Smithwick yelled, "Pull back boys, they'll cut us to shreds in there."

Andrews was on his knees, trying to catch his breath. Others were bent over doing the same. Smithwick and King were each on a knee charging their rifles. Felix cussed his pistol.

Smithwick slid his ramrod back into its keep. "We gave them a scare. Let's pull back and call it a win."

Ezra walked out of the Comanche camp. "Captain, we've lost Philip." Isaac remembered Philip Martin's fall. They found him on his side with an arrow sticking out the back of his neck. The fletching was just visible in his mouth.

"Lord God," Andrews said. "Shot him in the mouth."

Jo Weeks kicked a buffalo robe. "I can't find my damn Comanche. I seen the bastard fall right here. I hit him good."

Isaac pointed to the pink froth on the duff. Smithwick studied the gore. "That's lung blood. You hit him good all right, Jo. I imagine one of the savages doubled back and made off with him while we were after the others."

"Well hell," Weeks said. "I aimed to hang his scalp from my stock."

Wren shook his head. "We'd have waylaid them if I hadn't got lost in that damn draw."

Felix lifted one of the robes with his rifle barrel. "Like chasin' smoke."

Isaac fingered his chin. That Comanche boy was flesh and blood. And bone. Probably the one who killed Martin. He recharged his rifle with trembling hands. His chin would be blue in the morning.

He picked up a horsehide shield propped against a tree. Its weight surprised him. He fingered four dried scalps hanging from the rim. Three were black. He shivered. One was the color of Esther's hair. He walked out into the grass and retrieved the boy's bow. Arm length. Wrapped in sinew. He fingered the taut gut string. This was not the work of some ignorant savage. Someone had lovingly built this weapon. The young warrior would miss it. He fingered the sweat-darkened grip.

The rangers picked through the Comanche gear. Captain Andrews hefted a lance. "Well, at least we have their horses."

Felix said, "I still wouldn't call it even."

Andrews lowered the lance. "Don't get me wrong, Felix."

"We've got their horses, but they're liable to have ours if we don't get back down this hill," Smithwick said. "Isaac, fetch us a mule. We don't want to bury poor old Philip up here."

Twenty-One

THOMAS ADAIR swallowed a mouthful of biscuit, then chased it with coffee. He wiped his mouth and studied Isaac. "So how do you aim to make your way in the Republic, Isaac? You're young still, but a man has to lay his plans early if he's to have time to amount to something." He winked at Mrs. Adair. "I believe the wool on his jowls has growed a tad thicker since he last visited."

As usual, Adair's question caught Isaac with his mouth full. He chewed and nodded thoughtfully to hide his panic. Catherine was watching him with obvious interest. He lost his nerve, swallowed, and hoped no one noticed his watery eyes. "Yes sir." He cleared his throat. "After I finish rangerin' I'll farm my two sections. I've got my eye on a piece of bottom up the creek from the home place."

Catherine and Mrs. Adair looked at Adair to gauge his reaction. He nodded. "What'll you get started with? Corn don't just grow on its own."

"I'm makin' twenty-five dollars a month."

"Just because they print it don't mean it'll spend."

Isaac doubted his father had ever made that much in a year. "We've always swapped for what we needed."

"Yes. I expect you have," Adair said. "Mountain folks I've known have all been resourceful."

Mountain folks seemed to roll off the old man's tongue with distaste, but Catherine smiled at the comment. He'd take it as a compliment. "Our place ain't as pretty as yours, but it ain't bad. We don't go hungry."

Adair tapped the table with his fork. "I know of your daddy. Rough on the Creeks, I hear."

Isaac said, "That's what they tell me. He never said much about it to me. I believe it though."

Catherine said, "I hear you men smote a horde of Comanches."

"Smote? Caught a dozen sound asleep about two weeks ago. Every one of 'em got away and we lost Philip Martin."

Catherine cocked her head. "Lost him?"

Adair said, "Catherine . . ."

"We buried him outside the fort," Isaac said.

"Oh."

"We got their horses and mules though."

Adair pounded the table with his fist. "I'd call it a victory then."

"Yes sir. But they stole 'em all back four days later."

Adair jerked his head aside. "Thieving barbarians."

"Yes sir."

After supper, Mr. and Mrs. Adair made a show of being occupied with small tasks while Isaac sat on the front step with Catherine. Louise left the door propped open.

"So," Catherine said.

Isaac squinted sagely at the western horizon and tried to think of small talk. "Be dark soon," he said with much relief. Now she'd have to reply, giving him a chance to think of another remark.

"Yes. Soon." She smoothed her dress.

He'd hoped for a little more time. "I enjoyed the meal. I thank you."

She smiled. "Isaac, you men don't generally patrol by yourselves, do you?"

"No ma'am. King Sol came with me."

"King Sol?"

"He's a Tonkawa scout."

"Where is he?"

"Camped just over the hill. He was afraid your daddy would shoot him."

"Why would Daddy shoot him if he's helping you hunt Comanches?"

"If he was to ride in here unannounced, you'd want to shoot him. I promise. He's the best man that ever was, but he's Indian and looks like it. Got circles tattooed around his ti—on his chest." His ears turned hot as white oak coals.

She laughed, her face red as a plum. Here she was, real as the hills and trees, sitting next to him.

She cleared her throat and seemed to study the circle she was drawing with her toe in the dirt. But there was no mistaking the mirth in her eyes. "What brings you here tonight? Why would two men ride all the way down here from Coleman's Fort with Comanches about?"

Isaac watched her toe tracing the circle. Tell the truth and risk looking like a fool or lie and look like a fool for sure. "I s'pose I came to call on you."

She rested an elbow on her thigh, propped her chin in her hand. "You're a bold sprout, ain't you? Seventeen years old and calling on a widow."

"And an old, wore-out widow at that. Probably all of twenty."

"Just turned nineteen." She went back to her drawing.

"Uh-huh. Probably got suitors beatin' your door down."

She let go a bitter laugh. "Most old as Daddy with a long list of their assets. Gonna do me a big favor and take care of me. Daddy's been so hateful to them, most don't come back. He don't have much use for men too worried about their hide to serve in the Revolution or help with the Indian problem—no matter how prosperous they might be. He likes a scrapper. He loved Franklin.

Never resented him for running off to Béxar and leaving me widowed and expecting."

"A man would need a good reason to come all the way out here." He hoped she saw the compliment in the remark. "How you been? I mean I don't want to come along too soon after what all has happened."

"You're the first to ask. Franklin has been gone over a year now. Would've followed James Bowie clear to perdition. He was a good boy, but I suppose I'm about grieved out. The baby, though . . . Nights are bad sometimes."

"I imagine so." He felt terribly young. Here sat a woman. He counted the fingers of his right hand.

"What in the world are you doin'?"

"Countin' my assets. I was hopin' to have to go to my left hand, but I swear I didn't even make it to the thumb on my right."

She covered her mouth with her hand and laughed so hard she shook.

Twenty-Two

THE COMPANY spent more time hunting food than Comanches. The arrangement suited Isaac. April mornings, turkey gobblers announced their intentions to the local hens. Isaac thought nothing of calling in a tom by imitating the seductive clucks of a turkey hen. Every Choctaw in the Ouachita Mountains knew the trick, but the other rangers were astounded.

Most of the men preferred to hunt deer and occasionally bison that wandered from the plains to the oak savannahs. Isaac bragged that he could bring in half a ton of turkey meat by the time the others could kill, skin, and quarter a single head of big game.

Smithwick and Felix argued that turkey and squirrel hunting was wasteful of shot and powder, never mind that Isaac counted forty-one holes in the hide of a bison bull that gored Jo Weeks's horse before Smithwick could rush the beast with his pistol and put a ball into the side of its head.

Isaac considered riding back to the home place to fetch Sis but decided against it after considering the problems posed by a hound that often disappeared for days at a time and could be heard baying in the hills all night long. If he could hear the baying, then so could any savage who might be lurking within ten miles of the fort.

Still, the thought of roasted coon made Isaac's mouth water. Thinking of following a hound through the woods after dark in Comanchería didn't.

Smithwick's gray and black brindled cur, Hazel, was a passable hunting hound, though her voice was about as pleasant as listening to a dry axle. Half the pleasure of hunting with Sis was listening to her baritone voice. Hazel, on the other hand, was strictly a meat dog; she came when called and stayed within earshot until she struck game scent, which most recently led to a bull bison that barreled out of a draw to tree her master. Isaac arrived at the scene to find Smithwick six feet up an elm, long legs wrapped around the trunk, trying to work his ramrod while balanced on a three-inch limb. Hazel, yelping like a pup goaded with hot poker, worried the flanks of the enraged bull as it bellowed and butted the trunk. The incident provided several nights' campfire entertainment.

Whenever Isaac compared Hazel's homeliness to Sis's silky coat and handsome, houndy face, Smithwick countered by pointing to Squab.

Captain Andrews complained that if the men spent half as much time worrying about Comanches as they did horses and hunting dogs, the settlement line would be a good hundred miles further west by now. But Isaac, when unoccupied with hunting, contemplated Catherine, even when patrolling for Comanche sign.

Lately he'd visited her every two or three weeks. Captain Andrews, having tired of the men's bitter complaining, had become generous with leave. Isaac felt a bit guilty about spending his leave riding a half day to the Adair farm instead of heading downriver to visit his family. But not guilty enough to forgo Catherine's company. Never mind that he and King had to ride back to the fort in the dark the last two trips.

Catherine finally told her father about King. Thomas insisted the scout camp along the creek behind the barn, but warned that he mustn't come around the house lest Cedrick panic and shoot him.

Thus far Isaac and Catherine's courtship consisted of supper and doorstoop conversation about weather, family, and Indians. He learned that her Grandfather Porter took the grippe and died on the way back from Louisiana three weeks after the victory at Saint Hyacinth; that she longed to visit her baby girl's grave; and that she'd left her cabin south of Gonzales where she and her husband had lived for just over a year. On his most recent visit, she sang "Barbara Allen" and read to him from *The Life and Memorable Actions of George Washington*.

They'd not touched. He'd wanted to stroke her brown hair as he watched her eyes scan the pages, her brows arching with the inflections of her voice. He watched and listened in amazement; here sat the object of a far-fetched dream, this girl who'd owned his thoughts for two hundred miles. She sat within his reach, as if one ached badly enough for something, it would be delivered.

In other ways, she seemed beyond reach. She knew the world in ways he didn't. And she'd known at least one man in a way he could not fathom.

And the suitors. Isaac imagined town clothes and gray muttonchops and Catherine sitting coolly, listening to middle-aged bachelors' and widowers' promises of a life of genteel security, as if such a thing existed in the Republic of Texas.

• • •

"Snuck a kiss yet?" Felix asked. "I can't call it courtin' until there's been at least one smooch."

"You're tryin' to get me smacked cross eyed or shot by old man Adair," Isaac said. They rode at the rear of the column of twenty-two rangers heading northwest through the hills above the east bank of the Colorado. Somewhere ahead, Castro, who'd recently rejoined the company, and King Sol, were going about their scouting duties while making a show of ignoring each other, much to Noah Smithwick's amusement. Isaac adjusted his sweaty grip on his rifle. "I've damn sure thought about it a lot. Thought about that and a few other things too."

"A fine young scoundrel," Felix said. "Say she's a little healthier than when I made her acquaintance?"

"You ought to see her," Ezra said.

"Watch yourself, Ezree," Felix said. "Old Isaac was smitten by her first. He has first try."

Isaac spat. "Damn right."

Ezra said, "He'd better get busy then. I'll give him 'til fall, I s'pose. If he ain't swapped slobber with her by then, it's my turn to try."

Isaac didn't take Ezra seriously, but the comment irritated him nonetheless. "Might as well forget about her, friend. If I don't get her, some rich old widower from San Felipe or Gonzales will tuck her away in a fine frame house."

"Her mama let you sleep in the big house yet?" Ezra asked.

"I ain't stayed there all night since last fall."

Felix winked at Ezra. "Why, I hear she put the Captain up in a feather bed. Why ain't she put you up for the night?"

Isaac leaned out and blew his nose. "Afraid to. Afraid her little darlin' will be overcome, wake me up in the wee hours and make me take her away. An old woman gets more watchful when there's a fine young man eyeing her daughter."

Ezra laughed. "Horseshit."

Felix said, "I'm afraid the boy might be right, Ezree. Else the old man would've run Mr. Isaac off by now."

"He ain't even planted one on her cheek yet," Ezra said. He nodded at Isaac. "You've got 'til fall, brother. Ain't you glad I think so much of you?"

They rode into the cedar hills in search of Comanche sign. A four-day patrol southward to Webber's Prairie had turned up little. There had been no reports of outright raiding; only stolen horses and stock and tracks of unshod ponies. Now they were headed back toward the fort.

Late afternoon, Andrews ordered a halt on a scrub oak–covered hill; Isaac smelled smoke. He looked at Felix.

"I smell it son," Felix said.

Isaac looked southward. "We're still downriver from the Adair place, ain't we?"

Felix nodded. "First thing you think of, ain't it?"

Isaac swallowed. "Well."

Castro rode in from the north and spoke to Smithwick.

"What's he saying?" Andrews asked.

Smithwick turned to his men. "They've hit a farm. Let's ride."

They rode single file down the hill, struck a creek, then galloped toward the head. Two miles further on, they found a towheaded boy in the middle of the trail, scalped and pinned to the dirt by three arrows. A skim of dust covered his blue eyes. Some of the men cursed.

"Ride for the cabin," Andrews said. "Nothing we can do for the lad now."

"Lord, you can see his skull," Isaac said. "He'd heard of scalping; the stories had not prepared him for the sight. The boy may have been ten years old.

Black smoke rose above the live oaks. Just beyond they found the cabin burned to the limestone foundation. The blackened stone chimney stood defiantly above the still-glowing coals of the oak logs. A lean mongrel dog barked. They dismounted. Andrews said, "Keep an eye out; the devils might still be around."

Smithwick surveyed the damage. "They're gone. They'll be beating it northward for home. God help any farmers in their path."

King Sol knelt over a middle-aged man who'd been scalped and drawn. The Tonkawa looked up at Smithwick. "I ain't seen no women. There was a woman and girl here. I expect they took the horses and the women."

"How can you say for sure that there was a girl here too?" Andrews said.

The Tonkawa ignored him. Smithwick said, "Look at the tracks in the kitchen garden."

Toward the back of the cabin a milk cow lay on her side, struggling weakly, a half-dozen arrows in her neck, flank, and side. Isaac drew his blade and walked along the side of the cabin. He didn't look into her brown eyes as he slit her throat. He couldn't abide a useful animal suffering. He looked northward across the two-acre field of new corn. Castro rode out of the trees toward him.

Smithwick said, "We'd best get on; there's two farms between here and the fort."

Adams drew a deep breath and nodded. "Yes."

Castro rode into the yard and pointed north. *"Más humo."*

Smithwick started for his horse. "Another one burning, Captain. We can't help these folks; we'll bury them later."

They mounted and rode north toward the next creek bottom. Isaac's chest tightened. The raiders' course would take them within a half mile of the Adair farm. If King was right, they already had at least two women. Old man Adair was damned arrogant to move his family within range of Comanche raiders. He'd ridden roughshod over the Creeks and Kronks and Tonkawas, but these people were different. They hit the lonely farms and trappers' cabins, then beat it for home beyond any country known by whites. His money and slaves would do him little good here; the Comanches cared nothing for his reputation and hard-shell religion. Isaac thought of Catherine Druin tied to a Spanish mustang.

They rode through the oak then cedar brakes, topped the hill, then descended into the creek bottom. The smell of burning flesh and cedar logs hit them full in the face. He passed Felix and Ezra and rode alongside Smithwick and Andrews. "Captain, the Adair place is in the next creek bottom."

"First thing first, son," Andrews said. "We don't know what we'll find ahead and there ain't enough of us as it is."

"They might be there right now," Isaac said. "These folks here are already done for."

"Fall in, Webb!" Andrews yelled.

They rode down the creek bottom. Smoke billowed just ahead. Smithwick led them through the little cornfield. Two hacked bodies lay in the bare yard. They reined their horses. Smithwick said, "Captain, Isaac's gal lives on the next farm."

Andrews dismounted. "Damn it! Go then. Felix! Ezree! Jo! Go with him."

Isaac turned Squab. "I thank you."

"Go!"

King Sol was already headed north.

"Where in hell does that heathen think he's goin'?" Andrews bellowed.

Isaac rode after King; Andrews's protests faded behind him. Oak and cedar branches slapped his face and tore at his clothes. Squab plowed ahead unaffected. King was obviously taking the shortest path to the farm. There was no trail. Felix cussed behind him.

They rode down the hill and into the bottom. Still no smoke. King peeled away and rode for the woods along the creek beyond the barn. The cabin was dark. Horse hooves beat the creek bank. A shot rang out—King's musket. More hoofbeats.

Isaac reined Squab in the shadow of a live oak copse and dismounted. The three other rangers followed his lead. They ran for the cabin, keeping low. Isaac helloed the house. Catherine's feist lay pinned by an arrow near the barn door. No answer. Sweat dripped from his beard. "Captain Adair. It's Isaac Webb." There was no sound except the whisper of leaves and a mocker's squeaking wheel song.

The door opened a crack; nothing but darkness within. "Slip on in here, boys," Adair said. The three ran for the house. Isaac burst into the dark room. Late afternoon light slanted though the shooting ports.

"Thank God," Louise Adair said from a dark corner. The room smelled of sour breath and sweat. Felix, Jo, and Ezra followed him in. Their ragged breathing seemed unnaturally loud in the closed cabin. Isaac's eyes adjusted. Catherine sat beneath the table. Cedrick hunkered near the fireplace.

"Catherine," Isaac said. He took off his hat.

She exhaled as if she'd been holding her breath. "Lord, I didn't think y'all would come. Praise Jesus."

"Get away from the door, boys," Adair said.

Isaac took a knee. Catherine reached from beneath the table and touched his arm.

"I couldn't tell how many," Adair said. "The dog started throwin' a fit, and by the time I came out of the barn, he had an arrow in him. We all beat it for the house. I never saw a one of the devils, but they were here sure as I am. Catherine had just got back from the creek. Lord have mercy."

"Mercy sure enough," Felix said gently. "We just came from two burned-up farms south of here. Men all dead; they might've made off with some women."

"Rest of the company's headin' this way," Isaac said.

"Oh lord," Mrs. Adair said. "The Thorpes and the Manns." She looked at her husband in realization. "They might have Mary and Martha. Dear god. And Elsie."

"Rest of the company will be here anytime," Isaac said. "We'll ride the heathens down." He didn't believe a word of it.

"They're gone," King Sol said from the yard.

Adair cracked the door. "It's that Tonk friend of yours, Isaac."

Isaac got up and stepped outside. The others followed. King sat his horse. "I run your two horses back in the corral," he said to Adair. "There was two younguns had 'em." He held up a fresh scalp. "This one here won't be tryin' to steal your horses no more."

The women blanched.

King said, "The rest rode off. They knowed we was after 'em."

"How many?" Isaac asked.

King studied the scalp. "A good bunch. We won't catch 'em this time."

Mrs. Adair said, "You've got to try; they might have Mary and Martha Thorpe."

King looked to the northwest. "They've got those women, but that ain't our country up there."

"Where in hell is the Captain?" Ezra said. "We ain't about to catch nobody standin' around here."

"Might as well stand around here," King said. "It's about dark."

Catherine ran to her dog, dropped to her knees, and wept. Her mother went to her. Isaac stood watching, feeling mulish. "Be damn," he said under his breath.

King glanced up the creek. "Here comes Noah and them."

Twenty-Three

THEY FOUND the yellow dress, corset, and pantalets early the next morning. The dress had been torn away; the corset had been cut up the back. The rangers sat their horses and stared at the garments strewn about in the grass along a game trail.

"Tryin' to goad us," King Sol said.

Andrews spat. "You ought to know."

King ignored the comment.

Isaac imagined the naked women tied to the Comanche mustangs. They knew their men were dead and had little hope that anyone would come for them. How would he feel if he were looking at Catherine's torn garments? Or Esther's? Or his mother's?

"We ain't gaining on 'em sittin' here," Felix said.

They rode northwest above the east bank of the Colorado. Midmorning they came to the Comanches' camp, an opening amid a dense cluster of oak mottes. The coals were still warm.

"Big fire," King said. "Had 'em a dance last night."

The trail led into dry, rocky cedar hills and grew fainter. Castro, King, and Smithwick cast about in search of sign—a scuffed rock or a fragment of track. Isaac had recognized no sign for the past ten miles.

He sweated under the late spring sun. Dark stains ran down the men's homespun and buckskin. The air was still in the oak and cedar breaks; he slapped at the gnats and horseflies and struggled to concentrate on the trail and his surroundings. Smithwick and the scouts agreed that the Comanches knew they were being pursued. They estimated fifteen or twenty warriors.

They broke out of the cedar into open country—gentle hills, prickly pear, and, here and there, mature live oaks. King peeled away and looped eastward. Castro stopped and studied the ground. The rangers rode toward him. Isaac hoped the Lipan hadn't found another garment.

Castro made a sweeping motion north and south. "*Se separaron. Unos se devolvieron. Unos se fueron con las mujers, pero otros nos quieren pescar en una emboscada.*" He looked in the direction King had ridden. "*Ay que voltear y regresarnos.*"

"Lord Jesus," Smithwick said.

Andrews looked blankly at the ground beneath Castro. "What the hell, man?"

Smithwick said, "He thinks they might've doubled back on us. Maybe a few went on with the women, but a bunch more are layin' for us now."

"Oh lord," Ezra said. Several of the men cussed. Isaac searched the hills and horizon for King.

Andrews said, "Why the hell didn't our scouts see this comin'? We pay them to find the enemy and keep us from gettin' ambushed."

"Well, Captain, so far we ain't been ambushed," Smithwick said. "Maybe they're doing their job."

Andrews looked back at his men. "Hell with it anyway. There's more of us than them."

Smithwick took off his hat and wiped his brow with his forearm. "That don't give us the advantage. They know where we are; they might be drawin' a bead on us right now."

Isaac studied the savannah. The nearest cover was at least two hundred yards ahead. "Captain, I don't see much place for a Comanche to hide out here. We could see 'em comin' a mile off long as we stay out of the brakes."

"We'd be a damn sight better off in cover where they'd have to dismount to fight," Smithwick said. "One Comanche on horseback is a match for any five of us."

Isaac remained unconvinced. Give old Squab a hundred-yard advantage in broken country and no pony would catch him. Then again, you couldn't rescue stolen women while running for your life.

King Sol rode out of the trees just above the river. "Let's see what the heathen has to say," Jo Weeks said.

Nicholas Wren felt for his pistol. "Right now, I'll listen to him over any Christian."

Isaac marveled that anyone had the courage to ride around alone with Comanches on the prowl. Did King fear anyone? He'd ridden at dusk into the woods along the creek at the Adair place to recover horses and taken a scalp while Isaac and the rangers hunkered down in the house.

The Tonkawa rode up. "Noah, they got around behind us. We best ride careful."

Andrews said, "We came to fight. We're not turnin' tail."

"We're fixin' to fight. Don't matter if we want to or not," King said. "We just as well start headin' back. I like to fight closer to home."

"By god, there are three women up ahead."

King snatched a horsefly out of the air and crushed it in his fist. "We won't find 'em today. These Comanches know we're comin'." He tossed the dead fly over his shoulder.

Ezra said, "What the hell we s'posed to do then? Just let 'em run off with women and stock?"

King raised his musket off the pommel and rested the butt on his thigh so that the muzzle pointed skyward. "You kill Comanches by sneaking up on their camps. If they don't know you're comin', you got a chance. If they know about you, you never find them unless they want you to find them. They want us to find them today. We should come back another time. Sneak up on their camp." He jutted his chin toward Castro. "That Lipan knows this."

Andrews slapped his thigh with his hat. "Damn it! Tell that to those poor women."

"I'd listen to him, Captain," Smithwick said. "Live to fight another day. We can't do the ladies a drop of good dead and scalped. The further out we get, the worse our prospects get."

Isaac looked over the vastness to the west. Chasing Comanche raiders was like hunting cougars. You know they're out there; you see the remains of their prey. But you see your quarry only when it chooses to reveal itself. Now, he felt more like a deer than a lion hunter. That Comanche boy he'd fought could shoot a dozen arrows by the time a man could charge a rifle. He wiped a drop of sweat from his trigger guard. King had said there would be a fight. Isaac felt it in his bowels.

Andrews slumped in his saddle. "Let's ease back, four columns of five, scouts out front. Keep in sight. Noah, tell Castro."

"*Vamos a retroceder,*" Smithwick said.

The scouts rode ahead. Isaac fell in behind Smithwick in the column riding furthest from the river. A light wind soughed in the grass and trees. Each gust sounded like brush against the flanks of a mustang. To his right were fifteen other rangers. Maybe sixty yards to cover on his left. Beyond accurate arrow range but well within rifle range. And some Comanches were said to have guns. He drank from his gourd. His mouth tasted as if he'd licked his knife blade.

Movement a hundred yards ahead and to his left, in the scattered oaks. Pale mustang. "Captain?"

The rangers stopped. The Comanche rode back and forth in the trees. Isaac could see his braids bouncing against his chest and arms. Castro and King, fifty yards closer, sat their horses and screamed shrill insults in their own tongues. Isaac understood their meaning if not their words.

Some of the men took aim. Smithwick yelled, "Hold your fire. He's tryin' to get us to empty our rifles. Then they'll all ride on us."

"I don't see another soul," Isaac said.

Smithwick watched the distant rider. "They're here. We all get caught with our rifles empty, we're done for."

The Comanche rode away over a low hill. The rangers eased ahead, rifles ready. They rode into the dense oak on the hillside. "They won't jump us in here," Smithwick said. "They can't ride in this stuff."

The comment comforted Isaac little. He could see only a few yards and could never mount and fire his rifle amid the clawing limbs.

Hair stood on his arms. He expected an arrow in his chest or back at any instant. Felix and Jo Weeks struggled up the hill behind him. Ezra was out of sight somewhere to his right. He wanted to see the big man.

They topped the hill and started down the other side. The country ahead opened up again. He patted Squab's neck. Fanny would have long since raked him off against a tree limb. He suspected the Comanches could follow their progress by the racket they were making.

"Hair on the back of my neck is standin' straight up," Felix said.

They had just cleared the trees at the base of the hill when two warriors rode among them from behind, one shooting arrows left, the other right. Horses bucked. Erasmus Holt grabbed at his neck and fell. Isaac mounted his rifle and swung on the leftmost Comanche. Gunfire. Hoarse screams. Squab held his ground. The warrior rode beyond Captain Andrews. Isaac could see the jouncing braids, the back and forearm muscles. He squeezed the trigger, kept the rifle moving, ignored the hiss and boom. The Comanche twisted, dropped his bow, but held the rein.

More gunfire. A ball whizzed past Isaac's ear. "Jesus Christ!" He dismounted, took a knee, and dumped a palmful of powder down the barrel and tamped it with the ramrod.

Andrews and Smithwick were shouting at the rangers to hold their fire. Horses were running loose in the thicket behind them.

Men scrambled for cover. Someone moaned. Isaac wrapped a ball in a greased patch and rammed it home.

Smithwick was on his belly behind a big cholla. "Never had a shot." He caught his breath. "By god, Isaac, you hit one. I saw him jerk. And look there." He pointed to a blood-spattered clump of bluestem thirty yards out.

"Erasmus is hit," Ezra said from the knee-high grass to Isaac's right. He rustled forward. "Lord, he's gone. Right through the neck. Damn it."

"I'm shot, boys," Raymond Skaggs said. The wind scattered his sobs.

Andrews's hat inched above the grass. "Where are you, Raymond? Say again."

"Dear lord," the boy screamed.

Isaac dropped Squab's rein, clambered up, and churned on all fours toward Skaggs's voice. He found the boy facedown, an arrow protruding from his back just below his right shoulder blade. "I got you, Raymond."

Smithwick, Andrews, and King came crawling up. "It went plumb through," the boy said. "I swear, I can't hardly breath."

"Don't move, son," Smithwick said. He glanced at Isaac and shrugged.

King knelt. "Get him on his side."

The boy screamed as the men turned him. King drew his patch knife. Using his thumb as backing, he cut off the brass arrowhead with one hand. "Now then. Lay him back down." They eased the boy facedown. "Hold him down," King said.

Raymond sobbed. "Oh Lord God. Just let me die."

"You ain't dying," King said. He looked at Isaac. "Hold him good."

Isaac pushed against the small of the boy's back. Smithwick held his shoulders. The boy cried. King placed his left palm next to the entrance and jerked the arrow out with his right hand, then tossed it away. Isaac had never heard such screaming.

King jerked up a handful of dead grass and plugged the wounds while Raymond whimpered. With the boy on his side, he touched the entrance and exit wounds as if to judge the wound channel. He gave a satisfied grunt. "Put him on a horse."

Raymond said, "I can't ride no horse. It'll jar my insides out."

King stood up. "Leave him here then." He picked up his musket.

The other rangers were gathering horses. Ezra laid Erasmus Holt across his saddle. "Poor old Erasmus. He didn't have no business comin' out here."

Jo Weeks said, "Where's Otis?" Otis Crocker had been behind Felix. Isaac saw the old ranger's hat perched atop a clump of prickly pear. "There's his hat." He walked to the cactus and bent to pick up the hat. He stopped. "Here lays Otis. He took a ball in the face."

"Christ Almighty," Andrews said. "We've shot one of our own."

Smithwick dusted off his pants. "Old Otis. Lord. Those heathens ran right through the middle of us."

Castro rode in leading two horses.

"That's my horse," Raymond Skaggs said. Felix and King had him on his feet.

Castro said, *"Se fueron."*

Andrews stood by his horse, his rifle laid across the saddle. "What's he sayin' now?"

Smithwick slid his hands under Otis Crocker's arms. "Grab his feet, will you, Isaac? He says they're gone, Captain."

Ezra finished lashing Holt's body on the horse. He shook his head. "I swear, just two rode in amongst us and damn near killed us all. If the whole bunch would've come at us we'd all be dead for sure. I can't see why they didn't."

Isaac and Smithwick laid Otis Crocker across his horse's back. "Because they're no more eager to die than we are," Smithwick said. "If they'd thought they had the advantage, they'd have come for us."

As they rode away, Isaac looked back at the Comanche's darkening blood on the grass.

Twenty-Four

June 1837

ISAAC AND KING rode into Thomas Adair's yard and found Catherine snapping beans in the shade of a live oak. She snapped a handful and tossed them into her pot. "I never expected to see you two so soon."

They sat their horses. Isaac said, "Andrews gave me a day's leave."

She stood and smoothed her dress. "And you're using it to call on me?"

"I'll go take a nap," King said. He rode toward the creek.

Isaac dismounted. "Where else would I go? If I went home, Pap would put me to work."

Thomas Adair came from behind the cabin, carrying his rifle. "I'd put you to work too, but I'd never hear the end of it from this girl. You aim to put that ugly horse up or just stand there holdin' up supper?"

Isaac stroked Squab's muzzle. "I need to see what we're havin' before I settle in."

Adair laughed. "I'm bettin' you'll eat whatever we lay out. Go put that bug-eyed beast in the barn. I wouldn't leave a horse out, though I don't expect them heathens to come back after you boys put the fear of God in 'em."

Isaac thought of the yellow dress and corset. And Erasmus and Otis. Coleman's Fort was growing a cemetery. "I reckon not. Don't shoot old King. He's on the creek somewhere."

Adair waved and stepped into the cabin. Isaac said, "What in the world are you doin' sittin' out here where you could get caught and carried away?"

"I can't stay pent up forever. Besides it's burnin' up inside. You don't want me sweatin' all over supper, do you?"

"Might sweeten it a little," Isaac said.

She rolled her eyes. "Let's put your horse up."

He led Squab toward the barn. Catherine walked beside him, her arm brushing his. They walked out of the sun into the darkness and dust. Along one side, five stalls opened to the inside. Rope and tack hung on the poles. A wagon, plow, and heavy tools occupied the shadows. He stood for a moment while his eyes adjusted. He'd never been so alone with her.

Catherine held the rein and sweet-talked Squab while Isaac took off the saddle and blanket and laid them astraddle a narrow, waist-high bench built for that purpose. Their hands touched as he took the rein. He opened the gate to the far stall; Squab entered readily, then turned around. Isaac tied the gate shut, unbuckled the throat latch, slid the bridle off, and laid it beside his saddle. He felt Catherine's eyes.

He turned to stroke Squab's muzzle, but she caught his hand. "Come here." She pulled him into the adjacent empty stall, into a back corner. "Were you gonna spend all night with that horse?" She pulled his face down to hers and kissed him. Her lips were soft and knowing. He looked in wonder at her closed eyes. Shafts of sunlight cut the dusty air. He tried to follow her lead, but felt her lips tighten as she smiled. "Lord, you're a nervous boy." She squeezed his arm. "You that tense all over?"

"Uh . . ." He'd never heard of a woman suggesting such a thing.

She lifted her chin and kissed him again, slid her hands to his hips and pulled him tight against her. "Yes sir, I believe you are."

Sweat rolled down his sides. He felt her breath on his neck. She kneaded his back as he ran his hands from her shoulders, along her sides, and down beyond the hateful corset. "Lord," she whispered. "We ain't got long."

· · ·

Adair stirred his coffee. "About the time you get rid of one bunch of savages, you move a little further west and run into another more devilish than the last." He took a sip and studied his cup as if to decide if he was one grain of sugar over or under perfection. "First it was the Creeks. Then the Kronks— I thought they beat all I'd ever seen—and now we've got Comanches ridin' in here stealin' women."

Isaac nodded. He hoped the Adairs hadn't noticed his nervous glances at the bits of straw in Catherine's hair. Adair sprinkled a few more grains of sugar into his coffee. Catherine said, "Keep at it, Daddy, and you can just spread your coffee on a biscuit."

Her father smiled and waved off her comment. "We'll have to whip the Comanches just like we did the other breeds. You know there ain't been a Kronk seen in this country in two or three years. I believe we managed to kill 'em all out. Good riddance, I say."

"I don't believe the Comanches will go easy," Isaac said.

"Nonsense, son. We have the better weapons and tactics."

"Isaac, you shot one the other day, I hear," Catherine said.

Mrs. Adair looked sharply at her daughter. "Catherine Lynn, you're talkin' with your mouth full like a five-year-old."

Catherine shrugged, tore apart a chicken wing.

Isaac said, "Yes sir, in the woods, we've got 'em whipped. But out in the open, where they've got room to ride, a buck'll shoot a dozen arrows at you while you're tryin' to recharge your rifle."

"That's why an Indian fighter needs a sidearm."

"Yes sir." Captain Adair's Indian fighting had obviously been restricted to forest dwellers. "A Comanche fights from horseback. You ought to see it."

Adair grunted. "By the way, where's our Tonk? I suppose we ought to feed him."

"Cedrick took him a plate," Catherine said.

Adair wagged a greasy finger. "A Tonk, now, there's a useful savage, though I'm afraid folks won't abide their ways."

"Seems like they make fine neighbors," Isaac said. "Me and Pap take supper with King all the time."

Adair shook his head in exasperation. "There's no place for a man-eater in civilized society. And far as I can tell, they don't have a nigger's aptitude for agriculture and subservence."

"King won't be nobody's servant," Isaac said. He bit into a drumstick.

"That's what I'm sayin'. I'm afraid they'll eventually have to go like all the rest."

Isaac stopped chewing and wiped his mouth to hide his tightened jaw. He'd let it go for now. For Catherine's sake. Folks around Bastrop had always gotten on well with the Tonkawas. There was plenty of room in Texas for everyone that wanted to get along. But it wouldn't take too many like Thomas Adair to make the country feel crowded.

"Doesn't it scare you to bed down beside an Indian?" Catherine asked.

Isaac swallowed his food and cleared his throat to compose himself. "You mean King? I've knowed him ever since we moved to Texas. He's at our place so much we don't even pay any attention to him."

She laid the bare wing bone in her plate and wiped her hands. "Well, what about the Lipans?"

"Castro seems like a good enough fellow to me. I can't hardly understand him though."

"Meet him under different circumstances and you'll see him for the savage he is," Adair said.

Isaac nodded. "I wouldn't want him mad at me."

"Mad or not, you don't want to find yourself alone with him. Especially if he's got some of his own kind there to embolden him. Not a stand-up fighter among 'em."

Isaac shrugged. If Castro were there, he'd lift Thomas Adair's thinning hair over the remark. He was beginning to miss King and the boys at the fort. If Adair was so worried about Indians, why did he risk his women's safety out on the far edge of the frontier?

After supper, Isaac and Catherine sat on the doorstep. She touched him easily and often as she'd no doubt touched another young man less than two years before. Swallows dipped and rolled for insects. "What should we talk about?" she asked.

"I can't think of much to talk about, but I sure know of something to think about."

She laid her forehead against his shoulder. "Now you'll think bad of me."

"You know better than that."

"I don't know what got into me. Being married before . . . I suppose I just got used to some things."

"I hope I'm around next time you get to missin' it."

"We shouldn't take these kinds of risks, you know."

"Dangerous world we live in."

She laughed. Checked the open door and kissed his cheek. "You men ever swim in the river?"

"Rarely. Water's cold."

"You ought to."

"Why's that?"

She smiled. "You're rank as a wet dog."

"And just as randy."

"Lord."

They sat in silence. A gray hen flapped to its roost on a low tree limb. Catherine said, "Your ranger duty is about up."

"Be a year in August."

"Will you still come and see me after you've moved back downriver?"

"Why, I might enlist for another ten years just to stay close."

She smoothed her dress over her thighs. "Well. I figured you'd get busy working those two sections you'll have earned."

Isaac nodded slowly. "I s'pose I could do that too. Take me a year or two to get the place in shape."

Catherine said, "I haven't met your folks yet. Tell me about Esther."

"Pretty thing. You might think she's a little rough. We ain't prosperous farmers or planters. We're mountain folks and act like it, I s'pose."

She tugged his hand. "Does she have a fella?"

"Jonas McElroy. His family lives a few miles downriver. He's twenty. That's who she'll end up marryin', but she's sweet on Captain Smithwick."

"I ought to have known."

"I'll tie him up before I let him come by here again."

"I *do* favor a jealous man."

King Sol walked out of the barn carrying his musket and leading his horse. He swung into the saddle and melded into woods along the creek.

Isaac said, "We won't lose no horses tonight. If we had twenty more like old King, we'd have the Comanches whipped before Christmas."

"He seems awfully grim."

"Stoic, my mother calls him. He gets to laughing with Pap sometimes though." He looked toward the creek. "I suppose if I was doin' my job, I'd be out there with him."

She pulled his arm against her side. "You're on leave. Remember?"

Isaac held her hand and watched the darkening woods and imagined King out there alone, keeping a promise. He checked to make sure his rifle was propped against the cabin within easy reach.

Twenty-Five

ISAAC STOOD on the parapet, looking over the river bottom. The sun had edged above the hills behind him, lighting the mist above the river. On the far bank, the forested hill rose two hundred feet above the fog.

Normally he hated last watch, but he'd slept little since his tryst with Catherine two nights before. The encounter now seemed like a dream, though at instants he smelled her hair and breath. He had not known that a woman could be so desirous. He swung between torturous lust and heartache over their separation. Perhaps he'd see her again in another month if the Comanches stayed clear of the settlements.

Of course if they continued, he'd eventually get her in a family way if old man Adair didn't catch them first and shoot him. But he cast these concerns aside. Far more pleasant to dwell on Catherine's firm, slender bottom and the determined set to her brown eyes. He wondered if he could trust Smithwick or Felix with any of it. He wouldn't torture Ezra with it.

He glimpsed movement along the river. Hooves splashed. He strained to see through the fog and into the shadows. Horsemen rode up the hill along the switchback trail, through a sunlit clearing. They rode mustangs and carried shields. Castro and his Lipans? No, he'd pitched dice with the old chief last night.

He turned toward barracks and yelled, "Indians comin' from the river."

Jo Weeks, on watch on the far side of the fort yelled back, "What'd you say?"

"Comanches, goddamnit! Wake everybody up."

"You seen Indians?"

The riders came on. Long braids, naked torsos, breechclouts and moccasins. Eight men. Carrying bows and lances.

"They're about to ride up to the damn gate."

The barracks door opened. Tom Crosby said, "What's all the racket over?"

Isaac rested his rifle on top of the wall and drew a bead on the lead warrior, the first bald Comanche he'd seen. "That's far as you go!" The bald Comanche waved a white piece of cloth tied to the tip of a lance.

Jo Weeks was yelling at the other rangers to wake up. Smithwick came up the ladder and looked over the wall. "Love of god. Hold your fire."

"Parlar," the old Comanche said.

"I don't believe it," Smithwick said. "They want to parley."

Most of the company were on the parapet now, rifles trained on the impassive warriors.

"You surely don't mean to go down there, do you?" Ezra said. "They can't be up to no good."

"I'll talk to them. What can it hurt? Captain?"

Andrews shook his head in disbelief. "What can it hurt? Ask the Parkers."

"Some of the boys will go with me. Isaac? Felix?"

"Hell," Felix said.

"Good man," Smithwick said. "Captain?"

"I don't speak Mexican or Comanche, but I'll back you up," Andrews said.

Smithwick started down the ladder, stopped, and looked up at the men still standing along the parapet. "Close the gate behind us and keep it closed till I say open it. Cut 'em down at the first sign of trouble."

Isaac stood at the gate along with Smithwick, Andrews, Ezra, Jo Weeks, Felix, Castro, and King Sol. Nicholas Wren raised the bar and started swinging the door open. Smithwick said, "Nick, shut this gate behind us. If a fight breaks out, leave it shut. We'll have to make out as best we can."

The gate swung open. The old Comanche waved the truce flag again and smiled.

"Cordial old bastard," Felix said.

"Hush, Felix," Andrews said. "The devils might understand English."

They walked toward the Indians, rifles at port arms. The Comanches seemed relaxed, but Isaac remembered how quickly a warrior could arm a bow. The men in the fort watched in silence. Isaac felt their eyes and tension.

"Who ever heard of a bald-headed Comanche?" Ezra said.

"I wish I'd sliced his balls off that time on the Trinity," King said.

Isaac winced. Now was not the time for unresolved grudges to boil up. The sun shone on the old Comanche's bare pate. His braids began just above his ears and ran nearly to his waist. Isaac had heard that aging Comanches sometimes wove horsehair into their braids to gain a few inches.

They stopped a dozen feet from the Indians. Isaac recognized the young warrior on the far right as the one he'd fought that morning on the bluff above the river. The young man's eyes widened in recognition. He smiled and touched his forehead and lifted a new bow for Isaac to see. Isaac nodded and touched his chin.

"I expect you two pups'll be sittin' in the shade swappin' lies directly," Felix said.

"Hell, Felix," Smithwick said through clenched teeth.

The old Comanche looked back and said something to the other warriors. They laughed.

Smithwick laid his rifle in the crook of his arm. *"Buenos días, amigos."*

The bald Comanche grinned. *"Buenos días, Capitan."* His Spanish was slow and deliberate. *"Nosotros buscamos un trato."*

"¿Que propones?"

"Déjenos entrar para hablar de nuestros asuntos."

"What the hell?" Andrews said.

"They want to come into the fort and propose a treaty."

"And they can all ride straight to perdition."

"Is that what you want me to tell him? I believe I'll go back inside and yell it over the wall. You boys can stay out here if you want to."

Andrews studied the Comanches. "Tell him we'll talk out here."

Smithwick said, *"Hablamos aqui."*

"Adentro," the old Comanche said. *"No queremos pelear."*

"Captain, we'll either talk inside or we're liable to have a fight right here. We're a dozen steps from a hell of a lot of trouble," Smithwick said.

Andrews glanced up at his men. "We could tell the boys to open fire right now."

The Comanches frowned.

"They don't like us talking among ourselves," Smithwick said out of the side of his mouth. He smiled and nodded at the warriors. A few of them responded in kind. "We caught 'em sound asleep up on that bluff and never brought home a scalp. They'll just kill half of us and disappear like they did that morning."

Andrews nodded. "Well damn it," he said pleasantly. He turned back to the fort. "Tom, open the gate. Be ready to shoot."

Someone on the parapet said, "Good god."

"Just back up," Smithwick said. "Don't turn around."

They backed toward the gate, all smiling and nodding except for King and Castro, who appeared ready and eager to open fire.

As the Comanches rode into the fort, men took cover behind wagons, feed bags, and water barrels, rifles ready but not yet aimed. Several of the horses in the stockade nickered at the visitors. The warriors' eyes darted about. Most of the men still on the parapet had taken a knee and were ready to fire.

Tom Crosby closed the gate; the Indians jerked their heads to look back. Two of their ponies shied. Several rangers cocked their rifles. The old man snapped something in Comanche.

Smithwick said, "Easy, boys. They're as jumpy as we are. We've got the advantage now and they know it."

Isaac doubted it. Sweat ran into his eyes.

"They're inside now," Andrews said. "Ask them what they want."

Smithwick cleared his throat. *"Yo soy Smithwick. ¿En que les podemos ayudar a nuestros amigos?"*

The bald Comanche thumbed his chest. *"Yo soy Muguara. Queremos que uno de sus jefes nos acompañe al campo para hablar con nosotros."*

Smithwick glanced at Andrews. "They want one of us to go to their camp and palaver with their chiefs."

"Pig shit," Andrews said. "What kind of fools do these heathens think we are? Tell him hell no."

Smithwick nodded. "*Nosotros iremos a su campo.*"

Muguara said, "*Nó. Nomás un hombre. Queremos hablar de nuestros pesares y sufrimiento y ofrecer un trato. No le pasará nada malo a este hombre. Nosotros lo protegeremos.*"

Isaac's Spanish had improved during his months at the fort. He caught enough of the exchange to know that Smithwick had disobeyed an order. The young Comanche seemed to have relaxed and now regarded Isaac with obvious curiosity.

"*Nuestro jefe no habla Comanche o Mexicano.* I told him you don't speak Comanche or Mexican, Captain."

"Damn right I don't. And I don't aim to."

The old Comanche considered this. "*Regresa con nosotros, Smithwick. Nosotros podemos hablar contigo.*"

The young Comanche pointed to Isaac. "*No lo llevarmos a él. Yo lo conozco.*"

Isaac's stomach fluttered. The chief turned and spoke in a gentle tone to the young man, who looked disappointed.

Muguara sat his horse and waited for a reply. Smithwick said, "He wants me to go back with him."

"Hell no," Andrews said.

"Captain, they took a great risk coming here. I might be able to do some good. What can it hurt?"

"I expect gettin' scalped and roasted will pain you a fair amount."

"I trust them in this." He smiled at Muguara. "Captain?"

"I can't see it," Felix said under his breath. "I wouldn't go with them devils."

Isaac wondered how the Comanches would accept a refusal. Surely they would ride out of the fort without a fight. But they might return better armed and less affable.

"For god's sake, Noah," Andrews said. "Think about what you're sayin'."

"I know the risk. But we may never get another chance like this. Turn them down and we're sayin' we want to fight."

"We'd rather fight from here to hell and back than to give you up to these devils," Isaac said.

One of the Comanches, a tall warrior of about thirty, pointed to his own chest, laughed, and said, "*Diablo.*"

Isaac felt all the blood drain from his face. Smithwick said, "I ought to go."

"Damn it; how long?" Andrews said.

"*¿Cuanto tiempo?*"

"*Dos lunas,*" the chief said.

"Two months, Captain."

"This is crazy."

"*Yo ire contigo,*" Smithwick said.

Muguara grunted. "*¡Bueno!*"

"Now hold on!" Andrews said. He lowered and shook his head. "I reckon if a man is eager to die, I've got no cause to get in his way. Boys, fetch his horse and one of the mules."

Smithwick pointed to the cook fire. "*Amigos, desmonten y sientense a comer y fumar mientras que yo me preparo para nuestro viaje.*"

The Comanches dismounted and glanced nervously at one another as rangers led their horses to the stockade. Isaac followed Smithwick into the barrack. "Captain. Lord."

Smithwick rolled his soogan. "It ain't just the treaty. I ain't quite that noble. If they don't cook me, I'll know where their camp is—at least for now. And I might learn something about their captives."

Ezra came in. "What kind of grub can I get together for you, Captain?"

"Plenty of coffee and sugar. I expect they'll provide the meat and God only knows what else," Smithwick said. He tied the rolled soogan.

They walked into morning sun. The Comanches were squatting around the fire, smoking clay and wooden pipes of various shapes. Ezra nearly had the mule loaded. Smithwick's hands trembled as he lashed down his bedroll. The Comanches stood and emptied their pipes into the fire and started for their horses. Rangers stood about, watching gravely. Andrews paced back and forth in front of the little blacksmith shed.

Isaac ran back into the bunkhouse and took the Comanche bow from beneath his bunk. He'd hoped to show it to Cyrus, but even the smallest gesture of goodwill might save Captain Smithwick from horrible death.

The young Comanche sat his horse when Isaac walked out. The boy saw him at once. Isaac offered the bow; the boy started to take it, but looked down at the new bow in his hand. He pushed back the offering. "*Ahora es tuyo.*"

Smithwick swung into the saddle. The men gathered around him. He shook hands with all. The Indians watched with interest. Isaac could think of nothing else to say. He shook his head. Smithwick said, "I know, son."

Felix cussed and muttered something about fools and savages. Uncle Jimmy pulled on his jug. Choctaw Tom opened the gate, and Noah Smithwick, leading his pack mule, followed the bald Comanche chief out of the fort. Just then, Isaac noticed the lace on Muguara's truce flag.

Twenty-Six

COMANCHE RAIDING along the Colorado ceased. Isaac led two patrols, one northwest to the scarp above the river, another south to Bastrop. They found no Comanche sign.

After the first month, the company spent the days hunting, gambling, napping, and speculating on Smithwick's fate. Isaac visited Catherine weekly.

There were no more outbuilding trysts, though not because of lack of effort. Cedrick developed the irksome habit of sauntering through the barn whenever Isaac and Catherine left the doorstep. Isaac knew better than to suggest a stroll.

Thomas Adair fumed over the rangers' negotiation with the Comanches. "We need to be killing heathens, not palavering with them," he said one night over a bowl of plums.

They heard nothing from Noah Smithwick. Captain Andrews asked Isaac weekly if he'd be reenlisting; Isaac remained noncommittal. He had no desire to settle down and farm. But a full-time ranger accumulated little in the way of property that young women and their fathers deemed important.

Catherine talked as if his leaving the rangers were a foregone conclusion. He gave her no reason for doubt. She wouldn't wait long for him. He'd either get busy and make something of himself or she'd choose the security of an older, settled man. For that matter, she might make that choice any time. He was only seventeen; too young to marry. What prospect did she imagine? And was her father merely humoring her, allowing Isaac to call on her until some suitably solid merchant or planter arrived to secure her favor?

Then again, in another two years, she'd be only twenty-one, still a young bride—if he could hold her that long.

• • •

Late afternoon, August 3, 1837, Noah Smithwick rode up the trail from the river and hailed the fort.

Twenty-Seven

SMITHWICK loosened his saddle girth. "They've got some bones to pick. Made me squirm from time to time." He lifted the saddle and set it astraddle the rail. "We probably ought to listen to what they have to say."

"What the hell kind of a bone can a Comanche pick?" Ezra said. "We ain't runnin' off with their women and younguns."

Isaac thought Smithwick looked gaunt and haggard. "Did they feed you enough?" He'd nearly wept in relief at Smithwick's return.

"They fed me plenty. I just don't have much taste for tripe or curdled milk out the stomach of a buffalo calf. And I don't believe I slept more than an hour at a time. They don't go to bed of a night the way we do. Bucks gambling and younguns playin' and laughing all night long. They just nap whenever they feel like it."

"These bones they want to pick; what are they?" Andrews asked.

"They say we're running all the game out of their country by settling."

"What do they propose we do then? Leave the country?" Andrew's eyes were wide as if he'd just heard the most ludicrous comment ever spoken.

"They never said a word about us clearing out of the country. They just don't understand our way of living in it." He propped his rifle against the rail. "When game gets scarce in a place, they'll pack up and move somewhere else for a spell. Then move again. Before long the game moves back. They rest their huntin' grounds. We just come in and shoot a piece of country out and then go to farming."

Felix spat and nodded. "What'd you say to that?"

"Damn little."

Felix said, "Noah Smithwick caught with nothin' to say. Next thing you know Uncle Jimmy will swear off the jug."

"I suppose we'll all go to livin' in hide lodges then," Ezra said.

"Boys, we've serious business at hand," Andrews said.

"Serious sure enough. They've a message for President Houston."

"And just what do they want to say to him?" Andrews asked.

Smithwick rubbed his horse's neck. "They want an agreed-upon boundary at the base of the escarpment, west of which no white settlers ever cross."

Ezra said, "They expect us to just let all that land and game go to waste?"

"Hush Ezree," Andrews said. "I'm askin' the questions here." He scratched his ear. "They expect us to just let all that land and game go to waste?"

Smithwick said, "You're a stern inquisitor, Captain."

The men laughed. Andrews took off his hat and feigned a slap at Ezra.

"That's what they expect," Smithwick said. "In return they promise not to raid the settlements along the Trinity, Brazos, or Colorado."

Isaac found the offer generous. It would leave the Texians the bottomland in three river drainages. If the Comanches would settle for the dry uplands, then why quarrel?

"Preposterous," Andrews said. "But I suppose I'll have to refer the matter to Secretary Sawyer. I'd love to be a fly on the wall when old man Houston catches wind of this."

"Captain, what about captives?" Isaac asked. Talk of treaties was all well and good, but remembrance of those discarded pantalets and corset haunted his sleep. And how would it feel to be without hope, knowing you had no family to return to? Were Martha and Mary Thorpe and Elsie Mann alive, wondering why the ranging company hadn't rescued them? Did they wonder if anyone thought or cared about them?

Smithwick said, "A Mexican woman and white woman."

"Which white woman?" Felix said.

"Not one of ours. This one was raised Comanche. Wild as any squaw. Wouldn't even look at me. They kept me away from the Mexican woman. She finally slipped and told me they'd taken her out of Chihuahua when she was a girl. Cecilia was her name. They call her something else—I don't recall." He shook his head. "From what I could get out of old Muguara, our women are somewhere on the plains to the northwest. He said there was nothing he could do. But I imagine we can bargain for them. They want that boundary pretty badly. Comanches aren't without their own kind of honor. They never raised a hand against me and even run off a band of Waco that came lookin' to scalp the first white man they could find."

Andrews rubbed his beard. "I ain't heard of any horse thievery since you went with them."

"They're expecting me next full moon."

"Where are they?" Isaac asked.

"Thirty miles north on Brushy Creek. We've ridden within a few miles of their camp many times."

"I don't see why we don't just ride up there, clean the place out then," Ezra said.

"I saw at least fifty lodges, Ezra."

Isaac considered that figure about forty-five more than he'd attack with twenty men.

"Raise a bigger company then," Andrews said. "We'd have no trouble; folks won't abide a Comanche encampment so close to Bastrop."

"You'll ride on 'em without me, then," Smithwick said.

Jo Weeks walked up. "I thought you signed on to fight Indians."

Smithwick said, "I signed on to protect the settlements."

"Best way to protect 'em is to rid the country of Comanches," Ezra said.

Smithwick shook his head. "They gave their word. I gave mine."

"Hell then," Andrews said. "I'll take the matter up with Sawyer, and we'll lay around here knowin' very well that there's a camp full of woman-stealin' devils damn near in the middle of Bastrop."

. . .

The cook fire shone on Smithwick's face as he sipped his coffee. "Lord, that's good. Old Muguara laid into my stash and went through it in a week."

Isaac watched Smithwick. The man knew something; he'd seemed thoughtful and distracted since his return. "Tell us about 'em, Captain; not what they said they want; what they're like."

Smithwick took another sip, rested the tin cup on his thigh. "More like us than most of us want to admit. They laugh and hope. Love their younguns. More peaceable among themselves than we are." He massaged his temple. "But they can't understand us any more than we understand them; we're lookin' at the world from different places."

"Damn right. I can't understand any man who'd take a hide lodge over a nice, tight cabin," Ezra said.

Smithwick nodded. "And a Comanche buck would call you a fool for all of your hard labor. We call hard work a virtue; they call it demeaning. Work's for women and slaves." He looked into the darkness beyond the fire. "I keep thinking about that white woman. She'd been raised Comanche. Never wanted a thing to do with me."

"Didn't know no better," Isaac said.

Smithwick sipped. "Didn't know any different."

Felix laughed. "Now we know what's been ailing him. A woman spurned his attention."

"Offered to carry a stack of hides for her and she ran off." He laid a knot of cedar on the fire. "What I mean is . . ." He rested his chin in his hands. "There's a scrim between us and the world a Comanche sees. We might look through it and make out some things, but we can't see it all. We can carry on with 'em, even laugh at the same things, but we won't ever see what they see even when we're looking at the same thing." He studied their faces. "And they'll never see what we see because they're on the other side of the veil, looking from another place."

Ezra said, "Folks have opinions, Captain. Ways of looking at things. Some right, some wrong. If they're wrong enough, they need to be punished."

"It's more than that, Ezra," Smithwick said. "You and I might disagree on a matter, but we agree on certain truths. If we fail to agree on a matter, it's not because we're not lookin' at the same thing. But a Comanche starts with different truths; or what he believes are truths. Even Castro and King; they're here with us, but they're not living in our world."

Isaac said, "I don't see how we'll ever get along with people that think so different than we do."

Smithwick poured himself another cup. "Son, it ain't the differences that will lead to bloodshed. We can abide some difference. It's our similarity that I'm afraid we won't overcome."

The men watched their captain. Firelight flickered on their brown, oily faces. Isaac shook his head.

Smithwick said, "Take the Tonks. They just want to be left alone to hunt deer and buffalo, eat a body or two, and do like they've always done. We showed up, and, after a skirmish here and there, a little horse thievery, they gave ground. Same with the Lipans and Kronks."

"We never gave 'em a choice," Ezra said. "That's how it is. If they'd been stronger, they'd have turned us back."

"That's just it," Smithwick said. "They'd have turned us back. Each tribe merely wanted to defend its piece of country. But the Comanches believe it's all theirs, whether they happen to live on it or not. The Tonks and Lipans and Wacos are still there only because the Comanches put up with them for now. When they want it, they'll take it. Likewise, we live along a few river bottoms, but we consider the whole of the Republic ours. We'll take what we need as we need it. If Houston agrees to this treaty, we'll honor it until it behooves us to break it."

"What's the use in talkin' to them then?" Isaac asked. "Seems like we'd best get busy cleanin' 'em out."

"A treaty might save some bloodshed and suffering for a time. Let the next generation worry about its problems. Today, the Comanches can do as they please and we're powerless to stop them. We'll grow stronger with time. Learn their ways. As best I can tell, they barely birth enough babies to hold their number steady. I didn't see many younguns in camp."

Isaac found the assessment heartening. If the Comanches bred like the mountain families he'd known, there'd soon be a dearth of hair in the settlements. "What if Houston won't go along with their treaty? You gonna ride back to their camp and tell 'em?"

"They'll be expecting me."

Isaac said, "You ain't afraid of gettin' cut up or roasted?"

"They understand negotiation. They've outbargained the Spanish and Mexicans for two hundred years."

Felix laughed. "But they never run up on such a cunning horde of scoundrels as us."

"I wouldn't trust no Indian," Ezra said.

King Sol walked up and sat down next to Isaac. "I won that Lipan's knife," he said. "I wish I could've got his musket."

"I'd hide it," Ezra said.

"He can't steal it back. I won it in that card game."

"Why hell," Felix said. "He used to steal horses all the time. Probably still does when he can."

King drew his patch knife and trimmed off a sliver of thumbnail. "But he didn't lose those horses gambling. You can't steal somethin' you lose gambling. It ain't right."

Isaac said, "King, you'd best get busy playin' for Castro's musket if you're goin' with me. I'm headin' home first light."

Smithwick's hat brim shadowed his eyes. "Made up your mind."

"Yep. I gotta get busy makin' somethin' of my two sections. Besides, you've got the Comanche problem in hand."

"Well. I suppose that gal is looking for some sign of coming prosperity."

On the other side of the fort, Uncle Jimmy whooped and said, "Fork her over boys, I won her fair and square!"

Isaac laughed. "I guess I'll get used to lookin' at the ass end of a mule."

Felix said, "King, what'll you do with your pay?"

The Tonkawa shrugged. "I don't know nothin' about it."

"Just likes to fight Comanches," Ezra said.

"Only a fool wants to fight a Comanche," King said. "I ain't a fool."

"What'd you sign on for then?" Ezra said.

King looked toward the card game. "I told Cyrus I wouldn't let nothin' happen to this boy." He stood and dusted his bottom. "I better go over there and win that Lipan's musket."

Twenty-Eight

WHEN BIG EZRA Higginbotham twirled, Esther's feet left the good plank floor. Isaac heard her squeal above the fiddling of Noah Smithwick and Reverend Ezekiel Hodge. Others in the crowded room laughed and clapped. Catherine smiled wistfully at Isaac. She sat next to him in one of the many cane-bottom chairs that lined the walls of Anson McAllister's great room. Isaac supposed that McAllister, Bastrop's principal merchant, had invited half of the Republic to his niece's wedding dance.

A few hours prior, standing in McAllister's yard beneath the weak January sun, they watched Reverend Hodge marry Twyla Scrivener and Angus Stewart. Now the bride and groom, in wedding dress and store-bought suit, danced and mingled, brushing against wool and cotton, buckskin and silk.

Isaac touched the windowpane, one of the few he'd seen. It was sweating. He wiped the glass and peered into the blackness beyond. He ran his fingertips over the plaster wall and looked about the room. Three more doorways. A staircase. Candelabrum in every corner. A beautiful sister and friendship with Noah Smithwick opened doors.

Cyrus Webb started to spit on the floor but caught himself. He watched Ezra and Esther. "Light on his feet for a big boy, ain't he?"

Jonas McElroy sat sullenly on the other side of Cyrus. "I swear, I believe the floor's shakin'."

"If you'd get out there and twirl that gal, you wouldn't have to sit here and watch somebody else do it for you." Cyrus wagged his head whenever he lectured.

"I can't dance a lick."

"Then hush fussin'. You can't bring a girl to a dance and expect her to sit." He leaned across Isaac and touched Catherine's arm with the back of his hand. "I never meant nothin' by that, honey."

Catherine smiled. "I'm happy to be here, Mr. Webb."

So was Isaac, but he'd have been happier if she'd forget her Baptist upbringing and take the dance floor with him. Several good whirls with Esther, Ruth, and Widow Duty had him warm and loose and ready to do anything but sit in a chair watching all of Bastrop dancing to good fiddle music.

He wanted to slip his arm around Catherine's slender waist, squeeze her hand, feel his moccasins glide over the smooth floor. Dancing with the comely Widow Duty had only sharpened his yearning.

The fiddlers finished "Sugar in the Gourd" with a flourish. Ezra swept Esther off the dance floor with one arm. Her toes barely touched the floor as he whisked her back to Jonas. A wisp of blond hair lay on her cheek. Ezra wiped the sweat from his eyes. "Thank ye, Jonas. I'll borrow her anytime you'll loan her."

Esther laughed and put her hand on Jonas's shoulder. "Bless your heart; you're the best thing that ever was." Jonas looked miserable. Ruth Webb walked through the dining room door and crossed the dance floor. Esther took Catherine's hand and patted it. "Don't they make a fine lookin' pair, Mama?"

Ruth smiled and touched Catherine's chin. The girl blushed.

Reverend Hodge fired up "Pretty Polly"; Smithwick caught him after a few bars. Ezra bent over Cyrus. "Mr. Webb, I'd love to give your wife a little whirl."

"I can stand it if you can," Cyrus said.

Ruth laughed. "A true man steps forward." She took Ezra's arm.

Esther grabbed Isaac's hand. "Get up from there, brother." He looked at Catherine. She smiled, nodded.

Isaac had to admit that Esther was the prettiest girl at the dance. Beside her, Catherine, handsome as she was, seemed serious and self-conscious.

"I sure wish the Captain would take a rest from his fiddlin'," Esther said.

"Say it a little louder and I won't have to walk over there and give him a hint."

Esther let go of Isaac's hand to wipe a trickle of sweat from her temple. "Would you do that for your big sister?"

"I would. But I'm afraid Widow Duty might jerk you bald. Good lord, look out!" Ezra and Ruth brushed by. Other couples moved aside. Laughter rippled around the room. "Now there's a pair that cuts a wide swath."

Esther said, "I don't suppose it'd be Christian of me to charm the good Widow's beau out of her arms." She glanced back at Smithwick. "On the other hand, will you look at those new breeches?"

"I'd better take you back to Jonas right now."

They finished the dance and filed into the dining room for coffee and ham and biscuits. The fiddlers took a rest and joined them. "I never seen so many little plates and cups in my life," Esther said.

Cyrus looked at the Captain's stiff black shirt. "Good lord, Smithwick. Where's the corpse?"

Widow Duty laid a thin slice of cake on her plate. "He's just indulging my weakness, Mr. Webb."

Isaac admired the buxom, dark-eyed Widow. Brown curls on her shoulders, full lips, skin that rarely felt the sun. He couldn't blame Noah Smithwick for dressing up for her. He looked down at his own greasy buckskins.

The Widow added a spoonful of sugar to her coffee. "And how are you, Miz Druin?"

Catherine smiled. Nodded primly. "Very well, thank you."

Isaac supposed that Catherine was still too young to be called Widow Druin.

Cyrus patted Catherine's back. "Why, all this dancin' and fiddlin' is hard on a good Baptist girl, Widow." Catherine's ears turned red.

Ruth said, "Cyrus! Don't make sport of that child."

Cyrus arched his brows. "Who's makin' sport?"

Isaac had warned Catherine about his people, but doubted he'd prepared her. He didn't envy her stern raising. If a good dance tune invited sin, then he'd take his chances in hell. Thank goodness Catherine wasn't as pious as she led her parents to believe. He wondered how cold it was in Anson McAllister's barn loft.

They filled their plates, then took their seats in the great room.

Thomas Adair stood in the kitchen doorway talking and nodding gravely with McAllister. Catherine leaned to Isaac's ear. "Look at Daddy. Always doin' business."

Isaac said, "That's why he's prosperous and most of the rest of us are sowin' corn around our stumps."

"I expect you'll do better than that."

Isaac chewed his ham. "Cabin's done. We'll lay in a crop this spring."

"Don't get so busy you forget to come up and see me."

He chewed, nodded, smiled, chewed. "Never," he said, finally. He sipped his coffee. He'd grown accustomed to the twelve-mile ride up the Colorado to the Adair farm. Besides, the distance gave him a handy excuse to stay overnight. Lately he'd forgone the barn for Cedrick's shack. He found the old slave fine company.

Adair waved to Smithwick, left McAllister, and sidled up. "Reverend, I'd say a fiddle-playing preacher rarely goes hungry."

Hodge raised his coffee cup in greeting. "A man had best cultivate more than one trade in these backwaters, Thomas. I must say I'm surprised to see a handsome family of Baptists at our merry little gathering."

Adair smiled and nodded as if he'd anticipated the remark. "We're here to pay our respects to the bride, groom, and host. We'll leave the heathenish excesses to the baser denominations."

Uncle Jimmy Curtis came in the back door and spotted Cyrus. He wiped his mouth with the back of his hand and walked over. "How about a little fresh air, Cyrus?" He nodded at Hodge and Smithwick. "Reverend. Captain. Damn fine fiddlin' if you ask me."

Hodge laughed. "Why thank you, Uncle Jimmy. You smell like you've already breathed some fresh air."

Cyrus slapped Jimmy on the back. "I say we raise a jug to the baser nominations. Join us, Reverend, Smithwick, Thomas?"

Adair shook his head. Ruth shot Cyrus a dark look. Hodge grinned and waved off the invitation. "I need to keep an edge for my fiddle playin'."

Uncle Jimmy said, "Captain? What do you say?"

Smithwick set his plate in his chair. "I say fiddlin' is thirsty work." He punched Cyrus's arm and started for the door.

Adair cleared his throat. "Be rejoining your Comanche friends soon, Smithwick?"

Noah stopped and turned. "Soon as they come back from their winter hunting grounds."

Adair nodded. "I see. And we're to knowingly abide two hundred savages within a day's ride of Bastrop."

Smithwick said, "I'd say an agreement ought to mean something."

Adair smoothed his mustache. "Why sure."

Isaac glanced at Catherine. She stared at her plate.

Cyrus swallowed half a biscuit. "Sam Houston hisself lived with the Cherokee."

Adair smiled. "Enough said."

Mrs. Adair stepped out of the kitchen, concern on her face. "My, what a stern-looking group."

"Just discussing the Captain's approach to Indian fighting, Louise. You know my thoughts on the matter."

"I certainly do, Thomas. And I hope you won't tire these fine people with them."

Isaac laid his fork in his plate. "We ain't had a Comanche raid since the Captain paid a visit."

"Nor have we recovered Mrs. Mann and the Thorpe women," Adair said.

Uncle Jimmy crossed his arms on his chest. "I'd damn sure rather palaver with a Comanche as to have to outride one." He turned to Hodge. "Beg your pardon, Reverend. Come on, boys. Let's have a snort."

"So we'll sacrifice our women to avoid a fight," Adair said.

Reverend Hodge rubbed his palms together. "Gentlemen, let's not mar the occasion." He squeezed Adair's arm. "We Protestants just earned the right to worship openly. Let's not fight among ourselves."

Adair remained stern. Ruth patted Mrs. Adair's stout arm. Isaac looked at his feet. Hodge said, "Come on, now, gentlemen."

Cyrus leaned back in his chair. "Lord, Thomas, you sure you don't want to take a little pull on the jug? Might do you some good. You're all backed up."

"Why hell yes," Uncle Jimmy said.

Ezra laughed. Catherine turned to Isaac. "All backed up?"

Isaac pretended not to hear.

Adair looked at Cyrus with contempt. "I've been told you're a fighter."

Cyrus shrugged. "I am. When I need to be."

"We lost neighbors to those savages."

"We all have, Thomas," Cyrus said.

Ruth sighed. "Why don't we . . . ?"

Cyrus raised his hand. "The man's bound and determined to say his piece. I'll let him say it."

Isaac recognized the resolve in his father's voice. Cyrus had never offered an opinion on the emissary work, but he liked Noah Smithwick, and that was reason enough to engage Thomas Adair.

Adair gave a quick, knowing smile. "I believe I've said my piece. Louise, tell Mrs. McAllister that we'll be needing our wraps."

His wife said, "Thomas!"

Ezra and Smithwick looked out over the dance floor. Cyrus kept his eyes on Adair.

"No way to be," Ezra muttered.

Adair turned his head toward his wife without looking at her. "Louise . . ."

Hodge smiled and laid one hand on Adair's shoulder, the other on Cyrus's. "Gentlemen, surely . . ."

Adair said, "We'll be heading on toward the door. Catherine, Louise."

"I swear," Cyrus said.

Catherine looked pleadingly at her father. He locked eyes with her and shook his head. She glanced at Isaac, panic in her eyes. Her face was flushed.

Ruth smiled at Catherine. "Don't worry, dear. These hot-headed men will come around."

Isaac helped Catherine from her chair. "That's right. I'll be out in a few days."

Adair took his daughter's arm. "I wouldn't bother, young man. I don't expect to see you and that Tonk on our place again."

The color left Catherine's cheeks. She looked to Louise, who averted her eyes. Laughter and conversation continued around them.

Esther crossed her arms on her chest and looked solemnly at Isaac. His legs felt weak. He searched the faces around him, trying to recall the exchange, grappling for words. He saw Ruth move close to Cyrus, then watched, numb, as Adair turned and herded his wife and daughter toward the front room. Catherine looked back at him as she walked through the door.

"I swear, boy," Cyrus said. "I never aimed for that to happen."

Isaac nodded. He'd never heard his father apologize.

Hodge laid his hand on Isaac's back. "I wish I knew what to tell you, son."

Smithwick said, "Reverend, I'd say this calls for a lively tune."

Uncle Jimmy rubbed his jaws and nodded sagely. "Cyrus, you should've just shut up and had a drink with me."

Twenty-Nine

ISAAC SAT amid a clump of cedars on the hill north of the Adair farm. A raw wind whipped the trees above his head, but the air was quiet in his sanctuary and smelled of rain and juniper. It would be dark soon.

He watched Catherine step out the cabin door and toss table scraps to the chickens. She stood for a moment, looking down the bottom as if expecting someone, then walked back inside. Smoke from the chimney drooped eastward. Falling weather coming. He rubbed his eyes. He hadn't slept since the argument the night before. After lying until dawn in the brittle darkness, the resinous scent of his new cabin sharp in his nostrils, he kicked off his quilts and rode upriver. He had no idea what he'd say to her.

Cyrus was contrite, but too proud to offer more than a few words of regret that Thomas Adair was such a son of a bitch. During the ride back to Bastrop, Esther told Isaac he had no business marrying into a family of Georgia prigs. Ruth said nothing.

Cedrick walked out of the barn, ax in hand, knelt at the chopping block, and axed a slice of kindling. Isaac eased down the hill toward the creek. At times, the brush and trees blocked his view of Cedrick, but the quick, one-handed chopping continued. He padded out of the streamside brush and stood watching the old slave work. After a moment he said in a low voice, "If I was a Comanche, your head would be a tad colder by now."

Cedrick cut another slice. He didn't look up. "If you was a Comanche, you'd have this ax buried in your head about now. I never heard such a racket comin' down that hill." He looked up. "Anyways, you're late. Miz Catherine has about paced herself to death."

"You've heard then."

"Marster Adair has been bellowin' about it all day."

"Where's he at now?"

"Inside preachin' the women mad, I expect. Your name's been used in vain more than once."

"Be damn."

"Be damn sure enough, if he catches you."

"If he'd been anybody but Catherine's daddy, I'd have knocked him into next week for talkin' to Pap that way."

Cedrick chopped. "Uh-huh."

"I'd be grateful if you'd slip and tell her I'm here."

"Uh-huh. And risk me gettin' whupped."

"Well. I can't go knockin' on her door."

Cedrick laughed. "And risk you gettin' whupped."

"I ain't afraid of old man Adair."

Cedrick stood. "I'm fixin' to walk back in the barn. When I do, Miz Catherine will be along shortly. We been expectin' you."

"How'd she know?"

"We knowed where you'd come from. We had it all worked out. When I start choppin' kindlin' I don't need, it means you're here. When I quit, it means she's supposed to slip out here. Give her time." He started for the barn.

"I thank you, Cedrick."

"She's hurtin'." He walked away.

Isaac slipped back into the brush. He could see his breath. Chickadees flitted about in the branches above. Steam rose from the little creek. He heard a slight rustle. Catherine ran from around the corner of the barn and looked about. She wore her familiar work dress. A scarf tied beneath her chin covered her ears.

He stood up and hissed. She froze. "Isaac! Lord! I knew you were here and you still scared the life out of me."

He propped his rifle against a stump and waded the ankle-deep creek. "Now you've got your feet wet," she said.

"I'll carry you across; we can't stand out here. Your folks will see us."

"We ain't got long. They'll miss me. I told 'em I had to go." She put her arm around his neck and he swept up her legs and started back across the creek. Her cheek brushed against his beard.

"You're heavier than last time I carried you."

"I can't remember."

"I remember. I've thought about it every day since."

He eased her to the ground. Tears rimmed her brown eyes. "Isaac, I swear." She hugged herself and looked away. "I don't know why that had to happen."

"Pap can't keep his thoughts to hisself."

"Daddy started it. He's been hoppin' mad ever since he heard Captain Smithwick listened to the Indians. And your mama sweet as she can be. And Esther."

"They were smitten with you. We all are."

"I saw the way Esther looked at me when I got up to leave."

"Blood runs thick. She didn't mean nothing by it."

"I reckon it does." Her breath hung white about her face.

"Too thick?"

"What am I supposed to do, Isaac? Run away with you? Leave my family?"

"I ain't afraid of your daddy."

"That's not it. He's my father. I love him. And Mama."

"I'd think less of you if you didn't. But what about me?"

"You know how I feel. Look what I gave to you. I don't give it freely; I'll tell you that."

He nodded, swallowed.

"We can't make a good life without family," she said. "We've got to let this blow over."

"Your daddy don't strike me as a man to let go of a slight."

"What about your pap?"

"He'd do it for me. Hell, he'd do it for you."

"Daddy can't be wrong. That's just how he is. But he's the best man I know."

"I never doubted it. But that ain't got nothing to do with us."

"It's got everything to do with us! Can't you see that? Would you leave your family for me?"

Isaac looked up the hill. Nearly nightfall. "No sense worrying about it. I don't have to make that choice."

"What're you sayin'?"

He shook his head in exasperation. "Nothing. Catherine, it's gettin' dark."

"Damn it."

He smiled and ran his finger over her lips. "Baptist girl's got a mouth on her."

She hugged his neck and buried her face in his beard. "Just come back when you can. I can stand it long as I know you're comin' back."

"I don't know what else to do." He stroked her hair. "I'd better get you back across this creek. Grab ahold."

Freezing rain began to fall as he carried her across. She kissed him and ran for the cabin. He waded the creek again, picked up his rifle, and walked on numb feet up and over the hill. Squab nickered at his approach. He fingered the ice gathering along his rifle barrel.

· · ·

Isaac lay abed in the middle of the afternoon, dozing and staring at the coals in his new stone fireplace. It drew well, much to his satisfaction. He and Cyrus had spent the better part of two weeks selecting the wagonloads of stone along the creek. "You build a home around your fireplace," Cyrus often said. He needed andirons. He'd seen just the set he wanted at McAllister's, but he found his ranging company earnings worthless. He'd have to barter; he knew of three honey trees he'd visit come summer, and he and Sis had collected stacks of fox and coon pelts.

He'd gather his first crop next fall using Cyrus's mules. He'd picked his two sections a quarter mile up the creek from the home place. They'd already worn a path. He still took most of his meals with his family and did the same chores he'd always done. Esther stopped by daily to complain about his slovenly housekeeping. He needed his own place to show Catherine and her father that he was on his way, that he had potential.

He'd already built a small shed for Squab, but had in mind a barn like

Thomas Adair's. And there would be a corncrib and smokehouse. One day, Catherine would plant a little kitchen garden.

He and Cyrus had already cleared an acre or so for planting, and they'd clear more before spring. He'd burn or jerk the stumps out if he had to kill a half-dozen mules doing it. He'd grown up sowing corn in stump-riddled fields, but now he'd seen Thomas Adair's immaculate creek bottom plantings. Yes, his own holdings were hillier, with shallower soils, but he'd make the best with what he had.

As much as he loved and respected his father, he'd now seen Cyrus's limited ambition. Or his narrow view of things. You had to know about something to want it. Or you had to be able to at least imagine it. He suspected Cyrus had all he'd ever imagined.

He dozed. He'd spent the night shivering beneath the ledge over Walnut Creek, dreaming of Cedrick's toasty shack. He arose to a crystalline world; ice-covered grass and trees, limbs and trunks sheared by the burden. He made it home early afternoon, and built a roaring fire and climbed beneath his stack of quilts. He'd shivered while the burning oak warmed the single ten-by-twelve room. He was glad for the smallness, for it warmed quickly.

The idea of slavery vexed him. He had no idea how much a Negro might cost. Then, after you'd paid hard-earned money, what would you do if he didn't want to stay? If Cedrick said he'd had enough and wanted to go his own way, what would you do? Shoot a friend you'd worked side by side with in the fields? Run him down and whip him? What if he decided he wouldn't be whipped? And how pleasant would it be to live and work with a person who hated you? It might be a little awkward saying good morning to a man you'd tied up and whipped the day before. He might have to do without slaves. Maybe Jonas would marry Esther and settle nearby; then he and Jonas could swap work.

Sis whined and sniffed outside the door. She trotted up from the home place every afternoon to spend the night. Sunup, she'd sniff her way back down the creek to spend the morning with the other hounds. He crawled reluctantly from beneath the quilts and walked barefooted across the cold puncheon floor and opened the door. Sis barreled into the room, tail whipping, and reared up on him with wet paws. "Get on now," he said. He swiped at the muddy paw prints on his nightshirt and crawled back into bed. The big hound sniffed every corner, checked beneath the table for crumbs, licked Isaac's nose, then settled in under the bed for a good scratching.

The wind rattled the window latch and blew ice shards from the trees into the side of the cabin. Isaac burrowed deeper into the quilts, sank further into the feather tick. The oak coals warmed his face. Sis sighed. He imagined her curled into a tight ball, tail wrapped across her nose. Before long, he'd rise and walk down the path to supper. Chicken or venison. Maybe baked coon.

Cyrus had penned a fat possum in the corncrib the week prior, planning to clean him out with a diet of corn and table scraps. He forgot to tell Esther, who opened the crib and danced a jig as the terrified beast tried to run up her skirt. The possum escaped into the woods. Esther recovered in time. Cyrus still suffered for his carelessness. Isaac had been looking forward to nice, greasy possum and cornbread, but he consoled himself with the thought that as soon as the weather broke, King would show up with a mess of squirrels.

He imagined the smell of Catherine's hair and skin. *I can stand it long as I know you're comin' back.* Of course he'd go back. But why? To sneak down the hill and carry her across the creek for a few throat-aching promises?

She could not betray her father and be the girl he now loved. Surely she was thinking similar thoughts. Weighing the prospects. How long before some acceptable suitor broke through her resolve? A woman had to be practical on the Texas frontier. Thomas Adair wouldn't be around forever.

He could apologize. Cyrus and Smithwick would understand and let it go. But Cyrus had insulted Adair in front of family and friends; any apology would have to come from him, and Isaac knew very well that Cyrus Webb would not apologize unless he believed he was wrong and maybe not even then. And he had not been wrong. Adair had come looking for an argument, and Cyrus put up with more than usual purely for Catherine's sake.

And Smithwick believed in the Comanche emissary effort. Most of the settlers along the Colorado supported it. Free from fear of marauding Indians, most of the farmers in the outlying areas had planted and harvested their first good crop in several years.

But the Thorpe and Mann women were still out there somewhere on the plains northwest of the scarp. That was more than Adair and others could abide. Why could he—Isaac—abide it? Only because they hadn't taken Catherine or his own family members or neighbors.

He'd seen firsthand what bitter enemies would do to each other. The Thorpe and Mann bodies were hacked no worse than those of the Mexicans on the Plain of Saint Hyacinth. What the Texians saw as thievery and savagery, the Comanches saw as warfare. And it was. His own ranging company had attacked sleeping Comanches to annihilate them. They would have shot them all in their blankets. They made no plans to check for women or children.

A truce would end the bloodshed. Then, perhaps the Indians would surrender their white captives. How much use would the Texians ever have for the dry plains west of the escarpment? The Comanches could have them and the buffalo too. How could he build a life chasing raiders for twenty-five dollars a month? What good were 1280 acres if he had no time to work them?

Sis banged her noggin scrambling from beneath the bed to the door where she sniffed and whined, perked her ears, furrowed her long brow, and cocked her head, listening.

Isaac stayed in bed. She probably heard and smelled Cyrus or Esther. She'd growl and rattle the roof at the whiff of a stranger. "I swear, Sis, I need to show you how to work the door catch. Now I'm gonna have to get up again and walk on this cold floor."

Slow hoofbeats on the trail. Noah Smithwick yelled, "Anybody home?"

Sis whined. Scratched the door. Isaac smiled. "Go home, goddamnit. I ain't gettin' out of this warm bed."

"Your mama sent me up here to fetch you for supper."

"You're lyin'. If supper was ready, you'd be down there eatin' it and winkin' at Esther."

Creaking saddle and footsteps. "Why, the Widow has already laid claim to me. It'll take more than a pretty little blond-headed thing to distract a virtuous man like me." Scraping sounds. Probably the horse pawing through the ice to get at a tuft of grass. "And I've come all the way out here to see about you and you won't even come out from under the quilts."

A slush ball came down the chimney and hit coals with a hiss. Smoke and steam filled the room. Sis barked and shook her head. Isaac rolled out of bed and felt for his pants laid across the back of the chair. His eyes and throat burned. He gave up, flung open the door, and ran barefooted into the icy yard.

Smithwick stood innocently holding his horse's rein. Sis bounded up and put her paw on his chest. He scratched her ears. "I swear, Isaac, I'm not in that big a hurry. You should've put your boots on first."

Smoke billowed out the cabin door. Isaac laughed and scooped a handful of slush.

The Captain looked at the chimney. "Probably gathered around the rim and finally melted loose and fell in your fire. I swear."

Isaac packed the ice into a ball, threw it a foot wide of Smithwick, and hit the horse's shoulder. The animal grunted and rolled its eyes.

Smithwick shook his head. "Has a spot of bad luck and takes it out on a man's horse."

Isaac's hands and feet ached from the cold. "Damn you!" He ran back to the porch. It was always good to see Noah Smithwick. The cabin had about cleared. Sis beat him through the door and jumped on the bed. He propped open the front window. "Hitch your horse and get in here."

There were still plenty of hot coals. He stirred and repacked them with his spade and dipped a coffeepot full of water from the pail he kept near the fire. He shoveled aside a small pile of coals and set the pot on it. "Why would anybody ride all the way up here from Bastrop on a day like today? Ain't you got some smithing you ought to be doin'?" He shoved Smithwick into the single chair and took a seat on the bed. "Not that I ain't glad to see you. Goddamn you." He thrust his bare feet toward the fire.

Smithwick bent to warm his hands over the coals. "You know me. I can't sit still with a piece of business hanging over my head."

"What business other than horseshoes and guns and knives would a smith have in the middle of winter?"

"Presidential business, to be exact."

"I reckon Sam Houston has sent for me. Let me get my breeches on." The Captain loved to blow.

Smithwick shut the window and unbuttoned his heavy wool coat. "Word came from Sawyer through Andrews. Houston has taken a keen interest in our treaty work. He wants an emissary available at all times to soothe the Comanches."

"He's got one, ain't he?"

"For now."

"For now? Where you goin'? Sounds like a plum job to me."

"You ever tasted raw buffalo gut?"

Isaac banished the thought. Too close to supper. "Why, you'll soon have the President's ear."

"That's right. Just like I did during the war. He tells somebody who tells somebody who tells somebody who tells me what to do."

Isaac nodded. "Just a few limbs from the top."

"Ain't nobody in Texas far from the top."

Isaac took a rag from the hearth, lifted the lid off the pot, dumped five handfuls of coffee into the boiling water, then moved the pot just off the coals. "You didn't come all the way out here in this ice to talk about rank."

"No." He looked at the pot. "Thurza won't wait on me forever. I told her I'd put in another year. She didn't like it but said she'd abide it."

Isaac knew where the conversation was headed and didn't like it. Hadn't the Captain heard the argument two nights ago?

Smithwick said, "I've done my part. Somebody else has to step up. I ain't gettin' any younger, you know."

"Well." He'd let Smithwick say his piece. No sense walking into a trap. He banged the coffeepot on the floor to settle the grounds. Dumped in half a cup of cold water, banged again, and set the pot near the coals. "About ready."

Smithwick nodded. "And I'm about ready to drink it." He turned his hat in his hands. "I've been thinking you might take over for me."

Isaac rubbed his beard. "Let me see now; I've probably lost my girl for stickin' up for this treaty, and now you want me to buddy up to the heathens who carried off Catherine's neighbors. That'll go over big with old man Adair."

"Oh, so we're settin' all our plans toward pleasin' him. No matter that the Scripture-spewing slaver wouldn't know his ass from a posthole."

"I'm settin' my plans on marryin' Catherine, and I can't do it if her daddy won't let me on his place."

"Marrying that girl. Hell, Isaac, you ain't but eighteen."

"She ain't but twenty and she's already been married."

Smithwick waved off the comment. "It's different with girls."

Isaac poured a cup of coffee and handed it to his friend. "Not everybody wants to wait 'til he's a decrepit old shit like you before he takes a gal."

The Captain nodded his thanks; took a sip. "I prefer to think of myself as measured and particular. A man of discrimination."

"Yep. Slow."

"You were a lot less tiresome as a timid boy."

Isaac leaned back against the wall. "That was before I got to know you." He sipped his coffee. "You know, a man had best get while he can. There ain't many pretty women around Bastrop that ain't already spoken for. And I don't expect a big shipload to come sailing into Galveston anytime soon."

"Can't argue. But if you can't work this out, what makes you want to join her family and put up with her daddy the rest of his life?"

"She'll have to put up with Pap."

"Cyrus ain't priggish; he's just crotchety. Anyway, what makes you think she's half as smitten with you as you are with her?"

Isaac looked at him. Surely he'd catch on without an explanation.

Smithwick said, "Oh." He smiled and swirled his coffee.

They sat in silence. Sis laid her head in Isaac's lap. Smithwick said, "Don't forget about that little visit the Comanches paid to the Adair place."

Isaac stroked his hound's ears. "That's why I'm for the treaty." Smithwick was shifty and persistent, but his ploy wouldn't work. He—Isaac—didn't need another problem.

"What if we ain't got a treaty by the time I quit parleying with the Comanches and marry the Widow? Right now, Houston's balking at the idea of a boundary."

"There's better men than me in your company. What's wrong with Felix or Ezra? Hell, or Jo or Nicholas?"

Smithwick bent to scratch Sis's muzzle. The dog thumped her tail against the quilts. "Nothing. All good men. But their Spanish is shaky."

"So is mine. And they ain't tryin' to patch things up with a prospective father-in-law."

"Isaac, the man that goes into that Comanche camp can't make a mistake."

"Now that makes me want the job. When can I sign on?"

"The men you named might be as good as you—they're all good boys—but I can't say for sure."

"Then why'd you pick Jo and Nicholas to scout ahead with you that morning on the bluff?"

Smithwick smiled. "The boy never forgets a slight." He leaned back in his chair. "Surely you don't think I made that choice lightly."

Isaac shrugged. The returning hurt surprised him.

Smithwick said, "I never doubted the fight in you, but you'd never engaged Comanches. Now you have and you outfought every man in the company including me."

"Plenty of fighters in these parts." How could nearly getting your throat cut by a Comanche boy be seen as outfighting everyone else in the company?

"But it's not the fight in you that brings me here; it's the way you fight. You don't hate your enemy. I got men in my company signed on to kill Comanches or earn two sections or twenty-five dollars a month in worthless currency. You signed on to defend your home."

"I signed on because you talked me into it." And because Ruth finally let him.

"You're the only one in the company I had to convince."

"You've got a harder job of convincing this time."

"You're the best choice, Isaac. You grew up among the Choctaw in the Ouachitas. You don't hate Indians just for bein' Indians."

"The Choctaw ain't Comanches." He'd never seen a Choctaw piss from horseback.

"Somebody has to do it."

"Well. Captain, you know how much I think of you, but I'm not sure I want to be breakin' bread with Comanches, much less sleepin' on the same thousand square miles."

Smithwick laughed. "You'll wish it *was* bread you're breaking."

Isaac found the remark presumptuous. "I ain't gonna be wishin' anything of the sort."

Smithwick studied his face. Smiled. "There's a young buck keeps askin' about Isikweb."

Isaac's throat tightened. The Captain knew no shame. "Same one that like to have got my hair, I imagine. How'd the little bastard learn my name?"

"Me and you will do it together for a year until you get the hang of it. I've already told the old chiefs. They're expecting us this spring. They didn't like it at first, but I told them you're like a brother."

Isaac shook his head. "I'd say you're in pickle. What're you gonna tell 'em now?"

"Look at the good you'd be doing."

"I'd do it save for Catherine."

"We don't have to decide until spring. A lot can happen between now and then."

"I sure as hell hope not."

"I didn't mean it like that."

"You'll talk to some of the other boys?"

"Why sure."

Isaac snorted. A lie if he'd ever heard one. For once he wished Noah Smithwick would leave him to his guilt and heartache. Just two hours ago he couldn't see how things could've been worse. "Captain, I need to just be honest here. I just can't . . ."

"Looks Far is the boy's name."

"Huh?"

"The buck that keeps asking about you. He's quite a fellow. Already has two wives. He might be twenty, but I doubt it. Must be a real fighter."

"You ain't makin' me want to know him."

"You two have already made each other's acquaintance. Whether you know him as a friend or an enemy is up to you. If it was me, I'd choose to be his friend."

"Why is it just up to me?"

Smithwick sighed. Stared into his hat.

"What?"

"I've been trying to decide how to tell you this." He twirled his hat on his finger. "Well then." He paused, laid his hat on his knee. "This past fall as I was about to leave his camp after my last visit of the year, Looks Far asked me a bothersome question."

"What?"

"He asked if the comely brown-haired girl was your wife."

"Shit. Why would he ask that?"

"He said he saw you with her one night last spring. He and a few boys were there after horses. Said they would've made off with them, too, if it wasn't for that big, mean Tonkawa skulking around the place."

Thirty

CATHERINE LOOKED desperate. "Why you? It'll look like you're trying to goad him."

Isaac glanced beyond her, down the hill at the house. No movement. Thomas Adair wouldn't be back from Bastrop until after dark, and Louise Adair was busy darning. The earth smelled of spring thaw, though it was still January. A balmy breeze and a noisy flock of robins just up the hill, gorging on rotten hackberries, made whispering impractical. "I told you. The Captain don't believe you're safe unless we get this treaty worked out."

"Felix or Ezra would do just fine. Or Captain Smithwick can keep the job. He's done pretty good so far."

"The Widow's out of patience. He's got 'til the end of the year to work somebody else in."

"I suppose Widow Duty is more woman than I am."

"You know better than that. She's put up with it for half a year already."

"Why should a woman have to put up with her man living with savages? Whoever heard of such a thing?"

He wanted to tell her about the young warrior's comment to Smithwick but couldn't bear the thought of her living in terror. "Catherine, I swear; I'm doin' this for you. Trust me."

"For me. Like Noah Smithwick is doing for the Widow. If Daddy gets wind of this, he won't ever let you come around."

"I'd take my chances with your daddy before I'd risk losin' what there is to come around to."

Catherine turned and looked down the hill. Isaac suspected that Mrs. Adair knew what her daughter was up to.

Catherine said, "You still ain't answered me. Why you?"

"The Captain says I'm the best man for the job."

"Well, there it is."

"There what is?" All those years around Esther hadn't prepared him to argue with a woman. Little wonder his irascible father rarely crossed Ruth.

"You're flattered that he wants *you* to do it." She jabbed her finger at him. "Tell him no."

"I did."

"Then what're we arguing about?"

"He kept after me. Made me see some sense in it."

"So every time he wants you to go off and do something, you'll go no matter what I think about it." She crossed her arms and shook her head as if he were the most pathetic sight in the world.

"Goddamnit, Catherine. I'm tellin' you they'll be back if we don't come to an agreement. They know you're here."

"Don't you swear at me, Isaac Webb."

Cedrick peeped around the corner of the barn. Catherine waved him away. "If you know that, then do something," she said. "You know where they're at. I thought that's what you men are supposed to do."

"The Captain promised we'd leave them alone if they'd leave us alone . . . as long as we're palavering about a boundary."

"What makes you think you can reason with these people? If they were whipped like the other Indians, we wouldn't have to worry anymore."

"Whipped. I reckon we'll just ride in there and go to shootin'." He realized he was wagging his head like Cyrus. "Lose half our company and won't get more than two or three Comanches. Is that what you want? Think on it. Felix, Ezra, the Captain?" He thumbed his chest. "Hell, me." Catherine had been listening to her father.

For the first time she looked uncertain. "Of course not. But Daddy says they could be wiped out like the Kronks."

"Oh. Ride in there and shoot the women and younguns too. In a year's time there wouldn't be a farm left between here and the coast."

"Surely you men can outsmart Indians."

Isaac nodded slowly, surprised by his disgust. "What do you think went with all the Kronk women and little ones? Outsmarted, were they?"

The color left her face. "I won't hear of it. He made the settlements safe from those killers. And he's a veteran."

"I won't say he didn't." He'd stepped into dangerous territory; he'd never followed this line of reasoning before.

"Then don't you accuse him of things you don't know about." She wiped the corner of an eye.

A lump formed in his throat. A woman crying. "I never meant nothin' by it. It's just . . ." He looked away, along the ridge lit by the late afternoon sun. "You know I think a lot of King. I know his wives and younguns. I've taken meals with them."

"You meant what you said."

"I was just mad." The lie disgusted him.

She sniffled and looked at him with resignation. "Is that how it would be? Tonkawas comin' around all the time?"

"Huh?" He knew very well what she meant.

"You're a good man, Isaac. But we're different. Raised different. Expect different."

The path was clear. He shook his head; ignored his tears. "Well hell. I should've been expectin' this."

She daubed her eyes with her sleeve. "This ain't what I wanted." She looked at him through new tears. "This is how it would always be, though. Our families could never get along. It'd make us bitter."

"You think he's right, your daddy?"

"We've never been able to live side by side with Indians."

"That's what your daddy tells you?"

"That's what common sense tells me."

"And what does your common sense tell you about me?"

"Isaac, it ain't your fault."

"I know. Blood runs thick among us ignorant hill people. Poor old boy can't help hisself." He checked the sun. "Your mama'll be missin' you. And I'd best be gettin' back to my corn squeezings."

"Don't be that way."

"Let me help you across the creek."

Her expression hardened. "I'll wade." She turned and walked down the hill. He slammed the butt of his rifle into the soft hillside. Thomas Adair had gotten to her. She reached the bottom of the hill. He didn't care who heard him now. Let old man Adair ride up. He yelled, "If anybody but your daddy would've talked to Pap that way, I'd have stomped a hole in him."

She hesitated for an instant, then waded the creek.

III
COMANCHERÍA

Thirty-One

March 26, 1838

ISAAC CINCHED down the bundle on the packhorse he'd borrowed from Jonas McElroy's family. The huge dun, named Thud, stood calmly and sniffed the back of Isaac's head as he worked.

Cyrus watched, arms folded on his chest. "No changin' your mind, now, I reckon."

Isaac checked his knots. "I need to do this."

"Don't be mad at Mother. She'd see you off if she thought she could stand it."

"You think she meant what she said?"

"About not lettin' Smithwick back on the place? Nah. She thinks too much of him. She's just scared. And your sister would be here if it wasn't for Mother."

Ruth had been adamant that King should accompany Isaac until Cyrus pointed out that the Tonkawa had likely killed and eaten a few of the band's warriors and might not be well received. Esther, on the other hand, seemed fascinated by the prospect of Isaac living with Comanches and urged him to bring back as many tokens of his visit as he could carry.

Cyrus said, "No tellin' when you'll get a crop in. I hate to see the place go to hell after we've cleared these little plots."

Isaac scratched Thud's ears. "I'll let you borrow the place. Go ahead and sow it and keep it clean. That way you'll have somewhere to come every week when Mama throws a fit and runs you out of the house."

Cyrus eyed the cabin. "Hell, I might not wait to get run out. That sister of yours is gettin' worse than Mother."

"She got right upset about that snake," Isaac said. Cyrus had been prying loose rocks for his new springhouse when he discovered a den of hibernating blacksnakes. He disentangled one of the longer ones—a six-footer, according to Cyrus; a twenty-footer according to Esther. He carried the cold, stiff reptile home and tossed it on the ground behind the cabin, planning to show it to Isaac just before supper, then went about his chores. That afternoon turned unusually warm for March; Cyrus forgot about the snake. Next morning, Esther woke to find the fire-warmed serpent coiled around one of her bedposts.

"Whoever heard of a girl pitchin' such a fit over a blacksnake?" Cyrus said. "Of course, it came right on the heels of that possum."

Isaac smiled at the thought of Esther bludgeoning both snake and bedpost with the poker. "I'll miss y'all."

"I swear," Cyrus said. "I hope to God Smithwick knows what he's doin'."

"I'd say he does. Folks are gettin' used to workin' without worrin' about losin' their hair." He tightened Squab's girth, then went over his list: bedroll, flint and steel, coffee, cornmeal, rifle, extra powder, patches, and ball.

He looked up at slate gray March sky. "Smells like rain." He extended a hand to his father.

Cyrus squeezed it. "Be lookin' for you in about a month. I suppose you'll come straight home now that that gal ain't got you by the ear."

Isaac swung into the saddle. Cyrus's shoulders looked more stooped than he remembered; his buckskins a little baggier; neck cords showing. Isaac's throat stuck. He nodded.

Cyrus waved him away. "Get on, hell, before you get rained on." He handed Isaac the packhorse lead.

Isaac started down the creek bottom toward the river. A quarter mile along, he rode up a slight rise and looked back at his cabin. Cyrus was standing where he'd left him.

He kept to low ground as much as possible. Whenever fallen trees or the terrain forced him into the hills, the wind numbed his face and worsened his dread.

He'd last seen Catherine that afternoon in mid-January. She rarely left his thoughts. He imagined her in pain as sharp as his own; imagined her resenting her father and cursing herself for her words on the hill that day. Abed, alone with the dim glow of oak coals, he pictured her restless under her blankets.

He heard the river, turned Squab up a game trail, and rode up to a bench overlooking the confluence. The Colorado ran fast and menacing, high and green, with whirlpools, eddies, and braided currents.

He sat his horse and hoped that Catherine was worried about him. Had her anger and hurt subsided so that she could now see his sacrifice? How many white men had ever ridden into a Comanche camp? What if he unknowingly offended his hosts? Would they kill over some minor breach of manners?

Fortunately Smithwick would be in camp for several months yet. And he'd get a month's leave come May. He could make it a month—if he dared sleep. He tried to imagine closing his eyes his first night in camp.

He planned to rendezvous with Smithwick next morning at Coleman's Fort. They'd ride from there up to the Comanche camp on Brushy Creek. The Captain seemed confident the Comanches would be there after their winter buffalo hunting. Isaac hoped they'd found the living so good on the plains that they'd decided to stay. What if they'd changed their mind about the treaty and white men in general?

He rode upriver toward the fort. The air felt heavier, wetter. He'd have to hurry to reach the big limestone overhang before the rain began. And it would be a cold rain.

The sullen weather seemed to agree with Squab. His hair stood on end, and he held a lively gate and snorted and pricked his ears in challenge to whatever he scented on the wind. The packhorse barely kept pace and at times had to be urged on.

An hour before sundown, he rode west into the mouth of a broad creek bottom. A half mile further on, Squab picked his way up a narrow game trail through sycamore and water oak. The path steepened, and Isaac felt he might tumble off the back of the saddle. The great outcropping loomed overhead. The little gelding loped up the last, nearly vertical twenty feet onto the bench beneath the overhang. Much to Isaac's relief, Thud followed with aplomb, his great hooves trenching along the way.

Isaac picketed the horses out of the wind, well back of the edge of the giant slab, removed their saddles, and checked for rubs. Old Thud nickered and nuzzled Isaac and seemed pleased to be out of the weather. Squab stamped restlessly and lifted his nose toward the creek. Satisfied with the horses' conditions, Isaac gathered three armloads of dry oak and cedar and rebuilt an old fire ring near the center of the bench. The remains of several much smaller fires were scattered about.

He shaved tinder off a cedar branch, fired a knot of dried grass with his flint and steel, and set the shavings ablaze. He added progressively larger sticks; coals began to form. He scrambled down the bank and dipped a pot of water from the creek. Just after dark he lay back against his saddle, supped on coffee, jerked venison dipped in honey, and cold cornbread. The coffee warmed his insides; the fire warmed his face and hands.

The wind gusted and the first fat raindrops spattered on dry leaves just beyond the ledge. He ate the last of his jerky and cornbread and threw his blanket over his legs. The flames danced and gusts brought damp, chill air to his nostrils. Little worry of Indians tonight. They'd be snug in their lodges. He laid another cedar knot on the fire.

He looked forward to seeing Felix, Ezra, and the boys. Too bad he wouldn't have a few days at the fort before riding on to the Comanche encampment. His anticipation surprised him. He'd kept so busy the past several months, making and planning for a life befitting Catherine, he'd forgotten his friends and their shared history.

Was he cut out to be a farmer? His father farmed just well enough to provide for his family but hated the drudgery. Whereas prosperous farmers kept hogs and chickens and beeves, Cyrus and Isaac shot or trapped nearly all of the family meat. Their few bedraggled chickens roosted in the trees, too wild to be caught by foxes or bobcats, Esther or Ruth. Cyrus wouldn't waste a load of ball and powder on one, although he shot and ate the rooster that flogged his hounds. Blood ran thick.

The rain fell in sheets now. The fire lighted the drops against the blackness.

Isaac rose and checked the horses, then scraped together a mattress of dried duff. He checked his rifle, wiped and blew on the serpentine and frizzen, then crawled beneath his blankets and lay his head on his saddle. He looked up at the smoke-blackened underside of the ledge. Men had lain here watching smoke rise against rock long before whites moved into this country; had lain warm and dry beneath buffalo robes, content to be out of the weather. What did they dream and what would they think of him lying here now?

He woke shivering after midnight. The wind whipped the branches of the trees. Water dripped from the ledge and branches so that he had to listen carefully to be sure the rain had ceased. He reached from beneath his blankets and laid another cedar knot and a handful of sticks on the coals. The wood caught, and the fire blazed anew. He added larger sticks and luxuriated in the warmth.

• • •

He had Squab saddled and Thud loaded before dawn. The clouds had cleared during the wee hours; sunrise had yet to wash out the firmament. He stamped his feet and blew through his hands until it was light enough to see, then mounted and started Squab down the trail. The eager little mustang nimbly picked his way down the hill. Steam rose from his nostrils. Isaac let go of Thud's lead and hoped for the best. He looked back when Squab made level ground; the big packhorse followed, sliding, lurching, and plowing through the underbrush. He looked wild eyed and ready for Isaac to take the lead when he reached the bottom.

He rode north, back to the confluence with the swollen Colorado, then headed northwest above the river. The country grew hillier, which seemed to suit Squab. Some of the bottomland trees had already budded; the warming air smelled damp, clean, and fecund, and redwing blackbirds swarmed in the streamside brush.

Midmorning, he stopped at a ford to water the horses and fill his gourd. He'd make the fort by early afternoon. The river hissed and gurgled. The bottom seemed to hold the night's brittle cold air, yet mayflies hovered over the dancing currents. He breathed deeply, drank from his gourd.

A rifle shot silenced the birds. Isaac froze; the echo faded into the river's voice. About a half mile upriver, in the hills. He held his breath, listening. He heard only his pulse, and the tentative *peter, peter* of a titmouse, and the purling current. Then two shots in quick succession. He mounted and rode upriver at a gallop. What Indians would be shooting guns? Comanches usually carried only bows and lances. Surely the Tonks or Lipans wouldn't attack his fellow rangers. But would they jump one another? Or perhaps they'd ambush a lone white man they didn't know. Yet he doubted the Tonks would venture this close to Comanche country unless they'd been hired by the ranging company.

Sporadic gunfire continued. It sounded measured, as if the combatants had taken cover and were aiming carefully. At some point, he'd have to tether the horses and slip up on foot. What would he do about one breed of savage fighting another? Perhaps he should simply withdraw and mind his own affairs. The skirmish was out of earshot of the fort.

He heard shouting, but he couldn't determine the tongue. It could have been English or Spanish or Comanche. He found a sheltered draw and picketed the horses. Some of the gunfire seemed to come from the hills above; some from near the river. He ran up the hill, keeping low and holding to the draws and lower contours, thankful for the dense cedar. He was close now. He could hear the cocking of rifles and movement in the brush above. He dropped to his belly and slithered through the cedar. He saw moccasins thirty feet ahead and heard excited banter and what had to be cursing.

He snaked forward and peered beneath the drooping branches. Four men crouched, firing over a jumble of boulders at some unseen enemy along the river. One of the men turned to reload his musket. Raccoon eyes. Slits tattooed from the corners of his mouth. Wacos, probably. But who would they be shooting at?

He could kill any one of them from this distance. But then what? He'd escape through the cedar to the horses in the ensuing confusion. The gunfire from the river had ceased. Maybe the shooters there had died or fled. Perhaps he should just ease back to the horses now.

One of the Wacos fired again. Someone shouted from the river. Isaac could not discern the words or tongue. The Wacos laughed. What if one of the rangers was under fire? Isaac raised his rifle, rested his elbows on the ground, eased the serpentine back, and laid the front sight on the temple of the nearest man, who seemed to be searching for a target. Isaac drew in a ragged breath. Squeezed the trigger. The Waco watched the river. The rifle bucked against Isaac's shoulder, but he didn't hear the blast or wait to see the result. He knew where the ball went. The Wacos shrieked. He ran low, searching for any path through the cedars. Branches whipped his face. He grabbed his hat and ran with it. No time to reload. The horses should be down and to the right, toward the river. Two shots from behind. The balls cut the brush well to his left. He angled down the hill toward the horses.

Someone was running through the brush to his right. He stopped to listen. The rustling continued on. Someone on his left too. And above him. They were trying to trap him. He knelt to recharge his rifle. The rustling behind him ceased. He seated the charge, rammed home a ball, then listened. Nothing. He eased down the hill. A whisper of movement behind and to the right, then a slight rustle in the damp leaves. A squirrel? He tried to listen over his pulse banging in his ears. His rifle would be of little use in the heavy cover. For once he would have preferred a musket. Or a pistol. He winced; it might come down to blades.

Sweat dripped from the end of his nose. He eased forward a few steps, stopped and listened. The horses nickered below. The Wacos might just wait in ambush near the horses. If he moved, he exposed himself. How long would they wait in ambush? If he remained in hiding, could they slip up on him? He gathered himself, then eased to his belly and inched forward, alert for any movement, a moccasin, dangling breechclout, or dark braid or shin, anything out of place beneath the boughs.

He heard nothing but the light breeze in the trees and chittering birds and the river below. He slithered ahead. The horses were directly below now. He peered into the draw, cringing at exposing his head. The horses raised their noses and snorted. He eased back into the thicket and waited.

The shadows in the bottom crawled imperceptibly eastward until the sun shone directly overhead. The boys at the fort would be missing him soon. Maybe he could hold out until they came looking for him. But then they might wait a day or more. He drank from his gourd and tried to remain alert. He rested his chin on his fist and scanned the ground ahead. Lying prone left him vulnerable to ambush from behind, but he dared not sit up where branches would obscure his view.

He stopped in midbreath; just a hint of movement—shadow—through the bows of a cedar, to his right and below, near the edge of the draw. He could see the darkness, the bulk. He cocked his rifle. The shadow moved. He heard thrashing, then nothing.

He waited half an hour, then crawled down the hill. The horses were just over the edge of the draw. He eased to a crouch, slowly stood, and took a step forward. He stopped at the edge of a small, sunlit clearing. On the far edge, almost as well camouflaged as a downed quail, lay a Waco warrior, his neck torn open. Isaac fought the urge to stride across the clearing. He stepped back into the shadows. The sun was dropping toward the western horizon now, and it seemed even later in the long shadows. The cedar boughs shook and a man loomed before him. No time to fire. He grabbed his blade and thrust upward toward his attacker's chest; he smelled sweat and wood smoke. A brown forearm and pistol butt swung into view. He saw a red flash, and the cedar tops flew away from him as if he were pulled into a dark hole, and then the hole closed over him.

• • •

He opened his eyes just before dusk. His stomach rolled. He dared not move his head. He felt dry leaves and damp ground at his sides. He licked his cracked lips. The treetops swayed in the wind. The river murmured beyond his head. He smelled smoke and heard the popping of a small fire. He remembered the Wacos firing from the boulders. A face appeared over his, but he could not make out its features in the twilight. Trying to focus worsened his nausea. The head seemed lopsided. He smelled the familiar sweat, wood smoke, and tobacco.

"*Buenos días*, Isaac."

Of course. The head wasn't lopsided—just shaved on one side. Thick braid on the other. "Castro. Goddamn."

"You sound like a cricket. I didn't hit you in the throat." Castro spoke Spanish better than anyone else in the company.

"You like to have knocked my brains out. What in hell do you mean sneaking up on me like that?"

"I'm sorry, Isaac. I thought you were a Waco. And you were about to cut me with your knife. I'm glad you came along though."

Isaac touched his temple. "Sweet Jesus."

"I was riding to the fort when those Wacos started shooting at me. This used to be good country, but now there's a Waco everywhere you look. The Comanches chased them down here."

"That was you shooting from the river?"

"Yes. I had to shoot my pistol. I gambled my rifle away to that Tonkawa. I hope he comes back to the fort. I need my rifle." He squatted on the balls of his feet, staring closely at Isaac's eyes.

"What are you looking at?"

"Your eyes. I hit you a good lick, but your eyes look fine. I'm glad. Andrews would want to hang me if I broke your head."

Isaac's nausea subsided. He felt behind his head. Castro had made a pillow of several blankets. "Did those two Wacos run off?"

Castro slapped his thighs. "No." He nodded toward his gear stacked neatly by the little campfire. "Their scalps are drying over there."

"I never heard you shoot."

"They were looking so hard for you, they forgot about me."

"So that one I saw laying in the clearing wasn't shot."

"No. Sometimes a knife is what is needed." He smiled and patted Isaac's shoulder. "I took the scalp of the one you shot and hung it from your rifle barrel. I had to hunt for the top of his head. You made a fine shot."

"Damn."

"You were not aiming for his head?"

"I was."

"It was a good shot then." He rocked on the balls of his feet. "You can give the scalp to your wife to hang for your guests and children to see."

Isaac laughed in spite of the pain he knew it would cause. "*Gracias*. But I don't have a wife yet, Castro."

The Lipan furrowed his brow. "A warrior needs a wife. Several if he can take care of them."

"I had my eye on one, but her father hates me."

"Perhaps you need to offer more horses." He scratched his head. "You should have spoken of your need when we took those horses from the Comanches."

Castro's concern touched Isaac. "I'm afraid it would take all the horses in the world."

Castro stood and nodded gravely. "Some men are unreasonable. But there are other women and you're strong." He thought for a moment. "You nearly killed me."

"I'm glad I didn't."

"Yes."

Isaac sniffed the air. His mouth watered in spite of his throbbing head. "What are you cooking? Smells like fish."

Castro slapped his bare belly with both hands. "I went to the river and dug some frogs out of the mud. They're almost done."

Thirty-Two

FELIX STEPPED OUT of the barrack as Castro and Isaac rode into the fort. "I want you to look, Ezree. Two birds of a feather."

Isaac eased out of the saddle. His head throbbed. He raised his rifle barrel to show the dangling scalp. "Somebody in this company has to work." He wondered when he'd become so glib about killing. Maybe Castro and King were rubbing off on him.

The Lipan dismounted, and held up his battle ax. The three fresh scalps dangled from the butt. Men gathered. Castro swept his trophies grandly before his audience.

Tom Crosby said, "You and Noah won't be goin' to no Comanche camp now, will you Isaac?"

Isaac expected the question. Everyone assumed that the Comanches were the only hostile Indians in the area. "Wacos. They tried to jump Castro. Naturally, I had to show up and get right in the middle it."

Ezra leaned against the door frame. "Looks to me like the old killer didn't need any help."

Castro slipped his trophies in his saddlebag and sauntered over to the cook fire.

Uncle Jimmy peered around Ezra. He pushed the big man aside and stepped outside. "I swear, that boy blocks the sky."

Ezra laid a hand on the old man's back. "Beg your pardon, Uncle Jimmy."

Jimmy eyed the dangling scalp. "I knowed it. I told the Captain you'd run into trouble."

Smithwick came out of Andrews's quarters and pared his way through the rangers. "You're late. We were about to come looking for you."

"It's good to know you're cared about," Isaac said. "Let me swallow this lump in my throat."

Uncle Jimmy elbowed Felix's ribs. "Boy's salty for his age, ain't he?"

Early afternoon, Isaac and Smithwick, each leading a packhorse, rode out of the fort and down the trail to the river. The other rangers said little. Some waved. A few wished them good luck. All looked solemn. Once again, Isaac felt pulled along by some irresistible force, like Andy Dunn's raft on the Brazos. He'd felt that way the entire journey from Bastrop to Saint Hyacinth.

Smithwick rambled on about the surrounding country, Widow Duty's overbaked cornbread, honeybees, chiggers, and the foibles of the various Comanche chiefs. "Old Quinaseico, he's a dandy, now. Loves to hear himself carry on. Primps like a madam. You ought to see him."

"I'm afraid I will." Isaac didn't feel like talking, but he hated to ruin the Captain's fine spirits. "What kind of name is that?"

"Means eagle, I believe."

"Whoever heard of namin' somebody after a bird?"

"What's got you in such a sorry disposition? Still worryin' about that gal?"

"I'd about forgot about her. Until now."

Smithwick said, "Why, you might find one of these Comanche belles to your liking."

The thought stirred Isaac. It had never occurred to him that there were Comanche women. He'd always imagined a camp full of painted warriors. "A Comanche girl. End up gettin' my throat cut if I pay attention to you." He tried to picture a savage version of Catherine.

Smithwick said, "A man ridin' into Comanche country ought not have to put up with such surly company."

"A man about to get his balls cut off ought not have to listen to talk about Comanche women."

They rode north, away from the river and into the hills. Isaac said, "What do they look like?"

"Who?"

"Goddamnit now."

Smithwick looked at him innocently. "You mean Comanche women?"

"Hell no, I mean Mexican cattle." Noah Smithwick was enjoying all this entirely too much.

Smithwick laughed. "All at least a head taller than the tallest buck. And they walk around with big knives they use to skin and butcher buffaloes. And lusty."

"I ought to know better than to ask a straight question." He tried to imagine a young, brown woman six feet tall. Instead, he saw a slender brown hand gripping a butcher knife. "You laid with one?"

"Why, Isaac, a gentleman doesn't discuss his forays."

"That's what I thought. You never got within fifty feet of a Comanche gal. Afraid you'd lose your hair."

Smithwick laughed. "I hope you're a little more pleasant toward our hosts than you are toward me."

Isaac said, "You'd be cross too, if you'd just had your brains knocked out by a Lipan chief."

They camped amid the trees along a tiny creek. The night was clear and cold. After a supper of cornbread and jerked venison, they sat before a small fire, blankets wrapped about their shoulders, and sipped coffee. Isaac's head felt much better. Even in the cold air, he smelled the new spring growth.

"You really feel safe livin' with 'em?" Isaac asked.

Smithwick sipped, nodded. "They won't feel threatened by just two men. But we'd best not be talking too much among ourselves unless it's in Spanish and they can hear us."

"Well." He wondered if the Comanches would be watching him constantly. Or would they give him the run of their camp?

They rode northeast at daybreak. Frost covered the grass. Isaac rode with his blanket about his shoulders. The sun broke over the eastern horizon and warmed his face, yet he shivered so that his back ached. "I can't warm up," he said.

"It'll be warm enough in the lodges. We don't have far to go." Smithwick turned up the mouth of a broad creek bottom. "I believe this is the one. They'll be up near the head."

"You're sure they're expecting us?"

"We might have to remind 'em."

"What? You never said nothin' about that." Isaac's stomach churned.

"They'll remember. They set store by ceremony. They'd be insulted if we didn't show up."

Isaac shook his head. "I hope you don't do me this way when we get there."

"What way?"

They rode up the creek. Smithwick studied the ground. "I don't see any sign. I hope we ain't early. They might've had to stay longer to fill their larders."

Isaac welcomed the thought. He could do with another few days at the fort. Maybe the Comanches had moved to some other part of the Republic.

Smithwick stopped and studied the northern sky. "There they are. We turned up the wrong creek."

"They must all be dead. I don't see nothin' but buzzards." A small flock circled a mile northward. Isaac's hopes rose.

"Comanches won't be in a camp three days before they're drawing buzzards and crows."

Then Isaac pictured scalped corpses strewn about the creek bottom. "Lord."

Smithwick smiled. "They sling their scraps out of camp. That's one reason they move so often. Gets to stinking."

They rode north through the hills. After a half mile, Smithwick turned west. "They'll be looking for us to come up the creek. We don't want to surprise a little band of hunters."

"Hell no," Isaac said.

They rode two miles eastward along the ridge top, then down into the creek bottom. Smithwick pointed to the sandy ground. "Yep. Look there."

Horse shit littered ground churned by unshod hooves. Here and there parallel furrows cut the bottom. Isaac said, "What made the drag marks?"

"Travois. They use their lodge poles. Right clever, I think."

Isaac grunted. He wasn't ready to admire a horde of savages just yet. The sight of the unshod hoofprints brought back his shivers. He heard shrill yelling and laughing ahead. "My lord."

Smithwick seemed suddenly grave. "Just watch yourself. If you're not sure what to say, then don't say anything. Most Comanches speak pretty good Spanish. If you say something to me, say it in Spanish and loud enough for them to hear."

"Hell," Isaac said. His chest felt tight. He took several deep breaths.

"Don't be comin' apart on me now."

Isaac sipped water from his gourd. He'd been in tight spots before. He'd fought Comanches hand to hand. Why was this so much more terrifying? He took another drink. His tongue remained dry. This was different. He was riding into the domain of wild men. They could take him on their terms. "I'm holdin' up," he said.

Smithwick pulled a strip of white linen from his saddlebag and tied it to his rifle barrel. "About forgot," he said. He held the barrel up. The linen waved in the breeze. "One thing about Comanches: they never expect to be attacked. We're right on top of 'em and they haven't rode out to meet us yet."

Someone yelled from the ridge. Isaac saw several small forms moving through the oaks; black hair and pale buckskin. Smithwick laughed nervously. "Younguns saw us first. The bucks are all laid up with their women."

They neared a northward bend in the creek. Isaac heard approaching hoofbeats. He licked his lips and adjusted the grip on his rifle.

"Keep that finger away from the trigger, son. Just let her lay nice and easy across your pommel."

"Yes sir," Isaac said. "Sorry." Yesterday's jocularity now seemed distant. If the Captain ordered him to sing "Come to the Bower," he'd do it with gusto.

A half-dozen riders came around the bend. They wore breechclouts and leggings and quivers slung across their backs. Their torsos were bare. Long black braids flopped against their arms. They rode as if attached to their spotted mustangs. All carried short bows. Most appeared to be teenage boys. Isaac recognized the dark, stocky leader.

The rangers sat their horses, waiting. The Comanche boys reined their ponies to a stop ten yards away. Their dark eyes held curiosity but no malice. The leader, Looks Far, the boy Isaac fought that morning above the Colorado, smiled and raised a palm. "*Buenos días,* Juaqua, we have been expecting you." He looked at Isaac. "And Isikweb. *Buenos días,*" he said in effortless Spanish.

Isaac grinned and nodded.

Smithwick responded in Spanish, "Friends! I've waited all winter for your return. We are glad to see you at last. I trust you had good hunting. How are the great men? Muguara? Quinaseico? Potesenaquahip? Very well, I hope."

"They are anxious to see you, Juaqua. Follow."

Isaac hoped the Comanches would understand his Spanish as well as he understood theirs.

The boys turned their ponies as easily as Isaac would turn on the balls of his feet. He and Smithwick followed them around the wooded bend; the camp came into view—about fifty lodges strung along a grassy bench above the creek. The teepees were much larger than Isaac had imagined; tanned hides adorned with drawings of birds, horses, and buffalo drawn in red and black. Smoke rose from the tops.

Rangy gray mongrels howled and romped out to meet them, hackles raised. Two rushed Isaac's horse, but broke off their charge and ran alongside barking. Squab paid the dogs no mind. Naked little boys and little girls wearing pale deerskin dresses watched shyly as the riders entered camp. Short, brown women with black hair cropped above their shoulders turned from their work—buffalo robes, firewood, cook pots—to watch the procession.

Cook fires, low scaffolds, brush arbors, and gambrels were scattered about the camp. Isaac caught scent of what attracted the buzzards.

The boys dismounted and handed the reins to several young women, who led the horses away through the oaks beyond camp. Other women and children gathered about. Smithwick and Isaac sat their horses near the door of a large teepee. Isaac's Comanche counterpart pointed to Smithwick and said "Juaqua."

The children shouted "Juaqua!"

Looks Far gestured to Isaac and said, "Isikweb." A few little girls tried to say the name, but stumbled over the syllables and giggled. Some of the little boys mouthed the name, brows furrowed and eyes set in concentration. The young warrior laughed, pulled back the flap on the lodge door, and spoke to someone inside. He turned and motioned for Isaac and Smithwick to dismount.

Isaac swung out of the saddle; he felt the young warriors eyeing him, though he sensed no hostility. They were sizing him up. The body language was unmistakable. The self-conscious casualness; the furtive glances. He'd seen young white men do the same thing many times. He'd done it himself. He stood nearly a head taller than the tallest boy and outweighed any of them by twenty pounds. But all were sinewy, with powerful, slightly slumped shoulders, strong torsos, bowed legs, and hairless bodies. They held their bows with the same familiar ease with which he held his rifle.

The flap parted again. A bald pate appeared, then Muguara stepped out, followed by a younger man.

"Greetings, Muguara," Smithwick said in Spanish. "I've been thinking of my old friends over the long winter."

Muguara smiled. "Juaqua, our council seemed too small without you. We spoke of you often." He looked at Isaac. "This must be your friend . . . what is his name?"

Smithwick looked at Isaac. Isaac croaked "Isaac Webb."

The old chief cocked his ear toward Isaac.

"Isikweb," the young warrior said. "I told him to keep my bow."

Muguara laughed. "Yes. Isikweb. I remember now. Looks Far said he met you one morning last summer."

Isaac caught Smithwick's glance. He was expected to respond. "Yes. He almost broke my chin with his head."

Muguara slapped his thighs and grinned. Some of the young men laughed nervously.

"And how is my friend Buffalo Hump?" Smithwick asked.

The warrior standing behind Muguara—Isaac guessed him to be about thirty—said, "Very well, Juaqua. I trust you have good things to tell us."

"I have good things to tell you and good things to give you," Smithwick said.

Isaac didn't want to disappoint Buffalo Hump. The man seemed to lack old Muguara's sense of humor. Yet his countenance and bearing exuded dignity and intelligence. And perhaps ruthlessness. Broad, calm face; searching eyes; slender but well-muscled arms; long fingers. Half a head taller than any of the other Comanches. Probably a chief. Isaac wondered if all Comanche chiefs possessed equal authority.

Muguara said, "Later we will talk of these things. First we should eat." Several women dashed away. Smithwick unlashed a saddlebag.

Looks Far said, "I will see to your horses, Isikweb." He took the rein and stroked Squab's face. The mustang nuzzled his hand. "I'll keep him close by." He led Squab and Thud toward the trees. Another boy led Smithwick's horses away. Isaac wanted to ask what Looks Far planned to do with his saddle and bedroll, but he remembered Smithwick's advice about keeping quiet.

The two chiefs ducked into the big lodge. Smithwick and Isaac followed. Inside, it was dark, hot, and smelled of wood smoke, dust, and tobacco. Isaac stood for a moment while his eyes adjusted. A small pile of coals glowed in the center of the grass and dirt floor. A thin column of smoke rose through a small flue at the top. Muguara sat on a stack of buffalo robes opposite the entrance. He motioned for Smithwick and Isaac to sit at his left. Buffalo Hump took a seat on his right.

Isaac sat on a robe next to Smithwick. He followed the captain's lead and laid his rifle behind him along the wall. He had no idea Comanches lived in such roomy abodes. The floor was perhaps fifteen feet in diameter. The chief's weapons—lance, bow, quiver, and deadly looking battle ax—stood against the wall at the foot of his buffalo robe mattress. Parfleche bags of various sizes hung from the poles. Utensils and vessels of bone, horn, and brass lined the foot of the wall. Fourteen dried scalps dangled from a rawhide thong hanging just to the right of the door. Even in the dim light, Isaac could see blond and light brown, although most of the hair was black. He tried to relax and breathe.

The flap opened, and a grave old face appeared. The black eyes turned mirthful. "Juaqua! It's true!"

Smithwick said, "My friend Quinaseico. You look well."

The old man limped into the lodge and eased down beside Buffalo Hump.

The young chief elbowed him playfully. Two more middle-aged Comanches entered and sat across the fire from Isaac.

Muguara said, "This is Juaqua's friend, Isikweb. After Juaqua leaves us to tend his family, this young man will speak to Houston for us."

Isaac felt the dark eyes on him. Whatever he might say would pass through a dozen men before reaching Houston. He'd keep that fact to himself. Quinaseico said, "Juaqua, your friend is still a boy. What would you think if we sent a boy to parley with you and the other white chiefs?"

Smithwick smiled warmly, nodded. "Isaac Webb is one of my strongest men. He has already killed two Mexican soldiers and a Waco. He will be twenty summers when I leave you."

Isaac was relieved the Captain didn't tell the old man about the Comanche he'd shot up on the plains.

Quinaseico grunted. "A Waco. This is a promising boy."

Buffalo Hump spoke in Comanche to Quinaseico. The old chief looked at Isaac. "Buffalo Hump says you shot one of our warriors. He died that night."

Isaac swallowed. He felt Smithwick tense. "We were in a fight. He was shooting arrows at me."

Quinaseico blinked. "We are not at war now. I see no need to discuss this further." He looked at the other chiefs. "There is no need for wives or brothers to hear of this. Warriors die in battle."

Isaac breathed. He felt Smithwick relax. Muguara looked perturbed. "Our guests are hungry and we have no food before them. Where are the women?"

Smithwick opened his saddlebag. "We have gifts for our beloved friends." He pulled out several small sacks and passed them around. "Coffee and sugar."

Buffalo Hump hefted his sacks. "You never disappoint us, Juaqua."

A stocky young woman entered the lodge carrying an oak limb with a roasted venison hindquarter dangling from the end. She stuck the limb into the ground and supported it with a forked stick so that the meat hung about two feet above the little fire. Drops of grease hissed. Isaac's mouth watered.

The woman left, then returned with small slabs of hard leather that she placed before each man. Isaac studied her brown face. She didn't return his gaze. Buffalo Hump handed her the sack of coffee and spoke to her in Comanche. She hurried away.

The chiefs drew their knives and sliced off venison, which they ate with their hands. Smithwick leaned forward and sliced off a piece. Isaac did the same. The meat was tough but tasty. Isaac ate hungrily; this was his first hot meal since leaving the fort. He finished his piece, then waited for the Comanches to take seconds. After a few minutes it became obvious that one simply ate as much as one wanted. The group reduced the hindquarter to bone within half an hour. The woman came back with a bowl of water in which the men rinsed their fingers. She left and returned shortly with a dented, blackened brass kettle full of hot coffee. She passed out several dented cups and small vessels of horn. The chiefs dipped their cups into the kettle. Isaac dipped a hollow bison horn into the coffee, careful not to burn his fingers.

Buffalo Hump said, "Juaqua, we've missed your coffee." He took a sip and smiled. "And we've missed you." The Comanches laughed.

Smithwick said, "I have grown tired of beef and corn; I've been hungering for a fat hunk of bison to be eaten with good friends."

Isaac had no idea the Comanches were capable of such manners. These men were far more courteous then his fellow rangers. Then again, he'd never eaten in a room where scalps hung from the ceiling. Perhaps exaggerated politeness kept a man alive in a Comanche camp.

He sat pleasantly full. What would Cyrus think of him drinking from a bison horn? The Comanches stared at the coals. After a few moments, Muguara took a clay pipe from a bag hanging on the wall and began stuffing it with tobacco. Smithwick nodded slightly. Isaac dreaded the pipe as much as the talk.

The chief lit the bowl and handed it to Smithwick, who drew on it and blew a plume of smoke, then passed it to Isaac.

There was nothing to do but partake. The bitter, hot smoke burned his tongue; he hoped no one noticed his watering eyes. He blew a puff, passed the pipe to a portly middle-aged chief named Pahauco, then took another sip of coffee and quietly swished it around in his mouth.

Muguara said, "Juaqua, what does Houston say about our desire for a boundary at the white cliffs? I trust you spoke of this to him."

Smithwick seemed to take on the chiefs' grave demeanor. "Houston says that he understands your wish for a boundary and believes it would be right and good. But he must convince his other chiefs. Some of them are treacherous and greedy; he says that it will be difficult for him to keep the whites from crossing the boundary into Comanche territory. He asks for the Comanches' patience; in time, an agreement can be reached."

Muguara said, "Juaqua, we have already seen what happens when Tahbay-boh—white men—come to a place. More follow until there are Tahbay-boh lodges on every creek. Then the game leaves and we must move to search for food."

Buffalo Hump said, "We have not raided the settlements since you came to us, Juaqua. We have kept our word. Yet do you think we don't see Tahbay-boh moving further west? There are camps just below the white cliffs. Men and horses. All the things Tahbay-boh bring when they come to stay. We cannot allow this."

The pipe came around again. Smithwick partook and passed it to Isaac. "Houston praises the Comanches for their mercy and peacefulness. He asks for your patience while he makes the other chiefs see. Recall that Houston once lived with the Cherokee. He has invited them to live in the pine forests to the northeast."

"We cannot live on such a small parcel of land, Juaqua," Buffalo Hump said. "The Cherokee are a defeated people. They live where Houston tells them they can live and they rely on his mercy." He leaned forward. "Forgive my rudeness, Juaqua. We cannot be told where to live."

Smithwick said, "I take no offense; Houston is a great man like the chiefs sitting in this lodge. He knows of the Comanche power and wants only peace."

Muguara raised a hand. "That is enough stern talk for this day. Isikweb, tell us of your fight with the Waco."

Beads of sweat popped out on Isaac's forehead. "I was riding along the river to the fort when I heard shooting." The chiefs' eyes shone in the firelight; their foreheads glistened. "I crept up the hill and found four Wacos behind a rock shooting at someone near the river. I shot one, then ran down the hill and hid, waiting." What should he say about Castro? The Comanches and Lipans hated each other. "I lay waiting, but my friend came and killed the other three with his knife."

Muguara listened patiently to Isaac's labored Spanish. He smiled thinly. "Your friend must be a powerful warrior."

"Yes," Isaac said. Smithwick seemed to get tongue-tied at the worst times.

"Tell us, Isikweb; was this that big, ugly Tonkawa that goes with you to your woman's lodge?" Buffalo Hump asked.

"Don't be rude to our friend," Muguara said.

Isaac felt the sweat running down his temples. "No." What if they knew? If he lied, they'd never trust him. "It was Castro."

Buffalo Hump snorted in disgust. Muguara laughed. "That Lipan! I've wanted his scalp since I was a boy. He eluded me every time. Now I'm an old man." He seemed to think it a fine joke. "Juaqua," he said, "you will be my guest. My wives will prepare a bed for you."

Smithwick said, "I have looked forward to your hospitality."

Muguara said, "Isikweb, you will sleep in Looks Far's lodge. He would have it no other way. He is acting like an excited child."

"*Gracias,*" Isaac said. Sleeping in the lodge of a Comanche who'd nearly killed him and would have scalped him.

Muguara knocked the ashes from his pipe into the little fire. "You young men can spend the nights reliving your fight. By summer's end it will be the mightiest battle ever fought."

Thirty-Three

"I'M GLAD I didn't kill you, Isikweb." Looks Far was sitting on his stack of robes, studying Isaac as if he were the most interesting sight in the world.

"So am I. But you tried."

"Yes. You were too close when I raised my bow." He poked his little fire with a stick of green elm. His teepee was smaller than Muguara's—about ten feet in diameter—but comfortable. His bow and quivers leaned against the wall by his bed. "How did you find us up there on that hill?"

"We saw your fire from the fort."

He smiled. "We raided a Tonkawa camp to the south. We had ridden all day and were tired. Buffalo Hump warned us about building a fire in Tahbay-boh country. He was furious after the attack."

"I wouldn't want him mad at me."

"No."

Isaac couldn't imagine such hospitable people committing the acts they were known for. Then again, his own people were terrible when riled. The men who laid waste to Santa Anna's army on the Plain of Saint Hyacinth were now plowing and tending their families. And he'd done his best to kill this Comanche with his knife and rifle butt.

Looks Far slapped his belly. "It's time to eat."

Isaac said, "I am still full from the last meal."

Looks Far waved off the comment. "We have plenty, Isikweb. You should eat." He yanked a rawhide cord that ran beneath his lodge wall. "I'll summon my wife."

"How does such a young man come by two wives?"

"I traded horses for them. They're sisters."

Isaac felt a twinge of envy. "Where did you come by so many horses? I have only one."

Looks Far smiled. "I traded for them. If you Tahbay-boh would take more than one wife, you wouldn't have to trouble yourselves with small tasks."

The flap parted; a plump girl of about eighteen ducked in carrying a small brass kettle and two of the hard leather plates. Looks Far paid her no mind. She picked boiled meat out of the kettle with her hands, set it before them, then licked her fingers as she left.

Looks Far took a bite. "That's Feels How Deep the Water Is," he said, chewing. "She's the older sister. Eat, Isikweb."

Isaac bit off a chunk of the lukewarm meat. It was tough, fatty, and bland. Probably buffalo. He doubted the Comanches used salt. He nodded toward the flap. "Where is your other wife?"

The boy tugged another rawhide string, then continued his meal. After a few minutes he yelled something in Comanche, startling Isaac so that he nearly choked on his meat.

Looks Far said. "She's not in her lodge, so I have to call her."

Moments later the flap opened, and another girl, slightly taller than the first, ducked into the lodge and looked questioningly at Looks Far. Like the other Comanche women, she had shoulder-length black hair and wore a simple, knee-length deerskin dress and moccasins. She paid no attention to Isaac.

Looks Far pointed a greasy finger at her. "One More Girl. She's the younger."

One More Girl's eyes went to Isaac. Her husband said, "Isikweb."

"*Buenos días,*" Isaac said. She kept her eyes on him but didn't respond.

Looks Far waved her away; she turned and left. "She is the fleetest girl in camp. I bet on her often and she always wins." He wiped his mouth and jerked one of the strings again. Feels How Deep the Water Is reappeared with a roll of pemmican. She cut it in two, gave each man a half, then left.

Isaac enjoyed the sweet pemmican—honey, mesquite beans, and ground meat. "This is good."

"Yes. Does your wife make sweet food for you?"

Isaac said, "I don't have a wife yet." He never thought he'd be embarrassed to admit the fact at his age.

"That old man will not give up his daughter? What does he want for her?"

"He hates me. He'll never give her to me."

Looks Far laid his pemmican on the leather plate and wiped his hands on his leggings. "What have you done to him?"

"He doesn't want me to befriend the Comanches."

Looks Far took another bite and chewed thoughtfully. "He's angry because we tried to take his horses."

"Yes."

"Perhaps if we let him be, he would give his daughter to you."

"Perhaps." Certainly not, but at least Catherine would be safe.

"I'll speak to Buffalo Hump."

"I would be grateful."

"You need a wife," Looks Far said. "And this girl is comely." He jerked the string again. "I have comely wives. But One More Girl is too skinny."

Feels How Deep the Water Is brought a paunch of water. Looks Far took a long pull and handed the bag to Isaac. Drinking after a Comanche, he thought. Then again, he'd drunk after Uncle Jimmy. He gulped his fill, then handed the bag to the girl. She looked at his beard. He touched his jaw and smiled. She turned and left.

"Isikweb," Looks Far said, "there's pemmican in the hair on your face."

• • •

Isaac stepped out of the lodge into the cool night air and walked toward a stand of hackberry trees near the edge of camp. The warmth and snugness of the lodges surprised him. He checked the newly descendant moon. Nearly midnight, and children laughing and singing; men gambling, women chattering. The small fires lit the teepees like tallow candles. He felt uneasy walking about a Comanche camp alone, but Looks Far seemed unconcerned and told him he could piss anywhere along the edge of camp.

He walked toward the dark row of trees. A few of the camp dogs barked and skulked about, sniffing. His civilized life already seemed like a distant memory. It was a good night for sleeping under the stars.

He felt his otherness; felt conspicuous in his hat and homespun and beard. He'd been in camp less than a day and bare chests and faces and long braids seemed normal. One More Girl had looked at him as he would have looked at her if she were the only Comanche in Bastrop.

Back in Looks Far's teepee, he rolled out his bedding on the stack of buffalo robes.

"No, Isikweb." He pulled up a few robes and slid beneath them. "Like this."

Isaac looked at the pile of thick, wooly hides. God only knew what kind of vermin lived there. He pulled up a robe and slid beneath it, then laid the soogan beneath his head. Looks Far rolled on his side watching him like a boy with a new pup.

Isaac said, "I've looked forward to this visit." The Comanche penchant for silent eye contact was disconcerting.

Looks Far said, "We will hunt soon. And eat and gamble." He rolled onto his back, fingers interlaced on his chest, as if considering the endless possibilities for adventure.

Isaac found the hides heavy and itchy, although the stack beneath him made a fine mattress. He listened to the camp noises. A wolf howled to the south, probably along the river. Dogs barked and whined. Looks Far was already breathing softly, a young man with no concerns, secure in his station.

Isaac considered life with two wives. Looks Far would have no privacy as long as he—Isaac—stayed in his lodge. How would he lay with his wives? Did he bed both girls at the same time? And had he sent them to another teepee to make room for Isaac? Perhaps the boy would go to the women's lodge to fill his need. He'd find out in time.

The heavy hide walls seemed to breathe in the raw wind. He ran his hands over the woolly hair of the robe. His stone fireplace never seemed to warm his tiny cabin on a cold night, no matter how big the fire. The chinked walls seemed to absorb the heat; the dark corners remained brittle cold, unlike this round hide tent that held the flame's warmth and light, reflecting them inward.

He laid a hand on his rifle. Warm wood and cold metal. A comfort, though the weapon would be of little use in the confines of the teepee. He took his sheathed knife from his belt and laid it on his belly.

He woke at dawn to find Feels How Deep the Water Is kneeling over the fire. She kept her eyes on him as she snapped finger-sized sticks and fed the weakly glowing coals. He propped himself up on his elbow. "Good morning," he croaked.

She said nothing.

"Go back to sleep, Isikweb," Looks Far said. "It is early still."

He lay on his side, watching the girl. She eyed him as he might eye a rattlesnake. Keep an eye on it and you can go about your business without being bitten. The fire flickered to life. Looks Far snored softly. Isaac closed his eyes. The door flap swished and the flame hissed as a puff of air drew through the door and up the flue.

When he woke again, he found himself alone in the lodge. Looks Far's robes were empty, stacked neatly against the wall. The fire had again burned down to coals. He put his knife back on his belt, started to pick up his rifle, but thought better of it and pulled the door flap back and stepped outside to a clear, cool April morning.

Women worked about cook fires; small children ran squealing and chattering. Several women stopped their work to stare at him. He nodded and touched his hat brim, felt his foreignness again. He walked through hackberry trees toward the creek to empty his taut bladder. A tall, brindled mongrel raised its hackles and howled.

Isaac said, "Hush!"

The dog snarled and loped a few yards away and continued howling. Isaac walked deeper into the trees, looking for a familiar face, but no men seemed to be stirring. He glanced at the sun. Midmorning. Perhaps Looks Far was paying his wives a visit. Two wives at once. He tried to picture them as he made water.

Small birds twittered in the trees, their voices melding with those of the Comanche children. A horse nickered in the woods across the creek. Where was Smithwick? Probably laying it on thick with one of the old chiefs. Something about the wisdom of the chief Houston and his love for the Comanches. He smelled roasting meat. Maybe the Captain had a pot of coffee boiling somewhere. Surely everyone knew about their white visitors. He'd hate to surprise some warrior who'd missed the reception.

He started back toward camp, mindful of the dog. Did Comanches hunt with their dogs? He doubted such nondescript curs would tree anything. They didn't seem to take their dogs as seriously as horseflesh.

He walked toward the council lodge. A few young men were stirring. A gaggle of little boys ran by, oblivious to their tall, hairy visitor. Each carried a two-foot bow and quiver of arrows. No wonder the men shot so well from horseback. They'd been drawing bows since they were big enough to walk.

Near the center of camp, Looks Far's wives bent over a cook fire. Another rough cut of meat sizzled on a spit above the coals. The two were laughing and talking. They stopped when they saw him.

Isaac nodded. They stared at him, unsmiling. He wondered if Comanche women spoke Spanish and worried that there might be some taboo against speaking to another man's wife.

He approached the fire. One More Girl spoke to her sister, who gave a curt reply in Comanche.

He stopped a few feet away, pointed at the meat, then to his nose. *"Bueno."* He sensed no hostility. They were simply studying him as he would study a horse or a dog. He half expected them to circle him for a better look.

"Smells good," he said in Spanish.

One More Girl looked at the meat as if she'd seen it for the first time, then picked up a butcher knife from the dirt and sliced off a thin morsel and offered it to him. Pink juice dripped from her wrist. He could see the amber calluses on her palm.

He took the meat and held it up to cool. *"Gracias."* It was tough but delicious. Bison shank, he guessed. He nodded. *"Bueno."*

The girl started to cut another strip, but Isaac raised his palm. "We will bring it to you soon," she said.

"Gracias. Where is your husband?"

"He does not tell us where he is going," the older girl said. "He will be back when this meat is done."

Isaac stroked his whiskers. The girls gawked at him. He was looking about for a reason to walk away when Looks Far and one of the young men in yesterday's greeting party strode up from the direction of the council lodge.

Looks Far said, "Buffalo Hump has agreed to leave your woman alone, Isaac Webb. I arose early this morning to speak to him. This troubled me all night."

"I'm grateful." The day before he'd doubted that Comanche men rose at the crack of dawn for anything short of scalping and thievery.

Looks Far nodded toward the other warrior. "He is Best Cousin. He has been thinking about you, Isikweb. He wanted to come and look at you."

Best Cousin looked Isaac up and down. "Are all Tahbay-boh big and hairy?"

Isaac suppressed a smile. The boy was serious and might take offense at mirth. "I am taller than most."

"But not as tall as Juaqua."

"No."

"Best Cousin was not on the hill the morning of our fight, Isikweb," Looks Far said. "He has seen no Tahbay-boh but you and Juaqua. I told him your woman is pretty."

One More Girl sliced off another piece of meat, then draped it over the knife blade to cool. She licked her fingers. "What's her name, Isikweb?"

"Catherine."

"Catherine," she said. "What is that?"

"Nothing. Just a name."

She offered the strip of meat to Looks Far. The boy tested the temperature with his finger, then took it, bit off a piece, then tore the remainder in two and gave the halves to Isaac and Best Cousin.

Feels How Deep the Water Is scratched her ear. "Juaqua, Isikweb, Catherneen. I cannot understand these names."

"Our names are just names," Isaac said. He supposed that was true. He'd never considered it before.

Best Cousin chewed. "What is your chief's name? Hu . . ."

"Houston."

"Is he big?"

"I've never seen him, but I hear that he's bigger than Juaqua."

Best Cousin and Looks Far exchanged glances. "These Tahbay-boh are all big," Best Cousin said. "That's why all of their horses are so tall and eat so much."

Looks Far said, "No. Isikweb rides an ugly little horse. His feet drag the ground."

The girls' laughter sounded like coyotes yipping.

Thirty-Four

ISAAC RARELY SAW Noah Smithwick. He suspected the Comanches planned the separation, although Looks Far told him that older, respected warriors kept to themselves. The younger men considered it a great honor to be invited to sit in council. Although a successful warrior and hunter with many horses, two Lipan scalps, and several coups—one being his head butt to Isaac's chin—Looks Far had never set foot in Muguara's lodge.

A week into his stay, Isaac began to understand why Comanche warriors were so determined to hold on to their way of life. The rangers and other whites often conjectured as to why the savages refused to adopt the white lifestyle. Why sleep on a stack of robes in a hide tent when you could snuggle under a pile of quilts on a feather tick mattress in a nice, tight cabin? No sense roaming all over the desolate plains after wild meat when you could grow corn and vegetables and raise beeves and hogs and chickens.

Isaac now wondered why a man would want to spend half his life sweating behind a span of hard-headed, flatulent mules when you could rise well after daybreak, after your women had come in and stoked the fire, eat a breakfast of bison or venison, sit around camp, recounting your exploits, gambling, dozing, or wallowing in the robes with your best wife. Comanche men did no labor beyond hunting. The women did all the chopping, skinning, scrapping, cooking, fire tending, and child lugging.

The days passed and grew warmer. Isaac slept late and napped most afternoons. Feels How Deep the Water Is and One More Girl kept the fire going all day long. Isaac stopped by often to talk while their husband slept or gambled.

Both were eager to bear children, sons first, hopefully, to satisfy their husband, then daughters to help with the work. Although they'd both consulted Fox Tit, an ancient woman who purportedly possessed crow medicine and whose magic was responsible for the birth of most of the warriors in camp, neither had conceived.

The girls chattered and sliced off or ladled out whatever they were cooking. Isaac's breeches began to bind at the waist. Most days, One More Girl expressed concern that Isaac had no wife. Surely, she said, after the Comanches and Tahbay-boh agreed to peace, he would gain favor with Catherine's father. Perhaps she should take him to see Fox Tit about a spell. As the days passed, he began to consider her offer seriously. Feels How Deep the Water Is accused her younger sister of meddling.

One More Girl talked often of her terror of witches. Though no one seemed to have ever seen a witch, the dangerous hags were known to be working their evil. One day Isaac asked her if witches were Comanche or Lipan or Tonkawa. The girl's eyes widened at this horrible new uncertainty. Now she had to worry about resentful Tonkawa or Lipan witches who might have lost a husband or children to Comanche raiders. Then, Feels How Deep the Water Is assured her that witches were merely old, barren Comanche spinsters and widows who had grown bitter in their loneliness.

Early in the visit, Looks Far drank coffee all day and slept little. Isaac's snoring helped none at all. The bleary-eyed warrior woke him several times each night to tell him to roll over. By the end of the second week, the coffee was gone, and Looks Far slept for the better part of three days straight while Isaac moped about with a dull headache.

One morning, Isaac stopped by the cook fire for his pre-breakfast strip of roasted bison. Feels How Deep the Water Is tended the fire alone.

"Where's your sister?" Isaac favored One More Girl. He found her a far better conversationalist than her sullen older sister, and easier on the eyes as well.

"She bleeds."

"Cut herself?"

Feels How Deep the Water Is looked at him in exasperation. "She bleeds as women bleed."

"Well." Women were women, it seemed. And not just in their monthly bleeding. "She doesn't feel well?"

The girl prodded the roast with her butcher knife. Drippings fell hissing into the coals. "She feels good."

"Why isn't she helping you?" This girl was surlier than Esther.

She tested the meat again, more out of habit than necessity. "She's unclean. She cannot touch a man."

"What harm would it do?"

Her eyes widened. "It would destroy his power."

"Who says so?"

"Everyone says so, Isikweb. Surely you would not touch a woman when she bleeds."

"I wouldn't know unless she told me."

Her eyelids flickered as she pondered his remark, then patted her palm with the knife blade. "Looks Far would kill her if she touched him now."

"Well then." The girl was serious. He looked back at her husband's lodge. "We don't kill our women."

"Neither do we."

"You said Looks Far would kill your sister if she touched him while she's bleeding."

"Yes. He would."

"Then you said Comanches don't kill their women."

"We don't."

"I don't understand you."

"Our men don't kill their women because we don't come close to them while we bleed." She checked the roast again. The juice ran clear. "Do you want some now?"

Isaac gazed down the creek, beyond the line of lodges. "No. I am not hungry now."

• • •

"Isikweb, why do Tahbay-boh dismount to shoot?" Looks Far asked.

Isaac sat on a buffalo robe beneath a brush arbor, grateful for the light breeze and shelter from the midafternoon sun. "You cannot shoot straight astraddle a moving horse. And how would I reload?"

Best Cousin stuffed his pipe, much to Isaac's dismay. He'd as soon suck on a red-hot nail as draw on a bowl of Comanchero tobacco. "You should learn to ride and shoot," Best Cousin said. "That is a better way to meet your enemy."

"Maybe," Isaac said. He'd spill every grain of powder in his horn trying to reload on a galloping horse. "How do you know we dismount to fight?"

"I am glad you did not ride your horses among us when we were asleep on the hilltop," Looks Far said. "You are easier to shoot when you are on the ground."

Best Cousin lit his pipe and drew thoughtfully. "But your rifles kill us from a greater distance than our arrows fly."

"Sometimes," Isaac said. Problem was, by the time you saw a Comanche within rifle range, he'd be within bow range.

Looks Far took the pipe from Best Cousin. "I can stay hidden from your guns. When you see me, I will be shooting my arrows at you." He drew on the pipe.

Isaac watched in disgust. His turn next. Looks Far handed him the pipe. He tried not to wince as he puffed. Maybe a sprig of juniper would get the taste out of his mouth. He gladly passed the pipe to Best Cousin.

"I wish you would stay with us always, Isikweb," Looks Far said.

Best Cousin blew a plume of smoke. "You could go west and hunt with us. Or go south of the del Norte."

"What's south of the del Norte?" Isaac had no desire to be any nearer Santa Anna's army.

"Many horses," Best Cousin said. "And women. That's what Buffalo Hump says. I have not been there yet. I hope to go when the grass cures."

"I was there when I was a little one," Looks Far said.

"They took you to Mexico when you were a baby?"

Looks Far shook his head. He had lately adopted the gesture from Isaac. "No. Buffalo Hump brought me and my sisters out of Mexico."

That explained his excellent Spanish. "Do you remember this?"

"I remember mud lodges and goats and a man and a woman. Sometimes I don't know if I remember them or dream them. But this is what Buffalo Hump tells me. These people were my mother and father then."

"What became of them?"

"The man who became my father killed them."

Again, Isaac felt his otherness. "Where is he?"

"We shouldn't speak of the dead, Isikweb. Quinaseico sold one of my sisters to some Kiowas. I've seen her. She bore a son and a daughter. The other one became the wife of Pahauco. She bore him no children, but he still keeps her. If he threw her out, she would live with my wives."

The Mexican woman Smithwick spoke of. Isaac tried to remember her name. "Cece . . . Cel . . ."

Looks Far jerked the pipe stem from between his teeth and looked in surprise at Isaac. "No. Not Cecilia. That's not her name."

Isaac decided to drop it. He hoped the woman wouldn't be punished for talking to Smithwick. He wondered how far he could go. "What about the women you took from the farms on the Colorado?"

"That was before our truce," Best Cousin said.

"Yes. Where are they now?"

"They went with Comanches who live to the northwest," Looks Far said. "Buffalo Hump traded them for some robes and horses and two rifles. The rifles are no good, so we threw them in the river. Buffalo Hump wishes he had kept the two women."

"Where in the northwest?"

"These people move about more than we do," Best Cousin said. "They always come to us. We can never find them. We call them Wanderers. Their camps are filthy."

"Houston wants to buy them back. He might trade coffee and blankets or horses for them."

Looks Far puffed, nodded. "Horses maybe. If these women haven't been taken by a chief."

Isaac stilled a shudder. It was easy to forget that these people butchered men and stole women and children. He couldn't allow himself to forget that.

"I see no reason for you to leave, Isikweb," Looks Far said. "You should stay and we could hunt deer or ride to the Nueces and get horses from the Lipans."

"And gamble," Best Cousin said. "It is warm and we have plenty to eat. It is a fine time to gamble."

Isaac shook his head. "I need to go back to my family; my father and mother and sister."

Looks Far nodded gravely. "And your woman. Go speak with her father again." He arose and dusted his leggings. "Your leaving makes me sad, Isikweb."

Best Cousin tapped the ashes from the bowl of his pipe. "When will you return?"

"Two moons."

Looks Far snorted.

Isaac said, "You could come and stay with me."

"Yes, and we could spend our days cutting trees and digging in the ground. I will wait for you."

Thirty-Five

EZRA SAT on his haunches and studied the girl. "Right pretty, ain't she? Would be if she was cleaned up, anyways."

The girl, a Wichita captured as a child by the Lipans, sat on a dirty blanket beneath a brush lean-to, glaring at the gawking rangers.

Uncle Jimmy spat. "I'd say she's yourn, Isaac. Don't let her cut your throat."

Isaac sighed and looked at Smithwick, who shrugged. "What in hell am I supposed to do with her?" He'd just ridden through the gate after surviving a month with the Comanches; now this.

Felix's eyes darted from Isaac to the girl. "Old Castro just wanted to return a favor. Said you needed a wife and he had one handy."

"What does Andrews have to say about this?" Smithwick asked.

Felix said, "When the old devil showed up with her, Andrews said he wasn't having none of it. Then Castro allowed as how we could get a new bunch of scouts. Now Andrews says somebody ought to be able to make a house girl out of her."

"I just wish somebody would tame the little bitch," Ezra said. He nodded toward the girl, who eyed him with suspicion. "She keeps runnin' off and we keep havin' to catch her. Climbed up on the damn parapet and jumped over the wall the other mornin'. I can't see how she didn't break both of her legs. Landed just like a cat."

She did indeed remind Isaac of a cat. She squatted, rocking on her heels, as if ready to spring at someone's throat. Her hair was parted in the middle and plaited past her waist. She wore a buckskin dress and knee-high moccasins. "Just let her go or give her back to the Wichitas," Isaac said.

"Andrews thinks Castro would take offense, and we'd have to find new scouts," Felix said. "And which band of Wichitas would we give her back to? Would they even take her? Besides, I imagine Castro and them killed all of her folks when they stole her."

"Speaks pretty good Mexican, accordin' to Castro," Ezra said, "but she ain't said a word since he brought her in a week after you two left."

Isaac guessed the girl to be about sixteen. He doubted she was five feet tall. Her black eyes took them in and scanned the fort for any chance of escape. "Just where is Castro?"

Andrews stepped out of his quarters and walked over. "The mean old bastard dumped her off here, then headed back to the Nueces. We ain't seen him since."

Isaac wondered how long she could squat on her heels. All day, probably. "Well, I can't take her. That's all I need is to show up at home with a Lipan squaw."

"Wichita," Uncle Jimmy said.

Felix shook his head in exasperation. "Uncle Jimmy, she's dressed like a Lipan, has her hair plaited like a Lipan, and I imagine talks Lipan, if we can ever get her to say something. She's lived with the devils since she was a tot. She looks Lipan to me."

"A little darkish if you ask me," Uncle Jimmy said.

As usual, Smithwick appeared to be enjoying himself. "Why, Isaac, you don't have to marry the girl. Maybe that Comanche boy will keep her for you. That way you'd have a little belly warmer there when you go back this summer. I imagine he'll tend to her until you get there."

"Belly warmer hell," Isaac said. "Look at her lookin' at us. That ain't love in them black eyes."

"You've got two months to break her," Felix said.

"Break her. Felix, hell. She ain't a horse." He rolled his eyes and shook his head. "Why are these things always happenin' to me? I'm tellin' Castro I can't take her. I'm ridin' down to Bastrop to see my folks. I never asked for a wife, and I don't aim to take one 'til I'm ready."

"Castro ain't here, and if he was, I sure as hell wouldn't tell him that," Uncle Jimmy said.

"I ain't afraid of Castro," Isaac lied.

"He won't take her back, son." Felix said. "She's betrothed in his mind and that's that. Maybe if she was full-blooded Lipan, but he ain't takin' back a Wichita squaw that nobody in his camp wants."

"I can't see a buck not speakin' up for such a comely little thing," Smithwick said. "I believe he's beholdin' to Isaac and wanted to return a favor."

Felix laughed. "I'd say there's a good reason nobody wants her. There's no tellin' what the little booger has done."

Isaac felt the hopelessness of the situation. "I should've let the damn Wacos lift his scalp." But he liked Castro and would never abandon him during a fight.

Uncle Jimmy pulled on his jug and wiped his mouth with his sleeve. "Take more than a few Wacos to get that old heathen's scalp. You never saved him. I'd say you just got in the middle of his fracas."

Isaac started for the barrack. "I'm packin' for home. Leavin' first light. You boys can worry about this girl." He wondered what Looks Far would say if he showed up with a Lipan girl. He'd probably make his wives accommodate her in their lodge. He looked back at her; she caught his eye. Might she know a little English? Or maybe Castro had described him to her.

Smithwick followed him. "I swear, Isaac, you're gettin' to be a prominent man. Every young buck in Comanchería knows about you, and now Lipan chiefs are bringin' you women. Half the men in this company would give their eyeteeth to have that gal and would've already jumped her if they thought she wouldn't geld 'em."

"You want her?" Isaac plopped down on his bunk. It made a poor substitute for a thick stack of buffalo robes. The room seemed dreary compared to Looks Far's cozy lodge. Somebody ought to fashion a fire pit in the middle of the floor.

"Yeah, but then the lovely black-haired Widow would geld me."

"Maybe we can tame her and keep her here at the fort. Reckon she can cook?"

Smithwick laughed. "Probably nothing we'd want to eat."

"I ate some pretty rank meat in that camp. One day those girls dumped a sackful of live terrapins on the coals. Lord. I about lost my breakfast."

"That gal won't stay here and cook for us, Isaac, unless she takes up with one of us."

"Let her take up with Ezree or Felix. Hell, or Uncle Jimmy."

Jimmy's narrow frame appeared in the doorway. "I reckon not. She clawed furrows down Simon's face. He aimed to get him a little. By god, he got somethin' but not what he was after." Uncle Jimmy dug in his ear with a gnarled finger. "Then the ignorant bastard tried to strangle her, and she bit off the end of his little finger. You never heard such squallin'. Woke us all up. She was on top about to gouge his eyes out when we pulled her off. Nobody ain't bothered her since."

Smithwick laughed. "Where is old Simon?"

"Andrews got so mad at him over trying for that gal, he sent him home. Told him not to come back 'til he can act right."

"When is Castro comin' back?" Isaac asked. Nobody seemed to understand that he couldn't take care of a wild Lipan girl. He suspected that none of the men wanted to give her back.

"Who the hell knows?" Jimmy said. "Castro shows up when it suits him. Since there ain't much fightin' to be done right now, it might be a spell before he comes back."

Smithwick said, "Isaac, if we do some good with our emissary work, the old boy might never come back."

"I wonder if King might want her," Isaac said.

Smithwick said, "I imagine so, but I'd hate to have to explain that to Castro."

"Captain, that gal doesn't want anything to do with me."

"Not yet, she don't," Uncle Jimmy said.

"You lecherous old bastards just want a woman around," Isaac said. "You ain't foolin' me."

Uncle Jimmy raised his jug. Smithwick grinned and shook his head. "Leave for a month and the whole company goes to hell."

"I'm goin' home," Isaac said. "Andrews is giving me a month off. I ain't been thinkin' about much else for the last three weeks."

On the way to Andrews's quarters, they walked past the girl, who was still squatting on her blanket, watching her leering audience.

"I'd say you boys have done little else but stare at that girl," Isaac yelled to Felix, who sat on an overturned kettle next to the cook fire.

"Well, things have been slow since you two got cozy with the Comanches," Felix said. "I'm beginning to pine for a good scrape. Or a good roll in the blanket."

Captain Andrews sat on a stool behind a puncheon table. He stood as they walked into the dim quarters. "Leave the door open, boys. I'll take the flies over the heat. So what did you talk about with our Comanche friends?"

Smithwick said, "We spent most of our waking hours discussing weapons, scalp drying, hunting, horses, and various unmentionables relating to the female anatomy."

Andrews sighed and shook his head. "What about you, son?"

"We mostly ate and slept. I learned about witches from the women."

"And this is what I'm supposed to report to Sawyer."

Smithwick said, "Captain, they've already made their position clear. Isaac and I simply show good faith and friendship while our superiors figure out how to meet their requests or plan whatever treachery they'll use to steal their land."

Andrews stroked his mustache. "Well then. Good work, boys, I suppose. I'll report that negotiations are going well and the Comanches are looking forward to seeing you two again later this summer and would they please make up their goddamn minds about what to tell these people."

"I only report good news to the Comanches, Captain," Smithwick said.

Andrews smiled. "Damn right. Isaac, I reckon you're ready to visit your folks. You've earned it."

"I thank you."

"Don't mention it. That gal will be here when you get back."

Isaac snorted. Andrews said, "We'll manage somehow. We can't do without our Lipan scouts."

They stepped outside. The girl lay on her side on the blanket, but kept her eyes on the men.

"I don't imagine the little thing has slept a wink since Castro left her here," Isaac said. He walked through the crowd of men and squatted ten feet in front of her. "She got a name?"

"Inez," Ezra said.

The girl glanced at Ezra. For an instant, bewilderment replaced belligerence in her eyes.

"*Buenos días,* Inez," Isaac said.

The girl watched him.

"I am Isaac Webb. . . ."

"We done tried all that," Nicholas Wren said.

"Isaac," the girl whispered.

"Well I swear. First thing the girl has said since she got here," Uncle Jimmy said.

Smithwick shooed the men with his hand. "You boys find something to do. Let Isaac talk to this girl."

"This is all there is to do, Captain," Ezra said.

"Find something to do, or I'll find it for you," Smithwick said.

"I believe my bunk needs holdin' down," Ezra said.

The men sauntered away, glancing back at Isaac and Inez.

Isaac sat cross-legged in front of her. "Castro told you about me?"

The girl blinked. "Yes."

"What did he say to you?"

"That I was to be your wife." Her voice was thin and raspy, full of despair. Her Spanish was far better than his.

"Why?"

"My husband is dead. He has no brothers. We have little food."

Isaac watched her, transfixed, mildly aroused. He noticed the copper rings in her ears. Bracelets of copper wire, beads, and tiny white shells on both wrists. Scabs on her knees.

"We won't hurt you, Inez."

She rubbed her nose, drew in her legs.

"Are you hungry?"

"No."

"Getting enough to eat?"

"Yes."

"I leave tomorrow, but I'll return soon. You will be safe." He pointed to Smithwick, who sat watching from the bunkhouse door stoop. "He will protect you. Noah."

Smithwick raised a hand.

"Yes," Inez said. Isaac doubted she needed anyone's protection.

He slept little that night. Inez, Looks Far, and the Comanche girls visited his sleep. At dawn he stepped bleary eyed out of the bunkhouse to saddle Squab. Inez sat before her little fire, chewing a piece of jerked meat. The firelight danced off her earrings, bracelets, and hair. She watched him.

Tom Crosby descended the ladder from the parapet to open the gate. "Don't get fat and lazy on us, Isaac."

"I just finished layin' up and lettin' two Comanche squaws wait on me hand and foot for a month. Livin' can't get much easier."

Crosby pushed the gate open. "Them Webb women will slap some sense into you."

Isaac laughed and looked over his shoulder as he rode out of the fort. Inez turned and walked back toward her lean-to. She wore a doeskin smock. The luxuriant white tail hung down her back.

Thirty-Six

ESTHER STEPPED behind Isaac and snipped off four inches of his hair. "Sit still, brother, before you lose somethin' you need. Pap, look what a pile of mousy brown locks."

Isaac squirmed in the straight-backed chair. "I like to keep an eye on a woman with a sharp blade."

Esther laughed wickedly and worked the scissors close to his ear. "I believe I'm gettin' the shakes."

Cyrus sat on a puncheon bench, sipping his morning coffee. "Worse than shearin' sheep. If I'd known we'd have such a mess, I'd have made you trim him up outside. Isaac, I'm surprised you didn't come back wearin' braids."

"That'll take me another trip or two. I've been thinkin' about them plump gals. Pretty as day-old calves."

Esther said, "Don't forget about these scissors."

Cyrus sipped. "Them gals will feed you your balls, they catch you at the wrong time."

Esther stopped trimming. "Pap! That's no way to talk." She combed Isaac's hair out straight. "Would they sure enough?"

Isaac said, "I believe they would, if they were mad at a man. You ought to see what the bucks done to old man Thorpe."

"Ever hear of Mary or Martha or Elsie Mann?" Cyrus said.

"They're with another Comanche band somewhere northwest of the river. The Captain says there's one white woman, wild as any Comanche, been there since she was a tot. I never saw her. And a handsome Mexican woman. She stayed clear of me. Never would let me get close enough to talk to her."

"Devils," Esther said under her breath.

"That's just their way," Isaac said. "They treated me as good as any man has a right to expect."

Cyrus set his cup in the bench. "Yes sir, I can just hear them bucks talkin' about old Isikweb. 'Nice enough fellow when you've got him outnumbered and keep him full of fresh meat. But you wouldn't want to let the scoundrel catch you out by yourself. He's a mean one, sure enough.'"

. . .

Isaac sat against a blackjack oak and watched Catherine from the hillside above the Adair farm. She tossed table scraps from a dishpan to chickens gathered about her feet. She wouldn't see him, although he sat less than a hundred yards up the hill. Nor would Cedrick. The broken cover on the hillside hid him; yet in times past, he had felt exposed in heavier cover. His months with the rangers had taught him two things: A predator's eyes sought movement. And humans were, above all else, predators. You never saw the gaudy bobwhite cock until he flushed; you saw the deer's dark, moist eye only after it flicked its ear.

Isaac guessed that Adair, frantic man that he was, had cleared nearly half a section. How was it to know that you're right, to never question it, to push on single-mindedly, sure of your propriety? Men who questioned their motives rarely accomplished great things. Nor did those like Cyrus, drawn to fighting and coon hunting. Or those who lived in snug lodges and followed the bison, who moved in good weather but sensibly ate and slept and lay with wives when not after food or scalps or plunder. The fortune and the power went to simple, frantic, ambitious men like Adair. Isaac wondered if the man ever slept. He watched Thomas and Cedrick loading creek stone into a wagon. No split rail fence for this man. Crops laid; beeves pastured; hogs growing tallow from the fat of the land. We'll take these rocks from the creek and build a fence, for if we stop for an instant we might question or feel remorse. Get the stone in the hot wagon before we feel its coolness or notice the cloudy creek water filling the void. Don't stop; a bar of fiddle music might jump into your head, and with it the thought of a woman's warm hand and the feel of her waist and flushed cheeks and her breath in your face. Hell no, don't stop. When you're right and surrounded by evil and sloth and naked savages, there's little time. Catherine walked back into the cabin.

Isaac drew up his legs and rested his chin on his forearms. He was no farmer. If anything, he was more indifferent than his father. Cyrus had laid in a corn crop while he was away with the Comanches. In the week since his return he had walked along the rows and felt nothing. No affection or covetousness. His cabin seemed cramped and filthy, despite his and Esther's efforts at tidiness. He lay suffocating on his feather tick, thinking of the night beneath the ledge and the freezing rain and the swishing of the horses' tails and the brittle air in his nostrils and the warmth and the feel of his rifle stock beneath his blanket. For a month, in the Comanche camp, he'd thought of little but home and Catherine. Now, he could think of little but Catherine and Smithwick and Ezra and the boys, the fort, and the languid life of a man in a Comanche camp. Cyrus seemed to sense it and said nothing about Isaac's obvious lack of interest in grubbing in the dirt.

He arose and padded along the hillside through the moist oak and cedar duff toward the new pasture. He had planned to stay on the hill, but felt drawn toward the creek; he moved slowly, easily; soon he heard creek riffles and Adair's stolid voice and Cedrick's grunted replies. He kept to the shadows, stopping when the men stopped or raised their heads; moving when they lowered their heads to their task. They would never know. He noticed four horses—two brindled geldings, a piebald mare, and a big, handsome bay in the corral back of the barn. Louise Adair appeared along the side of the house and slung a pan of dishwater. She stopped and shaded her eyes to watch her husband and their slave.

So this was what Looks Far saw. Isaac had looked down on this farm more than a dozen times but he'd never seen it this way. Completely vulnerable. Farmers intent on their work, oblivious. There had been no Comanche raiding since the start of the Captain's emissary work. Had Adair wondered why he still had all of his horses? Isaac searched the scene for a gun. He saw none. Surely he had one nearby. Propped against the other side of the wagon perhaps. Even so, Adair now stood thirty feet away from the wagon, by the creek, searching for the next stone. The fool. Isaac could hear him clearly now.

Cedrick bent and hefted a milk pail–sized rock to his belly and waddled back toward the wagon.

"How many times have I told you not to bend your back?" Adair said. "Use your legs. Next time I turn around you'll be whinin' about your back again."

"I been doin' this way forty years."

Adair waved him off. "Well then, keep right on. Just don't let me hear you whine." He squatted, grabbed an even bigger stone, then straightened his legs. "See there?"

Cedrick heaved his burden into the wagon. "I see you standin' there holdin' that rock. I thought we was supposed to load 'em in the wagon."

Adair's shoulders slumped; he sighed. "I declare. I'm wastin' breath." He started toward the wagon. "You don't know how good you got it—you know it? Ain't many men would abide your sassy mouth."

Cedrick walked back toward the creek, his face sullen. He scanned the ground. "Yes, suh, got it good," he said softly. "Got it good."

The breeze shifted. Isaac smelled fresh sweat.

"Take off if you don't like it," Adair said. "We'll see how far you get."

Cedrick continued his search. "Got it good; got it good, praise Jesus, I got it good," he sang.

"Why, I wouldn't even come after you. Wonder how far you'd get before the Comanches lifted that gray wool?"

Cedrick closed his eyes. "Got it good, got it good, Lord knows I got it good!" He resumed his search.

Adair shook his head and waded the shallow creek. He stepped just inside the streamside brush and unbuttoned his fly. Isaac stood twenty feet away, peering through a greenbrier tangle. Adair looked past him and made water. "Cedrick, sing that one about goin' to the promise land."

"Well then," Cedrick said. He cleared his throat.

Oh my Lord.
Oh my Lord.
Keep me from sinkin' down.

I tell you what I mean to do;
I mean to get to heaven too;
I look up yonder and what do I see?
I see angels beckoning me.

"That's the one," Adair said. "I reckon all darkies can sing; I miss hearing Lucy."

Isaac fingered the butt of his knife handle. The mighty Captain Adair, a few paces away, pissing unaware. He could take him right now, if not for Cedrick. Put a blade in him and peel his head and leave him. Nobody would suspect anyone but Comanches. This man who thought himself worthy of the title of Captain. Isaac's calm surprised him. He could just feel his heart. No wonder the Comanches found the white farmers such easy pickings. Cyrus wouldn't walk to the corncrib unarmed. And here a former ranger captain, a man he'd feared and respected, stood within easy killing range. Isaac watched him button his fly. He wouldn't kill him, but he could if he wanted to. Anytime. This man who'd insulted his father and his captain and kept Catherine from him. Thomas Adair would go to bed tonight with no inkling that a man who hated him had stood within smelling distance with his palm on the hilt of a knife.

Oh my Lord.
Oh my Lord.
Keep me from sinkin' down . . .

The groveling he'd done in Adair's home disgusted him now. This man considered himself a fighter. Isaac wanted to show him. Just step out and put a blade to his throat. Don't cut him; just show him. Show him that nothing is for sure. Let him think on that along with his figuring on more cleared pasture and handsome stone fences and fine horses and slaves. Let him take that up with the Almighty. It would do him some good. Teach him to pay attention and keep his gun handy. The bastard.

Catherine's call startled him from his trance. She came walking from the house, carrying a biscuit pan and a cloth sack. Thomas buttoned his fly. "Dinnertime!" He waded the creek again. Cedrick dropped his rock where he stood next to the creek. Sweat soaked both men's shirts.

"Y'all about got a load, looks like," Catherine said. She sounded awfully gay.

"We'd have a load, if I could find a little help," Adair said. He took off his hat, ran his finger through his sweat-plastered gray hair, then took the pan.

Isaac backed away and eased up the hill.

Thirty-Seven

ISAAC RODE INTO Coleman's Fort and found Inez sitting bare-breasted beneath her lean-to, arranging her smock in her lap. About half the company stood in a semicircle, watching her. She seemed to be ignoring them. She looked up at Isaac. He dismounted, tied Squab to the rail, and tipped his hat. He'd nearly forgotten about her.

She said nothing, went back to her task.

Ezra sat on an overturned pail. "Only set of titties most of these boys have ever seen. She showed 'em for the first time the other day."

Several of the men looked flushed. Smithwick sat on a bench, his back against the barrack. "Of course, the sight fails to shake a worldly man like Isaac."

Isaac leaned on his rifle. "I've seen several pairs bouncin' around in King's camp." His mouth was suddenly dry. "You're awful quiet, Mr. Higginbotham." His voice sounded full.

"Gets a man thinkin'," Ezra said.

"I never expected such a warm welcome from you boys." Isaac ambled over to the coffeepot. "It's clear you're glad to see me."

Uncle Jimmy pulled on his jug. "Lipans can't be all bad."

"She don't think a thing about it," Felix said. "She thinks we're just ogling like we always do." He winked at Isaac. "See what you been missin'?" The more absurd the situation, the better Felix liked it.

Inez turned the garment inside out and pulled a seam though her teeth.

Felix chuckled and shook his head. "Beats all I ever seen." Ezra was speechless.

The girl repeated the process, then licked her lips.

"Combing the nits out," Smithwick said. "They must be pretty good."

Inez looked at them all with obvious contempt and prepared to clean another seam.

Felix said, "I reckon you'll be breakin' her of that, won't you, Isaac?"

Isaac's lack of revulsion at her nit-eating surprised him. "I won't be breakin' her of nothin'."

"A winsome sight." Smithwick stretched his legs and clasped his hands behind his head. "I don't imagine I'll lay eyes on a pair of white ones."

"I'll bet Isaac has peeped at that sister of his," Felix said.

"Never had to." Isaac knelt and jiggled the coffeepot.

Ezra broke out of his trance. "What in hell do you mean?"

Uncle Jimmy spat. "I'm ready to hear this."

"We were pickin' blackberries and she plopped down to rest on a bed of piss ants. Sat there for a spell scratchin' around before she realized they were all over her." He tossed the dregs from Ezra's cup, refilled it for himself, and waited.

"Go on now, goddamnit," Ezra said.

Isaac shrugged. "Not much to tell. She squalled and flapped and come out of every stitch she had on."

Ezra blinked. "What'd you do?"

"I took my hat and helped her knock them ants off." He sipped his coffee and tried to suppress a smile. The big man's mind would never be idle again.

Inez finished delousing and pulled her smock over her head. "Well, hell. Now we'll have to wait four or five days for another look," Felix said.

Smithwick said, "Isaac, I told her yesterday morning that you were due back, and she's been primping ever since."

"Let her primp." Isaac doubted she weighed a hundred pounds. She grabbed her long plait and pulled it over her shoulder for inspection. Evidently satisfied, she flipped it back. Her copper bracelets jingled. "Little bitty thing, ain't she?"

Smithwick nodded sagely. "Yes sir. But you'd know she's there."

The men drifted back toward the bunkhouse and the shade of the east wall of the fort. Isaac drained his cup, then walked over and squatted a few feet from Inez's fire. "*Buenos días,* Inez."

She watched him, unsmiling. "Isaac," she said tentatively, as if testing her voice.

"Did Noah treat you well?"

"He kept the other men away. But they still look at me."

"Yes." He hesitated. "They like to look at a comely woman."

Her eyes darted about as she considered his comment. "I don't know what to do. Castro won't take me home."

"I'll talk to him."

"He said I was to be your wife."

"I'll talk to him."

"He said the father of the woman you want hates you."

"Yes." He glanced back at Smithwick, who still sat on the bench looking about idly.

"He won't take me back. He has said."

"He will. I'll talk to him."

She furrowed her brow.

"I hope to marry this other woman."

"Take her. But I have nowhere to go."

Isaac sighed. Another problem. Maybe the girl could learn English and help out around the farm. His family harbored no hatred of Indians. Or perhaps someone else might take her eventually. Plenty of men would want her. Yet there had to be more to her story. Castro hadn't given her up because of lack of food or to repay Isaac for his help during the Waco ambush. Or not for these reasons alone. She'd done something, or refused to do something. He might never know.

He felt a sudden tenderness toward her. He wanted to touch her face, but had no idea how a Lipan girl might interpret the gesture. And Smithwick was still looking on, his efforts to appear disinterested notwithstanding. Isaac couldn't remember Looks Far ever showing affection toward his wives. But then, Comanche and Lipan ways might be different. King Sol sometimes fussed over his wife and daughters, laughing affectionately at their antics.

He smiled. Inez smiled for an instant, then seemed to catch herself. She watched him. Her forearms rested on her thighs. Hands dangled between her knees.

"How old are you?" Isaac asked.

"Older than Castro's youngest wife."

Isaac nodded. She didn't know her age. She was old enough to bear children and that was all that mattered. He caught himself still nodding. Inez was looking at him as if he were afflicted.

"I have to go back to the Comanche camp in two days."

Her eyes widened slightly. "They cannot be trusted. They want you to come to their camp so they can kill you and Noah. Then what will I do?"

He stood and looked down at her. "I'll come back and talk to Castro. You should go back to your family."

She turned sullen. "He won't have me."

Isaac looked around, trying to think of something to say. Inez got up and walked back to her lean-to. She lay on her blanket with her back to him.

• • •

Isaac lay on his bunk, suffocating, determined not to cough again. He'd taken a summer cold earlier that afternoon and had been hacking ever since, despite a cup of Smithwick's cough concoction of equal parts honey and Uncle Jimmy's homemade gut warmer. Now he tossed mildly drunk and was still suffering. He lurched and let go several dry hacks. Uncle Jimmy and Felix snored on. Smithwick rolled over. Ezra said, "By god, Isaac, you're rattlin' the roof."

Isaac sat up. "Sorry, Ezree." He got out of his bunk and started rolling his bedding.

Ezra whispered, "Now hell, don't go gettin' up. I wasn't fussin' at you."

"I ain't sleepin' a wink; no sense keepin' the whole company up." He pulled on his moccasins and stepped through the open door into the summer night. Inez raised her head. The dim light from the coals shone in her dark eyes and on her black hair. Dust hung in the air. The men had long since worn the grass and forest duff away, and there had been no rain in weeks. The water troughs all held a skim of dust. He'd be glad for fall.

He rolled his bedding out on the lightly trammeled ground beneath the parapet. Nicholas Wren had watch tonight; he paced overhead. Isaac smelled his pipe smoke and heard his soft steps. "Evenin', Nick."

"Evenin' to you, Isaac. You're bayin' like Noah's hound."

"You'll know when I tree somethin'."

Wren laughed and said, "I believe you've a mellower voice though." He padded on around the wall.

Isaac's coughing grew worse. Sweat beaded on his forehead and rolled down his sides. He sat up. The air under the parapet smelled rank, full of cedar and dust and rotting leaves and gnats. He pulled off his shirt and rolled it up to use as a pillow. He coughed again, and thought of his camp beneath the rock outcropping, and the winter sky. He dozed between coughing fits, dreaming of Catherine's hands on his face and her flushed cheeks; then he was lying with her in Looks Far's lodge, but Cedrick was heating a horseshoe in the lodge fire and beating it and sparks were flying about the lodge and Looks Far was laughing and Isaac was screaming at Cedrick to stop.

He woke to the smell of hair and sweat. Inez sat at his side, her hand on his chest. He saw only the outline of her face and smock in the moonlight. Nick Wren padded by above.

Her hand felt cool. "You are bad," she whispered. "Are you thirsty?"

"Yes." His throat was parched.

She rose and walked into the darkness. He missed her touch. She re-appeared with a gourd dipper full of water. He gulped it down. It tasted clean; she'd brushed aside the dust scum before she dipped.

"*Gracias.*" He lay back and closed his eyes and listened to her breathing. Again, she touched his chest; he covered her hand with his, felt her wire bracelets and delicate wrist. She didn't move. He said nothing, stroked her fingers. She kept her hand where it was and lay down beside him. He moved over so that she would not have to lie in the dust. Her face was even with his. As she adjusted her feet, her toes touched the side of his knee.

He felt her breath on his face; smelled her fresh sweat. He turned to face her and eased his arm beneath her head and felt the stiff hairs of the deer tail that hung down her back.

He coughed. "Damn it." She laid her hand on his side. He was fully aroused. Wren walked above them again. He wanted to slip his hand beneath her dress; she'd let him. But then what would be his debt? She had come to him out of concern, he thought, but she was also doing what she could to survive. He moved his hand to the small of her back. Did one kiss a Lipan girl? What if he tried and she thought the practice odd? He was about to take advantage of a desperate girl. She lifted her leg and laid it across his—doing what she had to do. Catherine had gone after what she wanted.

Nick Wren started down the ladder. Inez stiffened. Her breathing was still soft, but ragged now. From the shadows Isaac watched Wren walk to the fire pit, lift an ember, and light his pipe. He walked back and put his foot on the first wrung, then peered into the darkness. Isaac could see him trying to make out the shapes. After a few seconds, he said, "Oh . . . beg your pardon, Isaac." He hurried up the ladder and walked off toward the eastern wall. Inez's sides shook with laughter. He'd barely seen her smile, let alone laugh. He'd never hear the end of it now. Wren would tell the whole company, and word would eventually get back to Cyrus, and, God forbid, Thomas Adair. He lay still. After a while, Inez's breath became deep and regular. Isaac coughed little and slept through the wee hours. When he woke just before dawn, Inez was gone. He looked toward her lean-to. She knelt, feeding twigs into her fire. The coals ignited the kindling and the new flame lit her copper face.

At breakfast, he avoided Nicholas Wren's eyes and enjoyed the hot coffee on his raw throat. Inez went about her morning ritual of inspecting her plait and beating her blankets. She paid him no special attention.

He imagined the men's sniggers and their eyes on him, but saw or heard nothing out of the ordinary. They ogled Inez as usual.

Both his cough and his outlook improved with every dose of Smithwick's cough medicine. Sweet little Inez, he decided, ought to be looked after. A man had to live with himself, after all. That heathen Castro had left the defenseless girl in his care and part of taking care of a woman was seeing that all her needs were met. He watched her sewing the heel of Smithwick's moccasin. The Captain sat in the bunkhouse door with his bare feet before him. "First time they've had a breath of air in half a year," he said.

Isaac said, "Good lord, they might be breathin' but I'm holdin' my breath."

Smithwick nodded toward Uncle Jimmy. "Take another dose of medicine, and you'll breathe without a care."

Old Jimmy raised his jug in agreement. "It evens out a man's disposition. Just look at me."

Isaac had much rather look at Inez. Just doing what she had to do. Who could blame her? Good thing Castro had seen fit to leave her in his care. But he had to leave for the Comanche camp the next morning. He picked up his cup from the oak log the rangers used as a bench. He'd seemed to need to cut the spirit with honey less and less as the day wore on. Jimmy filled it a quarter full. It went down easy. He'd hardly coughed all day. He looked at Nick Wren dozing in the shade. Good old Wren. The sun was directly overhead, but the heat bothered him little. Still he looked forward to nightfall.

He woke nauseated and coughing in his bunk. Moonlight streamed in through the propped-open window. He didn't remember crawling into bed; last thing he knew he was lying on the puncheon bench in front of the bunkhouse, talking with Felix about Comanche women. The other rangers snored around him. He rolled onto his side, and the nausea abated. God only knew what he'd said that afternoon. He'd never hear the end of it.

Through the window, he heard the leaves whispering in the breeze, imagined the purling river and Inez's tiny hands. He rolled onto his other side and massaged his temples.

From the bunk beside him, Smithwick whispered, "A little sickish?"

"Damn."

"Well." He chuckled softly. "Go on outside if you want to. I won't say a word to the boys. I'll rouse you when it's time to load up."

"Why would I want to go outside?"

"Suit yourself, my boy."

He sat up and held his head. "Maybe a little air would do me some good."

"Sure it would. Go on. I'll wake you."

He stepped into the moonlight. The trees soughed above him, but little air moved within the fort. Inez lay on her blanket, her back to him.

His stomach rolled. He sat on the bench and hung his head between his knees until he felt better. He looked up to see Nick Wren watching him from the parapet. The older man lifted a hand. Isaac returned the greeting. Wren walked off toward the west wall.

Isaac coughed. Inez rolled over and rubbed her eyes. He went to her on unsteady legs. She sat up as he knelt. He stroked her hair; she smiled and laid her hand on his forehead. He closed his eyes, and she laughed softly and massaged his temples. Her fingertips felt cool, but rough and hard like Esther's, unlike Catherine's scalding touch. "Jimmy's jug made you sick," she said. "You are not used to it as he is."

"No. But your fingers feel good." He opened his eyes. She still regarded him with slight wariness. Holding back. What had she known in her early years as a Lipan captive? And how must he look to her with his shaggy hair and beard and green eyes and floppy hat?

He gently held her thick braid; ran his hand along its length. She averted her eyes. She was not comforting him in the darkness beneath the parapet now. He'd come to her and their faces were lighted by fire and moon. "Pretty," he said. She glanced up at him and swallowed. He bent and kissed her on the forehead, then looked back toward the west wall. Wren was out of sight, somewhere in the shadows. She touched her forehead where he'd kissed her, then touched his moustache and smiled.

She guided him onto his side and lay beside him. He pulled her to him, and she buried her face beneath his chin, her hands tight against her chest. He stroked her hair and felt the rhythm of her breathing. His head felt much better now.

After a few minutes she rolled onto her other side and shoved her bottom tight against his belly. She fanned her face. "Whoo." Sweat trickled off her jaw onto her neck. He felt the roughness of her knee, and had begun to move his hand along her hard thigh, but her breathing had steadied. He patted her hip and lay with the strong scent of her hair in his nostrils.

He woke to the sound of Smithwick stirring coals and making coffee. Inez snored softly. The air felt much cooler. He checked the Little Dipper; a good hour until dawn. Sadness and despair welled in him so that his throat ached. He had enjoyed his visit to the Comanche camp, but now he thought only of the drudgery and confinement of camp life, and Inez imprisoned in the fort under the lecherous gaze of men who hadn't seen their wives in weeks and some who'd never known a woman.

He listened with dread to Smithwick's footsteps. The Captain bent and shook him. "Coffee's about ready, son."

Inez sighed and propped herself up on an elbow. Smithwick patted her shoulder. "*Buenos días,* Noah," she said sleepily. Isaac rose, acutely aware of the sudden coolness on his chest. Inez fed the coals of her own fire, then walked into the shadows behind her lean-to.

Smithwick watched her go. "Sleep well?"

Isaac ran his fingers through his hair.

"It ain't exactly a secret," Smithwick said.

"Well."

"Ain't a man in this company gonna hold it against you."

Isaac pointed to the steam rising from the coffeepot. "You're fixin' to burn the coffee."

Smithwick hurried to the fire, moved the pot off the coals, and poured in a cup of cold water to settle the grounds. "Get up and fix a man's coffee and he complains. Just how will you take your breakfast this morning, sir?"

"I'm obliged, Captain. I know I'm cross."

"I'd think you'd be in fine spirits." He watched Inez step back into the firelight. "Layin' half the night with a pretty little thing. And the rest of us suffering."

"Layin' was all that was goin' on."

"Now there you go complaining again." He knelt and banged the pot against a rock.

Isaac laughed and held out his cup. It was hard to maintain a poor disposition around Smithwick. A little coffee and breakfast and he'd be fine. And a long ride through good country ahead. He watched Inez kneeling before her fire, chewing her jerky and hardtack. He wanted to go to her and reassure her that he'd return and that she needn't fear the other men or the future. But she seemed to expect nothing from him. As far as he could tell, she hadn't glanced his way since she awoke. "I don't know what to think."

Smithwick nodded and watched her. "She won't show what she feels the way a white girl would. She's just sittin' over there bein' who she is. She ain't no better or no worse; she just is. And you won't change her. She's a grown girl."

Isaac smiled and sipped his coffee. "A right healthy grown girl."

An hour later, Isaac cinched the load on Thud. Ezra slapped him on the back. "Watch yourself around them heathen women."

"I ain't afraid of a Comanche woman."

Ezra grinned. "Them too."

"Damn you."

Ezra threw back his head and laughed. "Did you hear that, Felix? He's goin' after Comanche women now."

"It's a good thing you don't care nothin' about my sister, since I'll have to tell her what a sorry bastard you are."

"Like I said, Felix, Isaac here is a courtly man of virtue."

"You make sure nobody bothers that girl."

Felix lit his pipe. "We'll watch out for her." His eyes were grave behind the smoke.

Ezra said, "Sure enough, I didn't mean nothin', Isaac."

Isaac smiled and nodded. "You just keep thinkin' about Esther's blond locks and how bad you'd like to get your fingers in 'em. Of course, Jonas McElroy's been her beau for a long time. I expect they'll get married before long, but I s'pose I could put in a word for you—if I was inclined." He swung into the saddle.

Ezra slapped Squab's flank. "Get on out of here." The little mustang jumped but Isaac sawed him to a standstill. "Maybe Esther will invite you to the weddin'."

Nick Wren opened the gate. "God bless you, boys."

Smithwick touched his hat brim. "That's what you said last time, Nick."

Wren said, "I'll keep sayin' it until you don't come back."

Isaac looked back at Inez. She sat staring at her little fire. He started through the gate, glanced back again and caught her eye.

They rode down the ridge toward the river. Isaac said, "I don't know what to do."

Smithwick cleared his throat. "Feelin' tender about her or just needin' a good poke? Sometimes a young man has trouble tellin' the difference, but he gets better at it as he ages."

Isaac said, "Both, I reckon." He realized he hadn't thought about Catherine in two days.

"An earnest young man. I swear, Isaac Webb, you've got a steep path ahead."

Thirty-Eight

ISAAC SAT HIS HORSE on the hillside and watched Looks Far and Best Cousin below coursing a ratty-maned buffalo cow. They'd caught a little band grazing in a savannah. A half dozen or so had escaped, crashing through the surrounding oak and cedar scrub, but the boys cut off the old cow. Now, Looks Far distracted her, rushing in, shooting arrows into her sides, while Best Cousin eased in on her left flank, looking for a chance to drive his lance in behind her last rib.

Isaac already had a young buck and a pair of turkeys loaded onto Thud, who stood dozing.

The cow faced Looks Far, but her hindquarters quivered and she lowered her head. Best Cousin rode closer. Looks Far dashed in and shot another arrow just behind her shoulder. She bellowed, tried to charge, but faltered. Blood flew from her nostrils. Best Cousin drove his lance down and in behind her last rib and into her vitals. She turned on his horse, but the little mustang skittered away. The buffalo took a few steps in Best Cousin's direction, the lance still protruding from her side, then dropped to her knees. The boys whooped and looked back at Isaac. He held his rifle over his head in acknowledgment, then rode down the hill.

Looks Far dismounted, eased up to the dying beast, and feigned an attack with his knife. The old cow kept her eyes on him, but did not move. Isaac could hear her rattling lungs fifty yards away. The young warrior leapt forward and slit her throat. A crimson spot spread on the grass.

Looks Far stood holding his knife, watching the old cow die. "This one is too old to have a calf. Look; she's dry."

Isaac reined Squab to a stop and dismounted. "Her hide will make a poor robe."

Best Cousin jerked his lance out of the beast's side. "But it will make a good lodge hide." The tortured breathing stopped. Best Cousin touched her eye with his lanced tip. She didn't blink.

Isaac knew the meat would be tough and dry, but he doubted his Comanche friends would mind. They'd eat fresh meat tonight, then jerk the rest. He rolled up his sleeves. Sweat dripped from his beard, and flies swarmed over the carcass. The two Comanches seemed in no hurry. They drank from their water bags and alternately squinted at the clear sky and their kill.

Isaac cut the hide along the base of the cow's neck. Looks Far and Best Cousin tied their bags back on their saddles and drew their knives. They were all sweating and swatting flies, carefully cutting and peeling to avoid puncturing the hide when Squab nickered. Isaac stepped back and picked up his rifle that he'd propped against a clump of shinnery. Looks Far took his bow from the grass and nocked an arrow. They hunkered and caught their horses. Squab's ears were pricked. Looks Far pointed to the trees on the hillside.

They'd just mounted when Isaac heard a wet slap and Best Cousin fell backward out of his saddle and Looks Far was specked with blood and bits of bone. Then the musket blast rolled over the grass. Isaac dug his heels into Squab's sides and rode for the hillside cover. He expected a ball in his back, and heard gunfire buzzing close to his ears, and prayed that Looks Far was still in the saddle.

Movement in the trees along the base of the hillside. Four riders closing from his left. They had the angle on him. He swerved right, but saw there was no hope. He could hear their shrieks now. He'd have to make his stand in the open.

Looks Far screamed curses behind him. He wouldn't have to make his stand alone. The riders were within fifty yards now. Isaac reined Squab, dismounted, dropped to a knee and aimed. Long braids and tattooed faces. Wacos. Looks Far rode by him. Isaac gritted his teeth. The bastard was leaving him. So much for all of the Comanche courage. The front sight settled on the lead rider's chest. They'd all shot their rifles, and were now coming with bows and battle axes. He squeezed the trigger and heard the sickening hiss of a misfire. No sense running. Fear rose in his throat. Nothing to do but wait. He might get one good swing with his rifle. He held the sight on the lead rider. They wouldn't know he'd misfired. Maybe they'd break off their charge. But they came on. He felt for his blade; still there. He wouldn't be taken alive.

He glimpsed movement to his right. Looks Far rode across the path of the oncoming Wacos. He had his right leg hooked over his saddle and lay to the lee side of his horse. One of the warriors lurched and fell. The Comanche wheeled his pony and rode at the attackers, who reined their horses and tried to turn to favor their bow arms. He came at them low, leaning forward, the side of his face pressed to the horse's neck, and split the attackers before they could draw their bows. Another Waco fell. Isaac got to one knee, primed his pan, and sought a target. Looks Far rode for the hillside cover again, the two Wacos in pursuit. Isaac had no shot. He mounted and followed.

The Wacos closed. Looks Far stopped, and the little mustang seemed to swivel on its hind legs, its belly nearly brushing the ground. He rode into the Wacos again, and Isaac saw the blur of arrows and another warrior clawing at his neck as he fell from his horse.

Looks Far and the remaining Waco whirled to face each other. The Comanche reached for another arrow, but his quiver was empty. He drew his battle ax from a saddlebag and cursed the Waco, who nocked an arrow.

Eighty yards, perhaps. Isaac dismounted, sat and crossed his legs and rested his elbows on his knees. Too late. The two Indians charged. Looks Far rode straight for the Waco, hand ax raised. The Waco drew his bow and leaned forward to shoot. Looks Far disappeared on the far side of his horse; the arrow flew and the Comanche popped up again as they passed.

They turned and faced one another again, chests heaving. Isaac shot the Waco out of the saddle. He caught Squab and rode to meet Looks Far, who was already over the dead Waco holding his head up by the braids. He looked wild eyed at Isaac.

"Your scalp!"

Isaac dismounted, started to step forward, then stopped, "You can take it."

"No! Yours!" Spittle flew from his mouth. What Isaac had thought was sweat were tears dripping from his jaws.

Isaac drew his knife and peeled off the scalp.

Looks Far mounted and went looking for the other fallen Wacos. He took two scalps, then followed a widening blood trail through the grass to a middle-aged warrior trying to crawl to cover with an arrow through his shoulder. He dismounted and kicked the man's face and shoulder, grabbed the Waco's braids, and held the knife to his throat. Isaac turned away. He was not in his world and would not interfere.

He climbed back into the saddle. "I'll see to Best Cousin." He heard the hum of the flies fifty yards from the boy's body and the bison carcass. He picketed Squab upwind, tried to clear his mind, then walked into the bloody grass.

The ball had hit Best Cousin just below his right eye. The Waco had made a long shot—well over a hundred yards. Isaac had always heard that Indians were miserable rifle shots, but at least one had been excellent or very lucky. From here on, he'd assume excellent. The boy lay on his back. Isaac tidied him as best he could, pulling together the already stiffening legs, folding his hands on his stomach. He took from his saddlebag a swath of cloth he'd planned to cut into patches and covered the boy's face.

In the distance he heard the Waco's grunts and moans. The man was no coward. There was resolve in his voice; no piteous whining or screaming. He knew his fate and was determined to take it with courage.

Isaac started to tie Best Cousin onto his horse, but he thought that perhaps the Comanches might have some ritual they performed on a fallen warrior. He dragged the corpse away from the swarming flies and sat down beside it. He glanced at Looks Far bent over the Waco, then looked out over the savannah and the dark green of the cedar-covered hills.

He'd killed another man, and only just now thought of it. Is this how it grew on a man? He pulled the wet scalp from beneath his belt and tied it to the rawhide thong along with the other one. He told himself he did this for Looks Far's sake. One had to follow the traditions of one's hosts.

He'd now killed more men than those who commanded him. What did this say about him? That he was a deadly fighter, or that he had a knack for getting into trouble? Had Looks Far not ridden onto the charging Wacos, he—Isaac—would be dead and scalped by now. He'd been lucky. Why had the ball hit Best Cousin instead of him? His calm surprised him. He looked at his hands; steady as if he were eating supper at home. Is this what he'd become? Yet he was alive. The blood drying on his hands felt cool in the late morning breeze. He smelled the rank grass and cedar and his own sweat.

The moaning stopped. Looks Far rode up, dismounted, and stood over his dead friend. Tears rimmed his bloodshot eyes. Gore speckled his face and bare chest and arms. He wiped his nose with the back of his hand. Isaac stood and held up his palms and shook his head in acknowledgment. Looks Far bent and laid his hands on the dead boy's chest. After a few minutes, he grabbed Isaac's arms, shook him, then lay his forehead on Isaac's chest and wept bitterly. Isaac felt the boy's hot black hair beneath his chin and after a moment he cried with him.

They tied Best Cousin's stiff body on his horse, trying to give it a measure of dignity, but their efforts only made the corpse look more macabre. Finally they gave up and just tied him facedown across his saddle.

They rode back toward camp. At the top of the hill, Isaac paused to look out over the savannah at the partially skinned bison and the scattered darkening splotches on the prairie. The sun was overhead now, and the first buzzards were drifting out of the hills.

He rode behind Looks Far, who led Best Cousin's pony. The sun shone on the dead boy's copper skin, and the tassels on the heels of his moccasins fluttered in the wind.

· · ·

Two little girls stopped playing with a pup and watched doelike as Isaac and Looks Far rode into camp. A woman wailed; a girl dropped an adze and clawed at her face, leaving bloody furrows on her nose and forehead. Boys ran for the lodges of their elders. Shrieks and hoarse curses erupted all over camp, and warriors ran from their lodges and crowded around the riders, faces twisted in anguish. Looks Far had pulled himself together and now rode with his head up, stoic, as would be expected of a warrior. The fresh scalp dangled from Isaac's rifle stock.

Smithwick and the chiefs ducked out of the council lodge. The captain caught Isaac's eye and shook his head. Looks Far sat his horse and spoke in Comanche to Muguara and Buffalo Hump and raised the three scalps, then motioned toward Isaac. Several women had gathered around and were unlashing Best Cousin's body.

Buffalo Hump stepped up and took Looks Far's forearm, shook it gently, and spoke to him. The boy squeezed the chief's hand.

Smithwick said, "I fear we've brought this sorrow. The Wacos attacked because Isikweb and Castro killed four in the battle on the river."

Looks Far said, "No. The first shot killed Best Cousin. Then Isikweb fought the Wacos."

Buffalo Hump snorted in disgust. "These Wacos thought they could surprise and kill these boys. Their reasons don't matter to me."

Warriors muttered angrily in Comanche. At first Isaac feared some of their anger was directed toward him, but their eyes seemed to soften when they looked at him.

The women carried Best Cousin's body away toward his lodge. One More Girl and Feels How Deep the Water Is came to take the horses.

In the council lodge, Looks Far retold the story. For the moment, the passion of the fight seemed to overcome his grief as he recounted the battle.

The older men looked to Isaac. He nodded. "That's what happened."

Buffalo Hump began preparing a pipe. "We will find their camps northeast of here on the Brazos. Every warrior will want to go and kill these miserable Waco farmers." He looked at Smithwick.

The Captain cleared his throat. "If Houston learns that we are raiding with our Comanche friends, he will send someone other than Isikweb and me to visit you."

Muguara grunted. "Then you will stay here with me while our warriors gather Waco scalps."

Isaac quietly let out a breath. He doubted the raiders would restrict butchery to other warriors. He wanted no part of it.

Late afternoon, he stood outside Best Cousin's lodge, while inside Looks Far and the boy's father and uncles prepared the body for burial. He could hear their sobs and the hushed tones of anger and bereavement. After a while, they emerged and tied the body in a sitting position on the horse. The procession started eastward, the two sisters riding beside the corpse, holding it erect.

With the sun just above the western hills, the men lay the body under a knee-high ledge near the head of a grassy draw and closed the entrance with rocks. They said nothing over the grave; simply mounted and rode back to camp, the women wailing all the way.

Isaac rode up beside Looks Far. "I know you'll miss him."

Looks Far looked at Isaac with bloodshot eyes. "Isikweb, we must not speak of the dead," he said softly.

Isaac could hear the angry whooping of the men and the shrieks of the women half a mile from camp. Looks Far said, "Buffalo Hump is calling for a raid against the Wacos. We will ride north after dark."

They rode in at dusk. A fire burned near the center of camp, and the children were bringing armloads of wood from all directions. Looks Far sat up straight in the saddle, his eyes bright now. They picketed their horses near his lodge, and Looks Far hurried toward the commotion.

Isaac followed at a respectful distance, and, much to his relief, found Smithwick standing well away from the din. The older man nodded. "Your grandkids won't believe you."

"I'm about ready to head for the fort."

Smithwick said, "I expect we'd best be still and keep quiet." He looked at the fire. "You're gettin' pretty hard on Wacos."

"Thought I was dead. I never seen anybody fight from horseback like that Comanche did. We don't want to fight these boys out in the open."

"The idea is not to have to fight 'em anywhere."

After dark, four drummers began a rhythmic beat, and the camp dogs started to howl. The young women chanted and sang. Occasionally one of the men would leap into the circle of firelight and shout in Comanche and feign a lance thrust or ax blow and point to the heavens and the women would shriek their encouragement and approval. At times, old men danced stiffly and spoke and the drummers stopped and the others listened respectfully.

"Telling a big one," Smithwick whispered into Isaac's ear.

Isaac and Smithwick sat in the dirt, petted a mongrel pup, and watched the dance. Home and family, fort and Inez seemed like scenes from some bland dream; the fire blazed a dozen feet high, and the dancers cast wild shadows on the lodges. Beyond the firelight, the children danced in imitation of their elders. The afternoon's sorrow seemed forgotten; here were men preparing for what they lived for. Isaac shuddered. He imagined such preparation for a raid on the settlers around Bastrop.

The night wore on. Sparks rose and blew out over camp, and shadows moved among the lodges and into the woods. Buffalo Hump left the gathering and walked to his teepee; other warriors drifted away. Isaac watched for Looks Far, who'd disappeared into the mass of bodies, but couldn't find him. He wondered if he was back at the lodge, grieving or preparing his weapons.

Someone placed a hand on his shoulder. Isaac turned and recoiled. Looks Far stood holding his bow and shield, one side of his face painted black, the other side painted white. He seemed bigger and older than he did only hours before. And utterly terrible. No longer the curious jocular boy, but a killer. There were no tears in his eyes now. He saw Isaac's reaction and seemed to leer.

The Comanche squatted on his heels, his face inches from Isaac's. His eyes shone with excitement. "We leave soon, my friend. I owe you much, so I will not leave you alone. One More Girl will see to you while I am away." He nudged Isaac's shoulder. "We should return in four days."

Isaac said, "I thank you, friend."

Looks Far rose and walked into the darkness.

Smithwick said, "I wonder who's gonna look after me."

Three dozen mounted warriors thrice circled camp to the chanting and clapping of the women, then broke away and rode northeast into the black hills.

• • •

Isaac ducked into Looks Far's lodge, propped his rifle against the wall, and flopped down on his stack of robes. The camp seemed strangely quiet now.

He'd miss his friend's company, but the women always seemed eager for conversation. He enjoyed their gossip and breathless conjecture about ghosts and witches.

He heard soft footsteps and sat up. One More Girl brought in pemmican and water, which she offered without speaking.

He chewed the pemmican, surprised by his hunger. He realized he hadn't eaten since just after sunrise. *"Gracias,"* he said with a full mouth.

She acknowledged him with a glance as she knelt and built up the fire, then studied him as he might size up a prospective mount. He finished his pemmican, drank the water, and handed her the empty gourd. *"Gracias."*

She took it and watched him for a few seconds, then turned toward the door. She looked back at him as she stepped out.

He lay back and thought of Looks Far and the other warriors riding all night for the Brazos. They'd ride out of the next setting sun to strike the Waco camp. God only knew what they'd bring back. Hopefully no captive men for torture. The little ones might fare well enough if they survived the ride and the first few weeks. Would the Comanches treat captives differently in his presence? He doubted it.

The little fire was a comfort, though he didn't need its warmth. The women seemed to know just how to build them. When he returned to the fort, he'd spend the first few nights adjusting to the dark bunkhouse. Then again, he might slip out and sleep with Inez beside her fire. Inez. What would he do about her? What did one do with a Lipan girl? Word would get out. Even though his lying with her was common knowledge among the rangers, he wouldn't feel right about openly lying with her. Never mind that every man in the fort would pile up with her in a heartbeat if he could do it without losing blood. He couldn't see taking her home. Ruth had in mind Christian marriages for her children. Whoever heard of marrying an Indian girl? Two months ago, he was still pining over Catherine Druin, and he still ached whenever he thought about her.

Wolves howled to the northwest; he pictured Smithwick and old Muguara talking gravely about the ever-breeding Texians or laughing over the appetites and carnal preferences of fat wives or joking over the length of their members. Or Smithwick would be writing on paper the names of the chiefs or objects that Muguara would point out, and the Comanches would politely approve.

The howling of the wolves and the flapping of the lodge walls faded and he was at the Adair table. Inez had followed him into the cabin, and he tried to explain that he didn't really know this girl, that she'd been left with him and the only Christian thing to do was to look after her until he could make arrangements, but she came to the table and nuzzled his neck and pressed her loins against him, and now Ruth and Esther and Cyrus were there, and Smithwick was saying, "Oh, don't be too hard on the boy, he's just being a young man, and after all he's no different than any other man." And Cyrus allowed as how when he was a young man he'd have taken a girl any way he could've.

Now Isaac was fully aroused and pulling Inez to him and sliding his hands beneath her dress, embarrassed but powerless to stop, and Louise and Ruth and Catherine were screaming in outrage while Cyrus droned on about being young and virile.

He woke drenched in sweat. The fire had burned to dim, pulsating orange and gray coals. He ran his fingers through his hair.

The door flap opened. One More Girl stepped inside. He couldn't see her face but recognized her profile and ferine motions. "What is it?" he asked.

"I heard you talking. I thought you called me."

"I was dreaming."

"Do you want me to come to you?"

"What?"

"My husband said I was to come to your bed. I thought earlier that you were not ready for me."

Isaac's pulse beat in his temples. "You don't have to do this."

"Yes. My husband said. Do you want me to come to you?" She stepped toward him, knelt beside him.

He could smell her now. And he was still aroused from his dream. Now this. He shivered.

She lay beside him, her face inches from his. "Yes? My husband said. He loves you."

His eyes adjusted, and he saw her broad face, the almond-shaped eyes. She brushed the straight, coarse hair from her cheek. He laid his hand on her forearm. It was hard and thick; he couldn't close his hand around it. She said nothing, watched him. Here lay another man's wife. He pulled her to him; she rolled on top of him. This was different. Her hair fell onto his face, and he ran his hands along the back of her thighs to her round bottom. No pantalets here. She groaned and lowered her forehead to his. So this was what Looks Far meant by taking care of his needs.

• • •

Isaac was sitting in the shade of Looks Far's lodge, leaning back on his saddle, when he saw the white woman. She looked Comanche save for her light brown hair, now streaked with gray. He couldn't discern the color of her eyes. And she was tall and thin, and too narrow of hip to be Comanche. But the sun had turned her skin tobacco brown.

She strode past him. Smithwick had told him she remembered no English. He decided to test the assertion. "Mornin'," he said.

She stopped and eyed him with obvious suspicion. He tipped his hat. "How're you this mornin'?"

She held in one hand a paunch full of water. It dripped at her feet.

"I'm Isaac Webb. How long you been here?"

She looked around warily as she parted her lips as if she were about to speak.

"It's all right. I won't hurt you," Isaac said.

She took a few steps toward him. "Don't know no more. Caddos caught me when I was a girl east of Nacogdoches, then give me to these. I ain't talked to a white man since I was a girl."

"You remember how though."

"Kept talkin' to myself so I wouldn't lose it. They's a Meskin out west of here. I see him when we move out there for the huntin'. He'll talk to me in my tongue. I never learned his."

"Me and the Captain might could do something. Trade for you maybe."

"Swap for me." She smiled, showing broken teeth nearly worn to nubs. "I ain't got nothin' to go back to. Them Caddos never left nothin'."

"Could take you back to the settlements; to Christian people."

She studied him; moved the paunch to the other hand. "They gonna take me in now? Least I got a man here. He's old but he keeps me fed. He's more than I'd have if I went back. These here quit beatin' me after a spell. My daddy beat the hell out of me 'bout every day."

"Well." He hadn't expected this. "I'm sorry about what happened. If I can do somethin', I will."

"I thank ye. I best git." She started to walk away. "They set store by you and that other'n. Don't be lyin' to 'em."

Isaac nodded. "We ain't. Good day to you." He watched her disappear among the lodges along the creek.

• • •

Late afternoon of the third day after the raiders' departure, Isaac climbed into the hills above camp and looked eastward toward Waco country. Heat waves shimmered above the grass and cedar; buzzards circled, rising and falling on thermals. Muguara told him the day before that they would be moving camp soon; the stench had gotten bad. Buzzards, crows, coyotes, and wolves skulked about the edge of camp, gleaning the offal pitched across the creek. He'd gotten so used to the odor that he didn't notice it until after he'd been out of camp, upwind, for a while.

He sat with his back against a cedar stump and watched the horizon. The raiders should be home soon, unless they'd been ambushed or had failed to surprise the Wacos. From what he'd seen, the Comanches could outfight the Wacos any day, but sometimes things went wrong, the way they did at Béxar or Goliad or—from the Mexican perspective—on the Plain of Saint Hyacinth. What would the band do if they suffered more losses? How many Wacos would they then have to kill in order to settle the score?

One More Girl came to him again the night before. Although she seemed willing and knowing, she was not as desirous as Catherine had been. Dutiful, perhaps. Yet he was grateful. She probably saved her ardor for her husband. How would it be between him and Looks Far when the raiders returned? If they returned. The young warrior's wives seemed unconcerned, as if his return were certain. Isaac and One More Girl had not discussed it.

He'd proven powerless in the presence of three women. Word would get to

Thomas Adair and then Catherine. But what difference did it make? He'd seen her contentment that day in the pasture with Thomas and Cedrick. As if there had never been anything between them. No broken heart that he could see. No resentment toward her father. The dutiful daughter.

The setting sun at his back lit the hills before him, turning the grass to copper. The sweetest time of day. He imagined Inez sitting on her blanket enduring the gaping, sniggering rangers. Ezra would be having a good laugh. Let him. He was just jealous. Felix understood it, although he made no secret of his pleasure in watching the girl.

A breeze stirred and dried the sweat on his face and the back of his hands. Nearly dusk. A mockingbird sang its rusty hinge song somewhere below. Swallows skimmed the grass and treetops.

He'd sit until dark. Three does crossed the draw below, halting, listening, sniffing. A dangerous place, but they'd soon have the cover of darkness.

After a while, he realized the swallows had quit for the day. But the mocker sang on. They'd be lighting the night fires in camp now, and the lodges would be lit from within. He didn't have to look down the hill behind him.

Supper would be finished back home. They'd be sitting around the dirt yard to avoid the heat inside the cabin. Cyrus would have his pipe lit. Maybe Jonas would have come by to see Esther. King might be there.

A point of light appeared on a ridge. Then another. In a few minutes, a half-dozen tiny fires winked in the distance—three or four miles away, Isaac guessed. Wacos or Lipans or whites wouldn't risk building fires in this country. The returning raiders wanted to ride into camp in the morning sun. The sight comforted him, though in different circumstances he'd be terrified. He tried not to think about what might be happening around those fires. He pushed himself up and walked back down the hill toward the glowing lodges.

• • •

He woke at sunrise to hoarse screams coming from the hills east of camp. One More Girl lay with him, her bottom shoved against his belly, snoring softly. He shook her awake; she froze for a moment, listening, then scrambled out of the lodge without speaking.

The crier continued in Comanche. Cheers rose, and Isaac heard footfalls as people poured from lodges. He took his rifle and stepped outside. Buffalo Hump rode down the hill at the head of the column of raiders. Best Cousin's mother, Sun Shade, doddered to meet him, carrying a four-foot pole. Buffalo Hump rode by, hung something on it, and continued on toward camp. The others followed and did the same. Isaac squinted into the morning sun to see what hung from the pole. The old woman turned toward her cheering band. Scalps. Easily a dozen.

The procession continued. The pole grew bushy, and Sun Shade handed it to an older boy and clapped her hands in delight. Their faces striped in vermilion, the raiders made a lap around camp, then rode through the center, churning dust and setting the dogs to howling.

Now the captives: seven young women, naked, rings tattooed around their breasts, tied to horses, and two screaming little boys.

The Comanche wives jerked the Waco women from the horses. The captives wailed and covered their faces. One More Girl had one by both braids, dragging her and kicking her in the ribs. Other Comanche women hastily sharpened sticks and laid them into the fire. The Waco children sat tied on horses, mouths stretched wide in terror and despair.

The warriors rode to their lodges, whooping and holding their weapons aloft. Old Muguara stood beaming, watching the women, pointing and laughing. Smithwick stood twenty feet behind him, pacing, running his hands through his hair.

Isaac had seen enough. He walked back to Looks Far's lodge and found him sitting on his stack of robes, beating his heels on the ground to some rhythm.

"The raid went well," Isaac said.

Looks Far's eyes carried no grief or anger; only the euphoria of conquest.

"We rode on them near sundown, Isikweb. The Waco farmers were not expecting us. We burned everything. Trampled their fields. They tried to run, but we rode them down. I took many scalps." He held up six fingers. He massaged his face with his palms and shook his head like a dog and smiled. "It is good now. We can go on." He laid his bow against the lodge wall and went back outside.

• • •

Just after dark, the women lit another pile of wood. Isaac watched as Comanche boys tied the welt-covered captives to a pole a few yards away from the blaze. Warriors appeared, faces freshly painted vermilion, and took their places in a circle around the fire.

The four drummers began their rhythm. The Comanche women danced around the captives, dangling the fresh scalps in their faces or slashing with knives just inches short of their throats.

Isaac and Smithwick again sat outside the firelight, speechless. The women's wails sometimes rose above the din. The two solemn Waco boys sat in the laps of the Comanche women who would eventually raise them. Occasionally a warrior would jump into the ring of light to recall his exploits, while the women clapped and chanted and the men watched gravely.

After a while, Isaac said, "I've seen enough." He rose and went back to the lodge. Just as he bent to step inside, a woman said, "It will not always be this way for them."

He turned. A thin woman stood a few yards away. Her hair and dress looked Comanche. But the moonlight and glow from the lodges lit her more aquiline features. Mexican. "You're the sister."

"I endured what they endure. In time the Comanches will treat them with kindness as they have me. These women will lay with men who killed their people. Sometimes I forget this."

Isaac studied the woman. She looked as old as Ruth, yet she couldn't be more than thirty years old. "But tonight you're remembering."

"Yes."

"Cecilia?"

Her lips trembled.

"Is that your name?"

"For twelve years, I've heard it spoken by no one but me."

"I'm sorry. What do they call you?"

"Say it again. My name."

"Cecilia."

She smiled. "My brother has prospered."

"What can I do for you?"

"I have to go. My husband will be hungry after the dancing." She hurried away toward the firelight and chanting.

He went inside and flopped down on the robes. The fire had burned to ashes. Light and grotesque shadows from the scalp dance played on the walls, and he longed for the relief that comes in that instant of realization after waking from a nightmare. He did not want to talk to Looks Far or any other Comanche. He wanted to hear English spoken and to see blond Esther and eat across a table from Cyrus and Ruth.

He lay on his side to hide his eyes from the shadows, then finally dozed. He woke with a start as Looks Far burst in with Feels How Deep the Water Is. He lay very still as they whispered and laughed. Directly One More Girl joined him; she said nothing, but this time there was nothing dutiful about her movements. She was sweating and desirous, and despite his horror, Isaac responded, all the more aroused by the writhing in the robes beside him.

He woke before dawn. The lodge fire had been rebuilt and the women were gone. Looks Far snored softly.

One More Girl greeted him cheerfully every morning for the next week, but she visited his bed no more. Isaac and Looks Far talked of hunting and weapons and a particularly comely Waco captive that Buffalo Hump had decided to take for a wife. After a few days, the Waco boys began playing with the Comanche children, laughing and squealing and testing the women.

On the last morning of June 1838, while Looks Far watched sullenly, Isaac and Smithwick packed their horses, said their good-byes, and rode south toward the Colorado River. They talked little. Isaac felt the tension leaving him, and he began to think about Inez and his family—and that last night with One More Girl.

After a while Smithwick said, "I believe I'm ready for Bastrop and a spot of fiddle playing."

IV
INEZ

Thirty-Nine

*Webber's Prairie, Colorado River, northwest of Bastrop
January 1839*

DR. JOHN WEBBER pulled his toddler son from beneath the chestnut table and set him in his lap. "The way to get by, Isaac, is to not give a good goddamn what anybody thinks."

Webber's wife, Puss, a tall, statuesque free Negro, stood with Esther, washing dishes at a small pine table near the hearth. Puss threw her rag into the steaming dishpan. "John! Right in front of company and with the baby in your lap."

Webber rolled his eyes and waved off her comment.

Esther dried a handful of forks and spoons, then sorted them in Puss's utensil drawer. "It won't hurt, Aunt Puss. We're all used to it."

"See there, Mother," Cyrus said. "It'll all be just fine. We've never cared what anybody thought and I don't see no reason to start." He rested his elbows on the table and drained his coffee cup.

Ruth laid her head on her forearms. "Lord. The child ate her entire meal with a knife."

Inez sat next to Isaac and stared at the center of the table.

"Nobody's learned her any different," Cyrus said. He studied her a moment. "Pert as a baby coon, ain't she? Look at them black eyes."

"Lord," Ruth said.

"How far gone is she?" Webber asked.

Ruth raised her head and glared at Isaac. "About three or four months, we think."

Webber rested his square, red-bearded chin on his son's head. "Sixteen? Seventeen?"

Isaac said, "I don't think she knows. Best I can tell, Lipan women don't keep up with their age. They're either too young, old enough, or too old."

"I see sense in the method," Webber said, laughing. "Suffice to say, I'm old enough. No need to elaborate."

Ruth folded her hands in her lap as if she'd suddenly remembered her manners. "But Dr. Webber, Puss is a virtuous Christian woman."

Webber looked at Ruth as if she'd uttered astounding news. "Well, I'll declare."

Puss threw back her head and laughed. Dishwater dripped from her elbow.

"This child is a wild heathen," Ruth said.

Cyrus plucked a coffee ground from the tip of his tongue and dropped it in his cup. "Why she'll come around, Mother. Long as we keep her away from Esther."

The Webbers' ten-year-old daughter, Rachel, ran in through the propped-open door, her little brother Caleb in tow. She was tall and narrow of hip like her mother. "There's baby mouses in here." She held up a grass sack.

Puss wrung out her dishrag. "They'd best stay in there too."

"They ain't got no hair on 'em," the little girl said.

"And there ain't gonna be no hide on your bottom if you don't get that poke out of this house right now."

Caleb bounced on his toes. "Let's feed 'em to the hog."

Puss slapped at the boy's bottom with her rag, but he arched just in time to avoid the swat. "Why you little devil! Go put them nasty things back where you found 'em." She wrinkled her nose and turned back to her dishpan as the children ran back outside.

"We can get Zeke Hodge to say a few words of Scripture," Cyrus said. "He'd do it. Then it wouldn't all seem quite so heathenish. What you think, Smithwick? You're bein' awful quiet for a man that probably had a hand in this some way."

"Don't try to pin any of this on Noah," Ruth said. "We know very well where the blame lies."

Isaac sighed, crossed his arms on his chest, and rolled his eyes to Esther, who grinned and shrugged. He had it coming. He wondered what Inez was thinking.

Smithwick, who'd arranged the visit, was leaning back in his chair, legs crossed, fingers laced on his belly. "I'd say we're beating a dead horse to death. Mister Isaac here is either gonna take this gal or he ain't, and I'm bettin' he is, else why is he sittin' here puttin' up with all this mistreatment? I had hoped the good Webbers could offer some comfort and counsel, which they have, in addition to a fine meal."

Ruth smiled, nodded. "Amen to that." Puss scrubbed a pot as if she hadn't heard the compliment. Ruth said, "A lot can happen in the next few months, though. What if she doesn't have this baby? She's awfully young, you know."

Cyrus held up both palms. "Lord, Ruth, this girl is sturdy as a little badger. She'll have this one and a half dozen more and won't break a sweat."

Ruth said, "Isaac Webb, this is not how I'd pictured things."

"No ma'am, I reckon not." He wondered why anyone bothered to picture anything.

"That sorry Catherine Druin had her chance, and she let it go," Esther said.

Isaac could have gone without hearing about Catherine. What would she say about him getting a Lipan girl in a family way? Thomas Adair would trumpet the news to the far hills.

Ruth's expression softened. "Well then." She held out her hand to Inez who looked at it as if it were a scorpion. Isaac nudged the girl's elbow; she lifted her hand from her lap, and Ruth took it. Inez kept her eyes on the table. "Bless her little heart," Ruth said. Isaac's chest welled with relief.

Smithwick sat up straight and placed his palms on the table. "I believe this is about all the attention this young lady can stand."

Ruth let go and leaned back in her chair and smiled at Inez as if seeing her in a new light.

"I reckon we'll grow on her, Mama," Esther said.

Smithwick cleared his throat. "Puss, what went with that big kettle you loaned King that time?"

Puss pointed at the door with the knife she'd just dried. "That's it sittin' out front. I set flowers in it every summer."

"Just makin' sure. I thought maybe you cooked the beans in it."

"I never cooked another thing in it. If I would've known they was goin' to cook somebody in it I'd have told 'em to keep it."

• • •

Isaac bedded in the hay in the Webbers' little barn, exhausted, but sleep eluded him. Cyrus, Smithwick, and two of the Webber boys snored around him. The women and girls and smaller children slept inside with Puss and John Webber.

He knew that Ruth would forgive him, but he wasn't so sure about Looks Far and the Comanches. Houston's term had expired and the new president of the Republic, Mirabeau Buonaparte Lamar, promptly ended the Comanche emissary effort. On their final visit in November, Smithwick explained to the chiefs that this was not his decision and that, in time, the new leaders would come to their senses and renew ties with the Comanches. The chiefs listened politely and assured Smithwick and Isaac that they bore them no ill will. Yet they refused to promise not to raid. Muguara, as he prepared a pipe, said that he would be watching the Tahbay-boh carefully and would act in kind.

Isaac and Looks Far were self-consciously polite. They hunted and lay about camp as before, but the coming separation loomed. One More Girl chattered with Isaac as if nothing had ever happened. Looks Far grew morose the last two days. As Isaac packed Thud, the boy said, "You can visit us without telling Lamar."

Isaac nodded as he cinched the load. "I'll do what I can, friend. You know that."

"You won't come back."

"I will if I can."

"You can."

"I have to do as I am told."

"I can do as I please," Looks Far said. "Have I not been generous with you?"

"Very generous. I am grateful." The Comanches were the most generous and polite people he'd ever known. And the most terrible.

Smithwick led his horse up, followed by the chiefs. Looks Far snorted in disgust and strode back toward his lodge. Smithwick mounted his horse. "My friends." He hesitated.

Buffalo Hump said, "Tell Lamar you want to come back."

"Of course we will."

Most of the band had gathered around them, but Looks Far was nowhere to be seen. The children watched solemnly. Isaac climbed into the saddle. He did not look at the chiefs or at One More Girl as he followed Smithwick out of camp.

Three weeks after Isaac and Smithwick returned to Bastrop, Comanche raiders stole thirteen-year-old Matilda Lockhart and four other children of the Putnam family from farms along the Guadalupe. Most Texians called for revenge. Isaac hoped the raiders were not of Looks Far's band.

• • •

He woke in the cold darkness to find Inez snoring softly beside him beneath a blanket of hay.

• • •

Two weeks later, he stood beside her in the Webbers' cabin while Reverend Ezekiel Hodge read 1 Corinthians 13 and Hebrews 13:4 in English, then haltingly in Spanish for Inez's sake. *Marriage is honorable in all and the bed undefiled. . . .* She listened, eyes locked on the preacher.

The Webbers had pushed the furniture against the walls. They looked on with Cyrus and Ruth, Esther, Smithwick and Widow Duty, Uncle Jimmy, Ezra, and Felix and his portly, blond wife, Francis. Webber children peered from beneath the kitchen table and from behind their parents' legs.

After reading the Scriptures, Hodge said, "Since you're both standin' there and ain't tied up, I figure you're here to get hitched and don't need me to be askin' if you'll take one another. Is there a ring?"

Isaac hadn't thought about a ring. He looked at Cyrus, who shrugged.

Hodge smiled and closed his Bible. "Well then. Far as the Lord and everybody here is concerned, you two are man and wife. I don't have no idea what the Republic of Texas thinks about it." He shook Isaac's hand.

Widow Duty sniffled. Ruth cleared her throat. John Webber slapped his belly with both hands. "Puss, we'd better feed the preacher."

Inez sat at the table next to Isaac, amid the raucous conversation and raillery, and ate her dumplings off the blade of a knife. Isaac started to correct her, but no one seemed to notice. Ezra finished his story about Uncle Jimmy falling off the parapet into the water trough. She licked her knife blade clean and joined in the laughter.

Forty

INEZ COLLECTED all of her possessions at the Webb place—deerskin smock and dress—and rolled them into her blanket. She stood in the yard with Isaac and the rest of the family, looking up the trail toward her new home.

Esther tossed an acorn at Isaac. "You two done got the best part out of the way."

He caught it and pitched it back at her. "Lord, Esther."

"You've got no business expecting mercy, son," Ruth said. She shivered in her gray woolen shawl.

Isaac noticed her raw nose and swollen eyes. "I reckon not." He looked up the creek. The weak winter sun lighted the riffles and the trunks of the sycamores. "Be dark soon. I'd best get a fire built." Why did that familiar quarter-mile walk seem like such a great separation now?

Cyrus drew his pipe from a coat pocket. "Well."

"I go home this way every night," Isaac said.

Ruth wiped an eye. "I know you do."

"No sense gettin' weepy on me." A lump rose in his throat. "I'll be back in the morning."

Ruth nodded and tightened her shawl. "I'll see you then." She went inside. Inez stood holding her blanket under her arm. Tears ran down her cheeks.

"We've upset this gal," Cyrus said. "She don't have no idea what all the cryin' is about. She might think she's the cause of it." He squeezed her forearm. "Little thing."

Esther sat on the step and wiped her eyes with her thumbs. "I swear, brother."

Isaac took Inez's arm. "We're gonna take this few dozen steps up the creek and we'll be seein' you about first light."

Cyrus stuck his pipe stem between his teeth. "Yessir."

Isaac started up the path feeling a greater tug than he'd felt when he first left for Coleman's Fort. Inez walked silently beside him, this girl who'd been blown around like cottonwood down. Yet she took it stoically and no longer seemed like the wild thing that had bitten off the tip of Simon Hicks's finger.

They walked into shadows thrown by giant live oaks. Though Inez had stayed at the home place since Christmas Eve, Isaac had never taken her to his cabin. "Our home is smaller than my father's."

She seemed startled by his voice. "It has a place for a fire?" She was picking up some English, but it was still easier to converse in Spanish.

"Yes. It draws well." He tugged her braid, and she smiled at him, something she hadn't often done. She looked at him in wonder as he took her bedroll. "I'll carry it; it's longer than you are."

They walked into the clearing. The little cabin looked dark and forlorn in the failing light. Sis ran past them, bounded onto the little porch, and waited expectantly by the door, tail whipping. Isaac remembered Felix's statement about the Lipans' taste for dog.

He held open the door and Inez peered in as if she expected a hibernating bear, then stood in the shadows while he kindled the fire. He felt better about his place after the flames lighted the clean-swept floors. Inez's eyes settled on the quilt his mother brought from Arkansas.

"It's yours now. Mine and yours." He sat on the bed and patted the feather mattress. She sat next to him and looked about with glistering eyes. He felt the hum of her mind. Soon the words would start tumbling out. He'd welcome them.

Inez rose and added two more sticks to the fire; knelt and arranged the burning oak just so; walked back to the table and ran her finger over the surface. "Ours," Isaac said.

Her eyes cut to the chest in the corner and the palm-sized mirror hanging over the washbasin. She'd gotten over her fascination with Esther's mirror, but couldn't resist Isaac's. She touched her face.

"Pretty," he said. He wondered how long she could resist checking the trunk. She'd likely be disappointed. A couple of ratty quilts and his Bible.

Inez took her blanket from the chair and spread it on the floor. Sis barreled from beneath the bed, leapt on the blanket, and began pawing and circling. Inez nudged her and said something sharply in her one of her Indian tongues. Sis licked Inez's nose. Isaac laughed. Inez said, "Whoo!" and spat into the fire.

He jerked the blanket from beneath his hound, spread it on the bed, pulled Inez to him. They lay staring at the flames. Inez's hair smelled of cured grass and horses. Tomorrow, he'd ask her to get back into her deerskins. The oversized cotton dress made her seem confused and pitiful and even tinier than she was.

Sis jumped up and went to the door, growling and sniffing, hackles up. Isaac rolled out of bed and grabbed his rifle from the corner. Inez beat him to the door and shoved her ear to the crack. There came a howl and clang of pans and tin cups and hoofbeats around the cabin. Shots rang out.

Isaac propped his rifle back in the corner. "Hell."

Someone pounded on the door. "I say it's time for a little snort in honor of the bride and groom!"

Inez cocked her head. "Jeemy?"

Sis howled. The din continued. Isaac pushed open the window. "Can't a man have a little peace his first night home with his bride?"

"By god, you've done had a little piece!" Felix Gross yelled from the darkness.

Another whoop, this one feral and hoarse. Isaac laughed, shook his head. "King." He jerked open the door, and big Ezra Higginbotham fell in facedown with Uncle Jimmy on his back.

Inez leapt back and danced on the bed. "Be damn!" she said.

Forty-One

THE FIRST MILD DAY in January, Inez stepped off the dimensions of her kitchen garden. Isaac thought the proposed plot awfully small—too small, in fact, to bother with mules and plow—but Wichitas and Lipans were said to be clever farmers; so he dutifully broke the ground with spade, pitchfork, and hoe, and Inez grubbed in manure and the carcasses and offal from Isaac's hunting and whatever other foul things she could find. For several days afterward, he wished they'd located the plot further from the cabin and downwind. But after a week or so, he no longer noticed the stench; he wasn't sure if it had faded or if he'd just grown accustomed to it. Once Sis stopped rolling in the black, crumbling soil, and Esther quit wrinkling her nose whenever she walked by, he supposed the earth had consumed Inez's offerings.

Isaac had assumed their little garden would grow potatoes, onions, turnips, and perhaps collards. He'd raise roasting ears and feed corn on the few acres he and Cyrus had cleared. Then he noticed Inez carefully inspecting the craws of the turkeys and quail he brought in. She'd tear out the seed pouches, lay them aside, and finish dressing the birds. Later, when the light inside the cabin was right, she'd gather the drying sacs and spread their contents on the table to examine and sort them, at such close range he thought her eyes would cross. Tiny piles of various kinds of seeds began to accumulate on the mantle in terrapin shells, deer hooves, dried bison horns. He began to wonder what the garden would bear and what Inez might expect him to eat. He thought about questioning her, but she went about her work with such aplomb, he was loath to expose his ignorance.

Finally he asked, "Why do you get the seeds from birds' craws?"

Inez plucked a black speck from a clot of larger tan seeds Isaac recognized as snakeweed. "I like to let the birds find the seeds for me. They see them on the ground better than I can."

None of Isaac's family seemed inclined to learn Spanish, so Inez began to learn the English names of things. Mostly, though, she and Isaac still conversed in Spanish.

Inez and Esther liked each other from the beginning and did their chores together whenever they could. Esther enjoyed plaiting Inez's hair and Inez returned the favor. Ruth had been cool toward Inez in the beginning, but soon fussed over her and chided Isaac for letting the pregnant girl lug armloads of firewood and pails of milk and water.

The girl had gone back to wearing her buckskins; Cyrus often yanked the deer tail on her smock whenever she walked by.

Isaac still caught himself thinking of Catherine or brooding over Thomas Adair's rejection. The thoughts came to him mostly as he went about his chores. He'd likely see her again and wondered how the encounter might go. At night, though, with Inez beside him, he rarely thought of Catherine.

Yet Inez rarely spoke. Isaac wondered if Lipan women talked with their men. He wanted to share his hopes for their little farm and speculate on the sex of their unborn child or describe the way Sis trailed a raccoon along the trunk of a tree that had fallen across the creek. Whenever he worked near the house, chopping wood, repairing a harness, working a new spade handle, he liked a bit of conversation, which generally caused Inez to stop working to listen.

"I love to split a fine piece of oak," he'd say. "See how pretty that stick split?"

She'd look at the pieces of firewood, his ax, then him. Storing it all away, he thought. Or considering his dementia. What sort of mad man enjoyed hard labor? No self-respecting Lipan or Wichita warrior would think of doing women's work.

Usually, they took supper at the home place. There were few chores to do in January, so most days they headed down the creek by midafternoon. Inez seemed most comfortable working alongside the women while Isaac and Cyrus talked or made repairs or did light chores. Sometimes he watched her and wondered about her Wichita family. Any that survived the Lipan attack surely missed her and wondered about her. And would she return, given the chance? Her affection seemed genuine, especially at night while they lay quietly listening to the fire popping. She sought his touch, but was she merely making the most of what she had?

Other times he felt fiercely protective of this tiny girl, stolen then cast away like chattel. He'd give her a good life; prove to her that things worked out for the better after all her misery. His wife. The idea seemed strange. Who was this girl, this tiny wild thing?

• • •

Two weeks after his wedding, Isaac rode out of the hills north of home. Thud lumbered behind him, hauling a pair of whitetail does. A low sky blocked the afternoon sun. A raw wind had roused, and the smell of wood smoke from his cabin eased him.

He rode into the hard-packed yard and found Noah Smithwick petting and sweet-talking Sis while Inez peered into the hound's ear.

Sis whipped her tail. Smithwick said, "I figured I'd best get up here and see to your hound and your woman."

Isaac dismounted. "Well, I'm back, so you can go on home."

Inez plucked a tick from Sis's ear, flicked it away, then rose and dusted her knees. She eyed the two deer with obvious approval and smiled at Isaac.

"I s'pect you came by to check on supper too," Isaac said. "And Esther."

"Miss Esther looks to be doing fine. Of course she did mention supper."

"Asked about the Widow too, I imagine."

"She shows the utmost concern for the good Widow."

"She's concerned about her sure enough."

Inez hurried into the cabin. Smithwick said, "Let's jerk the hides off the meat."

Inez reappeared with a pair of skinning knives, which she gave the men. She led the horses back to their stalls while Isaac and Smithwick hung the first deer from the gambrel. Isaac tested the edge of one of the knives by shaving a patch of hair from the back of his hand. "Inez keeps these blades sharp."

Smithwick grinned. "A Lipan gal never knows what she might need a blade for. Thousand wonders she didn't geld half the boys at the fort."

"She's grown on me." Isaac made a cut along the hindquarters, then gently worked the blade along the surface of the muscle as Smithwick pulled the hide away. "Understand, now, I'm glad to see you," Isaac said, "but I know good and well you didn't come out here just to visit and ogle all these fine-looking Webb women."

"Well, I'm a man of affairs, as you know."

"Affairs. A fair bet you'll try to talk me into gettin' shot or scalped. Lamar decided he wants me to palaver with the Comanches again?"

"No palavering this time, son."

"I always get a bad feeling when you call me 'son.'"

Smithwick nodded. "It's serious, but I don't know what to think about it."

Isaac stopped skinning. "Lord. What?"

"There have been some horses stolen around Bastrop and further up the Colorado since Christmas."

"Might've been Lipan or Tonk."

"I talked to King. Took him up to a farm north of Bastrop. He says Comanche and I believe him."

"Well. You'd never find 'em."

"Castro and his boys found a big encampment up on the San Gabriel. Colonel Moore is gettin' two companies together to ride on them. I'll be leading the Bastrop company."

Inez came back from the horse shed, rubbing her belly. Isaac said, "They'll ride without me. I imagine we know several of the boys in that camp."

Smithwick nodded. "I won't lie. Castro recognized Buffalo Hump."

Inez's brow furrowed at the mention of the name. She looked at Isaac. He touched the end of her nose with a fingertip. "You aim to ride on folks we were livin' with back in the fall?"

"Isaac, some of those stolen horses belonged to John Webber. Could just have easily been younguns stolen. It's only a matter of time."

Isaac thought of the Webber children peering at him from beneath their table. Then One More Girl. Thick hair in his face and her sweat mixing with his own. "We never held up our end of the bargain." He patted his palm with the side of the skinning blade. "And there's more to it than that."

"I know there is," Smithwick said. "One of the Lipans said he saw a white girl in camp. Said she looked about the right age to be the Lockhart girl."

"I feel for Colonel Lockhart. I truly do. But I fought beside Looks Far. I grieved with him."

"I know. There's a bond formed of shared hardship."

The wind had grown colder and the sky was close and dark. Isaac ran the back of his forefinger along Inez's long braid. "He shared more than hardship with me. You remember his younger wife? The tall one?"

Smithwick turned back to the deer and sighed. "If that don't beat all."

Forty-Two

FOR THE NEXT TWO WEEKS, Isaac went about his chores, wondering how his friends were faring. He didn't know Colonel Moore, but knew Smithwick would look after his company. He caught himself watching the path along the creek, hoping to see the Captain's familiar form easing up the path.

He tried not to think about what would happen if Smithwick fell into Comanche hands. The old chiefs, his former friends, might have pity, but they would show no mercy. At night, lying with Inez, he sometimes thought of Looks Far working over the downed Waco. And how would One More Girl treat him if he himself fell into her hands? The Comanches had broken no promises. Isaac felt sure that the emissary work would have kept them satisfied indefinitely. The Comanches had plenty of room in which to raid and hunt. They seemed content as long as they felt their concerns were being taken seriously by the Texians. He suspected that Mirabeau Buonaparte Lamar and Thomas Adair were cut from the same cloth. Never question your beliefs; act boldly, certain in your rightness. Never hesitate lest you question.

On a late February afternoon, he and Inez walked down the creek path toward the home place. A raw norther had passed through three days earlier, but now the southerly breeze smelled of spring and wet earth. A garrulous flock of red-winged blackbirds squawked above the rush of the swollen creek. Buds had appeared on the elms and sycamores seemingly overnight. Isaac looked forward to spring weather, but dreaded the work that went with it. Several acres of future cornfield awaited his effort.

Inez hurried along beside him, taking two strides to his one. It was unnatural for her to live with him a quarter mile up the creek. An Indian girl needed to spend her days working and talking with other women. He couldn't remember ever seeing a Comanche woman working alone or beside a man. She'd enjoy the cooperative spring and summer work. She chattered more with Esther and Ruth than with him.

"Pretty day," he said.

"Uh-huh. Nice and warm."

He realized they'd just had a snatch of conversation in English.

He laid his hand on her back. "You're gettin' good."

She smiled. Making the best of her lot. The girl could survive anything. She'd outlive him.

She pointed to her ear. "Noah." Just then, Isaac recognized Noah Smithwick's laugh. They walked into the clearing and found him sitting on the front step in the throes of an animated story. He had Esther and Cyrus's rapt attention.

"You never saw anything like it," he said. "Caught 'em with their britches down. Bucks pourin' out of their lodges; women squalling." He looked up. "Isaac, you've got to hear this."

Esther waved her hand impatiently. "What'd y'all do then?"

"Why, we retreated. What else would a gallant company of rangers do in a situation like that?"

Cyrus puffed his pipe and studied Smithwick. "I ain't followin'."

"I don't imagine you are," Smithwick said. "Neither did we. But Colonel Moore ordered a retreat. Next thing we knew, the heathens had us pinned down in a draw. Eastland got a notch cut in his nose by an arrow. Castro got mad and went home and took all the Comanche horses with him. Just left us. Of course, the Comanches got our horses and left us afoot. Fine piece of soldiering on Moore's part. I imagine he'll get promoted to general now." He looked at Isaac. "Joe Martin took an arrow in the spine. He's alive, but just barely."

Isaac said, "See anybody you know?"

"Yeah, and I imagine they saw me." He swallowed, cleared his throat. "If we'd have pressed home our attack, we'd have fixed our Comanche problem. As it is, I don't expect they'll stop at horse stealing."

Esther looked beyond the creek. Cyrus squatted on his heels and seemed to study the ground between his feet. Isaac said, "Do the Webbers know?"

Smithwick said, "I tried to talk them into staying in town with me for a while, but they wouldn't hear of it. I don't know where in hell we'd put all those younguns, but I'd find someplace. What about y'all?"

"I expect I'll just sleep with one eye open for a spell," Cyrus said.

Smithwick nodded. "Well. How's the young Mrs. Webb?"

"Fillin' out nice," Cyrus said.

Inez pushed her belly out and rubbed it thoughtfully with her fingertips.

• • •

Isaac and Inez got back to their cabin near dusk. He stopped a few strides from the door. Inez bumped into him from behind. His throat tightened. "Lord."

"Lord," Inez said. "Lord?" She stepped around him, hesitated, then plucked an empty coffee sack from the door latch and held it out questioningly. Squab nickered in his stall.

Forty-Three

DAWN BROKE CLEAR. Isaac and Cyrus kept their rifles close at hand while feeding their animals. The women stayed inside. The two men went together to Isaac and Inez's cabin to look for Comanche sign and to see if anything had been stolen. As Isaac suspected, everything was in its place. Looks Far had left his mark and nothing else. Isaac figured the young Comanche had carried his pemmican in the coffee sack he'd left hanging on the door latch.

They found the tracks of unshod horses along the creek, then searched upstream until they found the ford where a single horseman had crossed.

Cyrus laid his rifle on his shoulder and looked across the creek and up the hill. "That boy probably watched and waited until you and Inez left and came down for supper. You weren't gone long."

"I don't like him knowin' where we live."

"He let you be, though."

"For now. Just a matter of time until they're hoppin' mad about somethin'. If they saw the Captain when him and the boys rode into their camp, I'm surprised they didn't do more than leave a sack on my door."

"Maybe they never saw him."

"Hell. They saw him. The old boy wants me to know he was here and that he knows where I'm at." He tried to spit. "He probably figures I'll worry myself to death. Probably havin' a good laugh about now."

"You know where he's at too."

"Nope. I know where he was. They don't stay put like we do. Or the Creeks or the Choctaws done. A hide lodge is a lot easier to move than a cabin. Anyway, I've got no reason to go after him. Far as I know he might have just come by to say good evenin' and take a meal with us."

"Uh-huh." Cyrus nodded. His pale blue eyes watered in the cool wind. "They come around here again, I'm liable to feed their heathen asses to old King."

"I swear, Pap. You're gettin' gentle in your old age."

They walked back down the creek. The air smelled of dampness and new growth. If Looks Far meant him any harm, he would have at least stolen some stock. Perhaps he had just left a greeting. Then again, his camp had been attacked by a ranging company led by Noah Smithwick a few days prior. Perhaps the sack was merely a warning. Isaac would heed it as long as they left him and his family alone.

He and Inez ought to go home and work in the garden and fields today. He'd borrow his father's mules and jerk up a few more stumps. You couldn't let a band of savages keep you from making a living. He'd have to learn to live with the threat. A Comanche would have a hell of a time sneaking around his place if Sis was there. She'd followed him down to the home place the night before.

Isaac and Cyrus ate their bacon and biscuits standing in the yard, rifles propped near the door. The hounds woofed. "Here comes the Captain again," Isaac said. "Comin' at a trot."

Cyrus stuffed a biscuit in his mouth, chewed and looked down the trail. "Why sure he's in a hurry. Smell's breakfast and wants to get here before it's gone."

Smithwick rode into the yard. Esther stepped outside. "Mornin'."

Smithwick tipped his hat. "Miss Esther."

Cyrus said, "Hell, Smithwick, we could use a smith around the place. Why don't you save your horse and set up shop right here?"

Smithwick smiled weakly. "This ain't a social call."

"I swear, you look pasty," Isaac said.

"I feel it too."

Cyrus set his plate on the rock step. "Good lord, what's the matter?"

"Comanches hit the Coleman and Robertson farms last night. Killed Mrs. Coleman and Albert. Ran off with the little boy and a bunch of the Robertsons' slaves."

Isaac's stomach went sour. Cyrus said, "Why, that's just down the river and over the hill." He shook his head. "Those Colemans have suffered."

Smithwick dismounted. Ruth and Inez appeared in the door. "We heard," Ruth said. She was as pale as Smithwick.

Isaac said, "I reckon we're gettin' a company up."

Smithwick shook his head. "Not me. Not this time." He took off his hat and slapped his thigh with it. "Anyway, a company out of Wells Fort is on their trail. I hear it's running north, toward Brushy. A company out of Fort Wilbarger is supposed to be just a few hours behind. General Burleson's in command."

Ruth turned to Cyrus. "I can't live like this, Cyrus. I won't."

"Mother . . ."

Smithwick said, "What do we expect? I led a company against them last week, just like a fool."

Esther said, "But you thought maybe they had the little Lockhart girl."

"They see it as an unprovoked attack. They stole that little girl from down on the Guadalupe. They don't think like we do. They see us as a band from the

Colorado. They won't understand that an attack on any settlement is an attack on us. And I knew it. Now I've got the Colemans' blood on my conscience. We should've tried to ransom that girl back."

"Captain . . . ," Isaac said.

He held up his hand. "I'm through with it. I've done my part and then some. I'm marrying the Widow and moving up to Webber's Prairie."

They stood in silence. Ruth went back inside. Inez searched the faces around her, then followed Ruth. Cyrus said, "What makes you think you'll be safe up at Webber's?"

"I won't be safe. They know I led that raid. But I won't lead another. I'll fight if they come for me, but I won't go looking for them. Nobody's safe. We had our chance and we let it get away. Thank God they passed you good folks by last night."

Isaac pitched half a biscuit to Sis. "They never passed us by, Captain. They just didn't stay long."

Cyrus said, "That boy brought back one of the coffee sacks you two give 'em and hung it on Isaac's door latch. Just wanted to let us know he'd stopped in for a visit, I reckon."

"We'd best hope Burleson either don't catch up with 'em or kills every buck in the band," Smithwick said. "Else, I'm afraid, they might stay a while next time they visit."

Forty-Four

G ENERAL E DWARD B URLESON caught
up with the raiders, but it cost him his brother Jacob. Isaac heard versions of
the story from Smithwick, Ezra, and Uncle Jimmy, none of whom took part in
the expedition, but the crux of the account was that Captain Jacob Burleson's
company of fourteen rangers out of Fort Wilbarger caught up with the raiders
near Brushy Creek, a tributary of the San Gabriel River. After sending a few
scouts ahead, he ordered his remaining men to dismount and advance. Most
refused to leave their horses with Comanches in the area—a wise decision in
Isaac's opinion. The first rule of engagement with Comanches was to stay on
your horse as long as practicable. If he had planned to continue a career fighting Looks Far and kin, he would have had to devise a method of loading his
guns from horseback. Most Texians considered the Comanches childish savages, but in a close-quarter fight, the bow, which could be armed and fired
from the saddle, was superior to the rifle or pistol.

The mutineers rode back to General Burleson's larger force; Jacob took a
Comanche ball in the chest as he tried to join his forward scouts. Edward
Burleson's force arrived soon afterward to find a large party of Comanches
well positioned on a plateau above the creek. His assaults were met with show-
ers of musket balls and arrows. The rangers spent the night hidden in an oak
thicket, exchanging sporadic fire with the raiders. Next morning they charged
up the hill to find the plateau empty save for one of Robertson's slaves, who'd
been shot in the belly, leg, and shoulder by the Texians. Burleson and company left with four dead rangers and without Tommy Coleman and eleven of
the twelve slaves. No one saw the Lockhart girl.

Mulling the account, Isaac formed his second rule of engagement: When a
Comanche had the high ground, you turned tail and rode for home.

Isaac and Cyrus remained vigilant for several weeks after the Brushy Creek
fiasco; they kept rifles propped near to hand; flesh prickled whenever the
hounds barked, especially at night; the women stayed close to the house, even
after blackberries ripened. In May, news came that Captain John Bird and a
company of thirty rangers engaged a Comanche hunting party near the Little
River. Again, the Texians gave up high ground and dismounted. Bird died of
an arrow through the chest.

Some of the rangers claimed to have killed thirty or forty Comanches, including a chief, though as far as Isaac knew, they collected no scalps to prove the claim. Ezra Higginbotham, who often rode up to the Webbs' to help Isaac, smile at Esther, fuss over Inez, and take supper as his reward, and who rode with Bird on the expedition, admitted that he'd seen no sign of a dead Indian and felt damn lucky to have kept his hair. Isaac allowed that promotions must be in the offing, what with all the captains getting killed. Ezra said he'd pass.

Throughout early summer, Isaac rose each morning, toiled in his fields and woods, then flopped exhausted into his bed each night, thinking not of Comanches but of the work that lay ahead. His place was taking shape, and he drew pleasure from it. Inez's garden produced onions, beans, potatoes, and collards, as well as various flowering legumes and forbs from the seeds she'd harvested from bird craws. The leaves and fruits of these plants, which Isaac recognized but couldn't name, she boiled and ground into poultices to treat cuts, rashes, and red eye. Her little plot seemed a bit unkempt compared to Ruth and Esther's, but just as productive. The older women acknowledged as much and admitted an interest in growing their own medicinal plants.

Inez's belly grew; Isaac and Cyrus thought her ripeness agreed with her. It certainly didn't slow her work, or, until about midway through her seventh month, her desire. One muggy June afternoon, Isaac found her on her knees in the yard, stretching buckskin around a cedar slat to form a cradleboard.

Her own buckskins were soaked; sweat glistened on her sinuous forearms and dripped from the sodden deer tail hanging from the back of her smock.

Isaac and Inez conversed mostly in English now, occasionally lapsing into Spanish or pidgin gesturing whenever a piece of shared work involved an object or action new to her. Some nights, before they fell asleep, he'd talk to her of his plans and dreams, and she'd rub her bare belly while her eyes fluttered and respond, "Yep. Yep. Two more acres in corn," or, "Yep. A meat hog is good. Yep. Pap says that. We're gettin' good." Then her eyes would still and her breathing would grow steady, and Isaac would study her delicate features and yearn for her command of English to catch up with her cleverness.

He suspected she'd learn English much quicker than he'd learn her tongues. He and Cyrus often asked her to speak in Lipan or Wichita just to hear it. Cyrus would say. "I believe it's prettier than Spanish. If I wasn't so damn thick, I'd try to pick up a little of it."

Late afternoon, in early July, Inez swung an ax handle at a blue hen she'd picked out for supper. Isaac had just unharnessed the mules and was standing in the shade, checking the beasts for galling. He'd stopped to watch his little wife sidle up to her intended meal, the ax handle—nearly as long as she was— hidden behind her back. A Lipan on the hunt. He'd told her countless times to summon him if she needed help, but she evidently never felt she needed it. She'd grown too large to catch the hen, but her aim usually was quite good; Isaac rarely saw her swing the handle more than once. This time, though, the bird ducked just in time.

She dropped her ax handle and bent over, grimacing. He carried her to bed, then ran down the creek to fetch Ruth and Esther.

A few hours later, near dusk, he and Cyrus stood outside the cabin door, hungry for supper, listening to Inez's labor and Ruth's words of comfort. Cyrus puffed his pipe and Isaac chewed twigs one after another.

"You'll wear your teeth down to nubs," Cyrus said.

"You're gonna smoke up all your tobacco."

Cyrus nodded. Inez groaned.

"What do you think it'll be?" Cyrus said.

"I hope it's a boy."

"Son of a bitch!" Inez said. Esther howled with laughter. Ruth shushed her. Cyrus grinned through his pipe smoke. Isaac shrugged and spat his twig into the darkness.

Two hours before midnight, July 9, 1839, Inez gave birth to Sarah Ruth Webb. While Inez slept and Ruth and Esther hurriedly prepared a meal of cornbread and boiled potatoes, Isaac held and studied his daughter in the firelight. Cyrus took off his hat and bent over the infant for a closer look. "Saree Ruth. I swear." He touched the child's nose. "Have you ever in your life seen such a head of black hair on a youngun?"

Forty-Five

IN EARLY SEPTEMBER, Isaac and Inez took the wagon into Bastrop. Isaac had been dreading the trip; Cyrus could have gone for the molasses, dress cloth, and ax bits, but Isaac needed to see Smithwick about a weak spring that had lately caused his rifle to misfire. More importantly, he needed to know what he and his Lipan bride could expect from the townspeople.

He had never considered himself a part of the community of Bastrop, but his friendship with Smithwick and Reverend Hodge, his rangering, and his courtship of Catherine had drawn him in enough that he cared about what locals might think of him. And what they might say to the Adairs.

A part of him bristled at the thought of the wives of local merchants and prosperous leaders, whose husbands were too well off and important to leave their families and possessions to serve in the Revolution or help with frontier defense, sniffing at his marriage to an Indian. Inez might slit a man's throat, but she wouldn't waste a single heartbeat skewering his reputation.

Seven months of marriage had changed his feelings about Inez. Acceptance and comfort had replaced lust and guilt. Love? He wondered. Certainly, he loved his raffish, loyal, irascible father and bright, long-suffering mother and sister. And he supposed his affection toward Smithwick, Ezra, Uncle Jimmy, and Felix might be called brotherly love. But Inez? He'd heard the Bible verses about love between a man and woman, and had heard Esther and Ruth speak of it as if it were jolting and unmistakable. Now he wondered if it might be something gradual and growing, ripening, yet simple as affection and respect born of mutual help and comfort.

Perhaps the Almighty didn't appoint a certain someone for everyone, but allowed choice and circumstance to bring a man and woman together, then left it up to them to build love and a life together as they might toil to make a prosperous farm or business. He knew, too, that hardscrabble upland farms required more work than rich bottomland farms. Perhaps some marriages—and some lives—required more work than others, and some, like farms started by lazy or ignorant or indifferent people on thin, rocky ground, were doomed to failure and misery. His own, it seemed, had begun on the poorest of ground, and yet he had his family's backing. If he remained tireless and diligent and tough, as he knew Inez would, for she had little choice and knew no other way . . .

The Webbs would prevail over war and drought, poor ground, wolves and Comanches; perhaps they'd do as well against scorn. *The way to get by, Isaac, is to not give a good goddamn what anybody thinks.* Isaac suspected Cyrus adopted the philosophy long before he heard it from John Webber; he'd accepted and loved Inez from the outset.

They rode south along the river. Isaac doubted Inez had been more terrified the day Castro dumped her at Coleman's Fort. He smiled at her. She swallowed. Her wide eyes were moist; he'd never seen a sallow Indian before. Sarah Ruth slept in the cradleboard laid across her mother's lap. She reminded Isaac of a ground squirrel peeping out of its hole.

Ruth still hadn't grown used to a baby hanging about in a cradleboard. She'd walk by a shady outside wall of the cabin or an airy spot inside, preoccupied with some task, and look over to see a pair of dark eyes following her. "Well! We've left it hangin' on a peg and ain't payin' a bit of attention to it! Granny better hold it a spell."

A month after Sarah Ruth's birth, Smithwick brought Reverend Zeke Hodge up to see the baby and to pay his respects to the new mother. After the noon meal, they stood outside the door, talking in the shade. The baby hung asleep on a peg near the door. Inez bustled by and wrinkled her nose. "Whoo!" she said, taking the cradleboard from the peg. "I gotta take the shit out."

Esther and Reverend Hodge grinned at each other; Ruth hurried to the creek with a pail; Cyrus clamped down on his pipe and clasped his hands behind his back; Inez cooed to Sarah Ruth; and Isaac casually looked away toward the northern hills. Smithwick cleared his throat. "I swear, I was relieved to get this young woman away from that squalid fort. I knew she was picking up crude language."

Isaac chuckled at the memory. He glanced at his wife beside him on the wagon. "I know how you feel, Inez. I remember ridin' into that Comanche camp."

"Yea . . ." Her voice cracked. She cleared her throat. "Yep."

"But I got by fine. You will too."

"We'll do good."

"Sure we will." They rounded a bend. Log homes and frame buildings came into view. "Be fine," Isaac said. His stomach rolled. They rode into town. Inez sat stiff as a dried hide, looking straight ahead. Dust rose around them. A few dogs barked. A couple of men waved. A few women stopped to watch them. Mostly people seemed to pay them little mind. He turned the team and stopped alongside the dry goods store. He sighed, looked at Inez. "Let's go in."

She got down and swung the cradleboard onto her back before he could come around the wagon to help her. He led her inside. The store was dark and cool and smelled of cloth and flour, meal, lard, and iron. Isaac stood just inside the door while his eyes adjusted. He could feel Inez against the small of his back.

The shadow behind a counter piled with crocks of honey and molasses and baskets of turnips and onions became Anson McAllister. The storekeeper looked up, squinted, and smoothed his mustache. "Isaac Webb! I ain't seen you since Angus and Twyla's wedding dance. Come in here."

Isaac took off his hat and walked up to the counter. Inez, plastered to his back, replicated every step. Two other customers, an elderly man and stern young woman, looked up and nodded their greeting, then continued sorting through a pile of hoes and spades propped in a back corner.

Isaac laid his palms on the counter. "Yes sir. I'd like—"

"Who's that hidin' behind you?" McAllister said.

"This . . ." he looked around to his left; Inez peered from behind his right side. He stepped away and left her frozen in Anson McAllister's gaze. " . . . would be Inez."

The older man smiled and looked her over. "The little wife, huh? Well. Smithwick and your daddy have told me all about her. How are you today, Mrs. Webb?"

Inez looked at Isaac who said, "She's fine." Inez turned back to McAllister and nodded. "Yep."

Isaac said. "She's kind of nervous; never been to town before."

Sarah Ruth sneezed. Inez nearly jumped out of her moccasins. Anson said, "Scat Tom! Who's that?"

Isaac touched Inez's shoulders with his fingers and turned her around. "Saree Ruth; she's about two months."

"Why the little thing's bound up like a caterpillar." He leaned over the counter and stroked Sarah Ruth's head. "Don't she fuss wrapped up tight like that?"

"Only cries when she's hungry, and Inez won't let her get hungry too often."

"Well." He ran a finger over the beadwork on Sarah Ruth's cradle pouch. "Somebody spent some time on this."

"Inez did. King gave her the beads."

"King's wife did," Inez said.

Isaac said, "She gave them to King to give to Inez."

The old man finished looking at the tools in the corner and walked past them without looking up or speaking. The young woman followed. Isaac met her glance, and the sternness in her eyes changed to uncertainty. Inez nodded, her expression open, curious. The woman peeked over her shoulder as she stepped out the door.

McAllister sighed. "I reckon old Pratchett can trade down to San Felipe. I don't know how he managed to snare such a young bride."

"We never meant to cause you trouble," Isaac said. He watched the man and woman cross the road.

McAllister raised his hands. "No sir. Don't think a thing of it. What can I get for you today?"

"We thank you." He named the items. Anson led them around his store until they found everything they needed. Isaac eyed the andirons, but decided he could wait. He paid, thanked McAllister, and started out the door. Inez was giving him a little space now.

"Isaac," McAllister said.

Isaac stopped.

"It's good to see you. Come back anytime. I mean that. Give my regards to your mother and daddy."

"I'll do it." They stepped out into the glare. Isaac said, "See there?"

"I seen," Inez said. She set three jars of molasses behind the wagon seat. "That woman don't know what to think about me."

"You're just seein' the bad. Mr. McAllister likes you. And Saree."

"Yep. But that old man don't."

"Why hell, I don't even know that old man. Why give a damn what he thinks?"

"Old son of a bitch."

Isaac laughed as he pulled back a canvas tarp and picked up his rifle. "Lord. Let's go see the Captain."

Inez's face brightened. They crossed the rutted road and walked away from the river, past a two-story frame hotel, a stable, the land office, and a physician's shop. Near the edge of town, they stepped into a low log building to find Smithwick talking to two men in linen suits as he examined a pistol. He waved as Isaac and Inez walked in.

The little shop was hot and smelled of turpentine, grease, sawdust, and metal shavings. Rifles and muskets, barrels and blank stocks were propped in every corner and hung in racks over benches along the walls. The two customers left. Smithwick laid the pistol on a bench and wiped his hands on a rag. "What have you done to your rifle?"

Isaac eyed the gunsmith's leather apron. "Biscuits done?"

Smithwick pointed to his forge. "Why sure. Reach in there and grab you one."

"I've ate."

"Figures."

Inez eyed the cast-iron box and sniffed.

He took Isaac's rifle, worked the serpentine, pointed to a well-used Kentucky propped against the door frame. "Leave this one and take that one. Try not to break it on somebody's skull. I'll ride up in a week or two, and we'll swap and you two can feed me."

They met two young, buckskin-clad men as they stepped out the door.

Both had sandy-blond beards and were nearly as tall as Isaac, brothers probably. The two men stepped back and parted, nodded to Isaac, and tipped their hats to Inez, who ignored them. Isaac said, "Afternoon," and continued down the road toward the wagon. Inez hurried along beside him. The wind kicked up and dust devils roiled. People and horses and dogs bustled about, but Isaac saw no more familiar faces. Three mud-encrusted hogs trotted up from the river and crossed the road in front of the hotel.

As they neared the wagon, Inez said, "Those men are scared of you."

"Who?"

"At Noah's."

"Nah."

"They think you're a big old mean bastard."

"What? Why in hell would they think that?" She must've heard Cyrus talking about King.

"Yep." She adjusted her cradleboard straps. She seemed at ease now, eyes wide, taking it all in. "You look big old mean."

Isaac had no response. They came to the wagon. He held his daughter while Inez climbed into the seat. On the way out of town, the older men nodded and waved. Women and young men averted their eyes.

Inez looked up at him as she unlaced the cradle pouch. "See? I said."

He wondered when this had come about. He noticed that his sleeves were a good two inches too short. He studied his hands. Not quite as thick as Noah Smithwick's—smiths had huge hands—but no longer the boyish hands he pictured whenever he thought of himself.

A mile up the road, Inez lifted her smock and nursed Sarah Ruth. She hummed a tune he'd never heard and watched him. He'd seen that look before.

Forty-Six

Bastrop, February 1840

NOAH SMITHWICK leaned back against his puncheon workbench and studied Inez and Sarah Ruth. "Isaac, I believe that youngster is about as big as her mother."

Inez smiled and turned around so that the child faced Smithwick. The baby's eyes crossed when he touched her nose. "Lord, that hurts me when a child does that. I just know they'll stick that way."

"What way?" Inez said.

"Cross-eyed."

"Nope." She turned around and crossed her eyes. "See?"

"Lord, don't do that!"

Isaac shook his head. You could never keep Smithwick focused on anything other than food, gunsmithing, or a deadly fracas, and then only if there were no children or comely women about. He looked again at the letter he held:

> Isaac Webb:
>
> On March 19, a party of Comanche chiefs will arrive in Béxar to parley with representatives of the Republic. It has come to my attention that in the course of your service under Captain Andrews and Captain Smithwick, you served as emissary to the Penateka band on the Colorado River from April 1838 through November 1838. Secretary Johnston and I feel that your knowledge of Comanche beliefs and ways may be useful during negotiation with the savages.
>
> Therefore you are to report to Lt. Colonel William Fisher of the 1st Texas Regiment at the courtroom adjacent to the jailhouse on the Main Plaza no later than noon on March 19. At that time, Colonel Fisher will issue your orders.
>
> Col. Henry Karnes
> Commander, Southern Frontier Region

"I don't know Henry Karnes from a mule's ass," Isaac said. "What does he mean sending me a letter tellin' me I *am* to do this or that?"

Smithwick said, "He means he reports directly to Albert Sidney Johnston, who takes orders from no one but President Lamar, and you'd best have your ass on the plaza in Béxar come March 19."

"How come you didn't get a letter? You spent more time with the Comanches than I did."

"The chiefs would start nocking arrows the instant they laid eyes on me. Don't think they didn't see me there on the San Gabriel."

"You got me to go live with the heathens and now I've got to finish what you started."

Smithwick shrugged, grinned. "You ain't cut out to be a farmer and you know it. This'll get you out of a few days of honest work."

"You ain't seen my place this year. You wouldn't know it. Anyway, I don't like people I've never met tellin' me what I got to do."

"You come honestly by the trait."

Inez slumped her shoulders and adjusted her pack. Sarah Ruth jounced and rubbed her eyes.

Isaac refolded the letter. "And I expect I'll get about as much sympathy from you as good advice."

"I always try to dispense both in even portions." He winked at Inez. "Honestly, there ain't much to say. Just go to Béxar and try to stay out of all the wind that'll pass between a bunch of colonels and Comanche chiefs. You ought not lose more than a week. They won't pay a bit of attention to you if you go, but if you don't, they'll lay anything that goes wrong on you."

Sarah Ruth gnawed on her mother's braid. Isaac slipped the letter into his coat pocket then and tugged the braid away from the child. She started to cry but found her fist and gummed contentedly.

"I reckon so."

Inez said, "Sarruth's gettin' hungry."

"We'd best start back home and flop a tit out," Isaac said. "How's Thurza? I still want to call her Widow."

"Being married to me agrees with her. She's plumping right up. Of course it's awfully quiet upriver. A little company would be welcome every now and again."

Inez looked accusingly at Isaac, who said, "I reckon you do owe us two or three hundred meals."

"At least that many. Go feed that youngun."

They stepped outside. A dark wall of clouds sat on the northern horizon. The air smelled of rain. Isaac held his hat on his head. "Got colder while we were inside."

Inez hurried along beside him, seemingly oblivious to the weather. They waited while several riders splashed through the puddles, then crossed several sets of ruts to the other side. They walked past McAllister's door, then to the side of the building beneath the budding sycamores where the wagon and mules waited. Isaac held the cradleboard while Inez climbed into the wagon.

"Well, Isaac Webb!" Catherine Druin bustled around the corner of the store. Isaac shifted the baby to his right arm and jerked off his hat with his left hand. His face went hot. "Afternoon."

Catherine hurried toward them. She wore her familiar gray wool dress. He judged she filled it out a bit more than when he last saw her. She had her hair drawn back and tied with black felt ribbon. "I swear, I thought that was you going by the door!"

"We were about to head back." He'd once talked easily to her. Now he was back to stammering like that first night at the Adair cabin. Inez smiled, glad for the company as always.

"Let me see that baby. I heard you were a father." Isaac held the cradleboard out. Catherine touched the baby's head and cooed. Isaac felt awkward as a mule. "She'll be a year old in July. Name's Saree Ruth."

Catherine met his gaze, the beginnings of crow's feet at the corners of her eyes. She'd never liked a sunbonnet. "After your mother. Look what a head of hair."

"Like mine," Inez said.

"Well, Isaac, introduce me to your wife."

Isaac cleared his throat. Inez said, "I'm Inez. I used to be scared to come to town but now I ain't."

Louise Adair waddled around the corner. "Isaac! Let me come over there and get hold of you!"

Isaac looked up and down the road. Catherine said, "Oh, he's at the land office. He'll be there all day, probably. You know Daddy."

"I do, and that's why I'm watchin' out for him."

Louise rushed up and hugged him so tight that Sarah Ruth squealed in protest.

"Lord, we've missed you, Isaac. You ain't still mad at us, are you?"

"Wasn't me that was mad."

Louise shook her head. "That Thomas Adair."

"How is he?"

"Pig-headed and pious as ever, but don't think bad of him. He's just made that way." She looked at Inez. "I heard you took a bride. I reckon this is her."

"Yep," Inez said.

"I'd introduce her, but she keeps beatin' me to it. Inez, this is Mrs. Druin and Mrs. Adair."

"Good day," Inez said.

He glanced at Catherine. She was studying him. He struggled for small talk.

Catherine said, "Mama, looks like he's made a man."

"I'd say he has."

Isaac hoped Inez wouldn't say he looked like a big old mean bastard. He swallowed. "Speakin' of men, I expect the rich suitors are about to overrun your place."

Louise laughed. Catherine rolled her eyes. "Lord. Old and rich or young and sorry. I'm destined for lifelong widowhood, I'm afraid."

"I doubt it." She had her daddy to thank for it.

Now Catherine blushed, seemed to struggle for words. Her mother watched her. Was that sadness or resignation in her eyes?

Louise looked up the street toward the land office. "Well, Miss Catherine, we'd better finish our business." She touched Isaac's arm. "So good to see you again. I want you to know that I hold no ill feelings. I hope you don't either."

"None at all." Just a good measure of regret and resentment toward old man Adair.

They said their good-byes. Catherine patted Inez's hand before she walked away.

Mother and daughter crossed the road and skirted the puddles on their way to the gray frame house that served as the land office. The old man would be adding to his holdings. He'd need another slave or two.

Inez took Sarah Ruth. "The young one wants to be your wife. But you can't have but one."

Isaac wondered if that was an assertion or observation. He suspected the latter.

Forty-Seven

ISAAC WOULDN'T have believed Texas held as many people as he'd seen the past hour in Béxar. He, Ezra, and Felix had ridden into town late morning on March 15 to find the one-story limestone courthouse swarming with Texas Regulars but not a single Comanche. Ezra and Felix went looking for a drink.

Several drunken soldiers laughed at Isaac when he asked for Colonel Fisher's whereabouts. On his third lap around the plaza, he bumped into a hulking middle-aged man coming out the door of Sanchez's, a busy cantina. It was early afternoon, and the sun glared off the limestone and adobe walls of the plaza buildings. Isaac squinted at the man, who stood a good two inches taller than his own six feet. He had deep creases in his forehead and in the corners of his friendly green eyes.

"Pardon me," Isaac said.

The man looked him over. "Not a drop of pardon called for. I don't believe I've run into you before."

"I just got here this mornin'. You don't know where I can find Colonel Fisher, do you?"

The man scratched his bearded chin. "I imagine I could show him to the right man. Would that be you?"

Isaac pulled Colonel Karnes's letter from his coat pocket, handed it to the man, and wondered if he'd made a mistake.

"Damn. Isaac Webb. I figured you to be older." He thrust out his hand. "I'm Mathew Caldwell."

Isaac took the big hand and noticed the mottled gray, brown, and white beard. Old Paint. Why would Paint Caldwell have figured anything about him? Isaac shook his hand for several seconds, studying this big Kentuckian whose reputation as a soldier and ranger had reached Bastrop from Béxar. He snapped out of his trance. "Pleased."

Caldwell laughed. "Foller me. So you're here to watch the procession of heathens that's supposed to show up here any day."

"That's what I'm told. I don't know what in hell I'm supposed to do."

"I'll tell you what I'd do. I'd keep quiet and try to stand close to the door." He glanced at Isaac as they walked eastward toward the river. "But I imagine you know a lot more about how to act around Comanches than anybody here."

Isaac kept an eye out for Felix and Ezra. "Captain Smithwick did all the palavering. I just done what I was told."

"How is Smithwick? I ain't laid eyes on him since before Concepción."

"He's married and moved upriver a piece. Still doin' a little smithing in Bastrop. He's quit rangering though. He's a Houston man."

They walked along Gonzales Road past houses and low stone buildings. Grassy hills sprinkled with oak mottes rose beyond the city to the north. Isaac admired several winsome Tejano women. He'd be ready to lay hands on Inez by the time he got home.

Caldwell said, "Smithwick's a good one. I admire his idealism. I wouldn't say I'm a Lamar man, but I'd say I'm a pragmatist."

Isaac had never heard of a pragmatist, but given the context he assumed it meant Caldwell had little use for Indians. He started to mention that there were no Comanche problems while he and Smithwick served as emissaries, but he held his tongue. Captain Caldwell might prove a powerful ally, if not a friend.

He supposed this one road in Béxar saw more people and horses in one day than the road from his farm to Bastrop saw in a year. Wagonloads of soldiers and supplies, groups of men on horseback, well-dressed Tejano men and women in carriages, dogs and chickens, and the occasional goat or hog.

Caldwell left the road and cut between a pair of log buildings toward the river. They walked in the shade of bald cypress and sycamores. A camp loomed ahead—a pole corral and scores of tents, the largest set in the shadiest spot on a bench above the river.

Soldiers milled about, gambling and smoking. A young man leaned on his musket by the door of the big tent. He snapped to attention as Caldwell approached. "Go back to sleep, Nate." The boy grinned and held the tent flap open for Caldwell, who disappeared inside. Isaac waited, enjoying the shade and gurgle of the river.

The boy nodded shyly at him. "Cap'm."

"I ain't a captain. I'm just here so Colonel Fisher can tell me what to do."

His remark seemed to put the boy at ease. "They's supposed to be a bunch of Comanches show up, but I ain't seen a one yet. I don't figure they're comin'."

"They'll be here soon enough."

The boy grinned. "You know about Comanches, do you?"

Isaac was deciding how to answer when Caldwell appeared with a uniformed officer. He was short and thin with red hair and beard. Caldwell said, "Colonel, this is Isaac Webb."

Fisher extended his hand. "Mr. Webb. I hear you've done some excellent work with the savages. I suspect you might be of some help to us here."

"I'll do what I can," Isaac said. He glanced at Nate, who'd turned peaked.

Fisher said, "We'll find a place for you to camp, and if and when the savages arrive, you'll need to stay close to Captain Caldwell. We'll call on you as situations require." He looked at the boy. "Nate, help Mr. Webb find a comfortable spot to bed down while the Captain and I have a drink and a chat."

"Yes sir." The boy turned to Isaac. "I know just the spot." He led the way along the bluff to a shaded bench overlooking the river. "This is where I'd throw down," Nate said. "Spot's too little for a tent, but plenty big for a bedroll and cook fire."

Isaac thanked him, looked across the river to the hills to the north. He could like this country.

Nate said, "I didn't mean nothing by what I said back there. I was just makin' talk."

Blond, blue eyed, and skinny as a crane. Soldiering just to keep food in his belly, probably. "I took no offense," Isaac said.

"I didn't know you."

"Think you know me now?"

"Well, I know of you. Everybody talks about you and Captain Smithwick livin' with the Comanches."

"We went in under a truce. There wasn't no danger."

"I keep hearin' about how they do people, scalping and gelding and such. Like animals."

"I've seen what they do. Nothin' worse than what I saw on the Plain of Saint Hyacinth."

"You was there?"

"Caught the tail end. The fightin' was over when we rode in. But the killin' wasn't. I've buried farmers after the Comanches finished with them, but I never saw anything worse than what I saw layin' all over the prairie at Saint Hyacinth."

"Yeah, but you know what happened here." He nodded west toward the fortress of the Alamo. "People say they gagged for days after the Meskins set fire to the dead."

"I don't doubt a word of it."

The boy studied him. "I hope they come. I never seen a Comanche."

"You're apt to be disappointed. They don't look like much when they ain't riled up."

Nate's eyes narrowed. He gently bounced his musket butt on the toe of his brogan. Isaac hated to ruin the boy's imagination. Smithwick would have told his butcher knife–toting Comanche women story.

Nate said, "I best be gettin' back."

"Obliged. Be seein' you."

Nate jogged back toward Fisher's tent. Isaac thought about his rationalization of Comanche warfare. Those kinds of comments would make him unpopular in certain quarters. He'd never say such things around Colonel Lockhart, nor comment on the slaughter at Saint Hyacinth around Uncle

Jimmy. But slaughter it had been. He'd seen the three surrendering Mexicans cut down from behind, men who may have bayoneted rebels inside the Alamo, or, for all he knew, executed unsuspecting Texians at Goliad. They probably had acted under orders; did that make a difference? He thought of the Mexican musketeers forming up to fire from the bank of the Colorado. What would be the fate of a Mexican soldier who refused to follow an order no matter how brutal? And would he have done any different than Uncle Jimmy had the Mexicans killed Cyrus?

The sun hung just above the horizon. The river ran in shade. He picked up a few twigs to start a cook fire. Nearly twilight, his favorite time of day and no chores to do. He'd sit and watch the river and sip coffee. Rangering was occasionally dangerous and nearly always tedious, but it had its rewards.

He'd nearly dropped off to sleep despite the laughter, barking dogs, and general camp din when Captain Caldwell showed up with three soldiers holding a fuming Ezra and amused Felix at gunpoint.

Isaac propped himself up on an elbow. "What in hell?"

"Went into town and pulled these two out of jail," Caldwell said. "The big one here was invoking your name and demanding to see Colonel Fisher. One of the deputies came down and told me."

"Sons of bitches tryin' to tell me I couldn't talk to that girl!" Ezra said.

Felix nodded. "She was somethin'. That lieutenant thought so too."

Caldwell raised a hand. "I'm leavin' these two in your custody, Isaac. I trust you can control your big friend. Four of my men jumped him. They may have come to in the infirmary by now. One's nursing three broken fingers; the other will be gumming his hardtack and jerky for the rest of his days. I can't afford to lose many more."

"I'll talk to him," Isaac said.

Felix laughed. "Hell, I talked to him and they locked me up with him."

Caldwell said, "Isaac, come by and see me in the mornin'. I'll be taking breakfast at Ybarra's, three doors up from Sanchez's." He turned and disappeared into the darkness.

Isaac laid his head on his forearm. "Where's your bedrolls?"

Ezra kicked the grass. "Back at the damn livery."

Isaac rolled onto his back and pulled the blanket up under his chin. The night had turned pleasantly cool. "You heard Captain Caldwell. You're in my custody and I ain't gettin' out from under this blanket. I hate to see you boys sleep cold tonight. Best build up the fire."

Ezra snatched up Isaac's moccasins and tossed them out onto the riverbank. "I sure hope nothin' comes along in the night and eats them salty things. I'm fetching my bedroll." He turned and stalked off toward town. Felix chuckled and followed him.

• • •

Isaac and Ezra were lazing by the river, sipping coffee in the morning sun, when the camp burst into motion. Nate appeared on the bluff above them and shouted that the Comanches had arrived.

Isaac grabbed his rifle and ran for the council house. Ezra allowed that he'd seen Indians before and would be along after he drained the pot and took a nap.

The plaza was choked with soldiers and onlookers. Isaac could see no Comanches for the sombreros and ladies' hats. Holding his rifle barrel up, he worked his way through the crowd toward the courthouse door. There, in an opening created by encircled militia, Muguara, Pahauco, Quinaseico, Esanap, and several other chiefs Isaac recognized sat their ponies. Mounted Comanche women and children extended into the crowd behind them. Colonel Fisher stepped out of the council house, and the soldiers began pushing the crowd back. Isaac tried to break through but a soldier stopped him.

"I'm with Captain Caldwell," Isaac said.

He pushed Isaac back with his musket stock. "I don't know a thing about it, boy."

"Goddamn you." Isaac pushed back with his rifle stock. The soldier leaned into him; Isaac stepped back and the man fell on his face. Isaac stepped over him and walked into the clearing. "*Buenos días,* Muguara."

The chief looked at him with contempt. "Where is Juaqua? Is he ashamed to show his face?"

Isaac had to shout above the din. "He has taken a wife and moved to better country. Where's Buffalo Hump?"

"He wanted no part of this council. He has seen enough Tahbay-boh treachery."

Two other officers appeared and stood with Fisher. The sun glinted off Muguara's bald pate. More soldiers arrived and pushed the crowd back, and now the rest of the Comanche women and children moved into the clearing. Several of the children pointed to Isaac.

A young Mexican man moved up beside Fisher. The colonel said something into his ear. The boy shouted something in Comanche to Muguara, who turned and passed word back. Two Comanche boys about ten years old led a pair of captives astraddle a mustang from the middle of the column. There was a collective gasp from the crowd. Women covered their mouths. An emaciated teenage girl, her face covered with welts and bruises, her nose burned away, sat the horse. In front of her in the saddle sat a little Mexican boy, the hair on one side of his head singed so that his scalp shone white in the morning sun.

The Comanches seemed unconcerned. Isaac took the reins of the horse bearing the captives and led it around to the horrified officers. "What's your name?" Isaac asked the girl. He barely heard her croaking reply above the angry murmuring. "Matilda."

The soldiers let several women through as Isaac helped Matilda Lockhart and the boy from the horse. The women swarmed over the dazed captives and led them away across the plaza through the parted crowd.

The three officers stood tense, red-faced. Fisher said something to the Mexican interpreter who spoke to Muguara. The chiefs dismounted and handed their reins to their women and boys.

Isaac heard Caldwell shouting orders at his men and urging the crowd to make more room. The chiefs followed the officers and interpreter inside. Caldwell called the names of a half dozen of his infantrymen and ordered them inside as well. Isaac noticed that he was unarmed. The crowd quieted. Some drifted away. Caldwell stood at the door and motioned for Isaac to step inside.

The room was stifling, despite the mild temperatures outside. Sunlight streamed through the three barred windows. Constant buzzing of flies mixed with low murmurs and clearing of throats.

Three officers, including Fisher, sat at a table at the front of the room. The thirteen chiefs sat on the packed earth floor, each with a short bow and single arrow across his lap.

"Smells worse than a goddamn barn in here," Caldwell muttered to Isaac. He leaned against the wall on the inside right of the door. He directed Isaac to stand beside him. "We'll be the first out the door if trouble starts. Can you imagine balls and arrows flying around, bouncing off these walls?" He shook his head. "I'm tellin' you what. Locked up in a room with these wild bastards. I'd like to know whose idea this was."

"Who are the other two officers?"

"The pup there next to Fisher is Colonel Hugh McLeod—a West Point boy. The other one is Colonel Cooke." He pointed to a heavyset black-bearded man standing at the far end of the table. "That's Tom Howard. He's a good one. Serves in our ranging company."

Nate came in last and stood by the near end of the table. He shut the door at Fisher's order. The Mexican translator stood in front of the table near Muguara.

Fisher faced the chiefs. His eyes darted to the Mexican. "Tell them we're honored to have them here today and hope to forge a lasting peace with the Comanches."

The translator nodded and began speaking in very flat, deliberate Comanche. The chiefs listened gravely.

Muguara responded in the sonorous chant replete with the bursts and buzzes Isaac heard so often in the Comanche camp.

The translator turned to Fisher. "He says the chiefs are pleased and honored to be your guests. However, he is surprised there are so many soldiers at a peace council and wishes to point out that he brought no warriors other than his fellow chiefs. He trusts that their families will be safe outside."

Fisher composed himself with obvious efforts. "Sententious butchers," he said flatly. "Tell them they may rest assured—"

Someone knocked at the door. "What the hell now?" Fisher said. "Mathew, get the door."

Caldwell opened the door. A low voice said, "Sorry sir. A Mrs. Maverick says it's imperative that she talk to an officer."

"She'll have to wait, Corporal," Caldwell said.

McLeod and Cooke were shaking their heads in disgust. The chiefs sat impassively.

Isaac heard an urgent female voice but couldn't make out the words. The soldier said, "She says the Lockhart girl told her something you'll want to know."

Caldwell turned back to the officers. "Colonel, it's Mrs. Maverick. I think I ought to speak with her a moment."

Fisher leaned on his knuckles, sweat beaded on his forehead. "Make it damn quick, Mathew."

Caldwell stepped outside. Isaac could hear low, tense voices. The officers smiled and nodded at the chiefs. Caldwell stepped back in and leaned against the wall. He nodded and Fisher continued. "Tell them we are sorry for the interruption and assure them that we intend their families no harm." While the Mexican translated, Caldwell slipped a scrap of paper to Cooke, who read it, nodded, and slid the paper on to McLeod. By the time the translator finished, Fisher was looking down at the note. He said, "Ask them why they brought in only two captives when according to Mrs. Maverick's note, the Lockhart girl reports fourteen white captives in their camp."

Isaac wondered where they'd hidden fourteen captives during his visits. And he hoped the chiefs were as ignorant of English as the officers assumed.

The Mexican hesitated. "What's the matter?" McLeod asked.

"I have to think of how to say all that. How to make them understand about Mrs. Maverick's note."

"Just ask them why in the hell they brought in only two captives. Politely."

The translator cleared his throat and spoke. Muguara considered the question for several seconds, then responded. The Mexican translated: "Yes, there are many more captives, but they are in the camps of bands headed by other chiefs. I have no say in their affairs. Yet I believe that, in time, every captive can be ransomed. The sister of the girl we returned to you today can be purchased with good muskets for each of the chiefs here today, and blankets for every woman and child that came with us. We also require vermilion and two kegs of powder and ball. How do you like that answer?"

"Christ Almighty," Mathew Caldwell said under his breath.

McLeod ran his finger around the inside of his collar. Cooke leaned back in his chair, hands behind his head. "Bill, this is hog shit."

Fisher nodded, still smiling. "Captain Caldwell, summon a guard detachment."

Caldwell turned pale. "Uh . . . sir . . ."

"Mathew," Fisher said, pleasantly, "get the goddamn guards in here this instant."

"Yes sir." Caldwell pushed the door open, stepped out and spoke to his men.

Isaac felt woozy in the stale air. Sweat ran into his eyes. He eased along the wall a few feet to gain room to mount and swing his rifle.

A half-dozen militiamen filed in carrying muskets. They spread out to bar the door. The chiefs eyed one another and gripped their bows. Caldwell resumed his position.

Fisher crossed his arms. "Now. Tell our honored guests that they are under arrest and will be held until every white captive is returned. Then and only then will they be released and presents distributed."

The Mexican looked ill. He propped himself against the table. "Sir, I was a captive of these people for nearly two years. They'll die fighting before they'll allow you to take them prisoner."

Cooke stood and leaned over the table. "Salinas, issue the ultimatum, or you'll be spending the night locked up in a big cell with your friends here."

Salinas nodded, swallowed. He opened his mouth, but his voice failed. He eyed the door, cleared his throat, and began anew. The chiefs sat frozen as he spoke. He finished the statement, then broke for the door. One of the guards tried to grab him; Fisher said, "Let him go." Isaac felt the blast of fresh air. Caldwell eased the door shut.

Muguara sat considering Fisher's statement. There was only the sound of breathing and buzzing flies. Isaac heard his heartbeat. Muguara sighed. Fisher seemed to relax. The chief leapt up and drew his knife in one motion and thrust it into Tom Howard's ribs. The ranger drew in a breath and looked down in wonder at the hilt and handle. The other chiefs whooped and nocked arrows; some fired from sitting positions; others jumped up to shoot, then drew knives and tomahawks and ran hacking and slashing for the door.

Fisher and Cooke screamed "Fire!" Gun blasts reverberated off the stone walls; Muguara fell back clutching his chest. Isaac drew back from the melee, knelt, and tried to pick a target. White smoke filled the room.

Musket balls whined. Shards of wood and plaster fell from the ceiling. Caldwell went down cursing, and now Isaac could only discern the bunched mass of soldiers and Comanches fighting hand to hand near the door. Cooke and Fisher stood behind the table, aiming pistols. More gunfire and screaming. Smoke seared Isaac's throat and nostrils. Two chiefs cleared the door, and now shrieks and gunfire and cursing erupted outside. More soldiers and Comanches ran out the door. Mathew Caldwell was on his feet again, his left thigh covered with blood. He rammed a musket butt into Quinaseico's face; the chief went down, and Caldwell finished him with another blow.

Isaac ran out the door; sunlight blinded him for an instant and he felt vulnerable. He sucked in the fresh air and kept low until his eyes adjusted.

A half-dozen dead Comanche women and children lay scattered about the street. Someone shouted that the Indians were headed for the river. Sporadic shots. Women screaming. A man with blond muttonchops, dressed in a fine linen suit, lay on his back, a tiny arrow fletching protruding from his chest.

Isaac strode across the plaza toward the river. Ezra came running from the opposite direction, carrying a small Comanche girl in one arm and a woman in the other. Blood covered his shoulder next to the woman's face. "Goddamn it, Isaac, I had to shoot her. I shot this baby's mama."

Isaac saw that the blood on Ezra's shoulder came from a wound at the woman's collarbone.

Ezra shook his head in despair. "She was drawin' down on Nate. She'd have killed him for sure."

The woman was sobbing; her toes dangled half a foot off the ground. Snot striped the baby's lips. Isaac spoke to the woman in Spanish; told her they wouldn't hurt her or take her child. He held the little girl, and Ezra laid the young mother in the dirt. The baby screamed and held out its arms. Isaac knelt and held the child close to her mother while Ezra cut the deerskin blouse away to check the wound. "Lord, her little shoulder is about gone." She turned away as he felt her cheek with the back of his hand. "She's clammy as a fish."

Flames leapt from the roof of a house on the far side of the plaza. Ezra glanced back at the fire, then cut a strip of cloth from the bottom of his shirt and bunched it into the woman's wound. "Two of those old boys ran into the cook house. Somebody dumped turpentine all over the roof and lit it."

Sporadic gunfire sounded about town as Ezra worked. The woman lay still, looking up, blinking in Ezra's shadow. Isaac squatted on his heels and bounced the baby on his knee. Whenever he stopped, the child cried out and reached for her mother.

Nate walked toward them from the direction of the fire, unarmed. Isaac said, "Where's your rifle, Nate? Don't be going around unarmed."

The boy stopped and looked at his hands. "I swear, I must've laid it down somewhere." He stood watching Ezra and the Comanche woman. After a few seconds, he said, "Isaac, they split that old boy's head."

"Whose?"

"One of them old chiefs. He come staggering out of that fire. He was gagging, couldn't see nothin'. Had his hands over his face, and that fellar just split him in two."

Felix ran up and knelt beside Ezra. "Good lord, boys." He looked at the young mother. "Ezra," he said gently.

The big man stood, jerked off his coat, powder horn, and possibles bag, pulled off his shirt and began cutting it into strips. Blood dripped from his elbow.

Nate walked away toward the council house. "That old man couldn't see where he was goin'," he said.

• • •

By midafternoon, the soldiers had loaded the bodies of the thirteen chiefs into a burial cart. The three senior officers were nowhere to be seen. The prisoners—thirty-two women and children—were marched at gunpoint, hands bound and feet hobbled, to Mission San José. According to Nate, Fisher planned to send one of the women back to the Comanche camp to tell them of the fate that awaited bands that failed to free their white captives.

At the infirmary, the exhausted surgeon—a German immigrant who spoke little English—worked through the night to save injured whites. Ezra stayed with the unattended Comanche girl until she died in the wee hours.

Just after sunup they visited Mathew Caldwell. He sat on the edge of his cot, soothed by laudanum, studying his bandaged thigh. "That ball got nothing but meat," he said. As they were leaving, he added, "We've killed the captives we were trying to ransom as sure as if we lined 'em up along a wall and shot 'em."

Isaac saw no reason to report to Colonel Fisher. They rode east along Portero Street, past the outskirts of town. Just across the San Antonio River, the cannon-pocked walls of the Alamo loomed on their left.

Forty-Eight

Plum Creek Fork of the San Marcos, thirty miles southwest of Bastrop
August 12, 1840

ISAAC MISSED Noah Smithwick more with each passing second. One of his sardonic observations would have been a comfort. Ezra's exhortation, "Sweet Jesus have mercy on us," helped none at all.

A dust cloud hung over the low hills to the southeast, churned up by a herd of some two thousand stolen horses and mules driven by a yet unseen column of at least four hundred Comanche warriors and their women and boys on their way home from an audacious raid to the coast. They had ridden out of Comanchería, the bison plains to the northwest beyond the escarpment, skirted Béxar, then rode onto the coastal plain, laying waste to Texian farms and settlements.

Word was, a ranging company out of Gonzales under a Captain McCulloch struck their broad trail on August 5. By the next day, McCulloch had sent out the alarm and call for volunteers as the raiders sacked Victoria, then rode away with horses, mules, and captives. Two days later, the Comanches struck the little coastal settlement of Linville, killing, burning, and looting. They'd raided a warehouse and now rode with mules laden with women's finery and umbrellas and all manner of hats and gewgaws.

Word of the raid arrived in Bastrop early on August 11; Ezra rode breathless into Isaac's yard with the news. By the time Isaac reached town, rumor had it that the Comanche horde had sacked Béxar and was headed toward Austin.

Some sixty volunteers left Bastrop in the wee hours; before they'd gone ten miles, several riders were referring to their party as the Bastrop Militia. They arrived an hour past sunup to find a hundred or so soldiers of the regular Texas Army and volunteer rangers bivouacked along Plum Creek. Already, the dust cloud was visible on the horizon.

Mathew Caldwell limped up, much to Isaac's relief. The big ranger captain had proven solid in the council house fracas.

"What about Béxar and Austin?" Isaac asked him.

Caldwell laughed. "I don't know where that rumor got started. The heathens went around Béxar on their way to the coast, and you can bet they ain't lookin' for a fight comin' back. They're just wantin' to go back home with all them petticoats and top hats."

Caldwell told them they would be part of a flanking advance under his command and that he'd best get back to the other officers. "That damn Felix

Huston just showed up with a few boy soldiers and took command. It galled me, but I had to give it to him."

As Caldwell walked back toward the creek, Uncle Jimmy said, "Queer lookin' fellar, ain't he? You ever seen a man brindled like that?"

A dozen or so Indians ran out of the trees north of camp. Some of the men mounted rifles, but Caldwell and the Bastrop volunteers shouted them down. "Good lord," Uncle Jimmy said. "Whoever heard of Tonkawas goin' around afoot."

The column trotted closer. Isaac made out the old chief Placido and King, as well as ten younger warriors. The Tonkawas jogged into camp among the gawking militia. Their naked torsos shone in the morning sun. The young warriors bent at the waist and rested with their hands on their knees. Placido and King flopped down in the grass and lay back, chests heaving.

The rangers had been lazing in the shade by the creek. They walked out to meet the Tonkawas. "King, what went with your horse?" Isaac asked.

King moved his forearm just enough to look up at Isaac with one eye. "Caddos stole 'em."

"Hell; you lost 'em gambling," Felix said.

"You got to watch a Caddo," Placido said.

Ezra shook his head in disbelief. "By god, King, you've run thirty miles."

"Nope. We walked some too."

"There's some boys wantin' to fight, now," Ezra said.

King said, "We didn't have time to get no horses."

Uncle Jimmy laughed. "Hell no, you didn't have time to get no horses. All the people you could've stole 'em from had already left to ride down here."

"Damn Caddos," King said. "You should've heard my wife. . . . Where's Cyrus at? He ain't no older than I am."

"Lookin' after our places," Isaac said.

King snorted. "Staying with the women. Where's Noah?"

"I don't imagine word has made it all the way up to Webber's." Isaac checked the horizon. Dust rose like a pale thunderhead. He guessed the herd of stolen horses was still a good dozen miles away. But the Comanches surely had forward scouts that might come into view any time. What if they had already spotted the waiting Texians? "King, you boys best get down there and tell Captain Caldwell you're here."

King pulled himself up on his musket. "Who's he?"

"He'll be the spotted white man," Felix said. "You can't miss him. Brindled beard; brindled face and hands. What in hell do you aim to do without a horse?"

King said something in his native tongue to Placido, who spoke to the young men. They started toward the creek. "There's a lot of horses comin'. This is a good place to be if you ain't got a horse and want to kill Comanches." He walked stiffly away with Placido and the young warriors.

"Old shit's stove up already," Ezra said.

Isaac chuckled. "I still wouldn't want him after me." He sniffed the breeze and licked his lips. "I can taste the dust now." He could also feel his pulse. He moved his rifle from his right hand to his left and rubbed the former on his pants.

They watched and waited. Men began to form up with their captains: Caldwell, Burleson, Hardeman, McCulloch, and others Isaac didn't know. The fourteen Tonkawa scouts trotted southeast into the hills, white rags tied around their arms to distinguish them from the Comanches.

"It'll be a cold damn day I can't tell a Comanche from a Tonkawa," Uncle Jimmy said.

They waited. By noon, men began to seek shade. Huston walked to a rise and looked toward the source of the growing cloud. The men watched and speculated. After a few minutes he returned shaking his head.

Early afternoon, two of the Tonkawa scouts trotted in and reported to Huston, then left again. Isaac, Felix, Ezra, Uncle Jimmy, and one of the Bastrop volunteers, John Jenkins, sat in the shade of the creekside live oaks, watching. Jenkins lived and farmed just north of Bastrop. Isaac liked the look of him—short, solid, strong jaw and chin, and red beard, probably the only man in the company younger than Isaac. He wore a dark suit and gray hat. He'd fallen in immediately with the rangers. "I'd have thought they'd have been here by now," he said, whittling an oak stick with his patch knife.

Isaac wondered if Jenkins had ever faced danger. He appeared calm—or maybe just resigned. "I'd say their forward scouts smelled our little trap and now they're thinkin' things over."

"Whatever is churnin' up all that dust ain't standing around thinking," Felix said.

King trotted into camp, breath rasping like a crosscut saw. He slowed to a walk and made his report. Isaac watched as the old Tonkawa drank from a gourd, then staggered their way. Sweat dripped from his chin.

"King, you're gettin' awful moss-backed for this," Felix said. "Let them younguns do the runnin'. You and old Placido ought to sit here in the shade until the shootin' starts."

King sat with his back to a tree. "Comanches are comin' but slow. Some of their mules have quit on them. Loaded down too much. They even shot some of them. Just left their booty." He opened a pouch on his belt. "I picked up this." He held a set of wooden teeth. "They just left it layin' there."

Jenkins said, "They must be back a ways."

King jutted his chin toward the southeast. "The front riders are just over that first hill. They'll show shortly."

"Good lord!" Isaac said. "What are our officers doin'?" He pictured the Comanche horde riding over the hill, catching the entire Texian force napping under the oaks.

King seemed unconcerned. "The herd's a ways back yet. Them front ones will ride out here directly and try to get us to shoot at 'em while the rest gets by with all them horses and mules." He drank from his gourd. Felix stuffed his pipe. Jenkins whittled and Uncle Jimmy dozed. Isaac and Ezra paced about swatting gnats and wiping the sweat from their eyes.

Another hour passed. Caldwell strode up. "You Bastrop boys gather to the north, about eighty yards up the creek." Other captains were assembling their men. The Tonkawas came and went. King disappeared again.

They pulled up their pickets and led their horses up the creek along with the other Bastrop volunteers and members of Caldwell's First Regiment. There was little talk. The sun sat directly overhead, and there were only the sounds of the horses' breathing and their hooves on the knee-high prairie grass, buzzing grasshoppers, and the hum of insects along the creek. Isaac felt the relief that comes with impending action. He wondered if Looks Far was part of the Comanche host. Given the reported size of the column, he almost certainly was, though Isaac did not expect to see him. And the women. One More Girl. He was part of a militia about to fire on a woman he'd once felt closer to than Inez. He stroked Squab's nose, tried to dismiss the thought.

Inez would be washing clothes or weeding the garden or helping Esther and Ruth. Sarah Ruth would be crawling about, pulling up and trying to stand. Her face stayed dusty; Isaac had never known so good natured a baby. At thirteen months she already had enough hair for a tiny plait. Inez had seen him off matter-of-factly, had already started her morning chores before he was out of sight, as if he were riding to Bastrop to barter for coffee and flour. Did she worry, or did Indian women just take sudden death and hardship for granted? When Ezra came with news of the raid, Inez said nothing; just went to work bundling jerky and cornbread and boiled potatoes for his trip.

Four hundred Comanche warriors. Should he allow himself to be taken alive, if it came to that? Would he be seen as a traitor and subject to the most brutal treatment imaginable, or would his old friendship with the Penateka account for something?

Buffalo Hump. The young chief had not been among those ambushed in Béxar. Isaac suspected he was the leader behind this raid. What had it been like when the Comanche woman returned to camp and reported the slaughter of their great men? The frontier had become complacent after the council house fight. The Comanches had withdrawn beyond Austin. The feeling around Bastrop and Béxar had been that they'd learned their lesson. Isaac had mourned the dead chiefs, had despised Fisher's treachery and arrogance, but hoped the assessment was right, that the beaten Comanches had simply withdrawn. Instead they had been preparing for war. Gathering the other bands. Their raid reminded Isaac of Santa Anna's march to the coast.

He could not forget the sight of Matilda Lockhart and the Mexican boy. The welts and burned flesh. The humiliation. The girl burying her face in Mary Maverick's bosom, begging to be hidden from the sight of the gawking crowd. He'd like to hear Buffalo Hump's justification. Doubtless no better than the justification of the whites in Béxar for allowing the wounded

Comanche women to lay on the floor, bleeding to death on their blankets with no attention from the surgeon. Just heathens, vermin, the infirmary guard had said. And what did the Comanches call white captives?

Dust settled on them now. Running sweat cut furrows down horse flanks and coffee brown foreheads and bewhiskered jaws. The men had formed five ragged, jumbled columns behind the captains. Huston sat his horse out in front, facing the hills to the southeast. The rumble of the approaching horses seemed to have silenced the birds and insects. Horse tails swished. Men spat, spoke in hushed tones, watched the hills. Horses raised their noses to the breeze, snorted and nickered. There was no sign of the Tonkawas.

Isaac shook his powder horn. Dry, of course. August in Texas. He caught Felix's eye and thin smile. Someone said, "Shit!" Huston raised a hand. "Hold your fire. Stand to your horses." Some twenty Comanche men rode down the hill less than a hundred yards away. They wore top hats and had woven calico into their horses' tails. One wore a dark broadcloth suit coat, backward and buttoned in back, and held aloft an open umbrella. The riders screamed what could only be curses and insults, wheeled their ponies as if they were extensions of their torsos. Isaac squinted but recognized none of them. The rumbling grew closer; some of the Texians shouted to be heard by those next to them. Dust blew into their faces. Isaac drew his neckerchief over his mouth and nose, pulled his hat brim low over his eyes.

The raiders moved to the left and performed their feats of horsemanship before a live oak copse. "Breaking up their outlines," Felix said. "Harder to pick 'em out against them trees."

A dozen more riders, all adorned in hats and scarves, or buffalo headdress, some in dresses and lacy pantaloons, joined the diversion. "I never in my life," Jenkins said. He studied the riders as a man might look upon some spectacle of Creation.

The herd pounded over the hill and along the base, driven by boys, as more warriors joined the taunters. The Comanches moved closer and the horses and mules thundered by behind them, heading north. Caldwell looked over his shoulder and shouted, "Trying to hold us up till the mules and loot get by."

Huston motioned for the men to move forward. They led their horses forty yards. The women and mules appeared, the beasts laden and sweating, goaded brutally. Caldwell shouted, "General, now!"

Huston hesitated. Caldwell screamed, "Felix, for god's sake!"

The first of the mules passed by, but began to bog down in the marshy ground at the north end of Big Prairie. A huge Comanche in a top hat and pigeon-tail coat rode toward the Texian column, stopped and taunted only eighty yards away. He wheeled his mustang and shook his lance and shrieked and laughed. Caldwell glanced again over his shoulder. "Shoot him."

Isaac mounted his rifle and tracked the bobbing, spinning chest. Uncle Jimmy Curtis said, "Hell then," and shot the Comanche out of the saddle. The top hat went blowing across the grass and into the hooves of the mules.

The warriors shrieked their outrage. Huston yelled, "Fire away!" Men moved in search of open shots. Some knelt, others aimed offhand. Huston squatted and ducked, holding his hat tight on his head. Isaac laid his sight on the chest of the nearest warrior and squeezed the trigger. The hiss of ignited powder was drowned by the collective roar of rifle fire drawn out over seconds. Some of the warriors swung to the lee sides of their mounts. Others spun their horses and ducked behind their shields. Isaac heard the slaps of lead balls striking hardened shields and meat. Horses and riders tumbled. Batting flew from the shields. Warriors lurched and righted themselves and continued their threats and insults. Long, arching arrow shots scattered the Texians.

The captains were screaming at Huston to give the order to charge. Men mounted their horses. Isaac rammed home another ball, then swung into saddle. Huston shouted the order; Isaac touched the horse's flanks with his heels and rode screaming toward the waiting raiders, who now came bent low behind their shields, bows drawn. At first, the warriors seemed one shrieking mass of calico, painted hide, and mustang. Now Isaac saw the grim, dark eyes peering over the tops of shields; then a certain pair fixed on him and everything else blurred and he no longer heard distinct sounds.

The raider dropped his rein, raised his bow with his shield hand, and drew. Isaac was riding with his rifle across the pommel. He lifted and pointed it with one hand, fired. The Comanche flinched; the arrow hissed by high and left. The warrior raised a hand ax. Isaac heard and felt the air knocked from Squab's lungs as he hit the other horse's front right shoulder. Comanche horse and rider tumbled and Isaac fought to stay in the saddle as Squab reeled and staggered and wheezed.

Isaac looked back and saw the Comanche pony limping away toward the trees, his right front leg dangling. Its master lay on his back, his arm twisted beneath him. Dead and dying horses and warriors littered the base of the hill. The militia were pouring into the northern end of the prairie where mules and horses slogged up to their bellies in the marsh. Many of the Texians had dismounted to take careful aim; women and boys and a few warriors had taken cover behind pack animals. A few Comanches were trying to escape into the trees, and soldiers and rangers tried to cut them off. Squab seemed to recover; Isaac held him to a trot.

He skirted the slaughter in the marsh and rode toward the shade of the hillside oaks. Gunfire crackled. Shooting at the bogged-down Comanches ceased; boys and wailing women staggered out of the knee-deep mud and water.

Isaac patted Squab's neck. "Rough little sumbitch." The mustang pricked his ears forward and seemed to watch the scene below with great interest. Isaac drank from his gourd, amazed that it hadn't been smashed in the collision. Battle rage always left him quickly. He surveyed the carnage and wondered if Looks Far or One More Girl or Feels How Deep the Water Is lay among the dead. He wouldn't be picking through the bodies.

King and Placido and several of the Tonkawas walked out of the trees on the south end of the prairie. Isaac rode back down the hill to meet them. Placido held the hand of a small, crying black boy. Felix and Ezra peeled away from the marsh and rode toward the Tonks. King cradled a naked, infant white girl. He smiled. "This one needs a tit. We could find one up there amongst all them women."

The little boy was sobbing; tears ran down his dusty face; dried snot caked his lips. The younger Tonks were grinning and jostling his shoulder and patting his back. Ezra said, "Lord. It's all right, son. Where's your folks at?"

Felix whispered, "Damn Ezra. Don't bring up his folks yet."

The little boy looked at Ezra, chest heaving, as if trying to remember where his parents might be.

King shaded the baby's eyes with his hand and started toward the middle of the prairie where several of the officers had gathered. The other Tonkawas and the boy followed.

Other riders, presumably those who had been tailing the raiders, came in with more captives—a horribly sunburned young white woman wearing nothing but corset and pantaloons, young children, and a black woman. And bodies of captives. A black man who had been dragged to death after the soles of his feet had been sliced away. A woman shot full of arrows.

They sat their horses in silence, watching, listening to the reports. At least one Texian dead, several wounded, they heard. Still counting Comanches.

Shouts along the base of the hill. A Comanche woman on her hands and knees. A pool of blood beneath her. A squat Texian in a filthy homespun shirt standing over her. Jenkins yelling, "No, for Christ's sake!" The Texian kicked her in the ribs; she rolled onto her back. If he heard Jenkins's pleas, he showed no sign. He picked up a lance and pinned the woman through the chest. Isaac heard her shrill gasp. Jenkins threw down his hat, pulled his hair, cursing.

Isaac rode for the grinning Texian, who bent to take the quivering woman's scalp. Uncle Jimmy reached him first, rode by and swung his rifle butt into the man's mouth. The murderer spat teeth and blood, tried to get up from his hands and knees. Isaac reined Squab and watched as the old ranger dismounted and kicked the addled man's ribs, then bludgeoned him with the buttstock until he lay supine, blubbering and covering his face with his arms.

Jenkins had already closed the woman's eyes. He was kneeling beside her. Felix helped him up. Isaac went to retrieve his hat.

Uncle Jimmy wiped his brow with his forearm and looked back at the man he'd left wallowing in bloody grass. "There's always some that just can't get enough," he said.

Forty-Nine

Isaac's chest tightened when he saw Esther standing in the path along the creek, holding Sarah Ruth. He would have urged Squab to a trot, but the little Mustang had stiffened up after the collision with the Comanche horse. He'd spent the night before in the militia camp on Plum Creek, then started home at first light. On the steeper hills he'd dismounted and walked to relieve his ailing horse.

Esther waited, bobbing the baby in her arms. The sun had nearly disappeared behind the hills. Sarah Ruth pointed at him. He stopped in the path. "Where's Inez?"

"Get down, brother."

He dismounted. They'd gotten her. He held out his arms and took Sarah. Esther hugged them both. "This morning. She went up to milk and never came back. Pap found where they crossed the creek. He's tryin' to trail 'em, but he figures he's at least two hours behind 'em and it's gettin' dark."

Isaac's breath came hard. His Pap wouldn't catch them. God only knew what they'd do to her. He thought of Inez stripped and tied to a horse. Stolen by Lipans to endure only God knew what, then dumped at the fort, and now hauled away to be beaten and used.

He handed Sarah back to Esther and sat in the dirt. He should mount and ride, try to bring her back, but he'd only be killing his horse. He'd been seen at the council house and now at Plum Creek. This was Looks Far's revenge. Nothing to do but wait for daylight. The Comanche had seen the way the Plum Creek fight was going, had ridden away to steal Inez. He'd warned Isaac. The coffee sack on the door.

"Brother, I don't know what to tell you." She sobbed.

"Thousand wonders they didn't get all of you."

"Pap said there was only two of 'em. Or one and another horse. We should've kept her here. But we never thought . . ."

"Hell, nobody ever thought nothin'. Nobody ever does. The damn cow needed milking."

Esther eased Sarah to the ground. The child took a few choppy steps and fell into Isaac's arms. She smelled like Inez. He wiped his tears on her hair. "Where's Mama? Y'all shouldn't be here by yourselves."

"She's inside. Isaac, there wasn't time to do a thing. Pap had to go. Anyways, he said they'd got what they'd come for; that they wouldn't be comin' back." She looked across the creek into the dark timber. "It don't seem like they could've been here. You just don't think about it. It's like she'll come hummin' back down the path lugging the pail with both hands and it banging on her knees. I've never seen a Comanche. I knowed they was about, but I never really believed they'd bother us."

"He never came to bother you. He came for my wife." He rubbed his eyes. "Hell, for all I know we killed both of his wives yesterday."

"Lord. Don't tell me about it."

Squab nickered. Isaac looked up the creek. "That'll be Pap." He heard splashing just upstream. Cyrus rode down the trail toward them. Sarah Ruth squealed and bounced in Isaac's lap. "Yeah, it's Pappy," Esther said.

Isaac couldn't see his father's face in the twilight. The old man came on slowly. "I reckon you boys stirred 'em up."

"We didn't leave many."

"Left at least one that I know of." He dismounted, doffed his hat. "Boy, I'm sorry. Maybe a better man could've picked up their trail. I lost it no more than a mile from the creek."

Isaac nodded. The darkness hid his tears. Yet his voice gave him away. "It's dark. Nobody could've done any better. Not even King."

Cyrus slapped his thigh. "I've growed fond of her. No, hell, I love the girl. We'll raise a company."

"Well." Inez was gone.

Cyrus said, "I'll see to old Squab. Go see about Mother."

Isaac pushed himself up and hefted Sarah. He found Ruth inside bent over the fireplace coals, spreading a dab of melting lard in a skillet with a wooden spoon. She turned and shook her head, still holding spoon over the skillet. Tears mixed with her sweat. She shook her head again and covered her eyes with her free hand.

· · ·

Next morning they picked up the Comanche tracks along the creek, then promptly lost them in the hills. An hour later, Smithwick, Ezra, Uncle Jimmy, Ezekiel Hodge, and Felix joined them. They rode up draws, around the bases of hills, along the creeks. They looked for fragments of tracks, scuffed and overturned rocks, hair, tatters of clothing, blood. Early afternoon, King and Placido and a young Tonkawa warrior named Malachi joined them where the tracks crossed the creek, and they began their search anew. The Tonks rode horses cut from the Comanche herd at Plum Creek.

Isaac felt Inez moving away. He rode bent in the saddle, studying the ground. Twice he dismounted, then wearily pushed himself up from his hands and knees after realizing that he'd found part of a hog track. Once he found a patch of bare slope freshly scuffed. He called for King. The three

Tonkawas dismounted, studied the churned hillside from different perspectives, and talked among themselves. King swung back into the saddle and nodded toward the sign. "We scared some deers up this hill."

Near dusk, Zeke Hodge squeezed Isaac's forearm as he rode down a draw toward the farm. Cyrus said, "Nothin' else to do, son."

Isaac sat his horse on a bare knob, looking westward over the hills toward the bison plains. His eyes felt dry and gritty, his arms heavy. It seemed impossible that Inez would not be waiting for him at home.

King rode up the hill and joined him. They sat in silence. After a while the Tonkawa swept his hand across the darkening horizon. "They're farther away than we can see, Isaac. Farther west than I've rode." He watched the others ride into the open below. "If he came back, I'd make him tell where your wife is at. He'd tell me. But he ain't comin' back. If you want her, you'll have to go where she's at. Wait 'til morning is cold. Comanches hunt buffaloes then."

Fifty

THE NEXT ELEVEN MORNINGS, during the wee hours, Sarah Ruth woke crying. Without lighting a candle, Isaac found her sitting up on her pallet, sweating and sobbing. He felt her reaching for him. He carried her to his bed and laid her on his chest. Sis reared up to sniff her. The child quieted at once; her sobs changed to slow, easy breaths.

He lay thinking of Inez. Was she waiting for him to come for her? Or had her despair already turned to resignation?

Usually a breeze picked up just before dawn and he slept until the roosters crowed. Then he'd feel the coolness at his side, rise and dress, and carry Sarah Ruth down to the home place where Esther fed her mush or mashed potato or biscuit soaked in gravy.

He worked. Split rails for a fence to keep the cow out of the new corn patch. Cut shakes to repair the home place roof. Hauled rock for his own spring-house. Cleared another acre. He did not glance at Inez's work places—the beaten patch of yard where she stretched hides; her meat scaffold; her cook pit. Esther weeded Inez's garden. Sis sniffed about, listening at times, head cocked. Cyrus and Ruth said little to him, though he felt their eyes.

Most nights he dreamed that he woke to find Inez beside him. Or that he was lying with her in Looks Far's lodge, or that Inez lay with Looks Far while he—Isaac—lay with One More Girl, or Catherine. In these dreams, he wondered if he was dreaming.

Smithwick, King, and Felix visited often. Isaac talked with them about raising a company to rescue Inez. Surely he should be doing something. But they all counseled against it. You caught marauding Comanches immediately after a raid or hit them unawares during the cool months when they were hunting or waiting out bad weather. Wait, they said. Bide your time. If Comanches know you're after them, they can't be caught unless they want to be. But they'll grow complacent deep in their home territory.

The August mornings were sweltering. Word came through Ezra that Colonel Moore was raising another company to strike the Comanches come fall. Next day, Isaac rode to La Grange to sign on. Colonel Moore's representative told him to go home and stay ready to ride on a day's notice.

September came, and Isaac stood just outside his door at sunrise, eyes closed, feeling for the slightest hint of cooling.

By mid-September, the heat had abated little, but the afternoon light seemed richer, more canted. On the second day of October, a late afternoon shower cooled the air. The sky cleared just after dark. Isaac was laying Sarah Ruth on her pallet when he heard a faint clamor. He picked her up and strode into the yard, Sis at his heels. He searched the night sky. The din grew louder. Sis whined. Isaac set his daughter on his shoulders and said, "Listen, Saree. Geese."

Fifty-One

October 6, 1840

ISAAC REINED HIS HORSE and looked back in amazement at the bustle in Austin, President Lamar's new capital. Buildings and surveying crews, horses, wagons, and all manner of livestock on dusty roads where three years earlier Coleman's rangers had trailed Comanches.

Ezra rode by heading northwest. "You fixin' to get left, boy."

Isaac ignored him. Other men rode by, most of them strangers. He'd have plenty of time to get to know them. Somewhere ahead of the column of about ninety volunteers, Colonel John Moore would be scanning the hills and draws for the night's campsite.

They were hunting Comanches. Their orders from Lamar and the War Department were explicit. They would not burden themselves with prisoners. This was to be a punitive strike in remembrance of the suffering of the citizens of Victoria and Linville. Much, Isaac thought, as the Comanches sacked Victoria and Linville in retaliation for the massacre of their chiefs at the council in Béxar.

Yet he had resigned himself to the killing. He wanted Inez back. To go after her alone would be suicidal. He rode with these men—some ninety Texians and a dozen Lipan scouts—merely to give himself and Inez a chance. He had no doubt that Felix, Ezra, and Uncle Jimmy had joined the expedition for his sake alone.

Smithwick had offered, but Isaac talked him out of it. The man had suffered enough from the first Moore disaster. The death of Captain Coleman's widow and his stolen children still haunted him. He and Thurza had been comfort enough, and now they had a farm to tend on Webber's Prairie. And Thurza Duty Smithwick had already lost one husband. She had stood by Noah during his rangering and emissary days, and he'd made her a promise.

Isaac fell in behind Felix and pulled his hat brim over his eyes against the setting sun. He did not feel like talking. He remembered this country. The discarded garments of the Thorpe and Mann women. The skirmish with the raiders. His second kill. Comanches had the edge here. This was their world. A horseman's world. No place to take cover. He'd take Inez back and never return.

Ahead, toward the front of the column, he spotted the black, woolen coat of Thomas Adair.

Cyrus Webb rode up beside Isaac. "I figured I'd ride behind Ezree. Shade is right sparse in this god-awful country."

. . .

The nights grew colder. Isaac slept well. The country opened as they rode west above the north bank of the Colorado River. Squab seemed to grow stronger by the day, while most of the horses grew gaunt despite the grain carried in wagons. The little mustang thrived on nothing but the cured grass.

Isaac felt no closer to Inez. He watched the horizon, constantly reminded of the separation. And what if she was dead? What became of a Lipan girl's soul after she died?

Five days out of Austin, they began to encounter bands of bison and antelope and flocks of prairie chickens. At first, Moore wouldn't let them shoot at game for fear of alerting Indians. He relented three days later after their rations of jerky, cornmeal, and hardtack had dwindled to less than a week's supply. Most men tried their hand at buffalo and antelope, but the light balls barely made it through the thick hides of the bison, and an enraged cow knocked over Lieutenant Dawson's horse, breaking the horse's leg. The lieutenant survived with sore ribs and a broken wrist. He shot his horse and settled for a lesser mount from the small remuda. The men later dug thirty-seven balls out of the dead cow, most of them in the muscle just below her hide. Several men tried to crawl within range of antelope, but when they'd raise their heads above the grass to shoot, the animals would flee. Isaac guessed them to be twice as fleet as the fastest horse.

Isaac and Cyrus hunted the timbered creeks where distances were more easily judged. Most days they took both deer and turkey. Every time someone fired a rifle, Isaac imagined Comanches fleeing with Inez. He could not believe the company could simply ride along this river and find her. King's comment rang in his head. "They're farther away than I can see." Gone beyond the horizon; though the horizon changed, it remained unreachable.

They saw no Comanche sign. Dark buttes and square ridges rose in the distance, some shaped like steps, square as hewn timbers. The men speculated on their size and distance. Bets were offered and some threatened to ride out and see for themselves, but no one dared leave the safety of the company. The river grew shallower.

Isaac avoided Thomas Adair, but he often heard the basso laugh and confident banter. Cyrus had awoken stiff and cross the first few days out, but the riding soon hardened him and he rose in fine humor. Isaac wondered how the old man would fare in a desperate fight. Comanches were not Creeks or red-coated British soldiers.

They came to a fork and followed its northwest prong for four days. They rode through low hills and good timber. Isaac found the country comfortingly familiar. The river fork and its tributaries ran as clear as the streams back in the Ouachitas. He often saw the slim river bass holding in gentle current, and he wished for his fish trap. They ate well off the land; their larder grew, though most of the horses grew poorer for lack of grain.

At times, Isaac forgot about Inez and simply enjoyed riding in new country and the brisk, clear weather—good sleeping and eating weather, Cyrus called it.

Twelve days out, Moore walked among the campfires and told the men that come sunup they would be heading south. He squatted by Isaac's fire, a tall slim man with a black and gray-flecked beard and buckskins blackened by countless campfires. "We'll take another week," he said. "If we don't ride upon the heathens, we'll head home." He sipped his coffee. "I suspect we're halfway to Taos. Further out on these plains than any white man has been before."

"Or cares to again," Cyrus said.

Moore smiled thinly. "When I give my report, I'll call this some of the best country I've seen. It won't be empty of Christians long." He got up and walked into the darkness. Isaac had no idea of the location of Taos, other than it had to be west of Bastrop. He wondered how a man might venture to guess such things.

"He's an ambitious man," Cyrus said. "Sets store by bein' first somewhere and makin' claims that can't be disputed."

Two days later, they came again to the Colorado. The northern sky was slate gray. The air turned brittle and Isaac smelled rain. They crossed the river next morning in cold drizzle. They pushed westward, bundled under sodden wool coats and buffalo robes and blankets. The country lay open and gray before them, grass and shinnery and plum mottes, oak and hackberry along the creeks. That night, their fires hissed under intermittent rain, and they sat up dozing or sleeping fitfully. An old man named Garrett Harrell coughed and shivered throughout the night. Cyrus glanced at Isaac from beneath his hat brim. Firelight shone on his damp forehead. "We'll be leavin' him out here I'm afraid."

Isaac pulled the blanket tighter about his shoulders and moved closer to the fire until he felt the heat of the coals through the soles of his moccasins.

Morning broke gray and wet. Ice clung to the grass and branches of trees and brush. Fog hung over the river and along the creek bottoms. They kept to their fires, sipping coffee and waiting for Garrett Harrell to die. Isaac and Ezra dug a grave on a grassy bench above the river. They dug with flat rocks and limbs. Just as they finished, four men arrived bearing Harrell wrapped in a blanket. Isaac stood with raw, freezing hands and eyed the dead man's moccasins protruding from the rolled blanket. Castro and the Lipans rode west into the gloom while Moore recited Psalm 23 over the grave.

Five miles westward, they came to a small pecan grove; all of the lower limbs had been hacked off. "I don't believe squirrels done that," Uncle Jimmy said. Castro rode in and conferred with Colonel Moore. Thomas Adair turned his back on the conference and stared into the hills to the north.

Cyrus said, "If I was this short on shade, I wouldn't be cuttin' up my trees."

The word spread among the rangers: a large Comanche camp on the river four miles ahead. Sixty families. Twice as many warriors. Isaac's stomach soured. The rangers cast hard glances and cursed softly. Cyrus spat. "Be damn. Been a long time."

Isaac watched his father. Cyrus seemed gaunt and frail and nervous. But then so did Uncle Jimmy. All of the faces looked pale and wet. Men shook their powder horns and felt for knives. Isaac wished for a pistol. One rifle shot and he was reduced to carrying a club. If they struck with complete surprise, they could wipe out the camp. If the Comanches had time to grab their weapons, Texians would start falling from the saddle after the first volley.

He rode to the front of the column. Colonel Moore was conferring with Castro and Castro's son Flacco and two other captains. Moore looked up, smiled. "Isaac, is it?"

"Yes sir."

"What's on your mind? Fighting, I hope."

"Yes sir. My wife . . ."

"Yes, Smithwick told me. I'll address the men shortly."

"Yes sir."

Moore looked westward. "It'll be damn hard to tell who's who. If she was a white woman, now . . ."

"She won't be shootin' at us. She's probably been waitin' on me. Wondering when I was comin'."

"I'll speak to the men, son."

"Yes sir." He rode back to his father and friends.

"What'd he say?" Uncle Jimmy said.

Isaac shook his head. "I hope she ain't there."

Cyrus said, "What in hell? What'd I come all the way out here for?"

"He aims to kill everything that moves."

"If she'll just holler out in English," Ezra said.

The Lipans led them to a broad, dry creek sheltered by oaks. They dismounted and picketed their horses. The order came that there were to be no fires.

The rain had ceased, but the air grew colder. The men huddled out of the wind and talked little. Moore and the captains walked among the groups, talking and drawing in the sand. Isaac could hear Cyrus shivering next to him. Isaac moved against him. "Come on, boys, he's freezin'." Ezra grabbed Jimmy's skinny arm and pushed him against Cyrus. He and Felix and Isaac bunched around the older men. After a few minutes, Uncle Jimmy said, "I've breathed better air in a shit house." But he and Cyrus had stopped shivering.

The sky cleared after sunset. Isaac found the Little Dipper and the North Star. They were in for a long wait. He imagined the inside of a Comanche lodge, the robes and fire, warm flesh. He caught himself becoming aroused thinking of One More Girl, who hated him now if she was still alive. Was Inez keeping some warrior warm? Had she accepted it the way she'd accepted a life with him? She'd come to love him; could she learn to love her captors? And if she bore a Comanche child, would she want to leave it to come back to him and Sarah Ruth?

Around midnight Castro roused him. "Inez could be there. It's cold and they are in their lodges. I did not see her."

"What in hell is he sayin'?" Jimmy said. "Damn Mexican talk."

"Said he ain't seen Inez because they're all in their lodges."

"Damn right they are," Felix said. "I'm too cold to shoot."

Castro looked in fine spirits. He didn't shiver, though he wore only a deer-skin shirt and long breechclout and knee-high moccasins. "They don't expect an attack here." He grinned as he ran his finger like a blade across his throat. He hurried back toward the officers at the head of the draw.

"Havin' hisself a big time," Cyrus said.

The swarthy Georgian Captain Owens and Colonel Moore appeared out of the darkness. "Boys, you'll ride under Captain Owens here," Moore said. Owens nodded to them. Moore said, "How's our two old veterans?"

"Freezin' to goddamn death," Uncle Jimmy said. "I'm either gonna fight or get good and drunk."

Isaac was concerned that Cyrus didn't answer. He'd always taken his father's fighting skills for granted, but now Cyrus was an old man about to ride on a Comanche camp. Isaac had never seen him shoot from horseback or even ride a horse at full gallop.

Moore laughed. "Stay sober 'til sunup; you'll warm up then."

Isaac wanted to question the wisdom of waiting until the Comanches rose for the day; then he considered trying to distinguish women from men and Comanche from Lipan and Texian in the dark.

"We'll attack with only fifteen men on horseback," Moore said. "You boys, Captain Owens, and ten others I'll talk to directly. The rest will come in on foot." He looked at Isaac. "You boys will hit camp first, right through the middle behind the Lipans. I picked you because you know what the captive girl looks like. The Comanches will run for the river; I'll have a company of rifle-men waiting. Another company will come in on foot on the left flank. Isaac, don't get so busy huntin' your wife, you get yourself shot. You can't do her a drop of good dead." He stood and walked down the creek to another group.

Owens said, "Try to rest. I'll rouse you." He followed Moore.

"Crowd in here, boys," Cyrus said. "Or I won't be ridin' nowhere."

• • •

Isaac saw Owens coming at false dawn. He'd barely dozed since midnight. Cyrus and Jimmy had snored steadily. He hoped the old men could stand. He nudged them. Cyrus said, "Time to ride," pushed himself up, and stomped his feet. Isaac squeezed his arm. "Tough old shit."

"Don't shake me too hard or I'll break into pieces."

Men were stretching, lashing blankets onto their saddles, checking flints, shaking powder horns, blowing into their fists, stamping their feet, faces lit by a three-quarter moon.

Owens walked up leading several rangers. "I reckon we'll ride with these Bastrop boys," one of them said.

"Just don't get behind me; I'm feeling a little gassy," Cyrus said. They laughed and found their horses, then led them out of the creek behind Owens.

Faint pink showed on the eastern horizon. They walked their horses west along the river. The Lipans trotted ahead of them, bristling with muskets and tomahawks. Other men formed up to the right; more eased along just above the riverbank. There was only the sound of hooves and shins brushing against frozen grass.

A dog howled in the distance. Isaac swallowed, tried to slow his breathing. He caught a faint whiff of wood smoke. He looked at his father and touched his nose. Cyrus nodded. He'd be fine. At least the wind was in their faces. They topped a low rise, then the prairie sloped gently downward. Isaac felt the ripple of tension as the Comanche encampment came into view—scores of lodges dimly lit from within by dying coals, spread in a crescent near the river.

Owens swung into the saddle. Isaac and the other horsemen mounted. They moved ahead, casting long shadows down the slope. The new sun lighted the lodges.

They closed to within two hundred yards. The Lipans broke into a sprint, bounding over the frosted grass. Owens quirted his horse. Isaac touched Squab with his heels, and the mustang surged ahead of Owens. Dogs howled and ran out to meet them. Women screamed. Castro brained one of the mongrels with a tomahawk. Women and children ran from lodges; warriors tried to nock arrows as the Lipans cut down a half dozen with the first volley.

Isaac's own screaming surprised him. Hoarse curses erupted all around. Rifles cracked behind him. Men and women tumbled, clawing at their own chests and faces. Isaac rode through camp. A teenage boy squatted before his door flap, taking aim with his bow. Isaac lowered his rifle and shot the boy in the chest, knocking him back into the lodge.

He rode to the far end of camp, dismounted, and dropped to a knee to reload. Comanches ran for the river. He rammed home a patch and ball and looked for Inez among dozens of dark-haired women. He searched for a long plait, worried that the Comanches had chopped off her hair. Shots along the river. A woman fell forward on the baby she carried. The flanking column ran into camp, firing and hacking. Ezra rode up beside him and dismounted, his chest heaving. "Where's your pap?"

"I lost him!"

Isaac held the ramrod against the rifle stock and ran back into camp. A warrior with pink froth on his chin tried to pull himself up with his lance. Isaac ran past him, leapt over bodies without looking at them, ran to the biggest lodge near the center of camp. He started to peer in the door, thought better of it, ran to the back and drew his knife and split the hide, then leapt away. Nothing. He opened the slit with his rifle barrel. Empty save for stacks of robes and weapons propped against the wall. He ran to the next lodge, cut it open, found it empty. He ran down the row, checking lodges. He found old women shot in their robes, a Lipan peeling the scalp off a boy, a skinny Texian beating a woman in the head with the butt of his knife, shouting, "Bitch! Bitch! Bitch! Bitch!" The butcher stopped and looked up at Isaac, flashed a toothless grin and dropped the woman into the coals, then walked away.

Isaac dragged the dead woman from the fire and stepped outside. Comanches were screaming and flailing in the river and rangers were kneeling, taking careful aim. Bodies drifted in the sluggish current. Several Texians had remounted to try to turn the stampeding Comanche horse herd.

Isaac checked the bodies of women, glancing at each face only long enough to see that it didn't belong to Inez. He'd seen no dead or wounded rangers.

He jogged to the river, then along the bank, looking at the bodies, hardening himself against the small corpses. Still no sign of Inez or Cyrus or Buffalo Hump, Looks Far, or any of the Penateka he'd known.

Uncle Jimmy and three of the La Grange volunteers held a dozen or so shrieking women and children at gunpoint, Uncle Jimmy yelling, "Hush squalling; I ain't gonna hurt you!"

Ezra and several others had gathered at the edge of the trees at the east end of camp. The big man was shaking his head. Isaac's throat tightened at the sight of blood on the grass.

He pushed his way through. Thomas Adair lay on his back, an arrow protruding from his belly and sternum. His eyes were teary and wild with fear. Cyrus was gripping his hand. "Nothin' to fear, Thomas. Not a thing." Adair blinked. His breath came shallow, panicked. "You're ready for this, Thomas," Cyrus said. Adair swallowed.

"Lord," Isaac whispered. He caught Cyrus's questioning glance. "She ain't here, Pap."

Cyrus studied Adair's wounds. After a moment, he looked up at Isaac and sighed. "Well," he said.

Fifty-Two

ISAAC HELPED Catherine and Louise into the seat of their wagon. They didn't look at their cabin. Cyrus had brought his wagon, too, and Ezra and Felix had ridden upriver to help with the moving. The heavy tools waited in the barn and shed for the new owners, the Balt family out of San Felipe.

They headed for Bastrop. Cedrick rode the mule. The milk cow was tethered to the back of the Adair's wagon. The late November drizzle started again before they reached the mouth of the creek. Ruth and Esther and several local women were at the former Hicks place, a solid cabin at the edge of town, Louise and Catherine's new home. They'd have the place warmed and food ready by suppertime. Isaac wondered whether Mrs. Adair would free Cedrick. Would he stay with them if she did? He couldn't imagine her selling him. He'd help Cedrick build a little cabin near Catherine and Louise, or maybe the old man could move up to Webber's Prairie or even the home place. He'd be a welcome help and good company. Cedrick needed a woman, though.

Catherine had put on weight and carried it well. Brown face and hands. The same gray dress. The stern Baptist girl. Yet he remembered her heat and the strength in those fingers. He realized she had her father's eyes and high forehead.

It was dark when Isaac yelled across the river to the ferryman. They crossed the Colorado and rode up the hill. Light shown from the windows of the old Hicks cabin. Isaac sensed the bustle inside as they rode into the bare, muddy yard.

Louise Adair wept as the women came out to meet them. Catherine patted her mother's back. The men saw to the animals. Isaac thought of what his friends and family had meant to him in Inez's absence. Louise and Thomas Adair had been married twenty-eight years.

The women herded the men inside to the table. Sarah Ruth sat in Isaac's lap and helped him eat his ham and cornbread. She opened her mouth and followed the food with her eyes whenever he took a bite.

Catherine said, "Don't you ever feed that girl?" She held out her hands and Sarah went to her.

"Every two or three days."

Catherine walked away toward the door, bouncing and cooing to the child.

She turned and whispered in Sarah Ruth's ear and they both looked at Isaac and smiled. Sarah pointed at him. He drank his coffee. His chest felt heavy. Cyrus went outside to have a pipe with Cedrick, who'd taken his meal just inside the door.

By midnight, they had the beds in place and trunks and chests and chairs inside. Louise said, "We're fine now; y'all got to get home." The women all hugged her and sniffled. The men stood around clearing their throats and rubbing chin whiskers. Cedrick took his bedroll to the toolshed.

Catherine picked up Sarah Ruth, snugged her blanket, and gave her to Isaac. "Now then," she said. "I thank you, Isaac."

"No trouble. I wish I knew what to tell you."

Her eyes glistened. She gathered herself.

"Don't ever worry about bein' a bother," he said. "There's a lot to do and now's a good time to do it."

She nodded.

"Can't have old Cedrick sleepin' in your toolshed. I'll help him raise a shack."

She stroked the little girl's cheek, then led Isaac to the door. They all said their farewells. Esther climbed into the wagon next to Ruth; Isaac set Sarah Ruth in her lap. The wind rattled the treetops. A few stars shone through holes in the clouds.

V

KIN

Fifty-Three

January 1841

"I'LL MARRY YOUR SISTER if you don't care," Ezra said. He leaned back in the chair and crossed his arms.

Isaac checked the coffeepot. Almost half full. He poured a cup, handed it to Ezra. "Well, it's about damn time. Have you asked Pap?"

Ezra nodded. "He said he didn't care if you didn't care."

"I figured I'd be hearin' this. I been seeing a lot of you and none of poor old Jonas."

Ezra blew on the coffee. "She talked to him. I seen him the other day. He spoke. Pretty good fellar."

"I don't suppose you've told Esther you're fixin' to marry her."

"She told me. We'd tie the knot or I'd be eatin' up somebody else's hogs."

The wind rattled the door and window and moaned in the chimney. Isaac would be ready for spring when it came, but for now he enjoyed these lazy afternoons by the fire. "Speaking of hogs, where do you aim to light? You ain't taking Esther off to town."

"I earned four sections rangering. I was thinkin' of Miles Creek."

Isaac shook his head. "No sir. That's a good eight miles upriver. We can't do without Esther."

"You mean *you* can't do without her."

"I mean Mama can't do without her."

Ezra sighed. "That's what she said. I was hopin' you'd take my side. If you'd get busy courtin' Catherine, you might be able to find your ass without your big sister pointing it out to you."

"You know why I can't marry Catherine."

"She'd marry you in a heartbeat. Then you'd have her and her mother both around the place. Ruth would have all the help she could stand."

Isaac sat on the edge of the bed and leaned toward Ezra. "You stood right there beside me while Reverend Hodge married me and Inez. I can't just forget about her. I'm bound to her as long as she might still be alive."

Ezra waved off the comment. "Hell, boy, you'll go the rest of your life not knowin'. How many women have we got back from the Comanches?" He caught Isaac's expression, leaned forward and slapped his shoulder. "I'm sorry. Damn thoughtless of me. I'm just saying that if you courted Catherine, nobody would think ill of you. Even Esther said so, and you know how much she loved Inez."

"I know what you're gettin' at. I just ain't ready to face it yet."

Ezra smiled, nodded. "Fair enough. And I'll see what I can find a little closer in."

"There's two sections of bottom and then some right up the creek."

"Why, it just gets rougher and rougher above you. Your Pap got the best place right at the mouth. You got a good place and you're expecting me to grub out a living on a rough old hill farm. I could have all bottom over on Miles Creek."

"I'll help you get the place in shape. You'll just have four or five little fields instead of one or two big ones."

"You wouldn't help me if I lit a little further upriver?"

Isaac said, "I would. But then you'd be too busy gettin' your place started and wouldn't have time to come down here and help us. Pap's gettin' older in case you ain't noticed."

Ezra snorted. "You just want your sister around to look in on you."

"You got mules?"

"I can buy a span."

"You ain't got shit, and if you had it you wouldn't know what to do with it. You've done nothin' but ranger and round up mustangs."

"I grew up farmin'," Ezra said.

"Uh-huh. Until you moved down to Biloxi. How old were you? Five?"

"Eight." He chuckled. "I loaded a few hundred tons of cotton at Biloxi."

"That'll come in real handy around here." Isaac bent over and reached beneath the bed to stroke Sis's ears. "Go ahead and carry your stuff in. I know you brought it with you."

• • •

Sixteen days later, Isaac, Cyrus, and Ezra finished chinking a new dogtrot cabin a quarter mile up the creek. Two days later, a Saturday, with most of Coleman's rangers and their wives in attendance, Reverend Ezekiel Hodge married Ezra and Esther at the Webber place. Ruth cried; Cyrus fidgeted, pale and hound faced. Isaac stood with Ezra; Thurza Smithwick with Esther. Ezra looked dazed, huge hands shaking, black wool coat stretched across his back and unbuttoned in front, boiled shirt and black tie, new buckskin breeches and moccasins. Esther wore a yellow gingham dress, her blond hair tied up in ribbons. She seemed to enjoy Ezra's discomfort.

The rangers lined the walls and spilled over into the kitchen where Puss Webber shooed her children outside or under the table and dared them to utter a sound. Smithwick stood with his fiddle at his side. Zeke Hodge read the rites, and Isaac caught Catherine's eye and knew that Inez would have enjoyed this—all the women and gabbing and children, and he could have taught her to dance to fiddle music. A lump came to his throat, and for god's sake she was out on the plains, a captive if she was still alive and enduring God only knew what; and here was Catherine, his first love, and yes he still loved her and ached for her like you ache for something just out of reach, not like you love the familiar, like he'd loved Inez with whom he'd worked and sweated and froze side by side and made a life and started a family.

And, God, Catherine was still looking at him. Of course Ezra and Inez had been right. She wanted him and had all along, but couldn't tear away from Thomas Adair. This woman who'd been a pallid girl he'd picked up and laid on a blanket nearly five years ago along the road to Cole's Settlement. And could he live with himself? How would it feel with Catherine, knowing that Inez might be out there suffering and longing to get back to him? What if a company rode on a Comanche camp, and there she was? What then?

He knew how the community saw things: Inez was, after all, a promising young man's mistake. He'd done the honorable thing. People seemed sadder for him than for her. There seemed to be none of the rage, the blind racial hatred that rose whenever a white woman was stolen. He'd be bereft for a while, but then he could get on with his life. Marry a nice Baptist girl, the one he'd really wanted all along. She'd help him raise Sarah Ruth and, hopefully, bear more children. That would be the word around Bastrop.

But they couldn't know the feel of Inez's hand on his chest that night at Coleman's Fort. Or that she said whatever she thought and didn't mind if he swore or if Sis slept under the bed. Or that if he yelled at her or was cross with Cyrus, she'd follow him all the way into the fields or woods, telling him what a sorry bastard he was, "You sorry, lazy bastard; mean shit! Don't be thinkin' you're gettin' under this dress no time soon."

"Don't be talkin' like that in front of the baby," he'd say. She'd toss her head, and her plait would flip like a horse's tail and she'd say, "Sarruth knows how you are!"

There was the morning he laughed after the hounds ate a deer hide she'd scraped and pegged out to dry. She tore into him, and he told her that if she didn't hush he'd feed every goddamn hide he brought in to the dogs. By mid-morning, he'd had enough of her tirade. He saddled his horse and rode up the creek to hunt. Even in the hills, far out of sight of the cabin, he could still hear her shrieks. He rode in after dark with a brace of turkeys. She had the baby in her arms, and he picked them both up at once and hugged them. Gasping for breath, toes a foot off the ground, she said, "You're sorry, I reckon." He reckoned he was. As he sat eating his cold supper while Inez nursed Sarah Ruth and watched him, he wondered if she'd meant he was sorry for what he said or he was just plain sorry.

Nor could they know how much she loved a good story, especially Old Testament smiting and treachery. She'd listen respectfully to a reading, or a telling by Ruth or Esther. But she most loved Isaac's telling. He'd recount the tales from memory, filling in and embellishing as required, though he soon learned that he'd best fill in and embellish the same way every time. Inez especially approved of the Passover and the Battle of Jericho and David's slaying of

Goliath. She'd listen raptly as she worked or nursed the baby or lay beside him, so close he could feel her breath on his shoulder.

The great flood vexed her. The giant vessel loaded with two of every kind of animal. All animals? Deer and cattle of course. Dogs. Buffalo. Birds, perhaps. Bugs?

"Every thing that creepeth upon the earth."

And what did these beasts eat those 150 days? Surely Noah had extra goats or deer or chickens to feed the wolves and coyotes and panthers. And didn't the animals shit all over everything?

"All things are possible with the Lord," Isaac would tell her.

Yes, it must have been filthy. But not filthier than Squab's stall. And where was Moses when all this water covered the world?

Isaac had to think about it. "I don't believe he was born yet." He'd have to ask Zeke Hodge about that.

Didn't the flood drown the Gypchuns? Where did they come from? Surely not Noah's family.

"The Lord put 'em there."

Inez had little interest in New Testament stories beyond the miracles and healings. Why should the chosen people turn the other cheek? Why would *anyone* turn the other cheek? You'd just end up dead and scalped.

They couldn't know. The way she looked when her braid was undone and Esther brushed her hair. Or what she could do with those strong little hands and that she was unburdened by any supposedly Christian compunction against coming to him with her exact wants. No hinting or suggesting. Do this right now before the baby wakes or before you get sleepy. No, right here, like this. Uh-huh. *Damn. We're gettin' good.*

Now she was gone and Thomas Adair was dead. And Catherine hadn't given up on him. He glanced at her. She smiled at Esther. What if Inez was dead? But then Comanches rarely killed their female captives. Maybe one of the chiefs would take her as a wife. He'd probably never know. No one would notice a Lipan girl among a band of Comanches. If she were white, word would get around.

She might make out fine. She knew how to live like an Indian if she knew anything. She might be getting good with Looks Far, doing what she had to do. Or she might look like Matilda Lockhart.

He caught Catherine's eye again. The Reverend needed to hitch these two and shut his trap.

Esther and Ezra finished their vows. Ezekiel Hodge presented them. Esther blushed and Ezra stood like a mule confronted with a new gate. The attendees laughed nervously. Cyrus said, "Ezree, kiss your bride so we can eat."

Ezra bent and pecked Esther on the lips, eyes raised to watch his fellow rangers for sniggering or snide comments, but they all stood red faced, hats in hands. Thurza Smithwick clapped softly.

The women hugged Esther and the men stood in line to shake Ezra's hand.

Afterward, they filed into the kitchen where Puss Webber filled plates with pecan pie. They stood about the great room eating and laughing; Smithwick struck up "Fair Ellender."

Uncle Jimmy grabbed Esther's hand and pulled her toward the middle of the room. "By god, I'll be the first to twirl the bride," he said. And Ruth took Ezra's hand and said, "I know this one can dance!"

Then Smithwick started "Turkey in the Straw." Isaac finished his pie and laid his plate in the chair and moved up beside Catherine to watch the dancers. John Webber opened the door to cool the room. Catherine clapped along with the other women and tapped her foot. Isaac bent to her ear. "Careful, girl."

She smiled at him, red faced. "I guess I can clap."

"Clap on. I'll have you spinnin' out the middle of the floor before the night's over." He had to move close to talk over the laughter and foot stomping. His face was only inches from hers. No one was watching. His chest ached. She wiped her hands on her dress, then touched his, gently taking a finger, all the while watching the dancers. He moved against her, shoulder to shoulder, and took her whole hand. She squeezed; her jaw tightened, showing a fierceness he hadn't seen since that afternoon in Adair's barn. He felt the heat of her arm through their sleeves.

Smithwick finished his tune, and Esther kissed Uncle Jimmy's forehead. Smithwick started another lick. Jimmy delivered Esther to Felix. Other dancers paired up, but Isaac stood where he was and stroked the back of Catherine's hand with his thumb. There'd be time for dancing.

Fifty-Four

"ISAAC WEBB, you're gonna have to court me a little bit more first," Catherine said. She pushed him away and punched at his hands.

They'd been walking along the river in the shade of sycamores and oaks. The trees were nearly leaved out, but the afternoon was cool and the river purled below them. He had stopped to kiss her and had laid his hands on her bottom.

"Court you. I've already ate half your chickens. Then you've got to count all the long rides I made to your farm before your daddy ran me off. I'd say that's a bunch of courtin'."

"Just how much are you willing to do?"

"Much as it takes."

"To what?"

"You're a sneaky girl. I'd say I've been patient."

"So have I." She watched him.

"Patient enough, I suppose." He'd been expecting this. Inez had been gone ten months now. Everyone urged him to marry Catherine, and he ricocheted so often between grief and guilt and desire that he simply wanted to settle it. "Reckon we could get your mama to move upriver with us?"

She stood with her hands on her hips and mirth in her eyes. She had him. "Naturally, you couldn't just come out and propose."

"And of course you couldn't just say yes or no."

"You might have to build her a place of her own."

"Is that a yes?"

"Was that a proposal?"

He took her by the waist and pulled her to him. "Maybe I ought to just court you some more, then."

"No . . ." She closed her eyes and pressed against him. "Lord. Feels like you're about out of patience."

Fifty-Five

ISAAC EASED INTO the riffle and worked his basket trap into the tail of the pool, then stacked fist-sized rocks on either side to block fleeing fish. Ezra stood knee deep at the head of the pool. "By god, Isaac, this water is cold. I can't feel my feet."

"If you can't feel your feet, then you can't feel those sharp rocks either." He tiptoed out of the shallows and onto the bank. "I wonder if fish can hear."

"I don't believe I could point out the ears on one," Ezra said.

"I wonder if they feel you comin'. That's why I'm steppin' easy." He waded in next to Ezra. "We need one more blocker. This pool is too broad."

"Well, I want you to look," Ezra said. He yelled to Esther as she walked down the path toward the home place. She set down her two slop pails and strode across the fallow field toward the creek.

Isaac said, "If fish could hear, these would be deaf now."

"I had to get her attention. She gets set on a task and you've got to shake her loose. I could tell she had her mind on haulin' them slops down to your pap's hogs."

Esther walked down the bank. "Of all the things you two could be doin' . . ."

"I don't suppose you'll be helpin' us eat this mess of fish, then," Isaac said.

"What mess of fish?"

"The one we'll have soon as you get down here and help us drive this pool."

"I know good and well that water is freezing cold."

"We're standin' in it," Ezra said.

"Somebody with sense wouldn't be." She scratched her ear and eyed the trap and deep, green pool. "Suckers, you think?"

"And catfish," Isaac said. "I saw some the other day. Maybe a few bream."

"The little round ones?"

"Yes ma'am; your favorite."

"Well." She sat on the bank and started unlacing her shoes.

Ezra laughed. "I knew she wouldn't be able to stand it."

Isaac held out a hand. "Come in here, sister. It ain't over waist deep. By god, we'll eat tonight."

She took his hand and stepped in. "Lord, you two. Gettin' me wet."

"You've got all day to dry out," Ezra said.

"I guess you'll have Miss Catherine doing things like this pretty soon."

Esther staggered on the slick rocks until she stood beside Isaac.

"I'll have her mother in here. Let's just stay abreast and ease on toward the trap."

They moved into deeper water. "Whoo!" Esther said as she moved in up to her thighs.

Isaac said, "I can just see fish swimming into my trap."

Ezra stumbled. "Goddamn, there's a bunch of rocks in here."

"Watch your mouth, Ezra Higginbotham."

"Hush," Ezra said. "I wish I'd cut me a staff."

"Just keep goin'," Isaac said. "See, it's gettin' shallow again."

Ezra stumbled and grabbed Isaac who grabbed Esther who said, "Well shit." They fell over like a picket fence. Isaac let go of Esther, but Ezra held on to Isaac as he struggled to push himself off the bottom of the pool. Every time Isaac tried to put a hand down and regain his balance, the big man jerked him down and sideways. He tried to yell but swallowed a mouthful of water. Finally, he turned and grabbed Ezra's arm with his free hand and fell on top of him. Ezra threw Isaac off and flailed his way to shallow water. "I swear, you're about to drown me!"

Isaac clambered over the rocks at the tail of the pool and stood in the riffle. Esther was on the bank wringing out her hair. Sis loped up followed by two men on horseback.

The current carried Isaac's hat to the mouth of the trap. He snatched it up, shook it, and put it on. Ezra's beard hung from his chin like a dripping black icicle.

"Mornin'," Esther said. She shook her head like a dog.

Sis waded into the riffle to greet Isaac. He said, "Well, girl, I guess you'll bring us a band of Comanches next time."

The men sat their horses, smiling, obviously admiring Esther and enjoying the scene. One was small, thin, clean shaven, with dark hair and eyes. He wore black woolen breeches and a plain buckskin shirt. Early twenties. The other man, a big Tejano or Mexican with a thick mustache and heavy chin stubble, held a musket in a massive hand and nodded as if he'd never met a man who hadn't just fallen face-first into a creek.

"How's the fishing?" the little man said.

Isaac noted the accent. Tennessee or Kentucky. More educated than any of his own clan. "Pretty wet. Maybe we ought to quit tryin' to catch 'em with our hands."

Ezra snorted. The little man laughed. He and the Tejano dismounted. "I'm looking for Isaac Webb."

Isaac sloshed out of the creek and extended a hand. "I'd dry it off, if I had something dry to wipe it on."

"Think nothing of it. I'm Jack Hays." He nodded toward the Tejano. "This is Antonio Pérez."

Isaac shook Hays's hand. Delicate for a man's hand. Yet firm. Few calluses. Not a farmer. Pérez's hand felt like a cedar post. Isaac introduced Esther and Ezra.

"I hear you boys have been busy," Isaac said. "What brings a pair of captains all the way over here from Béxar?"

"We had business over this way," Hays said. "Unfortunately our counterparts disappeared in the hills a few miles north of here with two dozen horses and a seven-year-old boy. Our scouts are still out, though I don't hold out much hope. The trail was two days cold when we picked it up." He wrapped the rein around his knuckles, cleared his throat. "There's something else, too." He looked at Pérez. "Captain."

Pérez nodded. "I believe you know the Lipan scout Juan Castro."

"I do." He drew a shallow breath. Surely the old boy hadn't gotten himself killed.

"A little bunch of Comanche raiders burned a ranchero a half day northwest of Béxar. We trailed them nine days until we struck what must have been some fork of the Brazos—I can't say for sure, but it was almost too salty to drink. Castro and some other scouts were half a day's ride ahead. We ran low on food; couldn't find a thing to shoot—and that salty water. We made camp and Castro and his boys came in after dark. They'd found a little Comanche camp—maybe thirty men and some women. The old man swears he saw your wife. Inez, is it?"

"Lord," Esther said.

Creek water dripped from Isaac's hat brim. "How'd she look?"

"He didn't have much to say about that," Pérez said. "You know Castro."

"And y'all never caught 'em?"

Pérez shook his head. "Tried to. By the time we got there, they'd headed north again. We didn't have nothing to chase them with. Out of food. Horses about dead. I'm sorry. If there was a way . . ."

Isaac looked across the pasture at the cabin he'd built with Catherine in mind. The home he and Inez had made and that Catherine hoped to inherit. Esther touched his hand. "Brother?"

Hays said, "I know what you're thinking, Isaac. But if Pérez here says he was out of horse, he was out of horse. He'd have gotten her back if he could've."

Pérez held his gaze, nodded.

Isaac swallowed. "You two aim to help me or do I need to raise a company?"

Hays said, "I had hoped Colonel Moore's campaign would put an end to the plundering. About all it did was teach them to break up into smaller bands. You can't catch more than a few dozen together. Since the weather warmed up, we're getting word of horse thievery nearly every day. They've burned seven farms in the past month. Raise a company if you've a mind to, but if it were me, I'd go to Béxar and get ready to ride. They'll hit a farm or steal some horses. Sooner or later, we'll pick up a hot trail. If we're lucky, it'll take us to your woman."

Ezra said, "We can be there by tomorrow night."

"You need to stay," Isaac said. "Remember what happened the last time I rode off chasing Comanches."

Esther said, "No sir. We'll get by. He's going."

Sis pawed and sniffed at the top of the fish trap. Ezra waded into the shallows and lifted it. A dozen or more suckers and bream and small catfish wriggled on the woven bottom.

"I'd say the fishing was better than you thought," Hays said.

Isaac started across the field. "Little Inez knows how to build a trap."

• • •

Catherine was on her knees weeding her garden when Isaac rode into the yard. She stood and dusted her hands on her skirt, eyed the rifle, full saddlebags, and bedroll. "Afternoon," he said.

She searched his face. He looked down the road toward town. "Somebody's seen her, ain't they?"

"I don't know what else to do, Catherine." He started to dismount.

"No, damn it. Just stay up there." Her face was flushed. "Why would you get down? What are you gonna say to me?"

"That I'm sorry. That I love you. That I never meant for things to go this way."

"Oh, you love me." She nodded, jaws clenched, and looked out over the river bottom.

"Lord Catherine. Don't be that way. Where's your mother?"

She wiped an eye. "I'm sorry." She shook her head. "All that time, I never looked at another man. And there were plenty to look at. Even after Inez, I held on. I knew somehow you'd make it back to me." She smiled through her tears. "And you did. At a horrible price, I know. But you did. Just like you came to me after the war. I opened the door that night, and there you stood. And of course Inez is saying to herself, 'He's coming. That's how he is.'"

Isaac's throat ached. He fought tears. "I might not find her. What then?"

She rubbed Squab's nose. "So you love this girl?"

"I didn't when I married her, but I came to love her." He couldn't remember admitting it to anyone else. "We both knew this could happen. You loved Franklin, didn't you? What would you do if you were me?"

"I can't say for sure, but I'll say this. I told myself she was dead or gone forever. That's the only way I could make a life with you. But as long as there's a chance you'll find her—God forgive me—I don't want to see you. No. I mean I can't see you."

Isaac nodded. "I've got to know one thing."

She saw his tears and sobbed.

He said, "I won't say that I ain't hurt you. But with everything that's happened, am I wrong? Have I wronged you?"

She shook her head, covered her face with her hands, and wept. He dismounted and held her. After a moment, she pulled away and walked into the house.

Fifty-Six

LATE AFTERNOON on their fifth day in Béxar, the plaza bell summoned Isaac and Ezra from their camp on the riverbank. They found Hays and Pérez with about thirty Tejano and Anglo rangers gathered in front of the Council House. They were checking weapons and lashing bedrolls onto horses. Several of the men nodded and spoke.

"I believe I shot at some of these boys at Saint Hyacinth," Ezra said under his breath.

Captain Pérez waved and walked up in fine spirits. "Boys. A little bunch stole some horses eight miles south. Ortiz and Fajardo cut sign late this morning. Ortiz is still out there. We ought to catch him by dark." He slapped Isaac's shoulder and returned to his horse. Hays had already mounted.

The two captains led the company south past corrals and tumbrels, jacales, and gardens green with new corn and beans. Midafternoon, they passed a few hundred yards west of a low stone farmhouse, a corral, and mud and pole outbuildings, probably the site of the thievery. They veered west and rode through the chaparral. They flushed groups of peccaries, and young quail no bigger than sparrows ran through the bunchgrass between prickly pear and mottes of thorny brush. Clumps of white prickly poppies looked like patches of snow on the sides of low hills.

The sun sat just off the western horizon when Ortiz rode out of a mesquite flat to meet them. He conferred with Hays and Pérez and a little Tejano wearing sandals whom Isaac assumed was Fajardo. Ortiz led them westward to a creek small enough to straddle. At dusk, they filled their canteens and ate jerked meat and pemmican. Hays walked along the creek among the resting rangers, saying, "No fires, boys."

An hour after dark, they mounted and rode west. The moon, two days shy of full, hung overhead when Hays led them into a mesquite flat. "Throw down and get some sleep," he said. "I'll kick you awake before dawn."

"He seemed like a good fellar that mornin' on the creek," Ezra said.

Isaac had already stretched out on his bedroll. He hoped Squab didn't step on him.

• • •

Someone prodded his shoulder. "Time to rise, my friend." Isaac looked up though the mesquite branches at stars. He couldn't make out the face above him, but the baritone voice belonged to a white man, a Southerner. Old sweat and sour breath hung on the cool morning air. A fox barked out in the darkness.

They rode west. The country flattened as the sun rose behind them. By midday, Isaac's shirt was crusted in salt. Not a single cloud broke the horizon. Hays and Pérez occasionally halted the column, dismounted, and walked ahead to confer or to study a bruised cactus pad or fragment of track.

"I ain't seein' much," Ezra said. Isaac occasionally saw possible signs of Comanche passage—tracks or scuffed ground or mashed clumps of grass, but he failed to see how Hays and Pérez navigated between obvious sign. Clearly, the raiders had spread out and were seeking hard ground. Yet at some point, they'd have to converge. Isaac's gourd was two-thirds empty.

He swallowed the last drop of water just before they topped a low hill and saw vultures wheeling and gliding like a thick column of smoke rising above the mouth of a wide draw a half mile away. Hays turned and motioned for the company to retreat back down the hill.

They dismounted and squatted in the sun while the captains scouted ahead on foot. Isaac's tongue and lips felt like parched rawhide. The men spoke little. The horses swished their tails and flicked their ears against the swarming flies.

Ezra occasionally glanced at Isaac with bloodshot eyes and shook his head. After an hour in the sun, Isaac walked up the hill. Near the top he hunkered forward until he just peered over the crest. An expanse of mesquite savannah stretched to the mouth of the draw; to the north, taller grass and a line of dense brush. A creek, probably dry. But there might be a spring near the head of the draw. He licked his lips. Inez was unlikely to be with such a small group—probably a little band of hunters and raiders. Judging from the buzzards, they'd killed and butchered something. Stolen cattle, maybe, or culls from their horse herd. If the company could find water and wait, the raiders might lead them to a larger camp. If they couldn't find water, they'd have to attack at sunup—or sooner.

He glimpsed movement out in the mesquite. Two men coming at a fast walk. The men disappeared, then reappeared as the cover opened. After a few minutes they ran up the hill and Pérez nearly stepped on Isaac before he saw him.

"Hellfire. Get down this hill," Hays said.

"I didn't want you sneaking up on me."

Hays shook his head as he started down the other side. "You better have kept your damn head down."

Isaac pushed himself up and followed the two captains. "You've got no cause to talk like that. This ain't the first time I've been in a scrape."

Hays ignored him and called the men together. Pérez shot him an apologetic glance and shrugged. Isaac had known men like Hays. Cordial enough most of the time, but completely focused and ruthless under pressure. Still, the little bastard had no cause to call him down and then ignore him. He tried to spit.

Hays stood before the men. "We'll leave our horses picketed here. The wind's blowing out of the draw. One of our horses might smell theirs. Otherwise we'd ride."

Isaac said, "Captain, we might kill this little bunch. We might. But that's all we'll get. If we can find water tonight, we might wait and see where they'll take us."

Hays listened, nodded, looked off to the east. "There's a fair-sized camp down there. At least a dozen. And at least two women."

"What'd they look like?"

"Hell, I don't know. Little brown, bowlegged women."

Isaac's chest tightened. Ezra said, "Now hold on, Captain."

Hays jabbed a finger at Ezra. "Not another word."

Ezra's eyes narrowed. Isaac felt Pérez pat the small of his back. He missed Smithwick and Felix and Uncle Jimmy. Hays wouldn't last a week among the Bastrop rangers. Several of the men looked at their feet.

Isaac smiled. "I meant, were they young or old, *Captain?*"

Hays returned the stare, nodding slightly. "I couldn't say for sure, *Isaac.* I was on my belly in the brush and didn't have a real good perspective. I believe one was a good bit older than the other." He started to turn his attention back to the group, then stopped and looked again at Isaac. "And boys, try not to shoot the women."

Pérez whispered, "Easy." Isaac felt sweat running down his sides. He wondered how many of the men would turn on him if he knocked the captain on his ass. If Hays heard Pérez, he gave no indication. "My company will form a skirmish line and attack head on," Hays said. "Captain Pérez and his men will flank the savages from the hills south of the camp. There's good cover up there. We'll give them half an hour head start. We'll strike at dusk; we don't want the sun in our eyes. We'll move shortly. Isaac, step over here, please."

He walked away from the men and stopped in the meager shade of a clump of head-high cedar. "Isaac . . . look. I've got thirty men under me and I'd like to get every one back to Béxar alive, including you."

Isaac laid his rifle on his shoulder. "I don't need my hand held. And I don't need somebody tellin' me to keep my head down."

Hays pursed his lips. "You know, I thought I was doing you a good turn, telling you about your wife and allowing you to join my company, but I'm not above leaving you in Béxar next time."

"You know, Captain, I thank you for tellin' me about my wife and lettin' me ride with your company, but I ain't above stompin' a hole in you when we get back to Béxar, if I can stand to wait that long." He started to spit, then remembered he didn't have any.

Hays rolled his eyes as if once again he had to bear the weight of Man's ignorance. "For god's sake, Isaac. Get ready to move. We'll take this up later." He walked up the hill, shaking his head. Near the top, he took off his hat, dropped to his belly, and looked out toward the Comanche camp.

Isaac stood leaning on one leg, rifle still on his shoulder, head well above the shade that had covered Jack Hays, trying to decide if he'd put the pompous shit in his place or had just been shooed like a horsefly.

The sun just touched the horizon when Pérez and his men slipped away toward the hills. Half an hour later, the Anglo rangers topped the rise, spread out, and wove through the mesquite, Hays positioned in the center and just ahead, Isaac on his immediate right, then Ezra.

They advanced at a fast walk. There was no breeze, but the moccasins and buckskin made little noise. Someone flushed a pair of quail from a nest. Hays raised a hand. They stopped. Isaac's pulse banged in his ears. After a few minutes they moved on. A rattlesnake buzzed to Hays's left. A ranger named Scranton jumped to one side, but no one paused. A breezed kicked up; Isaac whiffed smoke.

Hays dropped to his hands and knees. The others did the same. Isaac crawled through the scrub, mindful of the rattlesnake Scranton had sidestepped. And what if the Comanches knew they were coming? A dozen could strike now and wipe them out before they could get up to shoot. He thought about how fast Looks Far emptied his quiver of arrows. Surprise was everything.

He inched along, the scent of spring grass strong in his nostrils. The birdsong had stopped. The brush seemed more open here; he saw light ahead. They were nearing the mouth of the draw. He wished he'd asked Hays how far back the Comanches were camped. He smelled smoke again. They were close. He peered through the openings between clumps of bunchgrass and mesquite trunks, but saw no movement save for skittering rodents and flitting birds.

He crept another few yards, and looked through the last few feet of brush. Eighty yards ahead, along the creek, seven lodges reflected the light of small fires. He heard men's voices and a woman's laugh. He saw no movement on the hills above the camp. But Pérez and his men were there. It was almost twilight.

Without a sound, Hays rose to a crouch; Isaac did the same and heard the soft swishing of the others rising and cocking weapons. The Captain broke for the camp.

Isaac surged ahead, leaping clumps of prickly pear. Hoarse yells rose from camp. A warrior stood up next to the fire, and Isaac slid to a knee and shot him in the chest. The rangers roared curses; a woman screamed. Thirty yards ahead warriors were grabbing bows and lances and running up the creek. More shooting. Isaac heard the hiss of the balls, heard them strike meat and brush. Two more Comanches pitched forward.

Shots from the hills. The Tejano rangers were running out of the brush to cut off the escaping warriors. A wounded Comanche, blood dripping from his mouth and chin, got to one knee, nocked an arrow, and let fly an instant before Isaac brained him. One of the rangers yelped, screamed, "Oh lord! God help me! Captain! Lord!" Further up the draw, the Comanche remuda stampeded into the hills. Isaac smelled meat cooking.

The Comanches turned away from Pérez's flanking attack and dove into a narrow brush-choked tributary. Hays yelled, "Get above 'em! Cut 'em off!" Isaac turned right and ran up the hill alongside the streamside brush. He could hear the Comanches in the creek, struggling through the thick oak and plum. He knelt and reloaded. Other rangers ran by him, took up positions above him to cut off escape. The Tejanos did the same on the other side. Pérez shouted orders in Spanish. Men uncorked powder horns, worked ramrods, cursed, and gasped for breath. Below them, the wounded ranger still begged for help.

"Don't nobody shoot across the creek," Ezra said.

Someone below answered, "Worry about your own goddamn self."

Hays yelled, "Shut up and get ready to fire on my command."

Isaac said, "Captain, for god's sake there's two women in there! Give them the chance to surrender; they can't go anywhere." No sound came from the creek.

Hays said, "Well hell."

The wounded ranger cried for Jesus to take him. Ezra shook his head and spat. "Somebody go down there and see about that boy."

Up the slope, Lycurgus Strawn, the man who woke Isaac the morning before, started down the hill. "That's right. Let's forget about our own. We've got to all gather around and shoot us an Indian."

Hays yelled, *"Tiren sus armas y salgan. No les haremos daño."*

Nothing. Hays repeated the surrender offer. An arrow hissed out of the brush below Isaac and struck Silas Cromwell in the right wrist. Cromwell dropped his rifle. "Shit!" He straightened up, staring at the iron tip and five inches of shaft protruding just below the heel of his hand.

Someone fired into the creek, then most of the company emptied their rifles while Isaac listened to the death screams.

"There's your surrender," someone said. Cromwell dropped to his knees. "I hope you're goddamn satisfied, Webb. Red nigger lovin' son of a bitch."

Ezra squatted on his heels, peering into the darkening brush. "Shut up, Cromwell, before I break your other damn arm. Isaac, hell. I never shot."

"I know you didn't." Isaac walked down the hill to Cromwell who sat holding his wrist. "I'll help you. Let me see."

Cromwell didn't raise his eyes. "Get away from me."

Isaac's arms felt heavy. He wanted to kick Cromwell in the side of the head and walk away. If Inez was in there she was dead.

Hays shouted, "Pérez, send a couple . . ."

A thin, quavering chant wafted out of the creek. *"Ha-ah-ha, hay-hah-ah . . ."*

Several men shot into the brush. Isaac said, "Lord." The chanting stopped.

"Reload and fire," Hays said. Serpentines clicked.

A woman screamed, *"¡No! Soy Mexicana. ¡No disparen por favor! ¡Por favor no disparen!"*

"Lord," Hays said. *"Salgan."*

A few yards down the hill, a small woman clambered out of the creek. Her gray-streaked black hair tangled in the brush. Something seemed to hold her from behind. She kicked. "*¡No! ¡Suélteme!*"

She slapped at someone behind her, but her arm caught in the brush. She looked pleadingly at the rangers who mounted their rifles. "Hold your fire!" Isaac said. He rushed at the woman and rammed his rifle barrel into the brush until it struck flesh. Someone grunted and the woman jerked free and scrambled out.

On the other side of the creek, Pérez yelled "*¡Agarrenlo!*" Bodies thrashed about. Fajardo yelled, "*¡Yo te cortaré la garganta!*"

The woman got to her feet. The index and middle fingers of her left hand had been shot away just above the joints. Blood dripped from a flap of flesh that had been her ear. A ball had clipped the hair on that side of her head. She looked at Isaac. "*Nuestro amigo Isikweb.*"

"Cecilia?"

"*Sí.*"

"You know this bitch?" Scranton said. "She don't look Meskin to me."

"I know her. She was Mexican a long time ago." The men gathered around. Isaac asked her in Spanish, "Is she alive?"

"She's alive."

"Where?"

"I wish I had died in the creek." She staggered, pale from blood loss. "You'll kill him."

"If I have to."

Hays and Pérez walked up the hill nudging a boy of about fifteen at rifle point. The young warrior held his shattered right forearm. Blood ran down his side and dripped from his breechclout. Pérez shoved him toward Isaac. "I doubt he'll tell you a thing."

The boy grinned. Isaac said in Spanish, "Tell me where he is."

"I think he is laying with that Wichita girl."

Isaac backhanded him across the mouth. The boy fell on his back, unable to break his fall with only one arm. He caught his breath and grinned, showing bloody teeth broken off at the gum. "He likes her more than his other wives."

Cecilia turned away. Isaac handed his rifle to Ezra, drew his knife, and drove his knee into the Comanche's chest, pinning him. He held the blade to the boy's throat. "You tell him to bring me my wife if he wants his sister. Or else we'll hunt him down and feed him to the crows. You tell him."

The boy looked at Cecilia. "I will tell him."

"Damn you, Webb!" Cromwell said. Someone had cut the arrowhead off and pulled the shaft out his wrist. He sat with his head hung between his knees.

Scranton said, "Captain, this little bastard will just run off and leave us stuck with this squaw. I say we either shoot 'em both or tie 'em up and haul 'em back to Béxar."

Isaac fought the urge to ram the butt of his knife into the boy's temple. "Go on back to Béxar then. I'll do this myself."

Hays held up a hand. "We'll wait four days. We've got water here." He asked the Comanche if he could get to Looks Far and back in four days. The boy snarled, "*Sí,*" then spat blood.

Several of the men grumbled and walked down the hill shaking their heads. A few Tejanos worked their way up the creek to check for more survivors. Someone cursed. A pistol cracked.

Hays said, "Clean this rascal up and put him on a horse. Isaac, give him our word that we won't follow him."

Fifty-Seven

SCRANTON STEPPED INSIDE the ring of fire-light. "And what makes you think a thousand of the devils won't ride back here and scalp us all? We're short ten men what with them boys takin' Cromwell back to Béxar. And that Buggs boy dead."

Jack Hays lay on his side on his blanket, propped on his elbow. "We got one of their women, Bill. And I've got pickets all over these hills."

Cecilia sat between Isaac and Ezra. An hour earlier, Isaac turned away when she spread the bad hand on a dead juniper root and lopped off the finger fragments at the joints. Tears furrowed her dirty face when she handed him his knife. He had no idea what to do about her ear. It had dried into a scabrous mess. So far she'd been unwilling to talk about Inez.

They had burned the Comanche lodges. After they'd watered the horses and filled their canteens and a few Comanche water bags, Hays ordered camp set in the hills south of the draw, where they were less vulnerable to ambush. Four other small campfires burned on the grassy knob, lighting the brown and bearded faces.

Scranton jerked up a handful of knee-high bunchgrass and threw it into the darkness. "Pure foolishness. We ought to be headed back to Béxar."

"Head back," Hays said. "Me, now, I wouldn't want to be riding this country alone."

Isaac watched Scranton. He ought to jump up and stomp his ass, but he didn't need trouble. He needed Hays's help. Only a few of the men had complained openly.

Ezra pulled a strip of jerky from a parfleche bag, then offered the bag to Cecilia. She ignored him. He shrugged and pitched the bag to Isaac. "I guess she ain't hungry. I might be a little peaked myself if I'd just lost two fingers and an ear."

"Why she'd cut off more than your finger and ear, given half a chance," Scranton said. "Captain we aim to tie her up, don't we? I won't sleep a wink with a squaw running loose in camp."

Hays said, "We'll tie her up to keep her from running off."

Isaac hated the thought of tying her. She had to be in agony already. But he hated even more the thought of waking to find her gone.

Scranton squatted and spat into the fire. "Webb, what makes you think your Comanche friend will swap a young squaw for this hag?"

"She's his sister."

Scranton snorted. "Yeah, but even a Comanche won't fuck his sister."

"I'll be damn," Ezra said.

Isaac pushed himself up. "I'll break your neck, Scranton."

Hays said, "Sit down, Isaac. Two companies are out here risking their necks for you." Only his mouth moved as he spoke. "Bill, get on before I turn these two loose on you. I ought to tell this old gal what you said about her."

Scranton smirked and walked away toward another fire. Isaac plopped down on his bedroll. He'd had about enough of Jack Hays's orders. But the man knew how to use authority. He'd get Inez back and be done with him. Be done with this whole Béxar bunch. Pérez was a good one though. He didn't act like God had ordained him to lead a ranging company.

They sat in silence. Cecilia covered her eyes with her bandaged hand. Laughter broke out in the direction Scranton had gone.

Fifty-Eight

MIDMORNING of their third day in the hills, Fajardo rode down from the head of the draw and spoke to Pérez. Isaac and Ezra were sweating in the poor shade of a mesquite. They'd pulled the night watch. Both had slept a few hours after dawn, but the morning heat chased them from their blankets. About half the men were drinking coffee, gambling, or dozing about camp. The others were on watch.

Pérez walked down the hill toward them. Isaac's stomach fluttered. "What?"

"Your boy's on his way in. That one you whapped the other day. Bolt of white cloth on his lance. Leading another horse."

"Just him?"

"Our boys ain't seen anybody else."

"There might be some others hanging back," Ezra said. "Just as well see what he's got to say."

They rode out of the hills. A plain of grass and oak mottes rolled away to the north. Hays sat his horse along with several of the Tejanos. They were squinting toward the horizon.

Hays pulled his hat brim down. "I've lost sight of him. He's coming though. He knows the boys are on him."

Isaac looked out over the grass. "I don't see him either."

Pérez grinned. "Hell no, you don't. You Bastrop boys are used to ridin' around in the woods. My boys are wild as any Comanche." He nodded. "There he is. You'd never know his arm is busted."

A sun glint a quarter mile out. A lance head. Piebald withers. The boy rode up a little rise and came straight toward them. A hundred yards back, on his flanks, Pérez's rangers wove their way through the scattered mottes, keeping to low ground.

"By god, Isaac, I'd say his mouth is smartin' him," Ezra said. "I want you look at his lip. He'll remember you."

Isaac laughed without humor. The Comanche was looking right at him. You could always depend on Ezra for words of comfort.

Hays smiled at the boy as he rode up. "Isaac, you can do the talking."

"Where is she?" Isaac said in Spanish.

"She is in our camp."

"Did you tell him?"

"I told him."

"Why did you not bring her?"

"Where is the sister?"

"She is back in camp. Why didn't you bring my wife to me?"

The boy arched his brows in defiance. "His sister is in your camp. That Wichita is in our camp. What is wrong with that?"

Isaac sighed. Surely the boy hadn't ridden all the way back and into a hostile camp unless he meant to bargain. The fracas at the council house in Béxar had shown the Comanches that a white flag was no guarantee of safe conduct. "Will he trade for his sister?"

"Bring her to our camp. Then we will see."

Hays said, "I wouldn't go anywhere with that heathen." The young man grinned, showing his broken teeth and swollen gums.

"I think he gets your meaning, Jack," Pérez said.

"See what?" Isaac demanded of the boy. "He gets his sister when I get my wife."

"He will trade but only in our camp. Only with you. None of these other men."

Isaac glanced back at Ezra. "Go get her."

"Lord, Isaac," Hays said. "Surely not."

"Go on back home, then," Isaac said.

Hays shook his head. "Hell no, I wouldn't miss this for anything."

"Just goin' to parley," Isaac said. "I guess they set more store in a white flag than Fisher did."

Ezra rode down the draw toward camp. They sat their horses and looked out over the swaying grass. A few minutes later, he rode back leading a horse bearing Cecilia. She dismounted and climbed on the other Comanche horse. She looked at no one.

"Well," Isaac said.

Hays doffed his hat and wiped his brow with his forearm. "We'll be waitin' on you."

Fifty-Nine

THEY RODE NORTH. Isaac kept to the Comanche's right flank. Early afternoon, they struck a narrow, brush-choked stream, watered the horses, then turned east. Neither Cecilia nor the boy looked at him or spoke to him.

Two hours before sundown, they came to a confluence. Just beyond, on the south bank in scattered blackjack oaks, a dozen or so lodges flapped in the wind. A dog barked as they approached. A few little boys ran out to meet them. Cecilia dismounted and wept as she hugged them. The boys grinned and pointed at Isaac and spoke into each other's ears.

Isaac's mouth was dry and tasted of metal. He'd get this done and head back before dark. He had no desire to spend another night in a Comanche camp. A few women labored over cook fires. They stopped to watch him ride in. He saw no gaiety in their work. Dust blew through camp. The meat would be gritty tonight. Feels How Deep the Water Is stepped out of her lodge and regarded him flatly. He looked away.

The young warrior dismounted; a boy led their horses away. Isaac dismounted and followed them between the lodges to the creek, leading Squab. Two dogs sniffed his leg and bristled.

Looks Far sat on a blanket beneath a brush arbor, smoking a pipe. He saw them and tapped the ashes out on the ground beside him. He stopped a little girl and spoke softly to her. She ran away toward the lodges. He didn't look at Cecilia. "Isikweb."

"*Buenos días.*"

"I am glad you came."

"I will always come to see a great friend. Where is Buffalo Hump? Well, I hope."

Looks Far studied him. "He is well. We no longer live together in one place. You and Juaqua will have to search for us. But you did not come here to talk of fighting."

"No. I brought your sister."

Looks Far's gaze moved beyond Isaac. Isaac turned. Inez stood holding a naked infant, dusty, hair cropped short like a Comanche woman, wariness in her eyes. She seemed even tinier than he remembered. One More Girl stepped up beside her. Isaac counted months; turned back to Looks Far.

The Comanche regarded him serenely. "I gave you a daughter."

"You speak of giving?" Sweat ran into Isaac's eyes. He tried to imagine returning home with a half-Comanche baby. Would Inez leave willingly if the Comanches refused to let her take the infant? A swarm of flies roared in the brush just beyond the edge of camp.

Looks Far's expression remained calm. He said something to One More Girl, who hurried away toward the lodges. He picked up his pipe and tobacco pouch. One More Girl returned and spread a blanket before him. He motioned for Isaac to sit.

Isaac looked back at Inez. Her eyes were moist and wide with fear. She swallowed, rocked the baby girl. A month old, Isaac guessed. Plump, with a head full of coarse, black hair. Sound asleep.

One More Girl squatted on her heels on Looks Far's right. A small, naked child stood beside her, tugging at her knee. Looks Far stuffed his pipe and motioned again for Isaac to sit.

Inez gently bounced the sleeping baby. Others had gathered. Old men. A few young warriors. All standing at a respectful distance. It was too hot for the council lodge.

The child next to One More Girl squealed with delight. She had light brown hair. Another captive child. She tried to push One More Girl over. Looks Far's young wife playfully fended her off. The little girl had green eyes, set close. A boy brought Looks Far an ember. The young chief lit his pipe. The green-eyed child stood on her toes and pushed One More Girl until she put down a hand to keep from toppling.

"Isikweb, sit with me."

Green eyes, close set. Graceful neck and long fingers for such a young child. She kept after One More Girl.

"Isikweb . . ."

"She looks like Esther." He'd lapsed into English.

"Isikweb, I do not understand this talk."

Isaac turned to Looks Far. "That little girl looks like my sister."

Looks Far puffed his pipe and studied the child, a horseman pleased by fine traits passed on. "Yes. And like you. As we might expect."

Sixty

"ISAAC, THAT GIRL'S gettin' a bottom on her." Cyrus sat on the doorstep, watching Inez and Sarah Ruth walking back from the creek with a goose they'd plucked. Inez carried the bird by its feet. Sarah ran beside her, tail feathers in both fists.

Isaac stepped out and closed the door. "Damn right." The late autumn sun lit the bare limbs and the few tenacious oak leaves and the shallow pools across the weedy field.

"Havin' babies will do that to a woman," Cyrus said. "What do you think this one will be?"

"She says a boy. I'd like to throw a son before I'm through."

Cyrus nodded. "I wish Esther and Ezree would have some luck. You know good and well them two are tryin'."

The door opened behind him. "Somebody's wantin' out," Ruth said. Isaac jumped off the step. The little girl they called Ellen waddled out, arms outstretched. She wore a simple wool dress and moccasins. Her dark hair hung about her shoulders. Isaac took her from the step and set her on the ground. She tottered toward her mother, who cooed to her.

Cyrus groped in his coat pocket for his pipe. "Bandy-legged little stink, ain't she? Them little ears will be gettin' cold."

Sarah Ruth ran to her baby sister and dusted her chin with the goose feathers.

Esther stepped outside, fanning her face with her hand. "Lord, she's run me out of there with that fire. I don't see how she stands it." She looked up the path toward her cabin. "Now I wonder where Mister Higginbotham is. Probably up there in the molasses again."

Isaac studied his sister. Green eyes, close set. Graceful neck, long fingers.

She caught his eye. "What, brother?"

He held her gaze. "Not a thing, sister. I just like lookin' at a comely woman."

THE END